THE DUFFER
by
BOB KOCHER

Published by FICTIONWRITERS
in association with
LULU Publications

Cover Design
by
FICTIONWRITERS

Acknowledgements

With sincere thanks to all my
old golfing buddies from over the
many years of hooks, slices, missed
putts, and shanks. Miss you guys.

Dedicated to:

All my lovers and wives who
endured so many years of my
being 'Missing In Action' at:
Oxen Run Golf Course,
Robindale Country Club,
Brandywine Country Club,
Lake Marion, Santee
and
trips all over the East Coast.
* * *
"Thanks, Patti Ann . . .

THE DUFFER

CHAPTER I

Being alone late at night, after a trying and difficult day, had become commonplace in recent months. Even weekends served little respite, allowing only limited spurts of self-indulgence in more enjoyable activities and relaxation. However, feeling sorry for oneself didn't fit into the forced busy schedule.

Really wanting to catch the late-night sportscast, last minute interruptions of 'triple importance' denied the opportunity. The news anchorman was signing-off at the program's end as the screen gradually drew to its proper focus. Totally dedicated to his new career, television not only represented a link with the outside world, it was an often welcome form of distraction and companionship. As disappointed as he was, stretching out on the bed felt extremely satisfying. Weariness, sometimes approaching near exhaustion, frequently counterbalanced the absence of a bed companion.

Preferring a 'Late-Movie' western with ol' Randy Scott over a rerun of 'I Love Lucy,' the benevolent sandman paid an early visit bringing needed sleep -- mercifully conquering the conscious mind.

Tomorrow was another day.

* * *

As if resting on a blanket of downy texture, the distant setting sun's fading glow of existence clung to the vaporous mounds of clouds like clutching fingers trying to delay its inevitable descent from Hack's small part of the world.

"You'll have to fasten your seat belt, sir," the stewardess stated, treading her way up the aisle toward the front of the plane and commenting to all those failing to heed the lit warning sign.

Snapping the buckle into place, Hack watched intently as her hips swayed in gentle motions, being especially attentive to the subtle ripples of her calf muscles becoming pronounced with each step, caused by the black high-heels she wore.

Suddenly, breaking the mood, a nasal voice speaking in monotone echoed through the cabin as if it were a single sentence. "This is your Captain speaking. I trust you've had an enjoyable flight. We'll be landing at Washington National in approximately fifteen minutes. The weather is clear at the moment with thundershowers predicted over the tri-state area, the temperature at sixty-one degrees. I wish you a pleasant evening and hope you'll once again choose Eastern for your next flight."

As the Captain finished his dialogue, minor turbulence shook the turbojet as it began to penetrate the storm they had previously been soaring above. Against the blackened sky, the plane's windows changed to mirrors reflecting clear images of its interior until bolts of lightning shattered the premature night giving the appearance of ghostly images cast by the shapes of surrounding clouds.

Glancing toward the nearby window, Hack's reflection revealed evidence of the distressful pangs he was feeling. Becoming aware of his facial expression, which was exposing all attempts at hiding inner emotions, he took a slow and lengthy deep breath of air while opening the last miniature of Canadian Club and literally tossing its contents down his throat.

A burst of light suddenly filled the environment as the plane broke free of the storm's chaste grip. The buffeting ceased, and save the continuing drone of the engines, there was no other evidence of being in the air until the metal bird groaned from its belly, dropping the landing gear into place.

Braving a peek through the window, he was astounded by the majestic picture unfolding before his eyes. The storm was now a foreboding wall receding in the distance. A rainbow streaked across the heavens still carrying hues of the waning sun. The terrain below passed very slowly, projecting concepts of being suspended motionless in space. Somewhat mesmerized, he settled back in the seat and blindly continued his stare, drifting into unconscious thought.

Zachariah Paul (St. John) "Hack" Arnold, including his confirmation and nickname, boasted of broaching six-foot-two in cowboy boots and represented the better side of being ruggedly handsome and athletic in build.

"Aw, shit," he inadvertently muttered out loud.

"Pardon me."

Startled by the response, he quickly looked away from the window into the eyes of the stewardess as she leaned to retrieve the cups and miniature bottles from his tray. "Oops, sorry," he apologized while blushing.

"That's all right." She smiled and continued her chores. "You did seem to be in rather deep thought. But, you shouldn't light that cigarette right now. We'll be landing in just a few moments." She nodded toward the no smoking sign.

Hack smiled and replaced the filtered stick of tobacco into its almost empty pack. Tucking it with the lighter into his inside coat pocket, he returned to gaze through the window and observed the rush of water and underbrush speeding beneath the wings. Pavement suddenly appeared and the plane jolted with its wheels making runway contact. The engines began to scream from reverse throttling and soon the giant vehicle lumbered its way toward the terminal.

It felt damn good to be in contact with Mother Earth once more.

* * *

"Taxi!"

A cab pulled forward from its waiting point and stopped only long enough for Hack to toss in his baggage and slide into the rear seat. Without waiting for instructions, the driver lurched from the curb and headed in the direction of downtown D.C.

"1018 Eighteenth Street, NW."

"Yassir."

"Okay if I smoke?" Hack asked.

"Yassir, you smokes all's you like." The cabby turned to smile over his shoulder. "Have a nice trip?"

"Pretty good. Yeah, pretty damn good to tell the truth." Hack ventured to smile at himself in satisfaction.

"Dere's been good weather here." He smiled again. "'Cept for that storm that jest buzzed through here."

"I know," Hack responded. "I've only been gone since yesterday morning on a business trip to New York. We went through the storm just before we landed."

"It was a muvver, you bet." His teeth gleamed even brighter.

* * *

Stopping at the office for the purpose of leaving several documents on Carin's desk for the following morning, Hack went to the bar in his room, poured a generous snifter of brandy, and walked to the front windows overlooking the street. The late workers were about all there was left of the rush hour, reminding him he, too, should be on the road. After swallowing the final contents of the glass, he moved to the phone and got halfway through dialing his wife before changing his mind and replacing the receiver on its cradle. He really wasn't in the mood to talk to her and easily decided it could wait until getting home.

Returning to the bar he grasped the brandy bottle around its neck, switched on the TV, and flopped on the couch with his legs stretched down its length. The picture sputtered and eventually came to focus exposing the evening news. Imbibing a bit more of the biting liquid, he watched as the sports announcer made an appearance and spent a great deal of his spot promoting the coming Masters Tournament. Gaining his full attention, Hack reached to turn up the volume and settled back to enjoy the program.

Not fully realizing the extent of his weariness, he fortunately rested in a position just uncomfortable enough to keep him from deeper sleep. Awakening in a startled manner and dazed stupor, he wasn't sure of the time.

"Damn," he muttered, looking hurriedly at his watch while jumping to his feet. It was nearly eight-thirty.

This time, he completed dialing the number only to reach a busy signal. Rather than wait, he quickly checked inside his valises to determine their contents, shoved one into the closet, and carried the other to the car, tossing it into the trunk.

There was little traffic on the way to the house. For still being early spring, the evening was unseasonably and pleasantly warm. Even though he dreaded having to face Alice, he looked forward to getting home, hopefully to relax. His mind drifted in varying thought as he drove, weighing the good with the bad.

10

Oblivious to his surroundings, and practically driving by instinct, he was totally unaware of the wailing siren and flashing lights of the police cruiser until it was abreast his side.

"Aw, for crying-out-loud," he complained. "What the hell have I done now?"

Pulling over to the curb, he waited in the car until the officer appeared at his window.

"May I see your drivers license and registration, please?"

Hack reached to his wallet for the permit and found the other document stored in the glove compartment. An open sleeve of condoms spewed its contents to the floor in the transition.

"Were you aware you have a tail light out?"

The registration card was sticky with a foreign substance. The cop handled it delicately between the tips of two fingers and after minimal scrutiny handed it back to Hack. A distinct odor indicated it to be covered with lubricating jell from a broken seal on at least one of the rubbers.

Hack couldn't control his reaction and exploded into laughter as the officer sniffed his hand.

"Get the hell out of here." He spun on his heels and stomped back toward the cruiser. Hack continued chuckling as the cop whipped his car in a U-turn and began speeding up the highway -- coding to beat hell.

Retrieving the small packages from the floor, he remembered Jerry asking him to buy them and having forgotten to give them to him, but puzzled as to how and why they had been opened. Under closer scrutiny, three or four spent casings cluttered the glove box. Shaking his head in bewilderment, he turned the ignition key and continued on his way. On second thought, one of his sister's kids was almost sure to be involved in the mystery.

There were no street lights in the neighborhood and in recent times it certainly wasn't unusual for Alice to ignore putting on the garage or porch light for his welcome home.

Turning into the driveway, he stopped at the bottom just short of Alice's car, switched off the headlights and ignition, and slowly managed to extricate himself from behind the wheel. Following the pavement to the house's corner, because of the dark, he decided to risk a brief shortcut across a small flower bed. On his second step, he felt a softness beneath his foot and cursed his stupidity at screwing up Alice's new planting. Hack reached down to doctor the disturbed area and became alarmingly aware the tender sod was actually dog-shit.

He half shouted, "Son of a bitch," gagging at the foul odor and frantically raking his shoe and hand across the lawn's damp blades of grass.

Totally irritated, he was primed for any crap Alice might have up her sleeve. With his hand still reeking with remnants of the thick goo, he stormed for the front door and stumbled awkwardly over various items strewn across the steps. Luckily landing on several of the objects, as opposed to full contact with the unrelenting concrete stairs, the end result could have been worse. As it was, he wound up only slightly skinning his clean hand in the process.

Still finding it difficult to adjust his eyes to the extreme blackness of the night, Hack strained to identify the obstacles by touch. They were his clothes and personal belongings.

Completely perplexed and befuddled, he turned and sat down in the middle of the pile, resting his elbows against his knees. Without thinking, he cupped the sides of his face with his hands. He jerked them away instantaneously; one because of the smell, the other due to the recent injury's burning sting.

"Damn. Is there no fuckin' end to it?"

Suddenly, the porch became brilliantly lit, coinciding with the not so gentle opening of the front door. Rather than bother turning to confront her, he sat stationary in his spot. There was no time to react to the crashing sound from behind and he felt the impact of a large object strike him across his back as it bounced down the steps. Golf clubs rained all around him. The bag slid past his hip and leg to the bottom of the stairs. "Welcome home, 'Sir' Arnold," Alice said. "I trust you'll find the more important things in your life ready for your leave."

"Aw, shit." He shook his head in disgust. "What in the name of God is this all about, anyway?" he asked in desperation.

"Come home once in a while and you might find out," she said as sarcastically as possible.

"For craps-sake woman, you know damn good and well I was in New York on business."

"Yeah. You and who else, that twit who works for you?"

"Holy hell, Alice. What do you want from me? I work my ass off; provide damn well for you, and your friggin' family; seldom have any time to myself, and have to put up with your hang-ups and bullshit every time I turn around."

"I . . ."

"Shut up, damn it, I'm not finished. You've got me standing out here in front of God and all his creations, knee-deep in half my personal belongings. And, dog-shit," he added. "If you had any friggin' sense, you'd at least be embarrassed to air our problems for the entire neighborhood to enjoy." Hack stood defiantly giving the finger sign to each and every nearby home he could see.

"You're a real asshole," she blurted, attempting to conceal an urge to laugh.

He stormed up the steps and into the house as she stepped gingerly aside to avoid his running over her. Alice smiled at the clutter she had wrought and followed him through the door. Hack went straight to the kitchen sink and began scouring his hands with Ajax and dish detergent.

She laughed. "You really did fall into some 'doggy-doo,' didn't you?"

"Yeah, and I stepped in it, too, smart-ass."

It wasn't until then she noticed stains on the kitchen floor. "Damn it, Hack. Haven't you got any brains at all? Take off your shoe."

"Screw it. It's my house, too."

"You're disgusting." She stomped from the room and returned shortly with a mop, sponge, and bucket.

In her absence, he removed and cleaned his shoes, sitting them carefully on top of an almost overflowing trash basket.

"Where are the kids? Thought they were supposed to be here."

"Your sister picked them up earlier."

"Thank God for that." His words were muffled through a paper towel while drying his face. "There sure are times I'm glad we never had any."

"Move. I want to get this up before it dries any harder."

After turning to the refrigerator, Hack selected a couple pieces of cold chicken and a can of beer and plopped in a corner seat at the table.

Alice continued swishing at the tiles and finally stuck the sponge end into the bucket, propping the handle against a wall. "Do you think we can discuss this in a civil manner?" she asked, while seating herself at the table's opposite end.

"Discuss what?" He couldn't stop his indignant attitude.

"Our divorce."

"Our wh . . . what?" He stammered, almost choking on the food. "You've got to be joking. "You're out of your friggin' mind.

"For such a romantic, caring and sensitive person as you're supposed to be, you sure have a gift for picking the right words to hurt."

"I'm sorry, Alice. I've never wanted to hurt you. It's just that you've got a knack of really rubbing my skin the wrong way. If you'd ever stop thinking about yourself for a few seconds, you might find a pretty nice feeling in thinking of someone else. Namely, me."

"That's unfair, damn it." She slammed the butt of her palm against the table top. "You're the one constantly blaming my family for all of our problems. Why don't you ever try to see their side of it?"

"Hold it right there. We're not getting into that tonight. In fact, I've had more than my share of it and don't want any more. Period!"

"That's the whole point. You won't give an inch."

"Give an inch? Good Lord. I've given a mile. No, tens of miles. No, hundreds of miles. Aw, shit. What's the use?" He shook his head and buried his face into his folded arms which were lying on the table. "And, furthermore," he said, suddenly raising his head to glare in her direction. "What's this crap about a divorce? You can't cope or take care of yourself half the time, anyway. How the hell are you gonna manage without someone aroung? I got you that car out in the driveway and that's where it sits. You won't even learn to drive."

Alice stared at him with a vacant expression.

"Oh, wow. That's it. How stinking dumb am I? There is someone else."

"Come off it," she said. "Wanting a divorce doesn't

necessarily mean screwing around, although that's about the level of your mentality."

"Yeah, yeah. Who's the dip shit you've got an ache for?"

Alice rolled her head and sarcastically responded, "Even if there were someone, what the hell difference does it make? You're never here. If we had kids, they'd know the milkman better."

"So, that's who it is."

"You're real cute." Her bitterness could almost be tasted in the air. "Ever since you opened that damn business of yours, I've been like a widow. You're never home; always away; day and night. Don't you realize you were only here five nights in the last three weeks?"

"Same old crap, over and over," he interrupted.

"That's just it in a nutshell." She calmed and reached for her cigarettes. "You'll never understand, and you're right, there never will be compromise. I'm tired, Hack. Tired and fed up. We've never been really happy. I don't think we ever could be."

Hack got up from the table and began to pace the floor. He started to speak a couple of times and each of the efforts fell short of a proper beginning.

"All right. All right," he blurted out, finally breadking the silence. "You can have it your way. The lawyers can fight over the details. I'm in no mood for it. I suggest you get . . ."

"I have one," she retorted. Her remark came as further shock, clearly indicating premeditation, opposed to spontaneity as being the basis for the current confrontation. By habit, he moved to the closet, but found it practically empty. Realizing his jackets, sweaters, and everything else already lay outside collecting dew, he headed for the front door.

"Where are you going?"

"To hell. Wanna come?"

"There's no reason for you to leave this late. Wait 'til tomorrow morning." A slight concern was shown in her tone. "And besides, you don't have any shoes on."

"Are you kidding me?" he blurted sarcastically, laughing loudly and looking at her as if she had lost her mind. "You've moved me lock, stock and barrel out on the lawn and you expect me to either leave it out there or move it back in. You've got to be shittin' me." Hack flung open the door and hopped through the maze to the bottom of the steps.

Beginning to collect his gear, he stuffed a few strewn articles of clothes back into the bags and proceeded to gather his golf items.

"Just think," she quipped -- referring to his clubs and avid interest in playing golf, as she tossed his shoes at his feet, "you can even sleep with them, now. . . . Oooooo, that's if your secretary-bitch doesn't mind."

She was good at hitting a nerve. "Get one thing straight once and for all. I work. I don't screw around."

Alice evidently came to the conclusion enough was enough and retreated into the house. Following the door slam, he could hear her bolt the inside latch and busied himself with loading the car.

Pulling out of the driveway, he toyed with the idea of peeling-wheels up the block and thought better of it. However, he couldn't resist honking the horn and waving a couple of times. The dash clock indicated it to be almost eleven. It was hard to believe the time had passed so quickly. On route back to the office, an all-night hamburger joint posed an opportunity for coffee and a chance to gather a few thoughts. After a second cup, he mustered the courage to place a phone call he had been tempted to make for quite some time. "Hello," the voice came sleepily over the wire.

"Carin. It's Hack. Is that invitation still open?"

"Are you kidding?" She perked to full consciousness. "It's about time. I thought you'd never ask. I'm awful lonesome." Her voice altered to a sensual whisper. "I've got something nice and warm just waiting for you." She giggled. "Either coffee, hot tea, or me."

* * *

A day off became a near impossibility the way things had been going. It was great to be busy and finally realize a return for the extra efforts, but pressures were taking a toll. Since signing a legal separation, thirteen months had passed. He still hadn't brought himself to completely believe Alice would follow through with the divorce even though she kept talking about going to Reno. His mind in wandering thought, almost by sheer instinct, the car inched its way amidst the congested flow of rush-hour traffic. It took the screeching of wheels from the car behind to rudely snap him to full awareness.

As the left lane started moving again, the new hardtop with good brakes pulled past on the inside. Behind the wheel was an old biddy glaring in his direction mumbling obscenities and offering a quick finger salutation over her shoulder as she gunned her motor. After waving back in a similar fashion, Hack made his turn and traffic began to sail better off the main drag. His eyes squinted in the direct sunlight. In the process of slapping down the visor, his lap became cluttered with an array of cigarettes spewing from half-a-pack long forgotten.

"What the hell, why get upset?" he said. "Damn it. Missed my turn."

After doubling back, another left, and a few curves, sprawling below at the bottom of the long winding street rested his gorgeous destination. Nine holes of public links that would unwittingly soon become a festering growth in his life. To be bitten by the golf bug, was one thing; to be damn near devoured, was another.

As the car ambled down the grade, he couldn't help but smile. It was like an oasis -- seventy-five acres of nature sprawling in a valley at the base of stacked tenement apartments, seeming forever-threatening and eager to pounce and devour the selfish space below. On two other sides, lower- to middle-class homes bordered the adjacent parkway. Across the street from the end nearest the clubhouse, fields of rolling land were still being tilled. In the distance, an old farmhouse and barn stood, defying urbanization. The landscape provided a rarely observed transition from city to country simply divided by a thirty-feet wide strip of pavement.

Pulling into the parking lot, Hack found it practically empty and easy to note Jerry was late. At least it offered the choicest of available spaces and the Chevy's front wheels embraced the curb near the entrance. While gingerly springing from the car, he rammed his kneecap against the window knob. Struggling with composure, while desperately trying to smile and rub the agony away, he was determined that nothing would be allowed to mar this wonderful and gorgeous day.

"Aaaww, geeze. Son of a bitch," he said, along with a pronounced groan.

Hobbling to the rear, he hauled his gear from the trunk. It included a second-hand set of nameless woods, 'Swingin' Sam's' signature irons, a mallet putter and a pair of Hush-Puppy spikes. After changing into the golf shoes, he limped inside.

Placing his bag in a wooden rack that stretched down one of the walls, he directed his attention to the snack bar area. The counter was void of customers. Three old gents were seated at a table near one of the windows, rehashing yesterday's rounds.

"Mornin', Suh. Coffee?"

"Uh, yeah, please," Hack responded. "Miss, on second thought, mind making that tea instead?" He watched the smile on the beaming black face fade ever so slightly. "Eggs, bacon, and toast, too. Soft scrambled?" From the looks of things, he wasn't sure what he might get.

Sitting and watching her move slowly through the ritual, he soused the tea with cream and sugar, took a long sip, and reached into the pocket of his windbreaker jacket for a fresh pack of cigarettes. Only after lighting up, did he realize it was the first of the day and felt pleased by the fact. Normally, he would be breaking into another twenty by noon.

The toaster popped as the front door opened. A final member of the old gent's anticipated foursome arrived.

"Mornin', you old sandbagger," the grayest spurted and laughed.

Without ever previously hearing the rhetoric, it was easy to detect that each and every morning the same group would meet, give or take one or two, and exchange the same old stories about the same old games. The most amazing part of the scenario was the endurance of the 'over-seventy-set.' Come hail or storm they generally got in at least nine and did their best to make it a full eighteen.

"What happened to you yesterday?" one of them bellowed.

The new arrival was the smallest of the bunch Hack recognized from having met on the tee the previous fall. A very nice, but talkative type -- Sam was seventy-two. Hack had quickly learned not to be fooled by age. The old guy sported a sixteen handicap, just three strokes worse than his own.

18

"Little Mama wanted me to help her clean the attic. I was afraid she might cut me off, so, figured I'd please her," he quipped, as he carried his freshly poured cup to their table. "Got over here late after y'all had already left. Played five holes and gave up. You sure missed a doozy though."

Hack found the morning paper nearby and opened it to the sports page. It was far too early for any Redskin's news and reading about the Washington Senators wasn't very exciting. The fact they hadn't played the night before provided space for a couple of editorials by aspiring young reporters otherwise seldom in print. Sam's conversation was distracting and proved to be much more interesting.

"Danny, what's his name? You know. The one that hustles a lot and sells that heavy construction equipment, I think. Anyway, Danny and two others got up a one-club match and played for a hundred a man."

"Phew," someone whistled.

"That ain't all. They got back in, started drinkin', and the ones that lost kept tryin' to talk him into givin' them a chance to get their money back. Danny wasn't about to hit the links again, so he cooked up some wild bet for the heck of it."

"Yeah, yeah." They were goading him to the punch line.

Sam was in seventh-heaven, with his audience spellbound. "Now, you've seen'em make bets on throwin' golf balls across the creek from the porch downstairs plenty a'times. Well, he makes the bet that he could throw three balls, all at one time. Now I tell you, that's from the balcony upstairs, across the creek on the fly."

"Got to be crazy," one of the others groaned. "I've seen 'em do it one-at-a-time, but all three," he questioned, shaking his head negatively. "Nobody could do it."

"Wow. You ever tried to throw a golf ball?" Another of the group quickly contributed his two cents. "Damn thing's so small and light, you can't hardly toss it."

Ol' Sam was laughing his head off. "That's what they thought, but the bet was agreed. While everybody else goes outside tryin' to get cross-bets, Danny goes to the pro shop and buys a sleeve of new balls and scotch tapes both ends of the pack and throws it that way. Should'a seen those guys. Thought they was gonna go bananas."

Hack chuckled to himself, and at the same time envied Danny's creativity. Laughter and an increased buzz of excited conversation erupted as breakfast was shoved across the counter.

"Dollar-seventy-five, Suh." She reached for the ten-spot near his arm.

The eggs were too dry, but palatable. The bacon, crisp --just like he liked it. About halfway through, Hack caught a finger in both sides of his rib cage and nearly gagged himself with the fork. Turning to see his brother, Jerry, plop on the adjacent stool, he continued to cough and grasped a napkin to his mouth.

"Bastard. You damn near choked me to death."

"Sorry I missed," he chortled. "How've you been?"

"Same as usual." Hack looked up after having resumed taking bites from his plate. "Getting much?"

"Hell, everywhere, but home. Matter of fact, you sure missed a wang-bang last night. Told Erica I was going out of town. The crew got a suite over at Victory Inn. Cripes. What an orgy. Better than golf."

"Shit. Now, you tell me," Hack shrugged. "Why not let a body know?"

"I did try. I left a word for you to call." Jerry projected an apologetic frown which quickly altered to a broad grin. "It figures."

"What figures?"

"I always figured that good looking thing you got answering the phones must be a better lay than a message-taker."

"Screw you."

"Don't get shook up. Things went so good we're gonna make Thursdays 'poke-her' nights from now on."

Hack couldn't avoid cracking a smile. "Okay," he grinned. "Hell. It's no wonder you're late. All that activity, think you can swing a club?"

Jerry groaned." It's a miracle I'm here."

"Let's go."

As contrast to the slight chill the early morn brought, the sun majestically embraced every object in sight; its growing warmth indicating, very shortly, sweaters wouldn't even be necessary. For once, the weatherman deserved a pat on the back instead of a boot in a more strategic location.

A small bird flew from its perch in a nearby spruce and returned shortly with sprigs of straw for building a nest. Its mate clattered loudly each time they met at the tree as if to be demanding exactly how and where the contribution should be placed in their abode. The scene brought unwanted flashes of Alice dictating to him under similar circumstances. He shook his head from side-to-side to help dismiss the thought.

Jerry finally arrived after taking a detour to the toilet and joined Hack on the porch. He apologized profusely about taking so long and moaned regarding his sudden diarrhea attack. They threw their bags over their shoulders and headed for the starter. While purchasing green fees, Hack had noticed the usual clubhouse group gathering. Even then, it was hard to fathom -- in such a short period of time, from possibly being the first group off the tee, they were suddenly fifth in line. However, the delay was somewhat welcomed after a couple of early practice swings. Bones, muscles and joints that had been passively responsive to normal and automatic motor commands, quickly engaged in a rebellion within their bodies. Among most golfers, groans and grunts during warm-ups were as much a part of the game as the use of choice four-letter words.

During final practice attempts, a brief debate on 'ups' for Jerry ensued and they settled into their usual dollar bet. Needless to say, the layoff quickly took its toll. Hack ricocheted one off the retaining wall to the left, looked around fruitlessly hoping no one saw it happen, then watched it trickle to a fairly favorable location near mid-fairway -- a little more than a normal seven-iron from where he stood. Jerry sliced his down the right side.

The round included a little bit of everything. Between the two of them, they managed to get into practically every kind of possible situation: in the water; under a tree; against the fence; and, occasionally -- in the hole. Fortunately, the course wasn't very crowded. With all their difficulties, they only had to allow one faster moving threesome to play through.

Walking off the ninth green, Hack felt great. The euphoria certainly wasn't the result of the lousy round he shot, although the putting was acceptable, but the special feeling of being exempt of problems and worry. It was a seldom experienced luxury in recent times, and the golf course, an ideal outlet to void frustrations.

"Damn," Hack muttered aloud and then directed the rest of his thought verbally to Jerry. "Why the hell couldn't we have learned the game as kids? Could've been pro, . . . maybe?"

"Oh, yeah. Sure," Jerry said, and made a beeline for the head as Hack climbed the stairs.

In their absence, the relative order and quietness of the room had exploded into chaotic activity and he wormed his way through the tables to a single remaining vacant stool at the far end of the counter. A few gin games were in progress and a series of laughs, 'screw-yous' and 'you're-ons' followed suggested matches and bets being offered.

"Yes, suh. Want somethin', mistuh?"

"Sure do. Couple of cokes, sweet-thing." Hack puckered his lips in an imitation kiss causing her to blush through her dark skin. She hurriedly set on the chore of dipping down in the chest searching for cold ones. Taking a seat on the end stool, he turned to lean against the wall and surveyed the room. Spotting several familiar faces without names, he couldn't help cursing them for their luck in having jobs or circumstances affording the luxury of playing every day.

From his vantage point, through open doors leading to the balcony, he could view a large portion of the course. His adrenalin still pumping, he was anxious to tackle the second nine to correct mistakes of the first round. Jerry finally appeared on the far side of the room and immediately moved toward a pay phone. When he eventually headed toward Hack, it was evident from the expression on his face and manner of walk he was profoundly disturbed.

"Hell, I'm sorry," he started, "that damned place won't give an inch. There's trouble with an account. I've got to go. Sorry."

After a few pointless exchanges, Jerry left mumbling about some half-assed rich bastard or something.

Hack remained sitting for a while slowly sucking on the contents of the bottle. With little difficulty, he concluded it would be damned stupid to head back to the office too early and ruin a great day. Conversations and activity in the room increased in pitch. In a matter of minutes, the majority flowed down and out, bags and all.

As the bustle subsided, he moved from the stool; pushed out a butt in a table ash tray; tripped on a chair leg; made a gracious apology to one of the surviving gin buffs; and, proceeded to the pro shop. Fingering the rows of clubs, he did his best to appear knowledgeable to any who might be watching.

Selecting a driver from one of the sets, he stood hefting it as if to feel its balance and changed his grip several times.

"You'll never hit it like that."

Totally unaware of anyone's presence, Hack was taken with complete surprise. He spun around in embarrassment managing a few stutters.

"No offense intended," the club pro said, with a smile. "I'm Wilt Hardin."

Hack nodded in recognition.

"I didn't mean to interfere, but I've seen you around several times. Your swing's not too bad, but you do have a few hitches."

"Don't I know it." Hack still fumbled for expression.

"Look," Wilt said, while physically moving Hack's hands to an altered position on the grip. "Using a death hold like you've developed will never do anything but murder the ball. Tell you what. If you've got a few minutes, we'll go down and hit a few."

The pro's sudden interest in his game was initially overwhelming. However, logic quickly indicated it an excellent approach in nailing down a good prospect for new gear. Hack didn't mind it a bit. An opportunity for improvement was certainly too tempting to ignore, no matter what the circumstances.

"Great. Sure you don't mind?"

"Hell, no. That's why I'm here. Besides, one of my scheduled lessons hasn't shown. Get the seven-iron out of that set over there and I'll meet you downstairs."

After ten or more minutes of beating the soil unmercifully, Hack was hitting a few shots he found hard to believe. His grip was changed to overlap from the old baseball style and the back swing slowed and abbreviated. With less effort, the ball sailed straighter and further than he could have ever expected.

"Now, there you go. You're getting the most out of that club." Wilt beamed with pride.

After finishing a small bucket of balls, heading back to the clubhouse, the satisfaction he felt was tremendous. His head whirled with excitement and fantasies abounded, urging him to attack the course with a rekindled vengeance.

"Damn, Wilt. Sorry. I don't know where my mind is half the time, anymore. The name's Hack Arnold," finally introducing himself formally. They shook hands while still walking.

"Aw, forget it," he replied. "In this business, you know people more by their swing than their name. Come on, let's get something wet." Wilt steered for the counter. "Couple of cokes, Marie," he ordered.

Mistuh Wilt, suh. Miz Blake done called whiles y'all was out. Said she had a flat or somethin' an cain't make it," she said, offering the two drinks.

"Hard to imagine anything flat about that little doll," he mumbled, laughing to himself.

Marie giggled and pushed a glass his way. They turned, moved to the closest table, and sprawled.

"Look, I really want to thank you for that lesson. I . . ."

Wilt interrupted and bared a broad grin. "In the first place, I can't stand to see that little pill tortured beyond a point. Second, you want more lessons, you can pay. Third, when you need equipment, remember me."

"See your point," he smiled. "Think there's any hope for my game?"

"It depends." He seemed to stall for the right words. "Really, most of it depends on what you expect it to be. Hell, you're luckier than many others. You're athletic and have a lot of natural ability. Knowledge, practice and experience is all you lack, but like anything else, it takes time and effort. You'll get out what you put in." It was quite apparent Wilt was in his glory -- delighted in promoting his professionalism, both for ego and financial potential. He continued. "Good grip; smooth swing; lots of practice; and most important, use your head. Think the shot out before you address it. That way, you concentrate on the ball and not the technical aspects during the swing. Concentration. That's it. He winked. "Now. If you want more help, I'll be glad to arrange a lesson or two. Can you get free during the week?"

"Yeah," he lied. "You name it and I'll make it."

"How about a bit earlier next Friday. Say, ten o'clock?" Wilt asked, while shoving his chair from the table and rising to leave.

"Sure thing." Hack followed him as far as the pro shop to get a bucket of range balls. Still filled with great satisfaction with the immediate results under the pro's instruction, his enthusiasm to get back to the tee was overwhelming and only delayed by the need to prove his recent improvements were not a fluke. Hack rushed to the range as if driven by an uncontrollable force and a deep-rooted necessity to overcome the transgressions of his swing, all in one day.

Three buckets of balls and a good deal later, Hack confronted the opposite flow of rush-hour traffic on his way back to the office and arrived somewhat earlier than expected. It would have been preferable if the staff had already left for the day, but there was still about an hour to go before normal closing at six.

Carin flashed a wink with the messages before he retreated to the bar in his office. Gulping a slug straight from the bottle, he then proceeded fixing a double vodka-martini. After returning several calls, he plopped on the couch, raising his head just enough to occasionally sip the soothing cool liquid. He was exhausted, but it was a pleasant type of weariness. The day had really been enjoyable. It was a satisfying feeling. Damn, he thought to himself. How wonderful it had been forgetting it all for a short while.

Soon after his final separation with Alice, taking over the remainder of the entire second floor of a three-story Georgetown row house had turned out better than anticipated. It took more than a month's hard diligent work, day and night, plus an investment of much needed funds, to refinish all five rooms. A hallway separated three rear offices from two up front.

Hack's room, the largest, about twenty-five by thirty feet with its own private bath, overlooked the busy street below. Walnut paneled walls, accentuated with natural burlap sections, reached four feet short of the towering ceilings. Suspended in the center was a crystal chandelier. An executive desk of matching walnut enhanced the coordinated decor of olives, golds and blacks. A plush black leather chair sat between the desk and a custom-built art table designed to fold into the wall when not in use. The combination created a handsome and efficient working arrangement. Except for these work necessities, the general appearance and atmosphere lent itself to be a plush bachelor pad.

A modern hide-a-bed couch sat in front of a stereo and bar built into the wall while the television was conveniently located in similar circumstances across from the couch. There was custom cabinetry and book shelves guarding the sides of a fully draped area covering the front windows. Basically, he and Carin had done it all. His talents were many and woodworking an enjoyable hobby. He was truly proud of the fruits of his labor and very pleased with the conveniences it afforded. As intended, it was impressive to business clientele, making his financial status appear better than it actually was.

Sitting the empty glass on the floor, he sank away to the fading chatter of the electric Royal in the next room. Deep sleep brought its reward.

Floating into a sea of grass heavily speckled with little white dimpled balls growing abundantly like flowers in a meadow, a dozen scantily dressed maidens danced through the mist, tantalizing him with erotic moves and gestures. Feeling one's warm breath on his neck, while another's lips teased at his ear, he raised up sharply and was pulled back equally fast, hitting his head on the arm of the couch with a thud. In the same instance, his blurred eyes found Carin's upside-down face six-inches distant, grinning like a Cheshire cat.

She had knelt at the end of the sofa, leaned over, and devilishly sent her splendid tongue practically to his eardrum while he dozed.

"Bitch," he said, hiding a grin.

"God, you're romantic." She moaned.

Swinging his feet to the floor and stretching his arms upward in a single motion, she now stood directly in front of him. The business suit he remembered her wearing was gone. In its place, she wore a miniskirt generously exposing her gorgeous limbs. From his angle of view, he could have probably counted hairs if she hadn't been wearing panties. In her hands she held two glasses, one of which she extended downward to him. Not hesitating to resist her offer, he took it and swallowed half the contents in a single gulp.

"Damn, lady, you look almost as good as the dream I was having." Hack smiled up at her.

"I could tell it must have been good. I noticed your pants swelling and decided to bring you around to save it for later."

"Bullshit, you know the old stud's got plenty to go round. By the way, it's way past quitting time, isn't it?" He struggled to his feet.

"I might have known," she said, with a moan. "You promised to take me out tonight. Damn. Half of the time I think all you want me for is to slave and screw. I don't see . . ."

"Cut it out," he said, in jest. "That shit-assed pout doesn't work, anymore. Anyway, you don't need it. Even though it slipped my mind, and I'm sorry, . . . it's a good idea. I'm starved."

"Oh, baby," she said, throwing her hands behind his head and yanking his face into her crotch.

"Keep it up," he said, with a gasp while jerking back quickly, "and we'll get no further than this couch."

"Don't worry lover," she said, in her most sexy voice. "Later. I need you, too."

* * *

The bed felt so relaxing he didn't want to move. It was amazing to be wide awake without the alarm, especially on a Monday morning. The long weekend had been perfect medicine - - to coin a phrase, 'just what the doctor ordered.' Saturday and Sunday were both spent at the course and the pro's advice from Friday had proven very worthwhile. Twisting to a crosswise position, he reached down for a pack of butts on the floor and, after lighting up, rolled to his back pulling on the smoke slowly while staring at the ceiling.

Trying to focus his thoughts on the days schedule, his mind inadvertently kept reverting to golf and things more pleasant. Realizing Carin would arrive early enough to prevent him from the intrusion of the rest of the staff, he lingered in his paradise of daydreaming.

Hiring Carin as his secretary six months before the separation, Alice, without justification, lowered the boom on Hack as quickly as his decision had been made. A fine looker, totally non-conservative after six, she was just the opposite during working hours. Not only being exceptionally efficient, she was a real blessing for his short memory, especially when it came to remembering his parent's and children's birthdays. The double doors slid apart and 'guess-who' peeked through.

"You've gotta be sick," she blurted in amazement. "I've never seen you awake this early on your own."

"I'm sick all right," he gagged. "Auuggh. It's lack-a-nookie."

"After Friday night, bull. You never had it so good. Come on, rise and shine. I've got your transfusion here, so get it while it's hot."

Crossing the room and placing the steaming cup of coffee on the desk, she picked up the strewn clothes from the chair and floor, moved to the walk-in closet, and shortly returned with a fresh outfit.

"Don't know what I'd do without you doll. I can't understand why some rich bastard ain't tucked you between the sheets to stay."

"I've got plenty of time for that," she responded in a rather disinterested way. "Besides, I can't imagine being tied down that tight to anything, or anybody, . . . except you." Her last two words were barely audible.

Hack pretended not to hear them as he ducked into the bathroom where she had water running in the shower and a basin full for shaving.

"Hey Babe," he called. "Soon as I get dressed, let's go across the street for breakfast."

Over the rattle of the water beating against his body, he distinctly heard her response.

"No doubt about it, he's got to be sick."

* * *

Basically, things went without any major hitches through the following week, primarily due to Hack's better frame of mind. Yet, with each passing day, the urge grew increasingly stronger to get away from the office. Most of the time escaping to the course was impossible, but outings to a nearby driving range were frequently squeezed between business trips in preparation for his first scheduled lesson with the pro. Carin had been well versed with an array of fabrications intended for any inquiring clients. She should certainly be able to struggle through the day without him.

After finishing the last group of layouts on the booklet he had been designing, it was nearly one-thirty. As tired and exhausted as he felt from the long and hectic day, he stretched out on the bed unable to sleep. After considering fixing a nightcap, he decided against it knowing one might lead to two and he wanted to be at his functional best in the morning. Still keyed from his efforts and anticipations of the morrow, Hack struggled to clear his mind of all thought.

"Screw it," he groaned, rolling over the side of the bed to an upright sitting position on its edge. "Damn, I hate this," he said, continuing to talk to himself. "Aw, what the hell."

Enough light filtered between the slightly opened drapes to allow a small degree of visibility in the darkened room. Rather than turn on the lamp, he inched his way around the back of the couch, feeling the cabinets to find the bar section. Lowering the door to its shelf position, he groped through the bottles in search of the brandy.

Assured the right choice had been made, Hack selected a buck glass and carefully poured the liquid, holding his index-finger against the inside and stopped when he felt it cover the second joint. Repeating his moves in reverse, he made his way around the couch to crawl back into bed as the phone rang.

"Who in the crap . . . ?" He never finished the sentence.

Strictly out of instinct, Hack lunged in the direction of the ringing instrument. The near corner leg of the desk suddenly fit itself between the fourth and fifth toes of his left foot. His drink flew through the air in the general direction of the sofa. Pain shot through his leg, stomach, chest, shoulders, fingertips, and even the top of his head. A blood curdling scream accompanied any number of writhing actions.

The phone persistently rang.

Supported by "ooohs, aaahs, unnhs," and several other more fitting four-letter words, he sprawled stretching across the top of the desk and snatched the receiver from its cradle.

"Damn it! Hello!"

"Maybe I better call back at a better time," he heard Jerry say over a background of noise and music.

"You dumb bastard. Do you realize what time it is?" He

strained his eyes trying to focus on the wall clock.

"I know what time it is. Do you know what time it is? I bet you don't." Jerry broke into a drunken giggle.

Hack scooted from his semi-prone position and gained access to the floor with his feet in a cautious manner. He turned and sat carefully in his executive chair raising his hurt foot across the opposite knee and snapped on the desk lamp, tucking the receiver under his chin.

"Oh, God." He gasped in shock. "I think I broke my fuckin' toe." He turned his foot to the light. "I did. I broke my fuckin' toe. Jerry, damn it. You broke my fuckin' toe."

"How in the hell could I break your fuckin' toe when I'm laying here dippin' my wick in a fine little thing."

"You asshole. Shut-up." His little toe did a right-angle in an outward direction at the halfway point. "I ain't bullshittin'. My toe's busted."

"You want I should call an ambulance?" He giggled some more.

"Up your's." Hack slammed the phone on its cradle and concentrated on the grotesquely protruding digit. Deciding to risk trying to correct the malformation, he gently moved the upper portion and it popped to its normal position. Apparently, instead of breaking the bone, it had simply separated at the joint.

Invading the medicine cabinet, he found gauze, but nothing to hold it in place. Ingeniously, a combination of scotch and masking tape sufficed in anchoring the toe to the rest of the foot for protection. Still mumbling about his ill-fated luck and his brother's stupidity, he yanked the brandy saturated sheets from the bed and decided to sack-out on the couch in its closed state. It was going on four o'clock by the time sleep came.

On awakening, it wasn't bad enough his toe was sore as hell, he had to also suffer Carin's smart-ass comments. However, being the angel she could be, after making a trip to the drugstore, she helped wrap the injury in such a way he could still wear a tennis shoe. Before being able to manage his escape to the club, he got stuck with repaying her kind attentions with a quick breakfast.

* * *

Placing clubs on the rack was part of the ritual. Wilt waved from across the room and simultaneously motioned to the counter for two coffees.

"Morning," Hack yawned.

"Rough night?"

"Just trying to do two days in six hours. Didn't want to miss the first lesson."

Marie arrived placing the cups on their table. "Yo tea, suh," she proudly spouted.

"Hell, I must be living right. A good looking chick like you remembering my drink," he laughed. "My wife couldn't even do that."

She returned to the counter wiggling her tail in a contented manner.

"Better be careful," Wilt chuckled. "she might blame you for that pot belly of hers. You know, . . . a 'Lil' Black Hack.'"

Hack ignored the remark and preoccupied himself with sugaring and then slowly sipping his tea, finding it a lot more tasteful than Wilt's ethnic comment.

Wilt changed the subject. "I noticed you were limping."

"That's a long story I'd rather skip for the moment." Hack smiled and slowly began to laugh. "I busted my toe last night," he said, deciding to confess and relate the details of the mishap. Before it was over, Wilt was almost in tears.

"You sure you don't want to cancel out this morning?" he asked, while wiping his eyes with a paper napkin.

"Hell, no. But, I'd like you to take a gander at the woods I'm using. They're old as the hills and I just can't hit that damn driver."

"Sure thing. Hey, Mitch," he said, calling across the room in the same breath as he motioned to a newcomer just arriving. "Come here. I want you to meet someone."

Walking in their direction was a rather tall well proportioned chap with slightly graying temples of a premature nature who didn't appear to be any older than his early thirties.

"Mitch, this is Hack Arnold. Hacker, . . . Mitch Flannigan."

"Hi'ya, Mitch. I've seen you around several times."

Mitch acknowledged his greeting with a head nod as they shook hands. "Seen you, too. How's the game?"

"Not as good as my bed life. At least, I've never shanked a

piece of pussy."

"A man after my own heart," Mitch laughed.

"Hack's got the potential for a pretty good swing," Wilt offered.

"He's being kind. He wants my money," Hack returned.

"Got him pegged already, I see," Mitch agreed with a smile. Wilt started to pout and then broke into a grin as he got up to go to the counter.

"Curiosity's got me." Hack directed his remark to Mitch. "I've noticed a lot of these guys seem to always be around. By their ages, most of them can't be retired. How in the hell do they manage so much time for golf?"

"Some of them never work." A bit of sarcasm mixed with envy could be detected in his tone. "They've either got a wife busting ass or some chick setting up a free feed bag. Some of the better players try to hustle bets and make enough to scratch through. There's another handful working nights bartending, or whatever; plus a handful of cops on disability.

"'Unemployment Haven,' huh?"

"You said it. Me included," he said, with a grin. "On the sly, three nights every weekend I'm at the Sundowner's night club working the door and got a couple of gals I sell myself to for spare cash. How about you?"

"I've been breaking my balls the hard way."

"Speaking about balls," Wilt interrupted. "We'd better get that lesson on the road."

"You got it," Hack responded and turned back to Mitch. "See you later if you're still around."

"I'll be here when you're done."

Hack grabbed his clubs from the rack and hurried after the pro. Wilt was headed toward the shop to get practice balls. "Hey, Pro. If there's time, I'd really like you to look at these clubs before we get started."

"Sure," he said as he came from behind the counter. "Phew, they are a bit done in," he commented, fingering the head of the driver. "Dime store Sam Snead. They're not a rare breed."

"They look like I got'em from a cave man," Hack said jokingly, mustering a weak grin.

It only took a few minutes more and Wilt let out a big

chuckle. "Hell, it looks like there aren't two that match. Craziest thing I ever saw." He gripped and hefted several of the clubs before weighing them on his equipment. "In fact, some of these shafts look like they're slightly bent."

"It's that bad, huh?"

"That bad," he shook his head affirmatively. "Believe me, this is no sales push. You'll have problems as long as you use them."

"Shit, should'a known better than trying to get a bargain buying something I don't know anything about."

"What'd you pay?"

"Not a whole bunch, but still too much. A hundred through a newspaper ad. I knew they were old, but hell, I thought . . ."

Wilt interrupted before Hack could finish. "Yeah, a lotta guys do. Somebody's always getting stung. It's easy to be fooled with a big name signature on a set of clubs. Most people don't realize it can be third or fourth-line equipment. Poor 'Ol' Swingin' Sam' probably signed a contract years ago when the money was bad on the tour and wishes to hell he could get out of it, now-a-days."

"That's par for the course; no pun intended," Hack muttered. "I generally learn the hard way. Sure would like some new sticks, but I can't handle it, just yet. It'll be a couple of months until I start getting returns on the new contracts."

"Hell, if that's the only problem, we can work something out. I don't need all the cash up front."

"Like what?" Hack's eyes beamed with interest at the proposal exposing his enthusiasm.

"A third now and the rest over the next three or four months," Wilt suggested.

Trying to restrain against self-indulgence proved impossible. As hard as he struggled with logic relating to his financial picture, the urge to accept the offer was too great a temptation to resist. "Sound's fine," he found himself saying.

"Great. What appeals to you?"

"Aw, I don't know. Something with a grip and a head on it, I guess."

Wilt chuckled. "Before you start, rule out the lady's clubs." He laughed, then sobered. "Swing weight, shaft-stiffness, and certainly feel, are the important factors. Off-the-cuff, I'd say you could use stiff-shafts with a D-2 weight. There's several here on hand. Or, if you can't find any, I can always order."

"What about these?"

"You are a business man," he goaded. "They're a closeout item; good price; right weight; but, wrong shaft."

"Shaft's that important?"

"Yep." He didn't hesitate. "Once you get to swinging properly, I really feel you're too strong for a regular shaft."

"Sorry to interrupt," the assistant pro made his presence known. "We got that new shipment of Haig's in this morning I haven't had a chance to unpack. Maybe he'd like to see them."

"Damn good idea." Wilt patted the youth on the back as he went toward the stockroom and called over his shoulder, "Come here a minute Hack, I want you to take a gander at these beauts."

"Haig's? Walter Hagen's aren't they? Pretty good name club, huh?"

"You bet your bottom," he blurted. "Cadillac of its competition. Try them on for size." He shoved a five-iron into his hands.

"Wow," Hack exclaimed, "that feels great. Ummm, super great as a matter of fact." He gripped a couple of the irons and tested the driver from the set of four woods. "How much?"

"Let you have'em for your clubs and, oh, let's say, three hundred and a quarter."

"Sold," he quickly responded. "One thing though, what in the hell are you going to do with my old clubs?"

"Cut'em down for kids."

Hack produced a big grin. Having finally succumbed to the decision in favor of himself, a few pangs of guilt subsided in realizing youth would benefit through it. Typical to his naive nature, he failed to consider there would be a buck-or-two involved for Wilt's pocket before a child would ever get their hands on them.

The lesson showed substantial improvement beyond his earlier initial assistance from the pro. Wilt lauded his progress and there was little doubt the new sticks had something to do with the added success. For the first time, he experienced sensing a golf club as being an extension of his arms. They worked with his movement, not against it. Most of the time, the seven iron was the instrument used in the lesson. However, unusual to Wilt's schedule, he moved to the five, and then to the three-iron before completing the hour.

Hack was elated, but not satisfied. His undying zeal goaded him to try another two buckets of balls on his own before calling it quits. Weary from the efforts, and his hand quite sore, he gathered his gear and went directly for the car. Stronger than his urge to leave was the desire to become more of a regular in this new environment. After exchanging shoes at the trunk, he returned to the club in search of Mitch.

They bumped into each other in the lobby area. "Where you been?" Mitch asked, as he smiled.

"I . . . well, I . . ."

"Forget it," he laughed. "It's got you by the nuts already. I can tell."

Hack grinned weakly and suddenly burst into a hearty laugh. It was an admission to having fallen prey to the dreaded golf-bug's bite.

"Don't stand there. Get your clubs. There's only three of us. We'll get a match."

"Wow, I'm really tired. I should really get . . . . What the hell." Hack turned away and trudged for the car and his gear.

* * *

Entering the workweek with an enthusiasm equal to having had a vitamin shot, by the following Friday night, with the television blaring out the National Anthem, it was time to call it quits. Five sixteen-hour days in a row was somewhat of an overexertion even considering the wonderful break experienced the previous weekend.

Pouring another drink from the bar, Hack's thoughts regressed to more enjoyable memories recently experienced. After getting his new golf clubs, and relenting to Mitch's insistence for another nine, he had the chance to truly gamble for the first time. Instead of betting on individual play, as had previously been the case between he and Jerry, the situation involved having a partner. However, because the foursome was comprised of players of widely varying ability, it was impossible to pair into permanent teams for the entire round. As an alternative, they decided on a "Round-Robin" since it provided the fairest chance for the weaker of the group. Each participant would have the other as a partner at least once; teams changing after every three holes. Under such an arrangement, even though partners would rotate, whenever a really unbalanced pairing occurred, the disadvantaged twosome received a proper adjustment. A best ball basis, match play, was the method of scoring. The lowest score of either partner determined that team's score for a particular hole; equally scored holes were considered halves; and, the most holes won determined the winners for that segment of the "Robin." Rationally, it seemed to be a rather fair approach, giving every player the chance to have the strongest as a partner. In hindsight, as usual, the best player still had the better end of the deal.

Even though losing a couple of bucks, practically speaking, it was worth the learning experience. Better than that, it provided the opportunity to meet a couple of other regulars from the club and a further chance to make headway into the clique.

He and Mitch were getting along rather well, and Hack received an offer to join his foursome the following day. That Saturday's match of thirty-six holes was repeated again on Sunday and the weekend represented another unique and total fulfillment.

Similar weekends, and certain days in between, were to become relished opportunities to partake in otherwise unforgivable absences from responsibility -- several weeks had passed since seeing the children.

Opening the couch, he beamed at the thought of teaching his son the game of golf. Hell, after all, he was almost twelve. Maybe he's still too young. Hummmm, I'll have to ask Wilt, he thought.

After pulling the sheet to his chin, his eyes focused on the barely visible ceiling for what seemed to be an eternity as his mind replayed each shot of every hole played in the prior weekend's rounds.

* * *

It was raining cats and dogs. Glancing at the desk clock, it served warning he had slept much too late. The phone disturbed the silence with a startling ring and he leaped to respond as quickly as possible.

"Hello."

"Hi, Uncle Hack." It was Josey.

"Hi, love bug. Bet I know what you want."

"You still coming to see me?" Her response was sincere and a pleading question of relative despair.

"You bet'cha. I wouldn't miss seeing you for the world. I'd have been there by now, but I worked awful late last night and overslept," he said, with a yawn. "How about the movies this afternoon?

"Hey, Cindy. Hey, Suzie. Hey, Billy, Uncle Hack's taking us to the movies."

"Sweetheart, I've got to get going and get ready so I won't be too much later. Okay?"

Josie offered no goodbye, just a loud click of her phone receiver hitting its cradle. Beaming with satisfaction, he headed for the shower and spun the taps in adjustment to body tolerance. Shedding his robe, he took time to squat on the bathroom throne and inadvertently began to browse through a new issue of Playboy magazine.

"You're on 'Candid Camera,'" Carin shouted, standing in the doorway snapping her fingers in mock gesture.

Her unexpected appearance scared him so badly he passed gas and it echoed though the bowl and room in undesired unison.

"Damn you, woman. You ain't so fuckin' funny," he yelled.

"If you could have seen the look on your face," she roared, "I'd have given a year of sex to have a picture."

"Damn it," he said, joining her in laughter. "You're fired."

"You can't fire me, it's my day off." Her voice faded as she disappeared.

Immediate response to Carin's quick wit was often difficult. "Well then, you can scrub my back." His statement rang through the office exterior as a demand as he stepped into the steaming shower. A few minutes passed and she entered the bathroom wearing his robe and carrying half the contents of her coffee in a buck glass.

"Here," she said. "Maybe it will improve your disposition."

"How come you're here today?"

"Do I need a reason?" She pretended to briefly pout and

changed her expression quickly. "Beasley called late yesterday, raising hell. He insisted the printer needed to have his job late this afternoon. Ted's coming in to wind it up and I've still got a couple of pages to type. And, I wanted to do some shopping while I'm downtown, anyway."

"Holy shit," he hollered. Taking a sip of coffee, he managed to spill just enough of the red-hot steaming liquid to burn the hell out of the end of his pecker.

"This just ain't your day, is it, hon?" She cooed sympathetically while dabbing softly with a hand towel. "Let mama kiss it."

* * *

The weather cleared by the time the movie was over. On the way back, Hack suggested the day wouldn't be complete without a visit to the drive-in for a fudge cake. At the last minute Sharon, his sister, had decided to tag along. Hack wasn't particularly pleased by her divorce and tried to spend as much time with her children as possible. Feeling bloated from an overabundance of popcorn and ice cream, they drove to the house where he kissed the kids and watched the four of them scamper in all directions to cram in a little more fun before sunset. Sensing a melancholic mood surfacing in Sharon, Hack refused her offer for him to hang around.

After saying goodbyes on the front steps, he headed back to find the office dark and uninviting.

Subconsciously, Hack had hoped to find Carin still there. Dreading the loneliness waiting above, he stalled long enough to buy cigarettes and a couple of magazines at the drugstore. Approaching the door to the front rooms, he burst out laughing. Hanging by a piece of thread from the top of the door was a band-aid with the imprint of Carin's lips in bright red lipstick across the pad. Pulling it down, Hack opened the door, tossed it on her desk, and headed for his room. Pushing the double sliding doors apart, the phone rang.

"Hello."

"Hello. Hack?"

"Yeah."

"This is Mitch. What are you doing?"

"Oh, Mitch." Hack's spirits elevated. "Just coming in the

door."

"Good. Glad I caught you. Got any plans tonight?"

"Not really. Figured I'd probably consult the 'strange book,'" Hack said, as a joke, while secretly wishing such a boon existed.

"Great, that's what I had in mind. I've got three gals on tonight and there would be only two of us to take care of them. Sound good?"

"Hell. Sounds about as good as getting one-up on a lock bet. What time and where?"

"Down at the Sundowner's. You know, on Rt. 301, in Waldorf."

"Got it."

"Make it about ten."

* * *

Waking up in the morning with a head like the 'Goodyear Blimp,' it took several minutes for Hack to realize where he was. Both beds in the room had been shoved together. At the far edge, long red curls drifted down a pillow and under the sheets. It was fairly evident by the lacy black lingerie strewn about, plus the cup size of a bra dangling from the center ceiling light, it must have been a helluva good time. Whatever he had done, his tongue felt swollen and as if it was almost glued to the roof of his mouth. The sensation was horribly enhanced by the rotten taste he was experiencing.

Rolling off the end of the bed, he reeled his way to the toilet and plopped on the commode. Resting his elbows on his knees with his head in his hands, he prayed softly -- "Oh, God. Help me through this one and I'll get through the next one by myself."

Following a run of diarrhea, Hack struggled to his feet and leaned forward on the basin counter unconsciously glaring into the mirror. With the realization of what he was observing, he made a ghastly grunt and began splashing his face with water from the cold tap.

There was shaving equipment and all other male and female needs. He vaguely recalled Mitch mentioning some rooms set aside for the night club owner's use whenever he was in town. Swishing around everything left in a bottle of mouthwash before feeling satisfied, he then gulped down the bubbling action of three seltzers. That, coupled with cold water from the shower beating over his head and body, eventually contributed to the attitude -- he might survive.

Toweling dry, he strolled quietly past the bed, easily detecting through the sheets that Mitch's tastes weren't at all bad. The door to the adjoining room sat partly open and he couldn't resist taking a peek. As he expected, Mitch was sprawled from corner to corner using his blond friend as a blanket. Gently shutting the door, Hack crawled back in the sack and slid across to cuddle up to 'Miss Thirty-Four C-Cup.'

Wiggling his nose through her tresses, he tenderly kissed her ear and the nape of her neck. She groaned softly, turned slowly, and buried her face in his shoulder. Circling his chest with her arm, the warmth of her body brought a surge of passion as she pressed tightly against him, squeezing his leg between hers. His fingers stroked her hair, continued down her back, and ultimately caressed the firmness of her buttocks. Her breathing increased to short rapid pants and her moist lips nursed gently on his neck. Rolling simultaneously, he pulled her to the top and felt the weight of her body mold to his. The throbbing in his groin increased as his growing shaft moved against the inside of her leg. She shifted slightly, so as to bring it in full contact, and pushed steadily down on the swollen mass. The enveloping warmth stirred his blood to a boiling point which began to revive the alcohol content from the night before. Her lips found his as an eager tongue forced its way deep into his mouth.

"All right, everybody up." The door flew open with a thunderous bang and there stood bare-ass Mitch.

Hack almost bit her tongue off. "Holy shit," he yelled, jumping up sharply as 'Reds' tumbled away head first to the floor.

"Son of a bitch," Mitch blurted, "I . . . I . . . aye, aye, aye, aye." He burst into a chorus of a familiar Spanish ditty, prancing and dancing in a circle with his balls flapping in the breeze.

"You crazy prick." Hack roared with laughter as Mitch was nearing tears.

Reds didn't think it was quite as funny and began to get further disturbed when Mitch kept laughing and rambling on about how she looked upside down and spread-eagled sailing through the air.

40

Settling down to a steady giggle, Mitch's blonde, having been wakened by the ruckus, stood looking at the both of them as if they had completely lost their minds. Eventually regaining enough composure to get dressed, the four had breakfast at the motel restaurant.

Following the meal and making an agreement to meet later at the course, Hack and Mitch drove their respective dates home. Reds had gotten over her earlier embarrassment and as Hack dropped her in front of her apartment, kissed him warmly, making a point they finish what had been left incomplete, sometime real soon.

Mitch made a quicker trip and had already set up a match with two other chaps by the time Hack arrived at the club.

"You sure you wanna make that bet?"

"Hell, yeah," Mitch positively asserted. "I know these guys and how they play. Mac's game is about like mine and the other guy's got nothing on you."

"Okay, if you say so. Match play, ain't it? Best ball?" Hack asked.

"Yep. Ten bucks a man."

The first tee was swarming with golfers. A few were regulars, but most weekend duffers. Hack welcomed the wait in having the chance to limber up with practice swings, a few chips, and several putts on the practice green until Mitch called him over to introduce their adversaries. Mac's partner Harry turned out to be one of the players involved in the earlier "Round-Robin" match.

Finally getting off the tee and hitting first, Hack was definitely relieved when his drive sailed straight down the middle of the fairway. After Hack sank a four-footer for birdie on the first hole, Mitch beamed with satisfaction at his choice of partners. Unfortunately, the glow wasn't very long lasting. Hack missed an even shorter putt for par on two. Since Mitch also bogeyed, they lost to their opponent's best-ball par and the match went back to even.

During the next four holes, Mitch managed three pars and a birdie on number six. "We'll press the bet," Mac declared as they moved to the seventh tee.

Not wanting to seem obviously ignorant, Hack waited until all had hit and were walking down the fairway before confronting Mitch. "What's this 'press-the-bet' shit?" he asked.

Mitch smiled. "All it really means is they're making another ten dollar bet for the last three holes." He noticed Hack's curiosity wasn't completely sated and continued. "Well, the custom is, when a team gets two down, they're entitled to a 'press.' It's simply another separate bet, generally made in the same amount of money as the original, for the remaining holes from the point the 'press' is made. In other words, we've already got them two down and there's only three holes left to play. For them to get out of the first bet and break even, they'd have to win two of the remaining three holes. Not very good odds, huh? But, by taking another bet, they only have to win one hole out of the three and halve the other two to win the press. That way, even though we've won the original, they've won the press, and everything breaks even. Comprendez?"

"Yeah. In fact, we could win both bets, or lose both if we drop the last three holes. Right?"

"Ya got it, Hacker, but don't talk like that. We got'em by the short hairs and we're gonna win it all."

Mac and Harry both fell apart and lost the last three holes. Mitch birdied the seventh and Hack sank a real gagger, fifty-feet at least, for a bird on eight. Being two down on the first press and out on the original with only the last hole to play, they pressed for a second time.

The ninth was one of the more tricky holes on the course. Slightly downhill from an elevated tee, it was approximately two hundred and sixty-five yards to the flag. Although not long, the creek crossed the fairway just in front of a huge sand trap guarding the green. A better hitter could make it across and possibly even drive the green by going straight at it, although there was a narrow margin for error with out-of-bounds close to the left and rear. Laying-up short of the creek with an iron, or hitting across to a wider landing area to the right, was the higher percentage shot.

Mitch drove across following Hack's successful safe attempt short of the creek. Mac pulled his shot too far left and watched as the ball took a single hop before diving into the water.

Harry hit the worse shot of his round, but luckily stayed in the

42

rough dangerously close to the out-of-bounds. However, his second shot wasn't much better. Having a bad lie, he sculled the ball and it dribbled into the sand trap. Hack and Mitch both made par while Mac's team's best score was bogey. With a sly wink from Mitch, Hack followed him and their competition upstairs, stopping long enough between nines to have a drink before trying to complete the eighteen. Being thirty dollars down, neither Mac or Harry seemed to groan much over the loss and by the time they were ready to play the next nine, the bet had been doubled.

Literally zipping through the back-side in record time, they were once again at the same table ordering drinks -- this time without the presence of either Mac or Harry. Fifty bucks richer for the day wasn't bad at all.

"Sorry I didn't do more to help that last round," Hack said.

"Don't be crazy," Mitch quipped. "Your making par on the third got the tie for us. It would've made a lot of difference without it."

"Ummph. I was damn lucky the way I topped that wedge close enough for a gimme four. If I could cut down some of those screwed up shots, I . . ."

"Don't worry about it. You're on the right track with Wilt. Just give it a chance and don't let up. Besides, from what I've seen of your short game, you could be on the tour." He continued. "It ain't how, it's how many. Don't you forget it. You'll soon find out golf can be a game of misses. One of the big differences between being a low or high-handicapper is whether you can come back with a good makeup shot."

"You think it's dumb to bet? I mean, the way I'm playing?"

"All depends on how and who you bet," he chuckled. "Don't jump on anyone you don't know, and wager small until you're sure. You got a good lesson today. A ten dollar bet can really grow in a single round."

"You're right. Never dreamed it would come out that good."

"Aw, shit," Mitch muttered after looking at his watch. "I've got to get going. There's several things to do before working tonight. I really enjoyed it though." He stood and shoved his chair to the table, shook hands in a brief but sincere manner, and sauntered across the room. When he reached the front door he turned and offered his own apology. "By the way, sorry about busting in on you this morning."

"Forget it." Hack laughed and waved his hand in a go-away gesture. "Next time, I'll know better and keep on pumping."

CHAPTER II

Contrary to earlier reactions, Hack found it increasingly difficult to concentrate on work or other responsibilities during the following weeks. At every chance, he used endless excuses to sneak a trip to the driving range or sandwich in a quick nine holes. With each outing, there appeared to be improvement in certain areas of his play, but setbacks in others. While the learning process offered encouragement, it seemed each time he would have one part of his game going well, some other phase would be suffering. Trying to get the irons, woods and putter all working at peak performance in combination, wasn't easy.

Daydreaming was also becoming an unwelcome habit. Initially, the enthusiasm generated by exposure to the game, with the chance of enjoying fresh air and sun, created a beneficial surge of energies in work matters. However, moderation was proving to be an extremely difficult condition for Hack when it involved anything to do with golf. The desire to be at the club was becoming a mental infestation hard to ignore.

Carin buzzed the intercom announcing Jerry's phone call. The interruption accomplished bringing Hack to a state of immediate awareness.

"Yeah, what's up?"

"Dresses and cocks tonight." Jerry laughed. "Can you make it?"

"Reckon so."

"Great. It's at the motel around eight. Room 'Three-O-Three.'" Click.

Instead of returning the receiver to its cradle, he hit Carin's button on the dial. In a jiffy, she popped through the door and perched on the corner of his desk.

"Got anything cooking this evening?"

"Planning on tinting the mop." She tugged at the tips of her hair. "Why, have you got something in mind?"

"Jerry's been trying to get me to one of his parties for a pretty good while. They've got one scheduled tonight and I thought you might get a kick in tagging along."

"It sounds like it might be fun. I'd love to go."

"Could be." He tried to subdue an impish grin and quickly turned to a more serious tone. "But, there's something you ought to know up front. I've heard it gets pretty wild sometimes."

"Here an orgy; there an orgy; everywhere, an orgy-orgy." Carin humped her hips a couple of times as she hummed her way out and back to her desk.

Hack tried settling into projects on the agenda, finding it difficult to believe it was still midmorning. His half-hearted efforts in attempting to muster interest in productivity were fruitless. Late in the afternoon, Carin left early to get clothes for the evening. Hack took the opportunity to stretch out for a short nap and didn't stir until she returned.

After lazing around for about an hour with cocktails, they rushed through showers and other details of getting ready. Clad in a towel, Carin appeared unusually appealing and the effect could be felt through his body. Auburn hair reached to her shoulders, although she frequently wore it gathered behind her head in a ponytail. Even though she was covered, he envisioned her youthful firm breasts capped by areolas of light pink softly blending into creamy white skin. For whatever the evening promised, he was well stimulated and sexually prepared.

Dinner at 'Duke's' sated physical hunger, but did little to allay expectations of what might be in store. While getting the car, the heavens let go. The downpour was so heavy it was extremely hard to see and Hack proceeded slightly above snail's pace. From before and after dinner drinks, Carin's condition hovered around being tipsy, adding to driving difficulties. She incessantly kept tickling the inside of Hack's leg and probing her finger into the opening of his fly. Finally arriving at the motel, they made a wild dash for protection under the overhang, climbed the stairs, and headed for the room. As they approached, it was odd to find the suite dark and appearing vacated and empty. The first knock received no answer. Following the second attempt, a grumbling voice responded. The door cracked ajar and one eye and a nose peeked through the opening.

Upon recognition and the proper password, Hack led Carin into a pitch black room as light sifting in from outside sources afforded a vague picture of what was transpiring. At least three couples were in one bed together; a foursome on the couch; a pair on the floor; and, another couple half-in and half-out of a chair. The door closed and the room was unbelievably dark once again.

Carin grabbed for the tail of Hack's sport coat as they threaded their way through the debris of bodies.

"Hell. I feel like I'm on patrol sneaking through enemy lines," Hack jokingly said.

Carin snickered and quipped, "Yeah, there sure are enough booby traps laying around here. Don't fall into some strange 'foxhole.'" She should have said 'knock on wood.' Catching her toe square in somebody's ass, she stumbled headlong into Hack's back. In turning to try and help her, they both lost their balance and sprawled on top of what turned out to be Jerry and some broad who went, "Ommph."

"Ohhhhh, shit," he groaned. "I've been shot. Medic. Medic."

"You've been shot?" The girl cushioning Jerry moaned. "You damn near made me explode. It felt like that rod of yours came out of my belly button."

A light flashed temporarily brightening the room long enough for everybody to roar at the twisted shapes on the floor. In an instant, it was dark with all returning to their particular thing.

Struggling to their feet, Hack and Carin searched and succeeded in locating the adjoining room. In opposition to the scene just experienced, three couples sat simply boozing and talking. Joining the reserved merriment, Hack and Carin settled down with sorely needed drinks.

Relaxing and exchanging names while blending into the open conversation, they quickly sensed the small select group preferred keeping sexual encounters a bit more intimate than their counterparts next door. The discussion initiated a surprising revelation to Hack that he felt the same.

* * *

Awaking almost simultaneously, Carin was still in Hack's

47

arms from the night before. Raising to an elbow, she brought her mouth to lightly touch his lips, kissed them softly and said in a low voice, "God, you've got bad breath."

He chuckled and pinched her ass.

"Ouch," she groaned. "I didn't deserve that."

They rolled and wrestled on the bed for several minutes until he pretended to be subdued. Leaping to the floor, her beautiful bare body scampered across the carpet and disappeared into the bathroom.

Hack sat on the bed long enough to finish a cigarette, heard the shower door close, and assumed he could get to the sink. After washing his face in cold water, he plopped on the commode and began brushing his teeth, attempting to spit out the excess suds into the toilet through the small opening left between his legs.

"I could do that easier than you," Carin quipped.

"Don't doubt it a bit."

"By the way," she continued, "what did you really think about last night? You know, the open sex, and all that?"

"Aw, I don't know. Guess I didn't turn on like I figured I would. Besides, I don't want anyone else to know how bad you really are." He chuckled.

"Bastard." She pretended pouting. "But, I love you for it."

He moved to the shower door and slid it open. Carin stood with the water sliding down her body from strands of saturated hair hanging near her shoulders. In the corner of her eye was a tear that might have easily been hidden among the shower drops had it been a moment later. "What's wrong, baby?" He moved to cup her face in his hands.

"Just being silly. You know me. Last night, meant a lot."

He kissed her tenderly on her nose. "See, no bad breath."

She smiled. Her arms raised and encircled him around his neck. Their bodies pressed tight together and he felt a softness in their embrace that seemed unique. Their lips met and lingered for precious moments. The sweetness of all her body began to flow from her mouth to his.

Peppering spurts of water stimulated every muscle into the spirit of the union. Hack gently lifted her upward. With legs circling his waist, her hips gyrated slowly at first, building to frantic movement as fingernails dug deeply into his neck. He pressed her back against the tiled wall, breathing heavily in her ear as she nursed hard on his shoulder. The thunderous roar of the falling liquid echoed with sounds of passion growing to a resounding climax. The water hitting the floor returned to a soft patter as they remained together savoring their satisfaction to its fullest extent.

Moving apart, Hack swept her off her feet, carrying her wet and lovely body in his arms to the bed. She lie silently, not uttering a sound, as he tenderly used a towel to caress away the dampness covering her skin. He leaned to kiss her breasts, neck, and finally her lips. Carin's eyes opened and met his in full contact.

"Got a dime for a cuppa coffee, Mac?"

"Shit." He laughed, shoving the towel in her face. "You can sure come up with 'em."

* * *

The entire crew was working in the back before the front offices were opened. Being well aware their boss used them for living quarters, the staff had grown accustomed and adjusted to Hack's occasional late mornings. However, Ralph, a one-time client and friend, had an appointment at nine and was usually a stickler for promptness. His rare tardiness was welcomed. When he finally arrived appearing somewhat disconcerted, Hack decided it best to give him his space. Ralph was the type to ponder over situations and problems before discussing them and always presented an overabundance of hemming and hawing in his approach. It was just a question of time for him to get to the point. Ultimately, he brought the matter to the fore and left much happier than he came. Hack's loan of two hundred dollars would save his life.

Considering the full schedule of the day, things went relatively smooth. Carin glowed like a Christmas tree, providing subtle smiles, winks and puckered lips at every covert opportunity. Hack left work late in the afternoon using a business meeting across town as an excuse. Carin pouted in realizing he hadn't included her in any special plans for the weekend. Still somewhat affected by their early morning experience, Hack conceded he would be in touch the following day.

It was nearly six o'clock when he dropped by the golf club. Sitting on the upstairs porch, he watched several foursomes complete play on the ninth hole. After putting-out, they systematically congregated behind the green to wait for the following players. It became easily apparent they were all involved in some type of large group wager. Hack spotted Mitch among the bunch and went down to join him.

"What say, old buddy?"

"Not much," Hack said. "How'd ya make out?"

"Don't know for sure, yet. Pretty good, I think."

After lingering long enough for them to settle individual bets, Hack and several others headed upstairs for a drink. Mitch, being in an unusually good mood, insisted on buying the round. Unfortunately, beer was the only alcohol sold. Hack's acceptance, as usual, was strictly an attempt to be one of the guys. By that time, Hack knew and had played at least once with each of the seven sitting at the table. The realization occurred he was gradually gaining acceptance into the select clan.

It was a completely new atmosphere for Hack as an adult. In childhood, he had sincerely enjoyed team sports and other endeavors involving male competition, often being the center of attention. However, responsibilities of early parenthood negated illusions of expanding on a fairly successful athletic reputation gained in high-school football. College was never seriously considered even though a scholarship had been offered. Marriage had led to deprivation of self-achievements and the alienation of many friendships. Finally being surrounded again by athletic counterparts, sharing in their fun and fantasies was an invigorating transfusion of spirit.

Preacher, a mild-mannered former minister in his late-forties, brought the conversation to a specific trip being planned to Hanover, Pennsylvania. "Dern," he said. "It's gonna be great. At least, it always has been every time we've gone."

Mac quickly responded, shaking his head in a wildly negative gesture. "You can say that again. But, I'll be damned if we're sharing a cart together this trip."

"Why? What happened?" someone from across the table asked, with a following chuckle.

"Shit," Mac continued, "I though I was a near goner." He

gulped a slug of beer from the bottle. "Look. It all started the night before the tournament. Wasn't much to do, so ol' Preacher here," Mac pointed with his thumb, "starts flirtin' with a little gal workin' in the motel restaurant where we was a'stayin'. Well, we were about 'two-sheets-to-the-wind' after killin' a fifth in the room. The little broad was kind'a cute, but sure as hell too young for that ol' bastard."

Preacher sheepishly smiled and succumbed to Mac's persistence to continue with the story.

"Well, can't say I blame Preacher, altogether." He poked him in the shoulder in a friendly manner and winked. "Although she was the next thing to jail bait, she looked a bit older, and, wow, what a set a tits."

"Dang it, Mac." Preacher blushed. "I didn't do nothin'."

"Bullshit." Mac rejected his emphatic denial. "Don't matter much, anyway. Even though the kid was only seventeen, she had got married and had a kid, and was already divorced. As it turned out, it was her ol' lady he had to worry about. Seems, on a bad night, he balled the old bag a couple years before and she remembered him."

"Crap," Hack jokingly said, "I thought this was gonna be a golf story."

"Well," Mac said, and laughed, "gimmie a chance. I was just gettin' to that." He wiped the corner of his eye. "You see, 'Preacher-Boy' talks the girl into showin' us where there's some action, but I don't go. I hit the sack early, and about six-thirty in the mornin', he comes bustin' in the room. Here we are supposed to tee-off at eight and he ain't feelin' no pain. I tried my best to get him straight. He just kept belchin' one minute and fartin' the next."

"Dern it, Mac." Preacher squirmed. "I told ya I ain't touched her. I passed out in the car. She finally got me up and I done took her home."

"Yeah, we know. She got 'it' up is more like it," a listener previously unheard goaded. "Go on, this is getting good."

"Well, I poured as much coffee into him as I could manage and tried to get him to puke without any luck. We got to the first tee and finally got off. And, I got to admit one thing. Ol' Preacher done hit the ball better drunk than I ever seen him do

51

sober. We got through the first nine in flyin' colors. Then, all hell broke loose. Now, look. Ya really gotta picture it. There's this par three hole that you gotta leave the cart on the path about halfway up this big hill. Even then, it must be a good forty steps straight up to get to the tee. We just hit our shots and heard some rustlin' sounds comin' through the trees in our direction. Shit. Would you believe it? Here comes that crazy ol' bitch draggin' her daughter by the arm, hell bent, straight for the Preacher. I never seen no one sober, so fast. We both ran down them steps, jumped in the cart, and flew down the hill plumb lickety-split. Don't know where my mind was to let him drive." Mac paused to wipe the corner of his other eye and swill another slug of beer. "Poor ol' Preacher must'a still had one too many in him for the road. He missed a turn and the next thing I know, we was sittin' in the friggin' middle of the lake."

The entire group roared with laughter. Mitch was in the midst of gulping some of his drink and spit it all over himself, coughing and gagging. By then, Mac was in tears. The entire clubhouse echoed with loud bellowing. "That . . . that ain't all." Mac struggled to continue.. "The ol' biddy waded in after us. She kept a'comin' just short of gettin' her dress wet while she's a pullin' the hem between her legs to the crotch and swingin' a long stick in her other fist, usin' every cuss word I'd ever heard, and a few more." He paused for a second to catch his breath. "Through all the dodgin', duckin' and alibis, you ain't never seen such high-talkin' like the Preacher came up with. He conned the pants off'n her. He wound up convincin' her that if she'd let us get on shore, he could prove he hadn't done nothin' to her kid. He told her he had a doctor's paper to prove he was impotent and couldn't get a hard-on no more."

Laughter that had never really ceased suddenly exploded into hysterics throughout the place. Preacher sank lower in his chair.

"Geeeezzzeee," Mitch literally moaned in agony. "Did he really have a 'no-hard-on sticker' to show her?"

"Hell, if I know. The second we hit solid ground he took off like a bullet and I was right behind," he said, almost crying. "Took him almost two weeks to muster enough nerve to even try and get his clubs back from the course."

"Dern you, Mac. I'll get you sooner or later," Preacher

mumbled while trying to subdue a grin.

"What the hell's gonna happen if you run into her again this time?" Hack asked, continuing to chortle.

Preacher groaned.

"He don't care," Mac offered. "Fact is, I figure by now he really got one of them certificates."

Preacher finally lost some of his religion. "Kiss my rosy ass."

* * *

Hack and Mitch decided to meet later for dinner at the Sundowner's.

Allowing just enough time to shower and change at his office pad, Hack arrived at the night club.

After struggling through tough T-bones and cold baked potatoes, Mitch anchored himself at the door while Hack took refuge at the bar. Even though the hour was still early, it was evident the owner's choice of a nondescript band for the night's entertainment was going to bomb. Simply from being a renowned singles meeting place, a few unescorted females arrived and were soon blanketed with attentions by a swarm of males in attendance.

Except for a couple of dances, a general mood lacking in sexual aggressiveness prevailed. As a result, they made an exit before last-call, stopped at a roadside for breakfast, and went to Mitch's place to hit the hay. The next day's golf ventures definitely held more promise.

The following morning provided continued sunny weather and neither Hack nor Mitch seemed to mind headaches that were slowly beginning to subside. Arriving at the course earlier than normal, they surprisingly found a huge crowd gathering of at least thirty players. Carrying cups of coffee, they began to circle among the group.

"Okay. Mitch and I'll wheel."

It wasn't the first time Hack had heard the expression, but he never completely understood its meaning. A sheet of paper began to circulate containing each player's name in a numerical order as they had arrived. Hack hovered behind several of the many participants eagerly awaiting their chance to enter what he observed and thought to be a series of numbers following each of the particular individuals names. Mitch went to the rack to change into his golf shoes. As he sat down, Hack, having followed close behind, asked, "I've heard some about wheeling, but what the hell's really going on?"

"Well," Mitch grunted in the effort of tugging on his left shoe, "a wheel is when two guys, in this case Gabe and me," he grunted again, "figure that we'll play our best ball score against any other two players that want to play against us."

"Lots'a four-balls, huh?"

"Yeah. In short, you've got it." He pulled equally hard on the right. "The only difference is that everybody's playing against the 'wheel,' and instead of having just a head-on bet with the players in your own foursome, the whole field is choosing any number of partners on the list to compare their particular combinations best ball against ours. In other words, if you want to play against us, you can take as many players for different partners as you like and each partner you have is like a separate match. You could win all of them; lose some; win some; or, lose'em all."

"That's sort'a like wheeling horses in a daily double."

"In a way, but not quite." Mitch smiled as he stood and seated his feet into the shoes before bending over to tie the laces. "With horses, there's only one combination that will ultimately win."

"Hell, you mean every guy here can do the same thing?" The magnitude of the possible number of betting partnerships became apparent.

"Yep, that's it."

"Damn. With as many players as there are now, if everybody takes each other as a partner, you could have about nine hundred individual matches. Nine hundred bets. Holy shit."

"Could happen, but it won't." Mitch continued to sound nonchalant. "The thing is, Gabe and I are a pretty strong team. Deciding on partners to take depends on each particular player's ability. Why take a chance with someone unless the choice represents a reasonable chance of beating us. And besides, most of this bunch are small betters, anyway."

"How much is each bet for?"

"It's up to the wheel to put a ceiling on it." Mitch moaned as he raised to a half-upright position, placing his hands on his knees to pause long enough for the throbbing in his head to subside.

"Phew, damn hangover," he managed, shaking his head. "We've got a five-dollar limit. It can be anything up to that."

"Aw, what the crap. You don't mind my playing against you?" "Hell no," he said, laughing. "You could win all yours, and depending on the rest, we could win everything else. Got it?" He winked and made a fake punch gesture at Hack's mid-section and strode across the room. "Pick'em good."

Mick was just finishing listing his choices and pushed the sheet Hack's way. He studied the paper for a few minutes and found it very simple to understand. As noted earlier, each golfer competing against the wheel was listed and assigned a number corresponding to their spot on the list. Rather than having to clutter the sheet with lengthy names, each player simply noted the particular numbers representing partners they desired to take. At the end, was a space for the amount of money per bet.

"Hurry up with that sheet," someone shouted across the room.

Hack sensed the urgency of allowing others access for their picks and quickly made his selections, opting on nine players at five dollars each. Surprisingly, he noticed his number appearing in several places on the paper following various other player's names. It indicated at least a few were beginning to respect his game.

The list eventually circled around to Mitch and he quickly made a rough total of all the bets. "Phew," he hissed. "There's got to be pretty close to a thousand riding."

"Got enough dough?" Hack asked.

"Yeah, think so. The wheel generally splits its wins or losses down the middle. At least, in this case we are."

"If you need any, say the word."

"Sure will." Mitch smiled in acknowledgment of the genuine offer. "I want you playing up front in our foursome, anyway."

Hack knew, from earlier observances, the honor of playing in the wheel's foursome was generally reserved for the strongest players and larger gamblers. He felt thrilled his virgin experience in the wheel would include being in the lead group.

Tradition had been established placing the wheel off the tee first so their best-ball score could be passed back to the following groups allowing them the advantage of knowing what they had to make to win or halve each particular hole.

Mitch introduced the fourth player of their group Jace, and his wheel partner, Gabe, to Hack on the first tee. Jace had all of the physical attributes normally identified with good golfer characteristics. He was tall and slim, but very solid, and swung with a fluid grace and rhythm surely indicating him to be a super player. On the other hand, Gabe appeared to be pushing twenty, small built, five-eight, a hundred and thirty pounds at most, with blondish-red hair and a freckled baby face. Choking down on the club a couple of inches from the butt of the grip, the little man's practice swing didn't seem to be anything overly exceptional.

Thoughts rambled through Hack's mind questioning whether Mitch might have used better judgment in getting himself into the situation.

Things soon got underway, and Mitch squared-off first, pushing it far to the right into an unplayable lie against the base of a large tree. As much as Hack wanted to win, he truly sensed the onus of pressure surely placed on Mitch's wheeling partner.

It was Gabe's turn, and all sympathetic feelings were soon dismissed. Never before in his life had Hack ever seen a guy so small, hit a golf ball so far. It looked like it would never land. Even more astounding was the accuracy of its direction, coming within a few yards of reaching the first green. Mitch's frown suddenly altered to a beaming smile. He strutted across the tee toward his bag commenting to Hack as he passed. "That was only a three-wood."

The wheel birdied the first hole, while Hack struggled after dumping his approach shot in a green-side sand trap. However, he played even with them through the next three holes, making all pars. On the fifth hole, Hack sank a long putt for a birdie and pulled back to being even on his own ball.

Mitch birdied the sixth and the little 'Mighty-Mite' drove seven. His birdie there, after the eagle attempt rimmed the hole, was followed by yet another birdie on the par five eighth, having reached the green in two. During this stretch of sub-par play, Hack bogeyed six, birdied seven and made par on number eight. He was two holes down to the wheel on his own score and realized he certainly needed help from his chosen partners.

Number nine, a potential birdie hole, especially for Gabe, turned out to be a nemesis for the wheel. With the ground hardened from the lack of recent rain, Gabe over-clubbed using a driver and banged it out-of-bounds beyond the green. Mitch put his tee shot in the trap while Hack and Jace laid-up short, requiring full pitching wedges to get home in regulation.

Mitch had to play a blast shot because of his lie. Hitting it a bit fat, his ball came to rest on the apron five feet short of the green. After compounding the problem with a bad chip, he two-putted for a bogey. Hack and Jace both parred and the four went upstairs to tip a few beers while waiting for the other groups to finish.

As each player came in, scores were immediately recorded from their cards to a master sheet translated to a series of 'Xs,' 'Os' and 'Dashes' depending on how they fared on each hole: the 'X' represented a loss; the 'O' indicated a win; the 'Dash' meant a tie on the hole. It was a clever coding system to make it easier in determining winning and losing combinations by eliminating the confusion of actual hole scores.

Hack had the advantage of being seated at the table as the computations were being made, providing him with an excellent opportunity to absorb the system. The room was filled with the chatter of players purging each other for particular hole scores to learn of their success or failure against the wheel. From his vantage point, Hack took every opportunity of scanning the sheet to attempt comparing as many of his chosen combinations as possible. Since he lost one down to them on his own ball score, and had already beaten them on the only hole they bogeyed, it was necessary that each of his different partners provide a birdie on at least one or more of the holes he had lost to the wheel, to either halve or win the bet. Final results indicated he won five bets; halved two and lost two; for a plus figure of fifteen dollars. After the total computation, Mitch and Gabe had won three hundred and ten dollars each.

"Holy shit," Hack exclaimed, shaking his head. "Where the hell'd you find that pygmy-tiger?"

"Gabe?" he questioned, trying to look overly innocent and then laughed. "He's home on leave right now from the Army and stationed down in Fort Bragg for the time. Great player, huh?"

"You bet your ass."

Gabe returned from the head, all smiles. "Let's go get a

'good' drink," he said in a high-pitched nasal voice, heavily tainted with a strong southern accent. "I need it."

The hangout for the nineteenth-hole was a small joint several blocks away called 'Pete's Suite.' Entering the dimly lit bar, after being exposed to the glaring sunlight, made it darker inside than it actually was. Hack's eyes burned and felt as though they were full of grit. Asking for directions to the men's room, he found his way, locating a basin to wash his hands and splash cold tap water generously in his face. While toweling with toilet tissue, since nothing else was available, even with his lack of total moral fortitude, he grimaced at much of the vulgarity covering the room's walls. As he stood before the mirror running a comb through his tangled hair, Mitch burst through the door.

"Move over, brother, I gotta unload real bad." Having the belt undone and fly unzipped on his way in, his pants were to his knees as he reached the throne. He squatted in a fashion attempting to avoid contact with the seat as his rear-end seemed to explode.

"Good Lord." Hack gasped. "You're dead and don't know it," he said, making a dash for the door to escape the pungent odor that would undoubtedly peel paint from the surrounding partitions.

Finding it much easier to see through the dim light and smoke-filled tavern, he spotted Gabe in a far corner pushing coins into an electronic bowling game machine. Several other guys from the club had arrived and were seated at the bar ordering drinks. Jace motioned with a wave of his hand and Hack responded.

"What would you like?" Jace asked. "I'm buying."

"Canadian and water, thanks."

"Come on, sit down and take a load off your feet."

"Thanks, I appreciate it, but I gotta get over to Mitch's table. We're supposed to have a sandwich ordered."

"You're a bit unconventional, but you've got a fair game," Jace said as he passed Hack's drink to him from the bartender.

"Pure luck. I sort'a got it going a little bit today for a change. You're the one that's got all the shots," Hack said. "You were even on your own ball, weren't you?"

"Yeah, but that was luck, too." He winked.

"Bullshit. Not with the swing you have."

"I'd almost swap that swing for your putting stroke in a second," Jace interjected without hesitation. "You've got a soft-touch that's fantastic around the greens."

"I make love that way, too," Hack said, and laughed.

Mitch walked past on his way from the head to their table near the bowling machine. "Hope to hell you left all your rotten parts in there," Hack called as he passed.

"Fuck you," Mitch said, holding his middle finger extended high in the air.

"Thanks for the drink Jace. It was great playing with you. I see the foods on the table and getting cold."

"No problem. We'll do it again sometime soon."

Mitch had insisted they order steak sandwiches. The initial bite made it clearly evident as to why it was a popular choice.

"That wasn't half bad."   Hack managed his comment preceding a belch. "By the way, what was with them not wanting you two to wheel again for the second nine?"

"Are you kidding?" Mitch returned. "They're scared shitless of the little man. The only reason we got the bet the first time was because they counted on him being rusty from not playing regular. Believe it or not, that was a bad round for him. I've seen the little sucker six and seven-under several times."

"Balls."

"No bullshit," he continued, as Gabe blushed. "The little runt don't fool no one, no more."

"Sheeeet," was all Gabe could manage, again in a discernible southern accent.

Mitch started chuckling to himself and it slowly grew to audible laughter. "Excuse me. I just remembered something funnier than hell about our little friend." He nudged his head toward Gabe. A smile began to expand across Gabe's face as he nodded back in agreement. "There's this buddy of ours," Mitch began. "Danny's his name. He's the biggest, smoothest, hustler you've ever seen."

"Seems I've heard his name mentioned a few times before," Hack said.

"Don't doubt it," Mitch agreed. "There's a million-and-one stories floating around about him." Mitch paused for a bite of his second sandwich. "Well, anyway, Danny agrees that they'll meet one particular day over at Annapolis Park and play in their wheel. Everybody knows Danny real well, but none of them had ever seen the little man." Mitch lit a cigarette and continued. "You've been around long enough to see all of the pissin', moanin' and groanin' that can go on trying to get a wheel off the ground. Well, everybody was arguing like hell about getting something fair going, and Danny just laid back keeping his cool until he saw Gabe coming up the sidewalk to the clubhouse." Mitch paused to sip his drink and chuckled in unison with Gabe. "Sooo," Mitch said, drawing the word out, "Danny jumps up all of a sudden and calls them all a bunch of cry babies without any guts and tells them he'll wheel with the next guy who comes through the door."

Hack swallowed some of the smoke he was inhaling and began gagging in a combined coughing and laughter spasm. "Holy shit," he barely managed, leaning and placing his head between his knees.

Gabe reached over and began pounding him on his back.

Finally able to reasonably control himself, Hack sat up and wiped tears from his eyes with the back of his hand. "You don't have to tell me," he coughed slightly as he spoke. "Gabe walks in and they wheel."

"Thought they were going to kill Danny before it was over." Mitch joined Hack's laughter.

The waitress, a cute, but slightly plump, little Hungarian-accented brunette, brought another round. With each visit to the table, she gave a little squeal as Mitch patted her well-rounded firm rump.

"Hummmm, that wouldn't be half bad," Gabe groaned. "Been so long since I had any, I forgot how to do it."

"Ummph, tell me another one," Mitch blurted.

"Naw. No kiddin'. Me and Betty ain't makin' it so good. I've been cut off for three, maybe four months."

"You mean nothing between?"

"Sheeeet. Ain't cause I ain't tried. Either got fouled up by the fuckin' duty or tried to nail a broad at the wrong time. Or, somethin.'"

"Well now, we'll just have to do something about that." Mitch winked at Hack. "We'll get together tonight and I'll set things up.

Okay by you two?"

"Fine with me," Gabe beamed.

"Sure." Hack nodded in agreement.

After Mitch excused himself for having to leave, Gabe and Hack decided to go back to the club for another nine. The original group comprising the earlier wheel evidently got something else rolling and were long gone. Managing to pick up a couple of stragglers, they made a small bet to make it interesting. Hack hadn't given it much thought, but practically all of his matches until that moment had involved Mitch in some way or another. It felt good for a change to play with a different partner.

After hitting their tee shots, they walked side-by-side down the first fairway. "Don't mean to be nosy, but I heard you mention Betty. Your wife?"

"Nope. Girl friend."

"Is she pregnant? You said something about being cut off."

"God forbid," he barked. "She caught me seein' some other broad, so she put a stop to us livin' together. Haven't been for a good while."

"Sorry."

"Don't be," he said. "Best thing ever happened."

* * *

As usual, they reached Hack's ball first, resting well short of Gabe's lie. Hack hit his next shot into the same trap as in the earlier round. For the rest of the nine, he seemed to be in some type of trouble on practically every hole. It would have been miserable except the conversation with Gabe continued and Hack was aware of a close friendship maturing quickly between them.

Instead of milling around the club, they agreed to split and meet later at the Sundowner's. Hack went straight to the car, threw his clubs in the trunk and headed back to the office. It was close to four-o'clock when he arrived. Carin had left a note from Friday regarding a phone call from his niece. Reaching for a tray of ice cubes from the bar refrigerator, he found they hadn't been refilled and decided to have milk instead. The children were out playing when he returned their call and he dialed Carin's number.

"Hello."

"Hi, doll."

She warmed immediately at hearing his voice. "Hi, 'bossy-wossy.' I was hoping you would call."

"Wanted to let you know I got the note and say hello."

"Miss me?"

"Don't I always?"

"You're teasing me," she said, and moaned. "What'cha doing tonight?"

"Going out boozing with a couple of guys from the golf club."

"Ooooh. I wanted you to come over."

"Damn. Sorry baby. I met a guy this afternoon. He's in the Army, and on leave. Hate to let him down."

"Hummm, a likely story; I bet he's got big boobs." She laughed a bit sarcastically.

"No kiddin', it's no broad." His light attitude was beginning to sour. "Even if it was, so what?"

"Now, you're mad," she said, with a groan.

"A little bit."

"Okay, okay, say no more."

He paused briefly to rid his voice of any bitterness. "Look, babe, we've talked about this enough times. I'm just not ready to settle down, yet. I never got the chance for any independence because of getting married so young. I just need some space for a while, and this sure as hell ain't the time to go into all this."

"I know," she soothingly said. "Forgive me lover. It's my time of the month and I get like a bitch in heat."

"You know what you can do to make it feel better."

"Yeah, but it's not as good as when you do it," she interrupted. "Promise me. If it's an early evening and you change your mind, come on by."

"Will do."

* * *

Hack's short nap did more harm than good, waking up with his neck as stiff as a board. Overall, he felt more tired than before lying down and struggled through the motions of getting bathed and dressed for the evening. Further adding to his blahs, the cubes hadn't completely frozen in the trays. After plucking bits and small chunks of ice into a short glass, he filled it generously with Canadian Club and a spurt of water.

Flicking the knob on the TV, it crackled into a wavering

picture. Following a change of channels and a minor adjustment to the tuner, he sank into his executive chair, leaned back, and propped his feet on the desk. The biting liquid slid past his lips and began to build a warming sensation in the pit of his stomach.

There was still a good twenty minutes of air time left showing the final holes of third-round play in the Western Open. Several big names remained near the top of the leader board. However, they were currently running second to some upstart young pro by the name of 'Champagne' Tony Lema, winner of the last British Open. But, Palmer and Nicklaus weren't far off the pace.

Hack sat for the balance of the program in a wonderful semi-daydream pretending to be in their shoes as each took their shots. Damn, it would be fantastic to be that good, he thought to himself; traveling all the time; all the new places and courses to play; good-looking broads impressed by a big name.

The phone rang shattering the spell as the show ended. It was a wrong number.

Dumping the balance of his drink into a paper cup, he carried it with him and headed for the parking lot. Regardless of all attempts, the Chevy wouldn't start and he reluctantly decided to get help. Fortunately, the service station he frequented was nearby and open all-night. However, the mechanic was on a road call, leaving no other choice than to agree to have the problem handled later.

The station manager, whom he had come to know quite well, was making apologies when Hack noticed Carin's Ghia sitting on the rack. They were late getting parts and missed having it ready by the time she left work. Since repairs had been completed, and by coming across with payment for the bill in cash with a sawbuck on the side, there was little problem in commandeering its use. For what it cost, a chartered flight would have been cheaper.

Running late, he lead-footed it all of the way. By the time he arrived at the night club, his two counterparts were already into their second round.

"Sorry I'm late. I had damned car trouble."

"Forget it," Mitch mumbled. "We've already ordered though."

"Hey." Gabe motioned for the waitress.

She sauntered over to the table and Hack gave a quick order without looking at the menu. "Sliced turkey sandwich; white toast; plenty of mayonnaise; and, a double vodka martini with an olive."

"That all you want?" Mitch asked in a concerned manner. "Steaks are usually worth a try."

"I'm not real hungry. Don't feel bad and I don't feel good. I grabbed a quick nap and ever since I woke up it's like I'm dragging."

"Probably comin' down with somethin'," Gabe said. "If you've got my luck, it'll be the clap."

The waitress sat what looked like a small fish bowl in front of Hack as she gave a scolding sneer at the little man, having overheard his comment.

"I wasn't accusin' you, you fat bitch," he mumbled low, flicking his middle finger at her broad ass as she waddled away.

"Holy shit. This is a double?"

Mitch laughed. "Don't ever ask for a king-size."

The martini was very dry and extremely chilled. It was needed, and did much to ease a now detectible ache in several body joints. "So, what's on for tonight?" Hack asked.

Gabe peered anxiously at Mitch.

"I made a couple calls earlier with no luck."

Gabe moaned.

"Cheer-up," Mitch continued. "I've never seen a Saturday night without a dozen or more good-looking singles showing."

"Don't be so sad, 'Gabey-Boy,'" Hack soothed. "There's always 'Joe' in the back room."

"Prick," he laughed. "On second thought, as horny as I am 'bout now, blindfold me. I might settle for it."

"Ten-to-one we get babes this evening." Mitch directed his dare at Hack.

"Knowing this place, that's a bet I don't take."

Gabe began to smile again.

Scooting off ahead of the other two, Mitch began working the front door. From their vantage point at the restaurant table, they had a good view of the entrance to the night club area. The evening crowd began to arrive, including a couple of stag female 'chubby-butts.' Overall, pickings didn't seem to get much better.

Deciding to stall for a while, they ordered another drink and discussed the current tour play they had seen on TV. Occasionally, a whispered lewd comment would be made between them regarding a "sweetie" hooked to some guy's arm, as they walked past their table.

Mitch motioned to Hack. "Get your drinks and come on in. I can't hold the table forever." He had chosen a place near the door.

Gabe strained attempting to scan the dark corners in his quest for a bed partner. "Well I'll be derned," he said. "I thought that son of a bitch would be dead by now."

Hack followed Gabe's gaze, picking out a table that was obviously his intended target.

"See. You see that big-ass lummox sittin' against the wall?"

Hack nodded in recognition.

"You've never met a bigger nut in your life, and I don't mean just physically. That idiot used to come over to the club pretty often. Then, all of a sudden no one saw him." He shook his head once again in disbelief and began giggling incessantly. "Man, I'll tell you. I know you've heard stories about guys losin' their cool over golf, but sheeeet, nobody would believe that one. Sheeeet." Gabe paused briefly trying for some composure. "Tommy Bolt's temper is kindergarten compared to him."

"After some of the things I've read, that's saying a lot," Hack cautioned.

"Top this if you can. This clown is out one day and through the first eight holes is shootin' way over his head. He comes to nine needin' a birdie to win an extra fifty bucks on his bet and winds up with about a fifteen-footer for an eagle. Sheeeet." Gabe took a quick sip from his glass. "Under regular conditions the guy's got hands like an elephant, but all day long he's been havin' the 'Midas Touch.' Still, we all figured him for at least two-puttin'. It turns out he takes three to get it down."

"I know the feeling. Lightning's struck here, too." Hack sounded empathetic.

"Haven't we all?" Gabe continued, with a remaining snicker noticeable in his speech. "But, would you get so upset that you'd get down on your hands and knees and start takin' bites outta the green?"

"You're shittin' me." Hack bellowed, causing occupants at nearby tables to express frowns of disapproval.

"No way, brother. This guy's got to be it." Gabe was still laughing at visualizing the occurrence. "He took a whole mess of chunks from around the edge of the hole before he realized his partial plate was in the middle of an earlier bite."

Looking at him across the room added to the imagination and only led to aggravate their funny spots. Their sides were aching from the infectious giggling mood that had surfaced.

The band started its first set. As if by magic, people arrived in greater numbers and soon the room was nearing capacity. By then, there were several tables of stags, both male and female. It was a kick to sit and watch the varying groups peer around the room as subtly as possible to locate the available contingents.

"There's a couple broads alone," Hack pointed. "Yeah, over there, a few tables from the corner."

"I've seen better," Gabe said with a groan.

"Squint your eyes. They don't look as bad that way," Hack suggested satirically. "Besides, beats sitting here playing with your knee."

As Gabe chuckled, Hack shoved his chair back and rose to snake his way through the crowd. He arrived at the designated table, leaned across an empty chair and boldly asked, "Wanna dance?"

The girl shrugged her shoulders in the manner of a "why not" response. They stayed on the floor for several fast selections and finally were confronted with a slow beat. It was the first chance they had to talk.

"I'm a bit pooped," she panted.

"You and me both. Outta shape, I guess. By the way, my name's Hack."

"Nina." She smiled and moved a bit closer.

"You dance great." Hack lied.

"Thank you."

"Come here often?"

"No. It's my first time. My girl friend does. You know, the girl I'm with tonight." The music stopped. Hack escorted her back to her table, donated a thank you, and got a promise for another go at it later.

Gabe smiled as Hack sat down. "Wow. You're good at that new dance style. Wish to hell I was."

Hack drained everything left in his glass and lit a cigarette. "It ain't so hard. Just move your feet and shake your ass to the beat." "Easier said than done," he complained.

Mitch walked over. "Those last two that came in are really ready. I've been lining one of them up for myself for sometime and there's supposed to be another one coming in later."

"Where the hell are they?" Gabe asked with a sense of urgency in his voice.

"Went to the head. When they come back, I'll sit them here. Remember though, the brunette's mine. You can fight over the other one."

"Okay, Gabe, give you first chance," Hack offered apathetically. "I'll wait for 'Miss Later.'"

"Deal."

Minutes passed before two of the finer things in the place sauntered up the aisle and Mitch made the introductions. Hack could have easily kicked his own ass. The blonde he so generously surrendered to Gabe was the same good-looker Mitch had in bed the morning he woke up with the redhead at the motel.

"Connie and Jill, this is Gabe and Hack."

"Hi'ya," both guys chimed in unison.

Jill looked at Hack and grinned. "Hope you're feeling better than the last time I saw you," He blushed.

Gabe frowned. "Uh . . . uh, you know each other already, huh?"

"Well, you might say we've observed some of the better parts of each other," she laughed.

"By the way," Hack choked slightly, "how is Reds? Seen her, lately?"

"Oh, you mean, Liz. As a matter of fact, she's supposed to meet us here later. She'll be tickled pink when she finds you here. Said you were supposed to take care of some unfinished business. She thought you would have called her before now."

Hack caught a definite change of expression on Gabe's face out of the corner of his eye. The little man was elated at having a clear shot at the blonde with big tits. Through the next few drinks, Jill and Gabe grabbed a few slow dances and Hack alternated between Mitch's girl, Connie, and Nina.

Jill suggested she call Liz and find out what was keeping her. On her return to the table, Hack lit a pair of cigarettes and offered the second to her. She sighed and bade the bad tidings received in the phone call she had just made. "Liz can't make it." There was no mistaking a definite frustration in her voice.

"Damn," Hack said. "Thought you said she wanted to see me again?"

"Her old-man's in town for the weekend," she whispered. "She really got upset when I told her you were here. Believe me, she wouldn't have canceled if it wasn't for him. He's a real bastard when he's around."

"I didn't know she was married."

"She's not. I guess you'd call him a sugar daddy. He's a dip-shit in my book."

"Didn't mean to sound pissed-off about it," he apologized. "Just a bit disappointed."

By twelve-thirty, Mitch's needed presence at the door was minimal and he began to occupy a great deal of Connie's time for the rest of the evening. Hack's earlier tinges of discomfort were slowly becoming increasingly pronounced. However, he still elected to make an additional half-hearted effort with Nina, noticing she hadn't settled in on anyone else. Taking her aloofness as a green light to make his move, he approached her for another dance.

"Say, babe," he started, "there's a small party over at the motel after closing. Would you like to join the fun?"

She didn't seem surprised at all, but slowly dragged out an, "I don't know. I wouldn't mind. In fact, I'd like to go. But, there's a problem. I drove tonight, and my girl friend rode with me."

"If she drives, let her take the car. I'll get you home. Or, we'll drag her along with us."

"She doesn't drive. If I go, she'll have to come."

"All right." He pulled her closer as the band played its slow soft beat. His leg purposely pressed between hers as they pivoted. She tilted her head to look in his eyes and he kissed her lightly on the lips.

Nina would never be signaled as a standout among a harem, but she did possess a quality of appeal, establishing her beyond throwaway material. After the slow segment was completed, Hack led her to his table and made introductions to the group.

Eventually, the last set of music began and Hack continued to focus his attention on Nina while dancing. Promptly initiating a few advances of her own, she clung so tightly during the closing number, her falsies felt like they were penetrating through his chest and out of his shoulder blades. The music having ended, walking off the floor, she went directly to her girl friend to explain about the party. Shortly, they returned together and the small entourage headed for the reserved rooms at the motel.

Jill and Gabe got there first and were mixing drinks. Within a five-minute span, all those invited had arrived. The majority sat scattered around sipping from their glasses and involved in trivial conversations while life-of-the-party Jill fumbled through various cabinet drawers.

"Hey, look at this." She squealed, having found a pornographic magazine showing everything that could possibly be imagined.

Holding it above her head, she flipped the pages quickly as if to tease everyone. Suddenly, she turned and declared, "I'm saving this for 'Little Gabey-Wabey' and me."

Gabe turned blood-red. Jill grabbed him by the hand and dragged him to the bed with her. "Come on, puddin'," she tantalized. "Let's get a little education." They sat on the edge of the bed as Jill slowly fingered through the pages, making comments and comparisons.

Sitting with Connie on his lap, Mitch leaned to Hack who was near enough to hear a whispered comment. "I told her about Gabe being a bit backward and his problem of lack-of-nookie. Watch this."

Jill suddenly grasped Gabe by the shoulders and pinned his back to the bed. "Oh, baby," she nearly shouted. "To hell with everyone else, let's fuck." She fumbled with his zipper as she rolled over almost on top and kissed him hard on the mouth. What was initially teasing torment, surprisingly altered quickly to determined desire.

Suddenly leaping from the bed, she exclaimed, "Come on, honey, this is going to be too good for any audience to appreciate. Let's go next door and make whoopie."

Gabe stood up -- his slacks fell down. Everybody roared as he groped for the pants restricting his ankle movement. Jill moved faster, grabbing a firm grip on his hard-on, pulling him toward the door separating the rooms. Gabe waddled through.

Hack sat on the arm of the chair where Nina was seated and turned to catch her reaction. He was surprised to find her in a semi-prone position, with her tail barely resting on the seat cushion's edge.

"Passed-out," her girl friend offered. "She's not used to drinking so much."

"Holy hell," was all Hack could manage to mumble.

Connie got a big kick out of the situation and Mitch echoed her sentiments. "This just ain't your day, lover."

"You can believe it," Hack said. "Come on, give me a hand and get her some fresh air."

They both grabbed an arm and struggled for the front door. Outside, the night was warm and still.

"Hell, this ain't gonna do no good. Help me lean her against this car. If you don't mind, I guess you better get her girl friend."

"Hacker. You're not leaving this early, are you?"

"Yeah, I guess so."

"Let her sleep it off inside, or dunk her in the tub, or something." Hack caught Nina under the tit with one hand and in the crotch with the other as she started to slide off the fender. "I'd just as soon get going. I'm really starting to feel ill, to tell you the truth."

"Okay. If you say so, I'll send her girl friend out. Do you need any help getting her in the car?"

"Naw, I'll make it."

Mitch looked over his shoulder and asked as he walked away, "Are you gonna play tomorrow?"

"Not if I feel like this."

Mitch disappeared and moments later Nina's other half arrived.

"Got your hands full?" she asked, giggling.

"Yeah. Slightly."

"Well, what do you think we should do? Uh, you know I can't drive, don't you?"

"Nina told me. By the way, she didn't mention your name."

70

"Shirley."

"Okay, Shirley, you open my car door and I'll stuff her in the back."

She took one look at Carin's small sports model and laughed. "This I've got to see."

It wasn't easy, but by letting her legs droop across the top corner of the front passenger seat and part way out of the window, they figured they might make it.

"Listen. I'm going back in and ask Mitch and Connie to bring her car when they leave. Give me the registration and keys out of her purse."

Following a bit of fumbling, she located the items and Hack departed to find Mitch. When he returned, Shirley was making the most of Nina's predicament. After slipping off her shoes, she tied a red piece of cloth on the big toe of the foot sticking out of the window.

By the twist of lousy fate, Hack's new partner turned out to be quite a conversationalist and didn't shut up the entire time driving her home. There was conclusive evidence she was higher than a kite and Hack wasn't quite sure her euphoria was strictly limited to the results of alcohol. In the process, he learned that she was Nina's older sister and they lived together with a third. Most of her jabbering was focused on how great she thought he was. There was little doubt in Hack's mind he was being handed a line better than anything he was even capable of contriving.

She snuggled as close as possible in the bucket seats, nearly breaking his neck with energetic squeezes of her arm hooked around his shoulders, and attempts at shoving her tongue in his ear.

As the car stopped in the dark parking lot, Shirley cooed, "Let's stay out here for a few minutes."

"What about Nina?"

"Hell, she'll be okay. Just too much booze and pot combined." She slurred her words while taking a small envelope from her purse.

"What say, good-lookin, wanna share a joint?"

"Not tonight, babe." He shook his head more emphatically than intended. "That, I don't need."

The packet disappeared and without warning she lurched

forward grabbing Hack with both arms, practically snatching him from his seat. Covering his mouth completely with hers, it was as if she were trying to emulate a vacuum cleaner and suck him entirely between her lips at any minute. Unzipping his fly with uncanny ease, she quickly reached inside applying a death grip. Holding his wrist with her other hand, she pushed his forearm up her dress jamming his palm against her crotch. It was at this moment he realized the red material dangling from Nina's toe had once been her panties. Stimulated to a hardened state by the relentless kneading of her fingers inside his trousers, Shirley tugged with her hand and pulled his cock through the pants opening, only releasing her hold to allow grasping his ass with both hands and force him between her legs. She writhed, twisted, and turned in tortured motions in attempting to cope with the small confinement of the car. Suddenly, an extended groan of complete ecstasy, coupled with a glowing emotional facial expression, indicated a success to her mission. He didn't have the heart to tell her she missed and had been rubbing on the gear shift knob, instead.

It took forever to get her out of the car. She continued raving about how good he could make love and the hardness of his dick. Finally accomplishing to calm Shirley's hyperactivity to a small degree, with her limited help, they managed to get Nina inside. Hack wasted little time making an exit, literally running down the steps and to the car.

Deciding it was closer to Carin's place rather than his own, he also rationalized she'd be able to have her wheels in the morning if they were needed.

Carin's apartment was dark. He fumbled in the pitch black and strained in front of the dash lights to see it was nearing five-thirty a.m. At this point, He didn't give a damn. It took every ounce of effort that could be mustered to attempt getting out of the car. He couldn't recall ever having felt so miserable. Complete exhaustion, aches throughout his body, and a nagging urge to vomit at any moment, were prompting his discomfort. After struggling up the flight of steps, the wait lingered into an eternity before she answered the door. "Who's there?"

"Just me."

The door opened as far as the chain would allow. "Hi, babe," he managed.

"Good Lord," she muttered, as the door closed quickly and the chain slid from its locked position.

"You look like hell. What happened?"

"Nothing. I've been getting sick all evening. Must've been something I ate."

Carin's expression appeared as if tempted to make a wisecrack about bad pussy, but evidently thought better of it. Instead, she quickly sped through a ritual of removing his coat and stacking pillows beneath his shoulders and head, as he stretched on the couch.

"God, you're burning up. You're getting your temperature taken."

He moaned. "Hope it ain't a rectal thermometer."

"Be quite . . . and behave."

Carin was enjoying playing nurse, and it almost made him feel better. At least, until he made a dash for the head and barely arrived in time, feeling as though his guts were going to go, as well. She hovered above in a genuinely sympathetic manner and eventually helped him into her room and into bed.

Hack was able to offer little resistance or assistance in her attempts to undress him. He began to shake from a chill. The room went dark and he felt the soothing warmth of her body pressing against his as she held him in her arms, running her fingers softly through his hair. Welcomed sleep finally came.

Awaking with a gripping pain in his abdomen, in a swift single motion he cleared the end of the bed and flew straight for the head. This time, the other end ran like a fountain. While straddling the stool, a sudden realization occurred. He believed he glimpsed someone unfamiliar glaring from the kitchen as he buzzed bare-assed through the hallway.

Carin's head peered around the door. "Are you okay?"

"I got the runs. They're really bad."

She entered the bathroom and placed her hand to his forehead and cheeks. "You're still running a fever."

"Yeah, I know. I feel terrible." He groaned with the effort of talking. "By the way, that was you in the kitchen as I came through, wasn't it?"

"Uh, well, no. Not really." She giggled. "You put on quite a show for my next-door neighbor. She just came over to borrow some milk and caught your act."

"Hell, I'm sorry. I woke up so fast, and had to go so bad, I never gave it a dream someone would be here."

"Forget it. I'd say you made her day. Now come on and get your nude little body back in that bed."

His return trip was a bit slower and more deliberate. He slowly oozed between the sheets. His absence, plus the air-conditioning, had turned them icy cold. Carin brought a tray of hot tea and toast. It was hardly touched before he again drifted into deep sleep.

The next time Hack opened his eyes, he was amazed to find the room dark. Groping for the wide side of the bed, Carin wasn't there. A small ray of light flickered beneath the bedroom door. Opening it, the TV was immediately visible and the program indicated the time to be after ten o'clock. Carin was sprawled on the couch asleep and he tiptoed quietly toward the toilet.

After grunting his way through the ordeal, he took her bathrobe from the back of the door, put it on, and flushed the commode. The noise of the churning water caused Carin to stir and her eyes opened as he sat on the edge of the couch near her waist. "How do you feel, doll?" he asked, and leaned to kiss her forehead.

"There's a few occasional cramps, but no big deal. More important, how are you feeling? It seems the fever's down."

"All gone. Feel dragged-out, and still got the runs, and . . . holy shit."

"What's wrong? She jumped to her elbows.

"Damn it. I was supposed to see the kids today. Damn. Damn it."

"Hold on, now," she comforted. "While you were asleep, I remembered you mentioning it the other day and I called your mother. I had her tell Sharon you were sick and wouldn't make it."

"Phew. You're unbelievable, sweets. Bless you."

"All in a day's work," she smiled. "By the way, you look adorable."

The rest of the evening was very quiet and pleasant. Except

74

for a few trips to the potty, the entire time was spent snuggled on the sofa soaking up TV. They never made it through the late show or even to bed before sleep came.

* * *

Summer slowly withered into fall -- the period proving profitable in more ways than one: business was fair; the love life on go; and, most important, the last three months evidenced several strokes shaved from his golf game. Having finally reached the plateau of being considered a full-fledged regular at the course, he accepted membership in the small club, making him eligible for any USGA tournament with a legitimate handicap for the coming 1964-65 season. Being an average public course, it certainly wasn't exclusive. However, what it lacked in prestige was overcome by an abundance of activities and fun. Since there was little if any overhead at all, with reasonable initiation, dues, raffles and very nominal event fees, the club easily prospered.

Marvelous weather stretched the current season far beyond its normal period. Considering it was early December, there had been very few really cold days. Hack had personally taken great advantage of the Indian summer by averaging at least five to six times a week on the links. It was fairly convenient by playing early and working late. The thing suffering most was sack time -- sleep that is.

Hack sat slumped in his chair, leaning back in a state of mind oblivious to his surroundings -- his thoughts drifting to a particular weekend, several months back. After having spent a span of three days averaging a few hours sleep each night, he had shown up at Mitch's night club, half-tanked. Instead of using the break to get needed rest, the two of them partied until the wee hours. Like a couple of idiots, the next morning, they allowed themselves to be talked into wheeling.

Doc, a general practitioner, and absolute golf addict himself, readily noticed their plight -- the 'wolves' were setting up their prey for a good killing. Calling them aside, he graciously provided a selection of capsules he insisted would ease their hangovers. It must have. After the round, Hack was three under par by himself and Mitch holed a bird where he had missed, it gave them a total four under best ball score allowing them to win

75

all bets.

Word leaked about Doc supplying the medicine and a deluge of ribbing about saliva tests ensued. Winning the money was fantastic, but secondary to the feeling generated by being the center of attention. It was unimaginable and represented one of the greater experiences of his life.

The intercom joggled Hack to awareness.

"Yeah. What's up?" he responded as he leaned and held the speaker button.

"Guess who?" Carin quipped.

"Babe Zaharias?"

"Who the hell's she?" Her tone attempted sounding concerned.

"Just a broad famous for playing with little white balls," he said.

"Oh. You had me worried for a minute. She's got nothing on me."

"Okay, smart-ass," he said, laughing at her quip. "What'd you want me for, anyway?"

"To remind you about your appointment at ten-thirty and the other one at . . ."

He didn't allow her to finish the statement. "Don't worry, I haven't forgotten a thing. I'll be ready to leave in five or ten minutes. Tell you what. How about cancelling . . . ? No, on second thought, you keep my appointment this afternoon."

"Oh, you thrill me so," she sarcastically returned. "Are you sure it'll be okay for me to be around that good-looking chunk of manhood? Especially since you owe him so many favors. Maybe he might settle for a trade agreement when he sees me."

"Bitch." Clunk went the phone.

The time spent with the computerized gent from IBM was rather rewarding and put Hack in a mood of celebration. Naturally, he headed for the course. Immediately on arrival, a quick call to the office with a trumped up excuse for the delayed return took only a few minutes. The usual group was already on the tee and he didn't dare miss the action. Rushing back to the car, he hurriedly pulled on his spikes and a sudden realization occurred like an emanation. It was a disease; he had the itch; he had 'golf fever.'

Subconsciously, a tremendous invisible force relentlessly and irrepressibly drew him toward acres of manicured fields dotted with strategically placed holes. There was no escaping the addiction. His mind churned in turmoil. Was it the game; the excitement of gambling; or both? He was becoming a real prevaricator, using every excuse but the truth to cover interruptions to business schedules and other responsibilities. It made him shudder to believe he could lose all control and succumb to anything so stupid. "Damn," he muttered while shaking his head violently hoping to clear away the self-recriminations.

His subconscious must have suffered deeply to find he was able to dismiss the matter so easily as he broke all records getting to the tee. After placing his bets, Hack found himself being the last leg of the final foursome.

No matter what he did, the harder he tried, the worse things got. 'Dogging' the ball on practically every shot, it was an absolutely hopeless round. Not only did he lose every bet, but a head-cover to boot, and felt too damn disinterested to bother tracking it down. After struggling up the stairs, he gave his scores to the wheel as they graciously smiled. Never could he have ever dreamed it possible to play so poorly.

An empty table across the room appeared to offer some refuge. He settled down in the isolated corner to curse the rotten luck and drown his sorrows with a beer in hand.

"Hey. Mind if I join you?"

In his daze, Hack wasn't immediately aware of the newcomer. As he looked up, he stuttered a belated response. "Uh, no," he answered, still jumbled in thought. "Excuse me, I really didn't mean to be rude," Hack apologized, standing up to shake hands. "Let me buy you a beer?"

"Not necessary, but accepted," he responded with a big grin. The recent arrival waved his long arm in the air indicating two more with his fingers. "By the way, I'm Danny. Danny Green's the name."

"Hack Arnold," he responded, as his hand was nearly crushed in Danny's grasp. "I know you pretty well, already. By ways of the grapevine, at least. Reputation, you know. Hellava game you've got."

"Just lucky," Danny said with a broad grin.

"Don't bull me, man. You're labeled the 'King of Hustlers.'" Hack smiled back in a faked sinister manner.

"Who, me?"

"I'm not lookin' at the bar maid." Hack chuckled with the remark. "What'd you shoot that nine, anyway? I understand you beat the wheel on your own ball. And, I heard about that putt you missed on nine. Three feet for a birdie, and you knock it past another three? Yeah."

"Can't make 'em all."

"Granted. Only when you have to, huh? Hack was getting a delight in goading his new acquaintance and only did so because it was evident Danny's ego was being elevated by the comments. "Hell. I could shank a turd from three feet and still hit the commode."

Danny gurgled in his beer. "I've heard you've got a much better game than you had today. What happened?"

"Damned, if I know. Just couldn't keep my mind steady. Been workin' too hard, I guess."

"Wow," Danny exclaimed. "You want to be barred for life. Don't dare use that nasty word around here. First commandment of the golf bums: 'don't ever let labor interfere with the game.'"

"Yeah, so they say. At the rate I'm going, that shouldn't be a problem."

"Nope, no kiddin'," he continued. "I've never let work, pussy, wife, weather, nor war, play havoc with my unending efforts for greater status in the world of hustling."

"Hell, that explains it. Why you're so good at it." Hack laughed with the response.

"Yuh-honor-me, Suh."

"Hi-ho, Danny-O," a voice interrupted.

The two of them turned to find 'Big Bad Mitch' moving through the crowd.

"Hey, brother, where you been?" Hack queried.

"Here a chick, there a chick, everywhere a chick, chick. Naw, not long for this world. I took a job at that sports shop I tried a few months back. They made a better offer."

"Hey, sweetheart. Another two, plus one," Danny called to Marie.

"I see you're in bad company." Mitch smirked with his sarcasm. "I thought you went to Arizona for good."

"Oh, you mean him." Hack pointed at Danny with his thumb.

"Damn, now I do feel inferior." Danny faked a pout. "Hell, I've had to sit here and have my ability and standing desecrated before you came. And, now, this?"

"Kitty-poop," Hack responded, shaking his head while turning to Mitch. "He's been doing his best to shaft me into giving him ups."

"That's a relief," Mitch blurted. "I thought for a minute he might have you by the short hairs."

"By the way," Hack altered the subject, "what's this I hear about you conning guys with the ol' ball-in-the-box trick?"

"How these fabrications get around is beyond me." He chuckled beneath his breath while relighting the butt of a cigar.

Mitch interrupted, "Don't tell me you got away with it again." He shook his head and continued. "I don't know how in the hell you do it."

"Naw. That was a long time ago. It still works out west, though." He chuckled some more.

The wheel took longer than usual to compute its results, and nearly another hour bantering and bickering about a fair bet before deciding to go another nine. Most of the players, having tired of the arguments and delay, had either left for home or scampered to the tee making independent matches. While the larger group had been haggling, Hack was on his way to being christened into the realm of 'hustle-hoodooism' -- making his first mistake by accepting a combination three-way bet of even, one-up and two-up for the nine from Danny. Classifying Danny as good or even great was, either way, an understatement. The man all but mastered every aspect of the game. It was practically unconscionable he wasn't on the tour. His swinging rhythm proved even more fluid than Jace's. And, his drives were at least as long, but much more accurate. Danny's shot-making repertoire included a short game of unlimited feel and versatility, handling his wedge as if it were part of his hands. Losing to Danny proved almost a pleasure. To play with someone of his ability was well worth it.

Having finished the round, Danny and Hack headed for Pete's

Suite and joined several other earlier arrivals from the wheel. Following sandwiches and throwing down more than a few glasses of booze, their group began to slowly dwindle. After Danny left, Mitch quelled a lot of Hack's curiosity. Danny was married; had nine kids with another in the basket; and, most devastating of all, developed a huge lump in the throat when in front of crowds. It explained a lot.

"Not to change the subject, but I'm curious about something, too." Mitch began his inquisition as he squirmed in his chair. "Where the hell did you get the name Hack? Something to do with golf?"

"Fuck." Hack groaned, as he flicked a bread crumb from the table with his middle finger. "If you weren't such a good friend, I'd tell ya to go screw yourself."

"I think it's pretty cool. Hack . . . Hacker? Sort'a fits with your golf game," he said and grinned. "What's the hang-up?"

"All right. Okay. But, damn it. You breathe a word of this to anyone and I swear I'll spread the word you used to hump your sister." He took a long draw from his glass as if to build courage and continued. "Well, it's like this. Because of my dad, I was raised Catholic. Sweet ol' Mama was a Southern Baptist, and boy, one of the staunchest kind." He paused to light a cigarette.

"I wasn't looking for your life history."

"Screw you. You want the story, or not?"

"Wow. We are a bit touchy about the subject, aren't we?"

Hack smiled. "Anyway, Mama converted over to being a Catholic. Mostly to please Dad, I think. But, that strict down in the country and heavy religious protestant upbringing kept showing through. She gave birth to three of us. All boys . . . Bartholomew, Jeremiah, and Zachariah."

While Mitch gagged on cigarette smoke, Hack suggested he choke to death.

"You got Zach . . . ari . . . ah?" He managed the clarification while still trying to clear his throat.

"Nope, you missed. I got Bartholomew," he corrected, adding with a sheepish grin, "In fact, 'Bartholomew Moses' to be exact." He chuckled.

"Aw, come on. You've got to be kiddin'."

"Yep, just joking," Hack confessed, holding his arms up in a surrendering manner. "Naw. I was the oldest and kind'a special to my ol' man. He was a cab driver and carried me around in the taxi with him when I was little. I really don't know if it came from his cab-barn buddies making a play off of 'Zach' or more because of the taxi connection. Probably both, I figure. Anyway, they started calling me the 'Little Hacker.' Shortened to Hack; it stuck."

He apologized while laughing. "Sorry I asked."

"Damn," Hack blurted, glancing at the wall clock. It was almost six. "Excuse me, I'll be back in a second. I should've called in before now." He jumped up to hurry to the phone.

"Want another?" Mitch shouted.

"Yeah."

Fumbling a dime in the slot, Hack spun the dial. A half-dozen rings followed and then a panting voice. "Hu . . . Hello."

"In bed doll, or just pooped from your afternoon meeting?"

"Damn you." Carin practically screamed her response. "Where the crap have you been? All hell broke loose this afternoon and I didn't know what to do."

"Whoa. Slow down, now. What's wrong?"

"Oh, not much. Josey. You know, your niece," she snapped sarcastically, "just happens to have had an appendix attack and Sharon rushed her to . . ."

"Holy shit. Are you kidding?"

"Do you think I'm crazy? Yes, I'm serious. "Her voice began to calm. "I had to go out and help get her to the doctor. We didn't know what to do. He put her in the hospital, right away."

"Oh, God." Hack pounded his fist against the wall.

"Look, don't get upset. She's doing fine . . ."

"Where's she at?" he interrupted.

"At the Center. I'll meet you there. But, please, don't get reckless. They're not going to operate until tomorrow morning. And, I'm sorry about the way I jumped at you. Just concerned. Okay?"

"Yeah, . . . sure. Listen. I want you to meet me in about a half-hour in the lobby. Bye."

Filling Mitch in on the situation took very little time. Much about the trip to the hospital was a blur, but recognizing Carin's car in the parking lot proved a great relief.

It seemed as if he hadn't slept all week. Between hospital visits and necessary business affairs, there was barely time to ponder missing golf. Carin begged him to spend a couple of days at her place. Even though very tempted, he felt too expended to cope with being around someone else, especially for a whole weekend. He insisted the entire staff leave early Friday and flopped on the couch.

An accident at the corner, accompanied by an ambulance wailing, disturbed Hack to consciousness. He stumbled to the window, more through instinct than curiosity, wondering why the hell he had bothered.

The desk clock read ten-thirty and a growing pang in his stomach reminded him he had missed dinner. Without really realizing it, or considering the time, he found himself dialing the phone.

"Hello," the voice answered briskly.

"Hi. Hope I didn't wake you," he apologized.

"That's okay. I've been kind of restless and lying here awake."

"How's Josey doing?"

"A lot better, but still a bit sore. She went to sleep this evening without any problem."

"How are the other three?"

"They're over at your ex's. She said she'd watch them for a couple of more days."

"Uummm, that's good." The second phone line rang. "Hold on a sec." He pushed a button.

"Hello."

"Still working?" Alice asked.

"No, not really. In fact, I just woke up. Guess it all caught up with me this evening. I sacked out about six."

"Bet you don't sleep tonight."

"Can you hold on a minute, Sharon's on the other line."

"Oh, I'm sorry. I'll let you go."

"No . . . no . . . we were just about to hang up. I'll be right back."

Hack exchanged lines and ended his sister's conversation.

"I'm back, we were just talking about Josie."

"How's she doing? Is she home, yet?

"Fine, and yes. Sharon said she came home this morning."

"Glad to hear that. She's a sweet child."

"You got that right."

"I'm hungry as hell right now, though. Missed both lunch and dinner today. Thought I'd hit an all-nighter and chow down."

"You can come by if you want. I don't have any bacon. Will pancakes and eggs do?"

"Don't sound bad, but, naw, it's awful late."

"I really don't mind," she implored. "I'm really not too tired."

"Okay, maybe I will. Give me about forty-five minutes."

"Good. Hey, by the way, if you've got a bottle, bring something. I could use a drink. I'm all out."

"Sure thing. See ya soon."

The moon shone brightly -- the temperature having dropped drastically, previewing a true sign of the coming winter. Hack breathed deeply, feeling rejuvenated by the cold air filling his chest. As he drove, he left the window down halfway and suffered some of the chill for the sweetness of fresh air in hopes it would help clear his head.

Why in the hell was he going out to the house? Was it because he was lonely? Hell, Carin had wanted him to stay with her. His mind rambled on in thought. Did Alice's being unable to give birth to children foster guilt feelings related to their divorce? Could it be his fault -- not hers? Had bumping into her at the hospital rekindled an old flame? Was there still a spark, reignited by the only thing they had in common -- sex? His mind rambled on.

Arriving at his destination, he shook his head attempting to clear it of thought and confusion.

Coasting into the driveway, he turned off the ignition and sat for several minutes staring at the house. It was typical middle-income, but a great buy for the price and the only real estate he had ever owned. They had been in the home eight months before the separation. New furniture; everything from top to bottom; now, it was all hers. He realized his generosity hadn't been based on solely benefiting Alice, but to appease any feeling of guilt he might share in the matter.

Grabbing the bottle by its neck, Hack slid from behind the

wheel, closed the car door, and headed for the front entrance. He chuckled in remembering the evening he had finally left her and his episode with the dog shit. Things had sure changed -- the porch light was lit, and Alice was waiting. "Hi. I see you brought some goodies."

"Hope you feel like scotch, I was out of Canadian."

"Better than nothing." She smiled. "Come on up, I've got some coffee ready and the batter's all made."

"Good. Are the kids asleep?"

"Like logs."

Sitting at the kitchen table, he watched Alice move methodically through her cooking chore and the conversation ranged broadly from the weather to her sore elbow. After Hack mixed her drink, she sat sipping its contents with much satisfaction while he gulped down the food. "More coffee?" she asked.

"No thanks. I'm not much for coffee anymore. Have it once in a great while. I've got to drinking tea mostly."

"How come?"

"Seems to help my stomach some, and better on the nerves."

"Maybe I ought to try it. How about some of your scotch?"

"Yeah, thanks."

Alice started to get up.

"That's okay, I'll fix it," he said, taking her near empty glass. He moved to the sink and made two generous drinks. When he turned, Alice had disappeared and he decided to get more comfortable on the living room couch.

"Just checking on the kids and everything's fine," she said, returning to sit in a chair across from him.

"So. How do you like being single? Been doing anything for kicks?" Hack asked.

"Not much, really. I went over to a new night club a few times with Sharon, and a Bingo game once or twice with a neighbor."

Alice was a great dancer and music one of the few things they mutually enjoyed. It was about the only recreation or entertainment she had ever found interesting.

"Cigarette?" He extended his arm across to her.

"Thanks," she said, accepting the offer. "Feel like hearing

some music? I've got a couple new albums you might like."

"Sure."

"Come on downstairs."

On the way to the rec room, he stopped long enough to freshen the drinks and visit the head. Leaving the bathroom, tones of soft music drifted up the staircase beckoning him to its source. As Hack reached the lower level, a sudden thought occurred. Of the entire home, he had enjoyed the rec-room most of all and found himself amazed at realizing how long it had been since having been in it. Nothing had changed.

Alice was still clad in her robe and sprawled across half of one of the two couches. He handed her a glass and sat at her feet on the floor. "Music's great. Billy Vaughan, isn't it?"

"Uh-huh," she agreed. "Could I have another cigarette?"

"How about a dance instead?" It sounded more like a suggestion than a question.

She smiled, stood up, and moved to the center of the floor. Hack pushed aside the huge throw-rug with his foot and they reached for each other. The music played from one selection to another and by the time the last on the album had begun, she clung to him as closely as she possibly could. Another record dropped into place and they turned and glided to the smooth 'twanging-guitar' of Duane Eddy. Hack found himself returning her embrace -- their bodies pressed hard together. He could feel the pressure of her legs against his, accompanying the beat. Her breathing became labored against his shoulder and his hands soothed her back and buttocks.

Hack guided their movement to the couch and sat down, gently bringing himself to a position where he lay on top of her. She gasped and moaned, pressing harder and more intensely between his legs. He reached up and turned off the light.

It was impossible to tell exactly how long they remained quiet and motionless. He wasn't sure if she fell asleep, or not. "I hope you're not sorry," she broke the silence. "We really shouldn't have, you know, but I'm not sorry."

"I hope not," he responded.

"Look, we've got a right." Raising to rest on an elbow, she continued with several comments as if they were a single sentence. "Even though we are divorced, you're not married.

Neither am I. And, we're still married in the eyes of the church. There's nothing wrong. Do you think so?"

Hack paused and lit two cigarettes, handing her the first. "Up front? No. I don't think it was wrong. You enjoyed it. So did I. On the other side, we shouldn't kid ourselves. Don't make something more out of it than it really is."

"Passion, but no feeling, huh?" she asked sarcastically.

Hack started to respond and instead raised and twisted his position to sit on the edge of the couch with his elbows braced against his knees and head in his hands staring through the darkness at the floor he couldn't see.

Alice interrupted his contemplation. "I'm sorry. Forget I said anything. Honestly, I didn't mean it. I'm really glad you came over tonight, . . . and everything."

Hack leaned and kissed her lightly on the cheek and began the search for his clothes. After he dressed, and Alice donned her robe, they returned upstairs to share some tea and a bit more idle conversation. By the time Hack made his departure, it was just getting light outside. Rather than confuse the children by his being there so early in the morning, they mutually agreed it would be better for him to come back later.

The car churned, finally kicked-over, and he had an increasing urge to go past Carin's place. He felt a strong desire for her presence and toyed with interpreting the reason. Sexually, the gratification he had just experienced with Alice was pleasing. However, there was a lingering emptiness he couldn't quite understand, and an urgency to fill the void.

It was close to seven by the time he got to Carin's apartment and decided to gamble she had forgotten the door chain. His key turned the latch, and luckily, there were no other locks in place. Quietly shutting the door, he slipped off his shoes and tiptoed into the living room.

Removing all of his clothes, he folded them neatly, placing them on the couch, and headed down the hall to her room. As silently as possible, he moved to the foot of the bed where he began to reach under the covers from the bottom and proceeded to tickle the bottom of her feet. With a start, she raised quickly upright in bed, and as the sheets fell to her waist . . . "Holy, shit. You ain't Carin."

"Rick." The girl screamed, leaping to her feet to stand at the head of the bed with her back plastered to the wall. "Oh, God. Rick. There's a maniac in here."

Frantically trying to gain cover for himself, Hack grabbed for the bedspread. Unfortunately, he also got hold of the sheet she held to shield herself. As he gave a hard jerk, both items came together and the poor girl tried desperately to hide all of her vital spots with her hands.

Hack threw the spread back in her direction and twisted himself in the white percale sheet as Rick came flying through the bedroom door.

"What the fuck's going on?" he shouted.

It was Carin's brother.

"Oh, man," Hack muttered. "What a relief."

Rick stammered a bit and broke into hysterics. "Son of a bitch," he said, bursting out into laughter. "You should've seen the look on your face."

"Damn it, Rick, who is this pervert?" the voice from the bed pled.

Rick tried to allay her fears in a soothing string of encouragements. "It's okay. It's all right. He's a friend. He's my sister's boss."

"Rick, I'm sorry. I didn't. I thought she was Carin."

"I know. Don't worry about it. Come on out here and I'll fill you in," Rick suggested while wiping his eyes with his shirt-tail.

As they headed for the living room, Hack caught a glimpse of himself in the dresser mirror and he did look ridiculous, although, on second thought, he might have made a reasonable candidate for an award at a toga party.

Rick sat explaining about the mix-up while Hack hurried getting back into his clothes much faster than a fireman responding to an alarm.

"So you see," he continued, "since Carin was at Mom's, I borrowed her key so I could have a place to bring my date. It just happened I was in the bathroom when you came in and, well, you can take it from there."

The bedroom door flung open and Rick's girl friend stomped down the hall and past the both of them like a storm trooper. Reaching and opening the front door, she shouted without turning, "Fuck you, . . . and your weird friends."

CHAPTER III

Sixty-five was supposed to be Hack's year, or at least so claimed his horoscope. There was no way he could complain about the last. Getting through the Christmas season without having to charge a single item was a first. It wasn't easy, but it was a real accomplishment. The holidays had been extremely pleasant, with a great deal of the time having been spent with Carin.

On Christmas day, he took the kids to the roller rink to try out their new skates. Josey had to sit and watch, but had a good time, anyway, with her share of hot dogs, cokes, and coins for the game machines.

Business was seasonably slow, affording free time for trips to the golf club on a regular basis. Carin's gift of long johns and thermal socks sure came in handy. A couple of days he had played were near freezing, including coping with snow flurries on one occasion.

Standing at his front office window, surveying the street below, he cursed the white blanket as it began to smother everything in sight. The clatter of chains and whir of snow tires further aggravated him to the point of total frustration. He felt like a child pouting about not being able to go out and play.

The gigantic flakes continued to fall. By two o'clock in the afternoon, it was getting so bad, some offices were beginning to close and Hack decided to let his crew go earlier than most others. Carin hadn't made it to work that morning and the silence of the empty rooms added greatly to his dismal attitude. He poked the TV button and settled down on the couch with the newspaper and a double martini -- scanning the sports section, then the comics and horoscope, and finally fiddling with the crossword. Getting stuck about halfway through, he lost all interest and fixed another drink. Hearing the main door open, its being slammed shut was followed by thudding footsteps coming up the stairs.

"Anybody home?"

"That you, Jerry?" Hack strained to see through the double door and around the corner.

"Yeah, just me," he answered as he entered the room.

"Damn, you look froze."

"You bet your ass." Jerry chattered, wringing his hands over the radiator for several minutes before moving to the head. He hung his coat on the shower rail and Hack could hear him shiver as he stood hovering over the commode.

"My hands are so cold I can hardly hold my dick."

"I can't see that being a problem. Shouldn't take you more than two fingers," Hack called back.

"Fuck you. Got any brandy?"

"It's already poured. What'cha doing around this neck of the woods?"

"Aw, business up the street," he answered as he returned and savored a sip from the pony glass. "I've been in a friggin' meeting since noon and had no idea it was getting so bad outside."

"Why don't you stay here tonight? Not much sense in traveling as far as you'd have to go."

"Exactly what I had in mind. I got stuck in a parking lot and couldn't get the piece of junk started."

"Playing any golf, lately?" Hack was sure he hadn't, but was fumbling for conversation.

"Nope. No time, and too cold. Heard you have, though. I understand you're getting pretty good."

"Little bit," he answered with a grin. "This suckin' snow really is enough to piss you off."

"Know what you mean. Listen, if you don't mind, I better call the old lady. I should let her know what's up."

"Just leave a dime on the desk."

Jerry decided to use Carin's phone in the outer office and it wasn't hard to tell by overhearing bits and pieces of the conversation, old 'Jere' would wind up on the losing end. "Hey,

Hack," he shouted from the other room. "I hate to ask, but I've got a problem. One of the kids is running a fever and, well, wait a minute, I'll be right there." He changed the direction of his attention from Hack back to the phone. "Yeah, honey, I'll be right back. Hack's in the other room. I'll only be a minute."

Jerry placed the receiver on the desk and re-entered Hack's office. "Damn, I'm sorry to do this, but you know Erica. Uh, could I, if you don't mind that is. Could I borrow your car? I gotta let her know."

"Yeah," Hack answered his plea. "If you feel you really have to go, sure. I think you're crazy, though."

Another attempt at bantering with Erica didn't accomplish anything more than her slamming the phone in Jerry's ear.

"You lucky bastard," he said, confronting Hack, as he returned. "You don't have to put up with shit like that. Wish I had the balls to set her straight."

"You said it. I didn't," Hack responded shaking his head in disapproval. "Why you don't either stand up to her, or get the hell out, I don't know. You *are* a real pussy," he emphasized.

Jerry did hang around for a short while and finally decided to leave around seven. He resorted to more grumbling as Hack helped him on with his coat and ushered him out the door. While finishing the last of the martini, Hack plundered through the cabinet looking for something in the way of a snack with little success. The thought of having to go out for any reason made him shudder. However, his stomach won the battle.

Stepping from the doorway, he plodded through the now knee-deep snow taking advantage of the paths made by the plows and tire tracks. Fortunately, the area was infested with restaurants. A favorite being quite close, he didn't have far to go. Nearing the corner, it was slightly cheering to note several other hearty souls fighting the elements. Abandoned vehicles dotted the streets in every direction he could see, being devoured by the relentlessly falling mass.

In front of the restaurant entrance, there appeared to be a semblance of an earlier dug trench curling its way to the curb. Actually, Hack's attention had become objectively focused on a gorgeous young lady walking just ahead of his pace. As she tried to step over an area of drifted snow, her heel caught in the process, causing a complete loss of balance. In a frantic effort, Hack lunged forward attempting to break her fall. One hand grabbed her square in the ass, and the other, under the arm. As a result, she wound up sitting in the middle of his lap.

They simply looked at each other in amazement, half-laughing, half-moaning, and too stunned to immediately move.

Several others behind, waiting patiently for them to unblock the passageway, provided some assistance in helping them eventually regain their footing.

"Are you okay?" Hack asked.

"I'm fine, I think," she answered, with a wonderful smile. "You seem to have gotten the worse end of the deal."

"No damage," he replied with a slight groan, helping to brush off snow. "Hell, it's not every day a guy gets a chance to save a beautiful damsel in distress. I take it you were heading into the restaurant."

"That's what I had in mind."

"Good. Maybe you'd like to join me. That is, since we've had such a proper introduction."

She laughed and shook her head in agreement.

Getting inside without further mishap, they checked their coats and headed toward a corner table that Andre had already chosen.

"Good evening, Mr. Arnold. Would the lady care for a drink?"

"Yes, thank you." She smiled with her agreement. "A vodka martini with a twist."

The maitre d' disappeared and their waiter shortly arrived with the cocktails, serving the lady first, and placing Hack's usual double on the table near his hand.

"I see you're well known here," she observed and seemed pleased.

"Well, enough. But, more important, though, is getting you to know me. I'm Hack Arnold."

"Hello," she acknowledged, with a beautiful enchanting smile. "I'm Terri Lakewood."

"Well Terri, the way the evening started, things were looking pretty dull until our exciting episode out front. Must say it made everything a bit brighter."

"Thank you." Again came her beguiling smile. "I'll accept that as a warm compliment, but I still feel bad about the jolt you suffered. I mean, even though it probably saved me an awful bruise in a very tender location."

The waiter returned with menus and as she sat across from him scanning the wide selections, he couldn't resist surveying her loveliness. When first walking in and shedding their coats, it was impossible not to stare at the near perfection of her body. She was truly one of the most attractive and beautiful women he had ever seen. All eyes had followed her graceful movements across the room. Hack marveled at his good fortune in their meeting, and was overwhelmed by his sudden change of mood.

Mutually, they decided to wait to order and had another round.

"I assume you're snowed in, too?" she asked.

"Well, in a way. But, if you mean, did I miss making it home? No. I have a combination office and apartment just around the corner."

"Oh, that sounds nice. What kind of business do you have?"

"A commercial arts studio and ad agency, combined."

"How exciting. I mean, well, I've always been enthused with the idea of modeling."

"To tell you the truth," he beamed, "it surprises me you're not in that profession already. You certainly have all the assets."

She blushed slightly.

"Have you ever been photographed other than candidly?"

"No, I'm afraid not," she said. "I take it you wonder whether I may or may not be photogenic."

"That's the idea. I seriously doubt you would have any problem. Tell you what. If you're really hep on the idea, let me know. I'll arrange a test. I've got a great photographer on staff."

"Wonderful," she said, showing excitement. "That sounds like fun."

Hack motioned for another round. "What kind of work do you do?"

"Actually, I'm in college at Maryland, but I do have what you might call a part-time job. Don't be shocked," she said. "I sell sports equipment."

"Shocked? What's wrong with that?"

"As a matter of fact, I work with my brother. He took the business over after Dad died. That's how I got interested in tennis. You know, the business in the family, and whatever."

"Damn. I thought your name was familiar. You've won several big local amateur tournaments, haven't you?"

"A few." She seemed very pleased.

"Wow, Milady. You are one hell of an athlete."

Again, she blushed with his compliment.

They finally ordered. The food was excellent and blended well into the pleasure of their mood. Tennis, golf, clothes and entertainment were major topics of conversation. Such a harmony in communication existed, there was never a lull or need to search for speech or expression.

Following dinner, they sat and savored the biting sweetness of Benedictine and brandy while words warmed to more personal discussions. At Hack's suggestion, they agreed to move into the lounge where there was piano music and a more cozy and comfortable atmosphere. A surprising number of people were already seated, but it was far from being crowded. Andre brought their unfinished drinks and, as they sat next to each other against the wall seat, soft music strains filtered through the room.

"This is wonderful," Terri whispered as she squeezed his hand. "I mean it. Everything is just perfect. I never dreamed I could be so glad about being marooned."

"Darn. I just realized I hadn't thought to ask. What are your plans? Have you arranged anything?"

"Well, in a way. In fact, I should make a call. One of my girl friends lives a few blocks from here. She works evenings and might be home by now." Terri reached for her handbag. "Excuse me while I try to phone her and powder my nose."

As she departed, Hack couldn't help watching her every move. It had been apparent all evening her presence was distracting to everyone in the place. She had beautiful charm impossible to go unnoticed. The fact that she was with him was a real boost to his ego. He sat anxiously waiting her return, lost in a million thoughts as to what to say or do, hoping not to be too forward or crude. Hell. So what, he thought. She's just another broad down under, but all the while his subconscious prayed he wouldn't blow it. Hack looked up to see her smiling down at him.

"A penny for your thoughts," she said.

"You're worth a lot more than that."

She blushed ever so slightly and sat down beside him, resting her hand on his leg. "You can be very sweet, you know."

The simple contact of her hand fueled the fire already raging deep inside. He lit a pair of cigarettes, giving her the first. "Get in touch with your girl friend?"

"As a matter of fact, no. It isn't as late as I thought. She won't be home until eleven. It's only ten, now."

"Good. That's great." He beamed with added enthusiasm. "We can spend more time together."

Her smile was an agreeing response.

"Terri. Please don't misunderstand, but I. . . . Hell. I'm really trying to invite you to my place for a drink. It would be even more comfortable." He bit his tongue with anticipation and fear of having overstepped his bounds.

She laughed softly making him feel she sensed his uneasiness. "Since we've had such a proper introduction, as you've earlier suggested, I don't see where it would be wrong."

Hack's grin spread across his face.

After paying the check and retrieving their coats, they began the trek through the snow -- Terri snuggled close under his arm for added warmth. They zigzagged side-to-side missing the mounds created by ruts from tires. Without warning, he reached down and swooped her into his arms, carrying her across the deepest drifts to his doorstep. He could feel the warmth of Terri's breath, then her lips, as they touched lightly on his cheek just before putting her to the ground. No words passed between them -- they weren't important -- the mutual feeling said it all.

At the top of the steps they stopped long enough to unlock the door. Once opened and the lights brightened the interior, Terri, without hesitating, rushed straight through the outer office and into Hack's room. He stood in the doorway watching her spin in a circle, arms outstretched, as if to try and gather all that surrounded her into one big embrace. She squealed, "It's wonderful. I love it," adding a tweak of her nose to emphasize her elation.

Her brief pirouette took her in the direction of the couch

where she gracefully collapsed.

Without asking, Hack went straight for the bar and poured two brandies. Terri knelt in a squat position with her chin on the back of the sofa watching his every move. He turned, stooped down, and kissed the end of her nose.

"Voila," he said offering a glass. "Your nose is cold."

She smiled. "I know."

"Really glad you like it." He stood up and pushed the stereo button and turned the dimmer switch.

"Ho-ho," she said with a laugh. "Sexy."

"I need all the help I can get."

The evening sped on much too quickly. He found her intellectual, but not stuffy, yet knowledgeable on just about any subject, with an excellent sense of good common reasoning. Their interests were of such parallel, neither of them regarded the late hour. Hack sat toward the end of the couch as she curled and rested her head on his shoulder. They sipped slowly on a brandy, shared together, saying little and simply enjoying the soft sounds of a stringed orchestra floating from the speakers.

The click of the changer lowering another album into position brought Hack to consciousness. He sat for a moment clearing his head and noticed the desk clock indicating it to be slightly past four a.m.

Terri slept soundly with her head laying in his lap and her long blonde tresses streamed across his legs in lovely disarray. God, how badly he wanted her.

Lifting her head gently, he rose, got a blanket and pillow from the closet, and after adjusting her as tenderly as possible, covered her lovely body, despising himself for denying his desires.

Not wanting to disturb her any more than necessary, he silently gathered additional bedding, turned out the lights, and gently pulled the sliding double doors to a closed position. From the rear offices, he retrieved a small foldaway bed and prepared it for himself in the outer-room.

The phone ringing woke him. He almost upset the cot flinging his legs over the side while hitting his foot on the corner of Carin's desk.

"Shit." He moaned, limping and leaning to grab the noisy intruder. "Hello," he barked.

"Well, good morning to you, too," Carin said.

"Ohhh, screw you." He groaned.

"Suppose I hang up and try again."

"I'll wring your neck if you do," he declared. "I banged my bad toe getting to the phone. What the hell time is it, anyway?"

"Eight-thirty. Ungodly hour, isn't it?"

"You're outta your mind."

"Look lover," she chided. "Just thought you ought to know there's no way I can get in this morning. Furthermore, I doubt that anybody will. Looked outside? No, I know you haven't. Worst damn blizzard you ever saw."

"You can't?" He didn't mean to sound so happy. Luckily she didn't notice. "Don't worry about it. You deserve some time off, and so's the crew. Listen. If things clear up later, I'll try to get by. Okay?"

"Can't wait." She smacked her lips in a kiss.

Hack hung up the phone and moved toward the double sliding door. The injured toe ached and he favored it with each step. Gently, he slid the doors apart enough to stick his head through.

"Hi." Terri yawned while stretching her arms before her from beneath the sheet.

"Good morning. Sorry you got disturbed," he apologized.

"Come on in," she requested.

"Just a sec, while I get some pants on."

Clad in partial garb of the previous evening -- his dress shirt completely unbuttoned -- he returned and found Terri wearing his lounge jacket. It covered her to a point just below the buttocks exposing her shapely curved legs as she stood gazing out of the window. Evidently, sometime after he had put her to bed, she had gotten up and removed her clothes. Terri turned and spread her arms as if to offer herself to him. Hack stepped into the embrace and for the first time felt the fullness of her caress. Their mouths met as he tenderly touched her lips with his tongue.

"Last night was wonderful," she whispered, burying her head in his shoulder. "I really respect what you did. I can't find the words to tell you what it really meant to me." She stood away from him and turned to the window.

Hack thought he detected her eyes watering. "What's wrong, doll?"

She again turned to face him. There was no evidence of tears, had they ever been there, only the glistening of her beautiful brown eyes. A beaming smile replaced the frown. "I'm just happy. And, confused, I guess. Everything's happened so quickly."

Hack sat on the corner of the desk, holding her hand between his, looking intently into her eyes.

Terri continued, "You could have easily taken advantage of the situation last night. Truth is, I probably wouldn't have minded it at all."

Hack started to respond and she placed her finger lightly over his lips.

"You didn't though. That's what's so important. I . . . I really want our relationship to be more than just sex. Do you understand?"

He nodded in agreement and raised her hand, kissing it gently in a long embrace. "Let's get some coffee." He pinched her nose.

* * *

Over the next couple of weeks, Hack was in the best of spirits. Unfortunately, the workload increased to such a degree, most leisure activities were cut to a minimum. Carin was delighted with the uplift in his general attitude and more than pleased to have him somewhat confined to the office and her presence. However, he often squirmed at the thought of her becoming aware of the hidden competition for his attentions. Terri frequently called, but always on his private line and generally later in the evening. The phone rang only at his desk and rigid laws had restricted anyone other than he to answer. There were several times opportunities to see each other had to be canceled, but they did manage lunch twice.

Golf was out of the question, although, except for a few flurries, it hadn't snowed since the big storm. However, the weather being colder than normal allowed little chance for a thaw. On the other hand, southern Virginia escaped the majority of heavy accumulation, catching barely enough to cover the ground.

Several friends from the club traveled to Greenhill, another public course slightly northwest of Richmond. On the plus side,

Hack's preoccupation with Terri helped divert his mind from the game. Otherwise, he would have undoubtedly been a frequent participator in the trips.

Having just finished putting final touches to an illustration due later in the afternoon, Hack reached across his desk for the ash tray and a pack of cigarettes.

"Want anything for lunch?" Carin popped in the door.

"Ham sandwich would do."

"Coffee, coke, tea, . . . or me?"

"Milk." Hack turned his head and stuck out his tongue at her. "Fooled you, didn't I?"

"You're a barrel of laughs," she chided as she turned from the doorway. "I almost forgot. Your bother's on line two . . . be back in a few."

Hack picked up the phone and carried it to the couch. "What say, Jerry?"

"Not much. What are you up to?"

"Just sitting here playing with myself."

"I know better than that. Not with Carin around. She hasn't cut you off, has she?"

"Nope, but if I ain't careful, she's liable to 'cut' it off."

Jerry moaned. "Hurts just thinking about it. I take it you've got something else on the hook."

"Yeah. I met this new gal . . ."

Jerry interrupted in the middle of his sentence. "Hold it 'til I get there. I'm just around the corner and wanted to make sure you weren't out fuckin' off. I'll be up in a minute."

Hack replaced the phone and barely had time to clean a few things from his desk when Jerry popped through the door.

"So what about this hot number you were talking about?"

"Phew. You wouldn't believe it, even if you saw it."

"Can't be that good."

"Don't you doubt it." Hack's tone showed a minor tinge of irritation. "She's the next best thing to a goddess. Ever hear of a local tennis star by the name of Lakewood? She belongs to Capital Country Club."

"You lucky bastard," he said and swooned. "Damn right I know her. Not personally I mean. Sure as hell would like to, though." Jerry had walked to the window and peeked through the drapes. "Remember last fall when I asked you to play golf with me and Quinn and you couldn't make it? Well, that's where we went. Saw her on the courts and could have stood and drooled all day if we hadn't been entertaining a client. How old is she, anyway?"

"Okay, Then you know what I mean."

"I know what you mean, but how old is she? You know: one; two; three; four . . . ?"

Hack mumbled lowly, trying to subdue his answer. "Nineteen."

"What?"

"Damn it, I said she's nineteen."

"Little young for you, brother, don't you think?"

"No, I don't think." Hack began getting a bit riled. "You can't tell me you haven't seen any number of girls standing on some beauty pageant stage even younger than her that's knocked your socks off. She looks and acts a lot more like an adult than some older broads I know."

"How the hell did you get close to it?"

"Might say I fell into it," he said jokingly.

"That had to be a hell of a fall."

"Let's change the subject," Hack suggested. "I wanted to talk to you about something else."

"Okay. If you say so," he answered, pretending to be real broken in spirit.

"Come on, I'm serious. I wanted to know your opinion on that deal we discussed. Are you interested or not? I've got to make a decision before long."

"It's not that I don't . . . . Hell, I just don't think I can. You know me. I had to discuss it with Erica, and, you know her. Damned stubborn Scandinavian."

"That's for sure."

"If I can help in any other way, let me know," Jerry weakly apologized.

"Appreciate it." Hack tried to sound genuine. "Got to have someone full-time though. Guess I've got no other choice than to hire Tony."

"From what I've heard, he'd sure fit the bill."

"No doubt about it," Hack said. "Only problem is, if I hire

him away from his company, I stand a better than good chance of losing that account. I do get a fair amount of business from them."

"Well, that may be a price you'll have to pay. You really think it's worth it. You sure he's really needed?"

"If the Hanford deal goes through, I'll need a hell of a lot more help than just him."

"Yeah, but what if it doesn't?"

"Cross that bridge when I come to it. Anyway, the administrative work around here's weighing me down. I need more time to work on the board."

"Did you say board, or broad? Cut down on golf and screwin' around," Jerry suggested.

Hack's tolerance weakened and his anger surfaced. "Kiss my ass."

"No, offense, but the truth can hurt."

"So can my toe up your butt."

Jerry continued pushing a sensitive issue and Hack's guilt complexes ran rampant.

"Oooo. Aren't we bitter, big-brother?"

"Yeah." Hack half-laughed.

"Seriously." Jerry's tone emphasized the word as he reached for Hack's cigarettes lying on the desk. "Where are you really heading? What are you looking for?"

Hack shrugged his shoulders and accepted one of the filtered tobacco sticks offered from his own pack. Jerry supplied a light. He took a long drag, inhaled deeply, and settled back in his chair.

Jerry sat on the corner of the desk and patiently waited to see if he was going to get a response.

"Why do I have to be looking for something just because I want to have some fun in my life for a change?"

"There's nothing wrong with having fun, Hack. But, you seem to be stretching the point a bit."

"Geeezzze . . . ." Hack drew the word into a long exaggerated expression as he rose from the seat and moved to the bar. "Want a drink?"

"Nope. Just an answer would do."

"You're getting pretty friggin' nosey, aren't you?"

"If that's what you think, okay. I like to call it concern."

Jerry fidgeted for another cigarette and continued his assault. "Look, damn it. You ask me to give up my job and come to work with you. What am I supposed to do, ignore potential disaster in the future?"

"You already refused the job."

"That's beside the point. It was more Erica than me. At least I got the opportunity for a pretty good inside look at your business. You've really got a hell of a thing going."

"Thanks. I know it."

"Crap. You've got tunnel vision. What the hell can I say to make you understand?"

Hack dropped a couple of cubes in his drink. Before they had time to get wet, Jerry took it from his hand. "Changed my mind."

Simply shaking his head, Hack started on a second as Jerry continued his onslaught.

"You're acting like a kid out of school; a tiger out of a cage. You could piss it all away." Jerry took a healthy swig from the glass. "You've got a great clientele, a super staff, and a knockout for a secretary whose nutsy-cuckoo about you. On top of that, you've got a God-given talent anyone in their right mind would give their ass for." Jerry was getting wound up and killed the last of the liquid and moved to pour another. "It's your talent your clients are buying, not your art director's, or the rest of the staff. They may do a fantastic job, but without your input, this place is just another production factory."

Normally, it was Hack's nature to retaliate. However, Jerry was having a field day putting in his opinions, and regardless of the fact he was hitting a lot of nerves, Hack still mused at considering Jerry could never confront Erica in such a fashion.

"I guess you've got a point," Hack meekly responded as a small degree of inner guilt-ridden sensitivities began to surface. "I've worked damn hard to get here," he said in defense, "but what the hell is any of it worth if you can't enjoy it."

Jerry knew to let him continue.

"There's a big difference between you and me. You put up with bullshit. I won't, . . . and don't. I did for years and where the hell did it get me? A wife I couldn't live with; responsibility after responsibility with her damn family, never having kids of my own. You know that." He began feeling further guilt in

102

having even mentioned children.

His original train of thought having been disturbed promoted a pause to attempt retrieving his direction of rebuttal. "I just need some time and some space. . . . Aw, fuck." He threw his hands in the air in a wild gesture. "Who the hell am I trying to fool? I am fuckin' off . . . and I really don't give a damn. The world out there is full of fun, if you look for it. I'm doing things now I never dreamed I'd be able to do when I was younger. When you come right down to it, I got married to my first piece of ass. I know that's a terrible thing to say about Alice, but the fact is, it's the truth. For all those years, I had nothing to compare with; no one to share with; only a combat zone."

"Got any more butts?" Jerry asked. "That's not a pun," he said with a grin. "Cigarettes, I mean."

"Yeah, in the top drawer. No, . . . the left side."

"You want to stop this persecution?"

"Up yours." Hack smiled and retorted. "I guess it does sound like that, doesn't it?"

"Strictly daytime soap."

Hack chuckled again. "You asshole. I just want to kick my heels for a while before even considering settling down to TV, beer and football games with another one-on-one. I'm not about to let anything screw-up this business, but I do want someone to share the responsibilities."

Jerry tossed the freshly opened pack to Hack. "Just wanted to make sure you weren't completely out on a limb somewhere. Clouds get pretty high sometimes and the feet have to touch earth once in a while. No offense intended."

Hack forced a laugh. "Yeah. None taken."

"Darn, I wasn't even watching the time. Got to get going. Your car's back at the lot," Jerry said as he jumped to his feet and headed for the door. "I just remembered. We're having another bash Thursday evening. If you want to come and bring that tennis doll, give me a call."

"Fuck you."

Carin slid past Jerry as he left, and plopped on the couch, sitting a box with their lunch between her and Hack. "Always end your conversations on a sexual level?" She smiled.

"Only when I'm happy, baby. Only when I'm happy."

"You don't look so happy to me. What was that all about? I could hear you when I came in downstairs."

"Business. Strictly business."

Lunch went down with a thud and Hack forced himself to start another project as anticipations for the evening ahead caused the afternoon to drag mercilessly along. Having planned a date with Terri, concealing his growing enthusiasm and excitement from Carin wasn't easy. He avoided her as much as possible until his private line rang near the end of the day, dashing his expectations for the night to pieces. Terri's mother was ill and alone. Terri seemed equally upset by the turn of events, and not for one moment did he doubt her excuse as being genuine. Since their first meeting, it seemed fate was trying its best to keep them apart.

Hack threw a rubber eraser across the room in disgust, then sat brooding and staring at the wall. Looking out of the window made him even more depressed at seeing the frozen blanket covering the ground. Suddenly, an idea hit him and he grabbed for the phone almost wildly.

Mitch and a handful of others were playing cards at the club. By the time the conversation was over, preliminary arrangements were made for a Richmond golfing weekend. It was decided they would leave that evening, stay in a motel, and play both Saturday and Sunday. He felt better already.

It took a little over an hour to clear some last minute details and pack a small bag as Carin continued hinting about tagging along. He convinced her she would be bored with nothing to do and blew her a kiss as he went out of the door.

The parking lot had the Chevy waiting near the front and he was soon fighting rush-hour traffic on his way to Mitch's pad. Being the first to arrive, there wasn't much to do but have a drink and chew the fat while waiting for the other two.

Eventually getting on the road, traffic was still heavy due to the weekend. The trip south was lengthy and tiresome. Efforts at trying to catnap were fruitless. His mind seemed to continually drift to Terri and toy with fantasies of what might have been had they gotten together. He thought of Carin and found himself both comparing her to Terri as well as weighing their assets separately. One fact was prevalent. They were the only two women in his life holding enough of his interest to possibly compete against his dedication to golf. What if he had to choose between them, he questioned himself in thought? If it should come to that, there was really nothing much to consider. It would have to be Carin. Rationally, Terri was nothing more than an intriguing challenge, while Carin had proven herself time and time again.

"You asleep? Mitch asked."

"Naw," Hack said. "Day dreaming."

"There's a motel just up the road. That okay by you?"

"Motel's a motel as far as I'm concerned."

"That is, as long as it's got hot and cold runnin' pussy," Gabe included.

Danny laughed. "You got pussy on the brain."

Following check in, the group headed for the restaurant, ate from a smorgasbord buffet, and eventually returned to their suite of rooms to play gin until almost two. None seemed to have any trouble sleeping.

Slightly warmer weather had been forecast, but the following early morning was still bitter cold. They decided to wait until midday to tee-off, when it reached the upper forties. To make a semblance of a fair match, Hack and the little man played Danny and Mitch a twenty-dollar Nassau. The ground was hard as a rock and contact with the dirt on the first iron shot sent tremors up Hack's arms as if he had hit both crazy bones at the same time.

At a disadvantage, compared to the other three, this was his first attempt at playing in such adverse conditions. Under-clubbing on every shot was an absolute necessity and, making the adjustment, more difficult than one might think. Regardless, it was great fun and any serious intent at the game dulled by hitting the brandy bottle almost as frequently as the ball. A third nine followed the first eighteen. How they completed the final round was a miracle in itself.

Back at the motel, Hack sacked-out while the others kept on the booze trail. About seven o'clock, the phone rang. He was supposed to meet them down the road for dinner. A quick shower and shave did a lot to make the body feel somewhat healed.

"Here comes 'Sleeping Beauty.'"

Hack gave Mitch a shaft-sign to the elbow and flopped in the vacant spot in the booth.

The waitress arrived almost simultaneously with the others' dinners and he immediately ordered.

Hack grumbled. "What the hell's the hurry, anyway?"

Mitch struggled with a mouthful of food. "Danny-O's done it again."

"Done what?"

"Oh, not much," Mitch countered, washing his food down with coffee. "He's just used his irresistible charm and set us up in this lonely little town."

"Hell, all I thought they had around here were sheep farms," Hack said, making a bad joke.

"This ain't local stuff," Gabe said with enthusiasm. "Danny's got some airline stewardesses comin' in."

Hack expressed a skeptical frown. "How'd that come about? There's no way a stewardess is going to have a layover in Richmond."

"Pulled 'em out of my hat like Merlin the Great." Danny glowed. "Naw. I met this Pan-Am goddess on a flight to the coast a good while ago and see her every now and then when she gets into D.C. Yesterday afternoon she called from New York after getting in from Europe with two other stewardesses. I told her to grab a fourth and meet us down here instead of back home. She's kooky enough to do it." He continued while spreading butter on a piece of black bread. "I talked to her earlier. She said she did; and they would; and, simple as that."

Hack glanced at his watch.

Danny noticed his reaction. "Their plane's due in at nine-thirty. We're supposed to meet them at a motel over near the airport at ten."

Dinner finished -- Mitch grabbed the check. After everyone contributed to split it equally, they were on their way.

In spite of taking a wrong turn and extending the trip a good ten miles, they found the place. Reaching the room, the door rested slightly ajar. Danny knocked and poked his nose through the crack. "Anybody here?"

"Come on in."

The motel room appeared typical with two double beds. Several assorted bottles of liquor sat on the vanity with setups and a bucket of ice. A guy from room service followed them in and began sorting out his orders, leaving chips, pretzels and more ice. Danny shoved him a fin as the old man left grumbling about his rheumatism.

"How about some introductions," the ringleader spouted. "This is Joan, Pat, Mortisha; . . . Morty for short, and I'm Sal."

Everyone nodded.

Danny did the honor by pointing. "Hack, Mitch, Gabe, and I'm Danny."

Amazingly, as if preplanned, pairings came almost automatically. In the blink of an eye, each began to match-up with a different mate. Danny stuck with Sal; Mitch got Joan; Gabe nailed Pat, and Hack settled on Mortisha. They were all good lookers: Joan the most attractive; Sal the best built; Pat the biggest boobs; then, there was "Mortisha." Morty was sultry as hell. Even though the name reminded him of the nutty broad on the 'Adams Family,' he pictured her more as floating down the Nile in a "G-string" and pasties.

The bullshit began to flow. Some of the lines being used were unbelievable. Morty smiled. "Okay, what's your story?"

Hack began with a short laugh. "Hell, they make me look like an amateur. Why bother?"

"Married?" she asked.

"Nope, divorced. Make a difference?"

"Not really. Got a cigarette?"

Hack reached for his pack, took two, lit them both, and handed her one. "Now, tell me something about yourself," he suggested.

"Hummmm. Born in a hospital; raised in a house; graduated from school; and, became a glorified waitress on an airline. Besides that, I'm nympho."

Not reacting to her unexpected remark was difficult. Calmly, Hack responded. "Look's like we've got something in common. I was born in a house; raised in an apartment; flunked out of school; became a golf bum; don't like sex; but, . . . but somebody slipped Spanish-fly in my dinner tonight." They broke into harmonious giggling together.

Deciding to get a drink, Hack and Morty got hooked into obliging everyone else.

Conversations were becoming more a group affair. Between jokes and innuendoes, laughter filled the room. A portable radio spewed rock-and-roll music and Sal began doing a rendition comparable to the moves of a stripper.

"Hey, are we going out somewhere or not?" Danny's voice carried loudly above the clamor.

A series of boos and hisses followed. By the fourth or fifth drink, things were beginning to get rather loose. Sal and Pat were dancing apart and trying to outdo each other with their bumps and grinds. Joan was half-crocked, sitting on top of the dresser yelling "take it off," while Danny and Mitch were doing their best to add encouragement.

Gabe stood with his mouth agape watching Pat's boobs wildly bounce to the rhythm. Morty sat on Hack's lap in a chair, running her tongue into his ear with snakelike jabs.

Sal fueled the competition by kicking off a shoe. Quicker than bunnies in heat, both were running a race to see who could strip the fastest. Any fears they would stop at bras and pants were soon allayed. Such was not the case. The contest ended in a tie.

Danny squatted on a trash basket turned upside down. As Sal turned, she plopped square in his lap. Without hesitation, she pushed Danny's head back and shoved her tongue far into his mouth -- the sudden action sending them both off-balance and tumbling backwards, head over heels. Nobody seemed to pay much attention to the calamity.

Mitch stood in front of Joan as she sat on the dresser's edge with both legs wrapped tightly around his waist.

Pat laid sprawled on top of Gabe, her huge breasts burying his face. Almost inaudibly he could be heard mumbling something about not being able to breathe. Danny and Sal occupied the floor doing their thing.

Hack tried to move to the bed, but Morty wouldn't let up. She managed to manipulate his zipper and he was now deep inside her. At first she moved very little of her body, using a technique of pulsating the muscles between her legs, driving him berserk. It was impossible to make it last. She began to gyrate wildly as passion neared its pinnacle. It seemed their throbbing climax would never end.

Sitting silently for several moments, he held her in a tight embrace. As temperatures slowly cooled, he looked beyond her shoulder to see Danny and Sal standing nude in front of the mirror pouring more booze. "How about one for us," Hack asked, while Morty resisted his efforts to rise from the chair. Even after succeeding, she tried to pull him to the nearest bed.

"Later, hon. Later."

Gabe was still pinned under Pat, her bare buttocks grinding relentlessly over his lower body. Mitch had undressed Joan down to her waist -- her skirt raised above the hips. He turned away from her toward the head, forgetting the pants draped around his ankles, and fell flat on his face.

Joan, hysterical with laughter, slid quickly off the dresser holding the remains of a drink in her hand. "My God, he's damaged. He's lost all his color," she cried out, while pouring the glass of liquid and ice over his ass.

Mitch screamed, struggling to his feet. "Mother-fuck, that's cold."

Joan drug a chair between them in an effort to remain at a healthy distance, as Mitch, with a handful of crushed ice, tried to shove it up her crotch.

"Naughty, naughty," Joan teased as she shook her finger.

He finally gave up and hobbled for the commode.

Assuming Gabe hadn't been suffocated, he was still at it.

Hack turned to give Morty her drink and realized her whereabouts by the groans and grunts coming from the bathroom. He handed it to Joan instead as they both plopped on the bed. Claiming she was thirsty, she practically guzzled its entire contents then laid her head in his lap. Her finger searched for his navel and slowly traced a path in a downward direction to find her need. Her head turned, followed by the caress of her lips. Hack lay there in combined pleasure and pain as her finger nails dug deeply into his thighs. Tightening his hands in her hair, he pulled her upward in a single motion and rolled on top of her back sending himself deep into her body. His hands moved beneath to cup her breasts. Spreading her legs even further, Joan raised her hips begging for more penetration. As he pumped and throbbed inside her, she, too, reached a climatic end. Hack kissed her on the back of the neck, rolled away, and sat on the edge of the bed. Danny and Sal had curled together in a chair. They were sound asleep.

Gabe was still at it.

Hack headed for the bathroom as Morty and Mitch were making their exit. Mitch gave a look of disbelief as they passed. Hack replied with a shrug of his shoulders.

Stepping into the shower felt better than good. After the hot, he stood facing up into an icy cold spray that trickled from head to toe. Satisfied his blood had began to flow again, he turned the faucet and stepped beyond the curtain to the tiled floor. Pat was sitting on the commode with a gleam in her eye. Lord, he thought. How the hell can I get outta this?

Trying to keep his back to her, in an attempt to ignore her presence, he began toweling himself dry. Grabbing him by the waist, she spun him toward her, burying her head between his legs. He stood motionless for several moments while earlier thoughts to resist rapidly dwindled. Pleading, she looked up. "Put it in me. Please?" Cupping her face in his hands, he gently raised her to a standing position with their bodies pressing close together. Turning to take her previous seat on the toilet, he pulled her to sit straddling his lap and entered her body. Her breasts were extremely large and full. She gained great stimulation from his hands and gentle nursing of her nipples. On her third climax, he pretended gaining his own satisfaction.

"Damn, that was wonderful," she said with a gasp.

Hack managed an exhausted smile of approval. This time, they both jumped into the shower; no hanky-panky; just water. After toweling each other dry, they headed for the other room.

Gabe was still at it -- with Morty this time. The other four were fast asleep.

"Damn," Pat groaned, as she spied the watch lying on the bureau. "It's almost seven-thirty."

"Okay, let's go. Everybody up," Hack yelled. There was no sign of life, except for the two sex-fiends on the bed. "Come on, Gabe. Time's up."

"Be with you in a minute," he said in a strained voice.

Gabe shortly fulfilled his obligation.

In the meantime, Hack and Pat struggled to revive the remaining scattered bodies. It took about an hour, but everybody made it. Even though room service brought coffee, breakfast would do a lot better. Walking through the cold air to the restaurant was like a tonic. By the time the meal was completed, everyone felt a bit more human and Danny had talked the girls into going to the course. Stopping back at the room long enough for the ladies to change into slacks and warmer clothes, they then headed for the guy's motel, where the men did the same.

Arriving at the club house, following a short drive, they found it fairly deserted. From a look at the parking lot, not more than a few groups could be playing. Danny and Hack led the way to the golf shop and requested four electric carts and four green fees. The pro looked at them like they were nuts. "It's rather embarrassing," Danny leaned over the counter and whispered as he pointed in the direction of the ladies. "Our wives don't trust us at all. It's the only way we can get out to play."

His explanation did little to improve the man's opinion of them. Nevertheless, they got what they needed and headed for the tee. Cart assignments resulted in being paired the way the previous evening had ended. Danny was still with Sal; Mitch kept Joan; Gabe got stuck with Morty, and, Hack rode with Pat. The girls drove while they played. There was plenty of booze, and to keep warm, they all had their share. Considering last night's excessive consumption, it didn't take much to stir the flow of remaining alcohol in their systems. Needless to say, the round wasn't the greatest example of golf. Even though Hack was the least quality player of the group, he had difficulty accepting three whiffs in a row on the first tee while everybody roared. To further complicate his dilemma, Pat operated the brake and gas pedal, but insisted on placing her hands between his legs, supposedly for warmth, while he steered the cart. He was having a hard enough time with his swing without the added bulging handicap growing in his pants.

At the par five seventh-hole, all the drives were fairly well hit and in the fairway. Danny and Gabe, as usual, were a good bit farther off the tee than the other two. The frozen ground allowed tremendous roll. Being a hole that normally played extremely long and definitely unreachable under regulation, it was brought to its knees by the fearless foursome. Mitch was just short, Gabe had rolled over, and Danny stopped pen-high on the elevated green. Hack's ball came to rest in the rough near a tree, and while he manipulated his shot and the rest waited, Morty and Gabe whizzed on ahead to locate his ball, somewhere beyond the hill.

Mitch and Hack were both on in three and relatively close to the pin. The entire entourage left the carts at the front and trudged toward the back of the green in search of the missing couple. As they all looked down, it was clear that Gabe's ball was in the trap — so was he — with Morty having a staunch hold on his pecker. While he stood urinating, she attempted to write her name in the off-white grit. In her zealousness to cross the 'T,' she squeezed a little too hard in pulling forward. Already unstable from intoxication, he plunged to his knees and then rolled in the sand laughing. Quite naturally, he was charged a two-stroke penalty for grounding his club.

CHAPTER IV

Having ended the day early, allowing the girls to get at least some rest prior to their return flight, it felt good to be home. Napping on the way back hardly helped.

Winning the struggle to get the couch open, Hack collapsed on the bed. Several times the phone persistently rang, but he couldn't muster the desire or strength to answer it and passed into unconsciousness.

Sounds of horns and motors revving stirred him to life. Opening his eyes into the direct glare of morning sun beaming through the unshaded window aggravated the pounding in his temples. His mind was still dull but able to sense he had been asleep since the previous early evening. Not having bothered to undress or remove any other paraphernalia, he consulted his watch and was tempted to snooze some more. He thought better of it and lumbered to his feet. His body felt poisoned and he reeled from dizziness before heading to close the drapes. Shedding his clothes along the path to the bathroom, he turned the faucet to cold, spewing icy shower beads that shocked his flesh to full reality. Jumping out much faster than he had entered the self-imposed torture, he swaddled himself with his bed sheet to avoid a chill. After flicking on the hot plate, he sat until the water boiled and with great effort made a cup of tea. The steaming liquid burned going down, but served its warming purpose.

Having moved to his chair, Hack sat facing the desk in several moments of solitude. First a smile, then a deep growing chuckle emerged, as thoughts reviewed the events of the past forty-eight hours. He recalled having a scorecard with the four names and numbers for future use, but couldn't remember where he put it. "Hell. Hope it isn't lost," he actually commented to himself aloud. "Fat chance of ever getting their numbers from the other guys."

Before starting to hunt for something to wear, he tried dialing Terri's number. The phone rang busy. "Holy shit," he growled after spying the pile of clothes forgotten for the cleaners. The only things in the closet not soiled were sports clothes. After making the most possible conservative choice available, he scooped up the dirty pile, shoved them into a plastic bag, and placed it beside the outer door. Pulling the pants on with one hand and cradling the receiver between his shoulder and chin, he tried Terri's call again. The phone rang repeatedly with no answer. "Damn it," he muttered.

No sooner had he zipped his fly and a key turned in the front door lock. "Welcome back stranger," Carin goaded. "Got something hot here for you."

"Thanks, but I already had some tea."

"Humph. What makes you think I meant something to drink?" She faked pouting.

Hack forced a smile with great difficulty. The mere thought of sex made his legs weak.

Carin stepped close and walked her fingers up his bare ribs.

He flinched.

"Well, I can see you're not in the mood," she said, placing her hands on her hips. He wasn't sure if she was acting or really disappointed. She turned away; looked over her shoulder; stuck her tongue out; and continued to her desk.

Monday mornings had become regularly scheduled for staff meetings, but not very much covered the current agenda. Some disappointment was noted about the fall in production and a decision was made to get a new coffee pot for the boys in the back. After the crew returned to the sweat shop, Carin and Hack sat and talked. Most of the conversation, initiated by Carin, inevitably drifted to his recent trip. Adeptly dodging the real events, he manufactured any number of exaggerations far short of the truth. He was able to sidetrack the issue by changing the subject to details of Jerry's refusal at accepting a position, and probabilities of hiring Tony. When he asked her opinion, she avoided an answer saying she'd like to think about it. That undoubtedly meant no. Ending their communicative session, they retreated to their desks and toiled away.

Trying to dial Terri's apartment again around ten o'clock without success, he decided to call her sports shop. Terri's brother answered the phone and informed Hack she had spent the entire weekend at her mother's and was still there. Hack graciously accepted the mother's number, scribbling it on the corner of his desk pad. Ending the conversation, he started to dial and suddenly changed his mind. Having second thoughts, and sensing an awkwardness in contacting her there, he finally completely dismissed the notion and leaned back in his chair.

Gazing at the ceiling, it seemed unbelievable. It had been little more than two weeks since Terri and he had met. Since that first night, they had barely seen each other. Yet, even considering the limited encounters, he felt as though they had known each other forever. Hack's mind labored in the fear of never consummating a relationship yet to exist.

Carin buzzed the intercom. "Tony's on line three."

"Damn. Tell him I'm . . . . Aw, hell. I'll take it."

Not being in the mood to get into a matter requiring such heavy discussion, Hack skirted Tony's query regarding the position by denying having been able to first talk to Jerry. Before putting the phone down, unable to restrain himself any longer, he dialed Terri.

"Hello." The voice was melodic.

"How you doing, babe?"

"Oh, Hack, it's really you?"

"Nobody else. Wait a minute, though, I'll be right back." With the receiver still in hand, he stretched the cord and pulled the sliding doors together. "I'm here."

"I thought you might have been upset about Friday night." She didn't pause long enough for him to respond. "I know it was at the last minute. You couldn't have been disappointed any more than I was. I tried to call you all weekend. Even last night, at least four or five times. Mother's been really ill and I just couldn't leave. You do understand?"

"God yes, baby," he agreed soothingly. "You had no other choice. I wouldn't have wanted or expected you to do anything less. But, about this weekend, I had to make a rather sudden business trip Saturday morning and decided to stay over with some friends."

"Oh, I'm glad. I feel much better," she sighed as she spoke. "You needed to get away from the office. You've been working much too hard."

Hack was certainly tickled she couldn't see the grinning embarrassment her remark provoked. "Just as soon as she's well, we'll get together. It seems like forever since . . ."

"Don't tell me," she interrupted. "I've had little else on my mind. Just think about how nice it will be when we do see each other."

"Be careful," he warned. "I might come right over."

She gave a little laugh and made a soft kissing sound.

"Call me tonight," he suggested.

It took several more moments to complete the goodbyes. Carin buzzed and wanted to know his plans for lunch. He succumbed to her persistence and visited the local cafeteria in the next block.

* * *

With his luck, it was bound to happen. Terri's mother had a setback. Nothing overly serious, but it was more than another week before Terri finally got back to her apartment. Their weekend plans had been canceled for a second time and, except for staying over a few nights at Carin's, Hack kept pretty busy. It was midweek and he hadn't been golfing since the Richmond spree. The itch for more play was increasing with each day. However, no sooner than plans were made to spend the afternoon at the course, it started to rain. Hack spent the rest of the day in a terrible mood, until realizing how long it had been since seeing Sharon's kids and made arrangements to have dinner with them that evening.

Being with the children was always enjoyable. Taking them to McDonald's and an early movie, their mother tagged along at his persistence. However, the minute he drove away after dropping them off in front of the house, his sour mood immediately returned. He hated the thought of being alone for another night and rationalized Alice surely wouldn't object to his stopping by, but there was no need to chance complications. Their one-time interlude shouldn't become two. Things had finally reached a happy medium between them and to risk fouling it up was stupid.

It was still fairly early. Instead of heading back to the emptiness of his place, he decided to head for the Sundowner's. It really wasn't on the way, but seeking companionship rather than solitude, he pulled into a station to get gas and use the phone. Dialing the nightclub in search of Mitch, he was shocked when Gabe answered.

"What in the hell are you doing there?" Hack's tone imparted an expression of disbelief more than a question.

"They finally mustered me out today. No more full-time soldierin'. Can you believe it?"

"That's great, but where's Mitch?"

"Ballin' some chick, I reckon. He wanted the night free and I told him I'd do the door."

"What's it look like?"

"Slow as a snail tryin'ta reach a piece of ass?"

"Want some company?"

"Sheeeet, yeah."

"Just getting the car filled with go-power. I'll be there, shortly."

"Hey," the attendant yelled across the lot. "Could you move your car? Other customers want to get to the pump."

Hack left the booth, paid his bill, and continued on his way. Feeling charitable, he stopped for a hitchhiker and during the ensuing conversation learned the youth was headed for Miami. The lad, evidently attempting to justify his reason for going, tried to convince Hack that "under the sun and on the beach" was the only place worth being.

"You play golf?" Hack instinctively asked.

"Yes, sir. Whenever I can."

"Have you played in Florida?"

"No, sir. I've never been there. This is my first time." He looked out his window. "Have you ever been there?" His returned question was as if it were nothing more than a polite response.

"Not yet. I really want to go though. I hear the courses are a lot different and I'd like to find out for myself." He reached inside his shirt pocket retrieving a near empty pack of cigarettes and extended it to his rider. The offer was refused. Shoving the lighter into the dashboard, he waited until it popped and lit one for himself. "Where do you play your golf? That is, when you can?"

"Connecticut. That's where I'm from."

As insipid as their conversation appeared to be, Hack's mind was embroiled in any number of fantasies, tantalized by the carefree personae of his temporary friend. Serving as a reminder of himself at a similar age, the boy at least had the spunk to follow instincts and fulfill his desires. He envied the lad. Seldom is there a second chance to live the freedom of youth and indulge in your dreams.

"You going to college down there?"

"Next semester," the youth answered and smiled. "I'm going to have some fun before then."

"That's great. Stick to it." Hack felt like he wanted to caution the boy against the pitfalls he would undoubtedly confront. A single mistake or a missed opportunity could be the difference between sentencing himself to a future of misdirection or propelling toward happiness, success, and even stardom. He suddenly felt very burdened by his own past.

"Well, this is as far as I go," Hack announced as he turned into the nightclub parking lot.

"Thanks a lot, mister," the lad said, bouncing from the car and retrieving his huge backpack from the rear seat.

Having a wide choice of parking spaces, he opted on a parallel spot to keep the drunks from banging the sides of his car, and glanced over his shoulder as he entered the main entrance noticing the boy had taken a place by the roadside holding a sign with the word Florida written on it. He continued through the door to locate Gabe, finding his 'rebel' buddy sitting at the near empty bar having a cup of coffee.

"Better watch out, that's pretty potent stuff," Hack joked, pulling a stool under his tail.

He laughed. "Yeah."

"Damn, this place is empty tonight."

"Tell me about it." Gabe's boredom with the situation surfaced.

"So, the Army dumped you, today, huh?"

"It's about fuckin' time. They've been pissin' around with my discharge for the past four months."

"Let's celebrate with a toast. I'll buy you another coffee."

"Kiss my ass." He laughed again. "I'll buy you one." He giggled some more.

Hack ordered a couple of drinks while Gabe responded to a phone call. He sat observing the small attendance wondering why the decision had been made ending "ladies night" on Thursdays. On second thought, the bands were no longer engaged except on weekends and, recorded music had never seemed to draw any crowds.

"That was Mitch checkin' in," Gabe commented as he scooted up to his seat.

"Where's he at?"

"Didn't say. Didn't ask."

There was a slight pause as the barmaid delivered Hack a second drink.

"You finished the first, already?" Gabe looked surprised. "You thirsty, or carryin' a load?"

"Both."

"So, what's the problem?"

Hack twiddled with the edge of his glass and shrugged his shoulders. "Just fed up with everything, I guess."

"Know what you mean," he agreed.

"I gave some young kid a ride on the way here tonight. It was sort'a like looking in the mirror and seeing myself years ago. He was on his way south to 'shake-his-legs' before jumping into college next fall. Nice kid. Hope he gets what he wants."

"Damn. You are on a downer."

"Yeah, guess so. I ought'a be content with the way things have been going with the business and all that. I don't know why I can't find the incentive for it like I used to have. You know, I never got into golf until not too long ago. Before the 'bug' bit me, I played once in a while with my brother, or maybe some client. After my old lady and I split, I started going more often and eventually got hung up in gambling and the group at the club."

"It's a nasty death." Gabe shook his head in an under-standing manner. "It's a hell of a lot of fun, though," he immediately added.

Hack smiled. "It's that all right." He raised the glass to toast his remark and then imbibed its contents. "My brother raked my ass through the coals the other day about all the screwing around I've been doing. The bad part about it is he's probably right, but unless you walk in a person's shoes, you just can't judge their need or why things bother them."

Another drink was automatically served and he paused to sip the liquid.

Gabe fidgeted on his stool and reached for Hack's pack of cigarettes and lighter. Almost rubbing his thumb raw on the flint wheel, he tossed it on the counter and fished through his pants pockets until he produced a crumpled pack of matches.

"I don't know," Hack continued. "I never had the chance to sow my oats when I was a kid. Hell. I was working practically full time when I was sixteen and had a degree in commercial arts two years later. I graduated from a vocational school."

"You're foolin'."

"Nope. Then, like a dumb-ass, I go and get married at nineteen for no good reason at all."

"You mean you didn't have to get nailed?" Gabe shuddered. "It's gonna be a cold day in hell a'fore I get hitched."

"Tell you a secret. My wife and I were both virgins on our wedding night."

"Are you sheeeetin' me? Why the hell'd you do it?"

"Stupidity, ignorance, hot pants . . . take your pick." Hack lit a cigarette from the smoldering butt lying in the ashtray and continued. "I've only had two vacations in the twelve, almost thirteen, years we were together. Never had any chance to take one alone. Other than a few weekends, since I met you guys, that's about it. Alice worked for a while after we got married, then when she began pushing about having our own kids she quit after she thought she was pregnant and never got another job."

"Sheeeet," Gabe expounded. "That's pretty friggin' bad."

"So, what have you got planned since becoming a free man?"

"Screw around for a while and probably blow my muster-out pay. I'll get a job later. Someday, I may even decide on settlin' down."

"Where you from originally?"

"Aiken . . . South Carolina," he replied, sipping his drink between words. "Actually I was born in Augusta, right across the river, and been thinkin' I might take a run down there. Haven't seen my mother or sister since before I enlisted."

"What about your dad?"

"He died when I was seventeen and left Mom with the controllin' interest in a big corporation. She's turned out to be a pretty good business woman. Anyway, I know the head-pro at her country club real well and he's been offerin' me an assistant job for when and if I ever got out. Might just head down that way and look into it."

"Want some company?"

"You serious?" Gabe spun on the stool to confront him face to face.

Hack smiled. "Never more in my life."

"Sheeeet. That would be great. We could have a hell of a ball. I'm ready to leave now."

"Not so fast." Hack laughed with his response. "There's a few things I've got to take care of in the morning. How about tomorrow afternoon?"

"Sooner, the better." He was elated. "I ain't got a car, yet. Can we take yours?"

"What about flying?"

"That's great with me. We can borrow wheels when we get there. That'll be no problem."

"Where you . . . ?"

Gabe interrupted his query as if he had read his mind. "Right here. I've got a room across the way."

"Good. I'll sack out here tonight and you can ride into town with me tomorrow." Hack turned on his stool leaning against the bar struggling to get his wallet from a back pocket. "Why don't you head on over to the room and try and make some flight arrangements for sometime after twelve-noon? Here's my credit card. Put the ticket reservations against it and we'll settle later. I'll hold the fort down here 'til you get back."

Gabe took off like a rabbit.

* * *

Sudden absences were becoming habitual for Hack. Carin didn't seem overly surprised at his unexpected plans, although, it

121

was unusual for him to be gone for more than a few days at a time. She was a bit taken by the fact this escapade could stretch beyond a week. However, knowing his disposition of late -- being the only person really sharing somewhat of an inside-track to his mind -- she ultimately assured him he deserved the break, but would be missed a great deal. He promised to keep in close touch.

Prior to the flight, Hack made a trip to the bank and withdrew two-thousand dollars in traveler's checks from his personal account. Landing at their final destination around six-thirty, having changed planes in Atlanta, Gabe's younger sister met them at the airport. She was seventeen; cute as a button; and her southern-belle accent, adorable. Following a big hug and kiss for her brother, and introducing herself to Hack as Bonnie, they loaded their transported belongings and drove to his mother's house. Except for the lack of acreage and cotton fields, the home itself resembled that of a grand southern plantation. Pulling through a stone archway guarded by an iron gate, the cobblestone driveway circled in front of the huge structure. The stark-white building, faced with several tall columns looming from the ground to the roof's eaves, was regal and impressive.

"Damn," Hack muttered. "You left all this?"

"Sheeeet," Gabe returned. "It's just another house. Take's more than that to be a home."

"Gabriel," his sister said, shaming him. "You shouldn't say a thing like that."

He flinched at the sound of his name and started to respond, but evidently changed his mind.

Before Bonnie could come to a halt, a middle-aged woman and a younger, seemingly sophisticated lady, appeared on the porch and rushed to the car. Gabe had no more than cleared its door and he was smothered in the arms of both women. Finally able to free himself of their embrace, he turned and motioned his arm in Hack's direction. "Here's a good friend of mine from Washington. This is Hack Arnold. And, Hack, this is my mother, Martha, and my Aunt Sylvia."

Offering their hands to Hack in a delicate gesture of southern hospitality, he responded in the proper manner. Sylvia appeared to be near Hack's age and refined in social behavior and mannerisms.

Bringing up the rear, as the group began to file inside, his attention focused on the firmness of Sylvia's buttocks. Her tight skirt strained to contain them. Wearing heels, she appeared to be almost as tall as he and very slim in figure. Without the horn-rimmed glasses and mousey-brown hair tucked neatly behind her head in a bun, he envisioned her as being more attractive than on initial appearance.

Gabe's sister disappeared immediately after they entered the vestibule. It was a large area with hardwood flooring, so highly polished, it mirrored near-perfect images of anything reflected in its surface. Proceeding into an adjacent room framed by double doors, appetizers and other gourmet offerings covered the better part of a small table near a bar cabinet. The decor was fourteenth century and reeked of expensive taste.

"Help yourself," Sylvia suggested to Hack. "We want you to feel completely comfortable and at ease during your stay."

"How about a drink?" Gabe added to her welcome.

"Yeah, . . . thanks. . . . Sound's good."

Bonnie seemed to pop out of nowhere, clad in a scant bikini. "Let's go swimming," she declared enthusiastically.

Hack gave her a puzzled look.

She cleared his mind of negative thoughts regarding the temperature. "We've got a heated indoor/outdoor pool."

"Now, Bonnie. They just arrived and haven't had time to settle or eat," her mother said in a scolding manner.

"That's okay," Gabe interjected. "We'll be there 'fore long."

Bonnie spun on the balls of her bare feet and made a retreat through a smaller door at the room's opposite end.

"I don't know what I'm going to do with that child," Martha said, directing her remark to Sylvia.

Sitting and listening for almost a half-hour to Gabe answer queries regarding his period away from them was becoming increasingly boring. Hack suffered through the conversation, occasionally responding to a remark or comment focused to his attention, understanding the importance of affording her time to dote on her wandering male child. Eventually content he had fulfilled his obligation, Gabe expressed his desire for them to be excused and join Bonnie at the pool.

"There will be a late supper at nine," Sylvia called as they left.

* * *

Opening his eyes to the sculptured ceiling, it took a visual survey of the room and several moments more before realizing where he was. Hack had been given the older sister's former bedroom to use since the guest wing was currently being redecorated. The bed proved comfortable and he had slept well.

A compelling urge to remain tucked under the covers was combated by better judgment and he flung his legs over its edge.

Drapes covering an entire wall practically shielded the room from daylight. He walked to the corner in search of the cord and drew them apart. Standing at the window, the area at the rear of the house wasn't as large as he had imagined. Half of the swimming pool jutted from a retractable enclosure attached to the house into the patio area. A narrow stretch of lawn, abutted by a long hedge, separated the property from a golf course fairway. A large pond complimented the near side of a green surrounded by sand traps, positioned to the right of his view. On a distant hill, in the same direction, a majestic club house towered over the meadows. The scenery was beautiful and stirred his desires to hurry to the tee.

Gabe poked his head in the room to let him know he was up and raring to go.

After a quick shower, Hack hurriedly dried his hair, dressed, and they met in the kitchen. "Good morning."

"Hi, Hack." Bonnie chimed her greeting, and immediately placed a plate of sausage and eggs for him at the table. He joined Gabe, already well into his meal. Bonnie brought a plate for herself and a fresh pot of coffee.

"Bonnie and Sylvia are going to play with us this mornin,'" Gabe said between bites. "Hope you don't mind."

"No, that's fine," Hack responded without hesitation -- lying through his teeth about his true feelings on the matter. Playing with a bunch of women duffers wasn't his idea of a having fun. "Got a tee time?"

"Yeah, nine-fifteen. There's no rush."

"Sylvia's already gone ahead to practice," Bonnie added.

* * *

From the club terrace, he could easily see the house. The hole

124

running behind the property was the seventeenth on the championship course. A second and shorter eighteen holes spread across even more hilly terrain on the far side of the grounds. Sated in his survey of the area, he joined Gabe as he was heading for the golf shop. After an introduction to Stan, the head professional, and arranging for carts, they went looking for Bonnie, finally locating her leaving the ladies room. "Where's Sylvia?" Gabe asked.

Bonnie shrugged her shoulders. "Still at the driving range, I guess."

"Hack. Why don't you buzz on over and tell her to shake a leg while we get the gear loaded?" Gabe suggested. "There's only three foursomes ahead of us."

"Which way . . . ?"

"That way." Gabe pointed in the opposite direction Hack had intended to take.

A curving walkway sheltered by tall hedges on both sides twisted down a slight grade to an open area. Rounding the corner of a small building housing the ball attendant, he stopped abruptly in total amazement. Sylvia was addressing an iron shot and the pass she made at the ball was that of an expert. He watched as the pellet soared through the air landing almost on top of the hundred and fifty-yard marker. There was no doubt it was her target. He couldn't move and was compelled to watch her repeat the feat. She did -- with almost identical accuracy.

Finally controlling his disbelief, he strode in her direction. Once again he stopped short of actually interrupting her. This time to marvel at the difference in her appearance. As he had earlier imagined, the change to a well-coordinated sports outfit, combined with wearing her hair in a pony tail dangling beneath a visor cap, totally altered her appearance. She still wore the heavy rimmed glasses.

Turning to reach for a different club, she noticed him ogling her. "Oh, hi," she said, slightly embarrassed.

He blundered for the lack of any other remark, "Damn, you're good,"

"Thanks." She smiled in acceptance of the compliment. "Are we on the tee?"

"Yeah, pretty soon. Here. Let me help you with the bag."

* * *

Hack could never have dreamed playing golf with women would be so enjoyable. He and Sylvia teamed against the other two -- the losers being liable for lunch. It was a tough match. From the men's regular tees, Sylvia was almost as proficient as her nephew playing from the blues. Bonnie's game had to be qualified as better than average, shooting from the ladies' tees. As it resulted, they finished in a tie and the three mutually agreed to put the meal on the mother's tab.

Compared to other country clubs Hack had visited, this was without question the most lavish and prestigious. The dining room was immense and the food outstanding. They delved in idle conversation through the meal and drinks that followed. Gabe excused himself and left the table to join the pro and several other men gathered in a far corner. "How come you've never taken the game more seriously?" Hack asked Sylvia.

"I've been on the ladies tour," she corrected.

It was his turn to be embarrassed. "I'm sorry. I had no idea."

"Yeah." Bonnie entered the conversation. "She was pretty good, too."

"Why did you quit?" Hack was sincerely interested.

"She got pregnant," Bonnie blurted.

"Damn it, Bonnie. Don't be so crude." Sylvia was mad.

"Excuuussse me." Bonnie disgustedly slid her chair from the table and made an exit.

"Forgive her. She's still quite young and wiry." Sylvia's ire had completely passed. "I did get pregnant and eventually lost the baby," she explained, then added, "unfortunately, my husband, too."

"Oh, I'm sorry."

"I just never developed the interest to try the tour, again."

Hack noticed Gabe returning at a rather brisk pace. "Hey. I got us a match," he beamed, as he neared their table.

"Time I took my leave." Sylvia stated.

Hack wanted to ask her to stay. Instead, he rose and moved to assist her with the chair.

She smiled her appreciation. "I'll see you back at the house."

"Did you hear me?" Gabe plopped in his seat and reached for a glass of water. "I got us a good bet."

"Who with?"

"Two members sittin' over there with the pro. I finagled a hundred-dollar Nassau."

"It better be a good bet," Hack cautioned.

"Don't worry, it is. We're playin' egos, not skill."

Since it was later than first realized, they agreed to play nine and meet the following morning for an entire eighteen. The two older gent's games weren't quite as bad as Gabe had originally implied, but certainly well within bounds of anything they should be able to handle. Having the opportunity to easily beat their opponents two ways, they settled for a single win and finished a hundred apiece on the plus side.

Delighted by the challenge of new blood at the course, Hack's and Gabe's opponents suggested the four meet for breakfast prior to an early tee time rematch the following morning. Placing their golf equipment in club storage left them unencumbered to walk back to the house. A threatening cloud hovered in the distance promoting fears rain might ruin their plans, while the breeze carried a growing chill unsuitable for the sweaters they wore. Picking up the pace, they soon skirted the hedge and crossed the lawn to a lower rear entrance.

"This is some kind'a pad," Hack imparted, observing the recreation room sprawling beneath nearly half the house. It contained two complete contemporary living room settings separated by a circular fireplace. A grand piano occupied one corner, while an adjacent area served as space for a crescent-shaped bar with the capacity of accommodating at least a dozen people. There was a dartboard, billiard table and Ping-Pong, as well.

Gabe took a cue from a rack on the wall. "Come on, I'll shoot you a game of eight ball."

* * *

Hack spent most of the evening in the rec-room with the family after dinner and was in bed at a reasonable hour. He retired about the same time as Sylvia. Bonnie and her brother remained curled on the couch engrossed in a TV movie special. Even then, the morning came too quickly. Hack awoke feeling almost as weary as if he had little rest at all. He struggled into the shower and exited feeling reborn. "You ready, yet?" he heard

Gabe call from the outer room.

"Just getting dressed."

"Step on it. We're runnin' late."

He breezed through a quick hair-dry and left the room still zipping his fly. Sylvia entered the hall as he rushed past. "You are in a hurry," she joked at his struggle with the zipper.

He stammered and settled on a blushing smile.

"See you later," she called as he tripped down the stairs.

Gabe met him at the bottom and they went directly out the front entrance. A gleaming black Jaguar touring car sat in the driveway. Gabe rushed to the driver's side and opened the door. "Let's go."

"Who belongs to this?" Hack was aghast.

"Sylvia. She must like you."

"Don't I wish?"

* * *

Finding the opposition in the men's grill, they served themselves from a breakfast buffet and joined them at their table. "Good mornin', gentlemen." Both returned the greeting. "Ready for a 'get-even' round," Dave, the older of the two asked?

"Yes, sir," Gabe meekly responded, forcing a smile.

"Bill and I've known your mom for quite some time. What brings you back down this way?" Dave queried as if he were truly interested.

"Stan asked me to consider bein' his assistant."

"Son of a gun. That sounds like a fine idea. You plannin' on acceptin'?"

"Haven't made up my mind, but I might do it."

"And, Hack. Are you also aspiring to be a pro?"

"No, sir. I've got a graphics business in DC. Gabe and I are good friends."

"Graphics, huh? Don't know much about that." His voice trailed in volume with the end of his statement.

Bill entered the conversation for the first time. "We about ready?"

Before teeing off, a few ground rules were changed allowing either team to press at any time as long as the other approved. After the first six holes, Hack and Gabe had them three down and their opponents continued pressing the bet. Having lost four hundred dollars apiece after the front nine, Bill and Dave suggested doubling the back-nine wager. Gabe's game had suddenly returned, but he still seemed to play only as good as the situation warranted, leaving all the right opportunities for Hack to salvage certain holes. They each finished the day on the plus side of a thousand bucks.

Bill and Dave avoided joining them in the grill after completing the round and went directly to their cars with the excuse of getting home to the wives. Hack felt relieved in not having to make a bunch of false apologies about taking their money.

"Son of a bitch," Gabe whispered. "We sure made it a day."

"Yeah," Hack responded. "But, tell me. Am I wrong, or are you lying back?"

"Who me?" He acted insulted and then broke into a growing smile.

"Asshole. You had me worried for a minute."

Ordering sandwiches and a pitcher of beer, they enjoyed the food and continued to revel in their success. As usual, Mom caught the tab. Convincing Gabe to assist him in his long-iron play, they went to the range with a bucket of balls. In a half-hour, Hack was having much greater success than exhibited earlier on the course.

Their opponent's early departure had taken them by surprise. It had been assumed they would be eager to try another eighteen in the afternoon. Leaving the last couple of practice balls lying idle on the tee, they gathered Hack's clubs and returned them to storage.

"What're you planning on doing?" Hack asked, after ordering his drink.

"Head back to the house, I guess. Mom's buggin' the hell out of me to go over to my grandmother's with her. Maybe, I'll do that." He scratched the end of his nose. "What'da you want to do?"

"Hadn't thought about it. You think Sylvia's home?"

"I know she is. We got her car."

"Considered given her a call," Hack mumbled to himself. "Think she might like to play?" he asked in a louder tone.

Gabe laughed. "Dad, don't you ever talk about me again.

You can't keep cunt off'n your mind."

"Screw you. I enjoy playing with her. Golf, that is."

"Give her a buzz."

Sylvia was thrilled to hear from him and tickled pink to accept the invitation. Gabe used her car to drive home. She returned with it a short time later. Hack had already arranged for a cart and their clubs were loaded and set to go. Without thinking, he made a bad joke about playing for each others bodies and was a bit surprised when she retorted with a cute negative remark as opposed to a put-down. Profoundly pleased, he found her extremely interesting and increasingly more open and aggressive each time they met. Enjoying their play, at a rather rapid pace on the near empty course, there was no problem in going on with the second nine. Finishing shortly before dark, they had drinks in the lounge and left for the house around seven. Finding a note in the kitchen, it indicated Gabe, Bonnie and their mother had kept the date at the grandmother's. They wouldn't return until quite late.

Deciding to first shower and change, both went to their respective rooms agreeing to invade the larder immediately thereafter. Dressing in a new sports outfit of shirt and slacks, he primped in front of the mirror attempting to look his best. Timing couldn't have been more perfect. They met in the upstairs hall and descended to the lower level holding hands.

"Hungry?" Sylvia asked.

"Starved."

Scanning through the refrigerator, she selected several items and carried them to the table.

"Need some help?"

"No. . . . Yes. You can get the silverware. It's over there." She pointed to a cabinet in the corner.

"How come you wear those heavy frames? Your eyes are beautiful."

"To see."

"Touché." He could have bit his tongue.

"That's okay." She laughed and playfully punched him on the shoulder as he walked past. "My eyes are so bad, and the glass so thick, lighter frames are out of the question."

He returned to stand directly before her and used both hands on each side of her face to gently slide them lower on her nose. Her eyes, which appeared large and full behind the lens, were now much smaller and less impressive.

"You're right," he said, shaking his head in a negative manner, while moving the glasses to their original and proper position. "I like you better with them."

"Smart-ass," she countered and burst into laughter.

"Now you know the real me." He joined her light levity.

* * *

They chose a cold fillet roast enhanced with imported mustard and homemade rolls; scrounged a salad together from leftovers; and, transported the meal to the rec room. While Hack commandeered a bottle of sparkling rose and a pair of stem glasses from the bar, Sylvia selected an FM station offering soft orchestrated music. They sat on the floor at a low coffee table enjoying the food and each other's company. Without asking if he cared for more, she made the next trip to the bar and returned with a second bottle of wine. Hack deftly removed the cork and was applauded at the sound of its "pop." They laughed and talked, finding a unique rapport of a light-hearted nature neither would have believed possible on their first meeting.

"Do you like to dance?" she asked, while he refilled their glasses.

"You bet."

Sylvia had already gained her feet and was moving in the direction of the radio. Changing to records, she placed a disc on the turntable and the sounds of Sam Cooke began to sift through the room. "How did you know he's one of my favorites?" he asked.

"Because he's one of mine." She smiled, taking him by the hand, pulling him to his feet.

"Oooh, gettin' old," he grunted while stretching out the kinks.

Moving to an uncarpeted area of the floor and stepping into each other's arms, they began to glide to the beat. It was as if they had always danced together. She followed his style without problem or mistake. To Hack, dancing represented more than simply having the opportunity to feel the nearness of a woman's body. At the right time, and with the proper partner, it was the intertwining of emotion expressed with grace and movement; an act of becoming one in the intercourse of rhythm; a total communication of physical response between companions. He and Sylvia immediately shared this unique experience and compatibility. She, too, sensed the special aura generated by their coordinated movement. There was never need to concentrate on the next step. Their bodies interacted as one.

Sylvia was deeply affected by the beauty of the moment and trembled while he still held her in his arms as the music ended. He rocked gently to an even slower beat totally in tune with their feelings. Kissing her tenderly on the forehead, they held hands returning to the couch. He sat on the floor at her feet. There was no need for conversation. Their nearness sufficed.

Confused before, he suffered an even greater dilemma at the present. It was impossible for him to believe he could desire any woman as much as Terri, whose immediate appeal had been overpowering, and of such a magnitude it was mind-boggling. On the other hand, the attraction to Sylvia occurred more gradually. Each time he saw her, he detected another captivating quality. And here he was, wanting her emotionally and physically more than any woman in his life. Yet, he was making no move to be aggressive. They barely knew each other. Was he reluctant because of her relationship to Gabe? Could it be from subconsciously fearing rejection? His record in having success with women was practically perfect, or at least until it came to someone he truly wanted. Carin was the only exception.

"Would you like more music?" Sylvia asked, breaking the silence and his spell.

"I'll get it," he offered, while rolling to his hands and knees. "What would you like to hear?"

"You look like a puppy-dog." She smiled.

"I don't think I've heard that song before. How does it go?"

She swung at him with a small throw pillow and sat back laughing. Hack jumped to his feet and went to the stereo. Having lost their earlier program of soothing sounds, he spun the dial until finding another with instrumental music. Soft harmonious chords filled the room. "That's nice," Sylvia commented.

"What time do you think they'll be home?" Hack asked, altering the mood.

"Maybe midnight. It's at least eighty miles each way."

"Oh." He sat again at her feet.

"How long will you be here?" The quality of self-assurance normally in her voice faded to reflect insecurity.

"Maybe this time next week."

"I don't even know what you do."

"I'm an artist."

Sylvia slid from the couch and came to a sitting position next to his. "An artist? That's wonderful. I know you're really good."

Hack blushed. "So, so."

"I'm sorry. That wasn't very tactful. I was just excited with the thought of your talent." She tucked her arm under his and gave a gentle squeeze. "Sensitivity exudes in your dancing. You have hands and fingers that paint emotions in their touch. I should have known you were either an artist or musician."

"I think you know I desperately want you." Hack couldn't suppress his inner-feelings any longer and surprised himself with his sudden boldness.

She tightened her grasp on his arm and laid her head on his shoulder. "At this moment, I don't think I've ever wanted anyone more than you." Raising to an upright position, she released her grip. "But, I can't. I just can't." Hack stood, offered his hands, and pulled her in an upwards motion. She gained her feet and walked to the bar with him close behind. They sat on adjacent stools. "I'm sorry. Truly sorry. I'm not much for one-night stands. I really don't know how to put it more delicately. In less than forty-eight hours you've managed to tear down practically every barrier I've had against men. I'm not accusing you of being the instigator. I'm not sure that it isn't completely of my own making. Either way, you possess a quality I never dreamed existed. You frighten me and at the same time give me strength and hope. I can't love you today and lose you tomorrow."

She astounded Hack. There was no denying her emotional stress, and yet, she maintained composure beyond any level of human expectation. He found her rejection easier to accept than his inability to recognize the depth of feeling capable by such an unusual woman. "I'm the one that should be apologizing." He moved from his perch to stand between her legs straddling the

133

stool and held her by each arm. "You are undoubtedly the most sensuous and appealing woman I've ever met. There's a quality I can't describe. But, you're right. Beyond magnetism, even compatibility, you and I might as well be from two different worlds. I doubt that you could release yours any easier than I could give up mine. You're a truly beautiful lady I'll probably regret losing for an awful long time." He leaned and kissed her cheek.

Sylvia's self-imposed walls were crumbling. She fought with all her ability to withstand the urge to be carried away in his arms. Pausing for several moments to gain her senses, she gave herself in the only way possible. "Let's always remember these moments and believe we may have found something so special, it may be furthered shared in another life."

They kissed with only their lips touching in a soft embrace, then, gazed silently into each other's eyes as if communicating through telepathy. They held hands leaving the room. Reaching his bedroom, he stopped and watched her walk slowly to the end of the hall and disappear behind the door.

CHAPTER V

"I hear y'all took some of the starch outta Dave and Bill, yesterday." Gabe blushed at Stan's remark. "They never did have much sense. 'Specially that Dave. He's got more money than he knows what to do with, and an ego that's bigger than the Empire State Building." The pro broke off a piece of bread and began to chew on the crust. "Don't be surprised if'n he comes back at ya."

"Hope it ain't with a gun," Hack joked.

Stan laughed. "Doubt that, but he's got a memory like an elephant. Sort'a acts like one, too. If'n he gets the chance, he'll try to get it back one time or another."

"Reckon we scared everybody else away?" Gabe's tone hinted regret.

"On the contrary. There's a whole slew of em waitin' in line to get a chunk of you two'uns."

* * *

For the better part of the following week, they played match after match, often thirty-six holes each day, and were not reluctant to face any pairing. When the competition appeared too unbalanced in their favor, the pro acted as a judge to determine a fair handicap adjustment. Losing twice during the entire period provided weak proof they could be beaten. However, enough diehards were left to keep testing their skills and luck. As a team, Hack and Gabe were relentless, winning over six thousand dollars a piece.

Making the decision it was time to return to Washington was difficult. Gabe temporarily refused Stan's offer, but wanted to remain in Aiken a little longer. Having ran into one of his high-school girl friends, he planned to chance his luck with her before leaving.

Hack had seen very little of Sylvia since the evening they spent together. However, after the car had been packed, she arrived to say her goodbyes and make the promise of letting him know should she ever be in his area. There was a definite sadness in the parting. He sensed Sylvia felt more isolated than ever and, for their final moments together, they shared in that loneliness. She watched, waving, as Gabe pulled the car from the gate.

* * *

It was dark and cold walking from the terminal, and Hack was irritated at not having called Carin to meet him. A porter hailed a cab and loaded his gear in the trunk. The flight afforded time and opportunity for a lot of self-analysis. It accomplished nothing, other than making him feel even more like a lost soul, searching for a goal that had no identity nor meaning. The taxi ride from National brought back memories of his return trip from New York and the following confrontation with Alice. It seemed so long ago.

"This the place?" the driver asked.

He looked from the window to be sure. "Yeah. This is it."

Unloading at the curb, the cabby helped move the luggage inside the front door, sitting it at the bottom of the steps. Carin, evidently working late, heard the minor commotion and flew down the stairs and into his arms. She didn't want to let go -- neither did he.

* * *

By Friday afternoon, Hack still felt listless and forced himself through a series of scheduled appointments. When he returned after the last, Carin made a drink as he slumped on the couch thumbing through a new issue of Golf magazine. "Damn it. Why not?"

"You talking to me?" Carin asked as she gave him a puzzled look.

"Uh. No. Just thinking out loud." He couldn't wait. After searching his brain for an excuse, he sent Carin to pick up his cleaning. That was long enough to make a call. Terri was supposed to leave work early to get ready for their date. He prayed she was already home. On the seventh ring, she answered.

"Hello." Her voice raised his heart beat.

"Hi, hon. You just get home?"

"The phone was ringing as I came in."

"If you've got a minute, I've got a great idea," he suggested. "There's been some business I've been wanting to handle down south," he lied. "The thought occurred to me that we've both been pressured so much recently, well, what I wondered was . . ."

She didn't let him finish the sentence and attempted to complete it herself. "Would I like to go with you for a half-business and pleasure trip?" Her excitement couldn't be concealed. "I'd love to go. How far south?" He found himself stunned at the complete lack of any reluctance. She repeated, "I'd love to. Where are we going?"

"Mi . . . Miami." He stammered his response.

"Oh, Hack," she squealed. "That sounds marvelous. I've never been there. When can we leave?"

"Soon as you're packed." He beamed with satisfaction. "I'll be there in a couple of hours."

"Okay. I've got to go if you want me ready."

"Yeah, but first, do you have any preferences about either driving or flying?"

"Not really. Whatever you prefer would be fine, although I hear it's really nice to see the changes of scenery if you travel by auto. Besides, we could have a problem getting reservations on such short notice."

"Sounds good. We can drive. I'm in no hurry, are you? The only catch is whether or not my wheels are up to the strain."

"Not at all. The more time we can spend together, the better. And, the car is the least of any problems. We can take mine."

It was like being in another world. He floated around the desk, grabbed two suitcases, and began to pack. Carin walked in and eyed him suspiciously. "What's up?"

"Golf trip," he lied. "Got a call while you were out. One of the guys canceled and they asked me to take his place. They've got reservations, plus they'd be without a full foursome, so I decided to fill in."

"It should be fun." She didn't sound too happy. "Where will you be?"

"Florida."

"That'll take more than any weekend," she commented, as if

wanting to be wrong. The fact he had barely returned from being south and would be away again wasn't easy to handle.

"Yeah. I'll be gone about a week."

He began to feel really guilty as she started to help him pack without asking.

* * *

Terry was ready and waiting when Hack arrived at her apartment. She had already loaded many of her things into a brand-new El Dorado parked in front the buildings entrance. He met her coming out of the door carrying additional luggage.

"Wow. That's some boat you have there." He whistled.

She laughed and handed him the luggage. "It's really a company car and actually belongs to my brother. I've been using it while they're fixing my Corvette."

"Now, that's the kind of brother to have."

"He's okay. Nope, he's really great," she corrected. "He's one of those guys with a car fetish. I'm not sure how many he really has. It's a real hobby with him."

"Be right back. I want to get the stuff out of my jalopy."

Terri waited until he returned and, after pausing for a full embrace on the sidewalk, they held hands while making their way upstairs to retrieve a final load.

Hack felt like a king. The excitement of the trip; the luxuriousness of the automobile; and, Terri--beautiful Terri--by his side was more than anyone could expect. It had been around seven-thirty when finally pulling from her driveway. They hadn't been on the road very long and Terri turned reaching into the back seat and produced a large hat box. As the lid was removed, it exposed sandwiches, fruit, candy and whatever else one might imagine. There was even a well-chilled thermos full of martinis. "I thought it would save an early stop."

"You're a doll. A real doll," he exclaimed as he squeezed her knee.

Making only a slight dent in the supplies, Hack did request a second on the drink as Terri fumbled in her purse for change. They were approaching the first toll gate near Richmond. Conversation between them seemed endless and made the time pass quickly as the odometer steadily clicked. Not thinking to set the gauge before leaving, rough calculations indicated they had traveled somewhere over two hundred miles and were well into North Carolina. "Getting tired?" she asked, raising her head from his shoulder.

"Not too bad," he responded. "Though, I figured we'd stop at the next motel that looks good. Not much sense in going any further tonight."

"Look. There's an ad," she observed as they sped past a giant billboard indicating a Quality Inn was just ahead. Slowing into the exit lane, he turned from the highway and followed a short road leading to the motels main entrance. Terri stayed in the car while Hack registered and soon returned with their key. Driving around the corner of the complex to the last building, he spotted their number. Parking as near as possible to the door, Hack hurried around to help her out of the car. Arm-in-arm they walked to the room. The key turned in his free hand and the door swung open. He stood aside as she entered. A light coming from a corner lamp dimly lit the cubicle. The decor was modern and the furnishings appeared new. As motel rooms go, it was fairly small, affording space for only one double bed. It helped explain the rather reasonable cost.

Hack gently took Terri's shoulder and turned her into his arms. He was surprised to sense something lacking from their embrace. Something ever so slight, but a definite hint of hesitancy on her part. Their kiss ended and he held her against his chest. His mind fumbled trying to decipher her reactions and what might be wrong. The conclusion: a combination of the late hour and it only being the second time they had been alone was more than enough reason to justify any uneasiness. Stepping away, he kissed her on the forehead. She kissed his chin.

While Terri went to the bathroom, Hack returned several times to the car to gather bags and items they might need. "You okay in there?" He called to her while opening the suit and dress bags in hopes of saving wrinkles.

"Un huh," she responded affirmatively.

Having made one final visit to secure the Caddy, Hack took the key from the lock, laid it on the dresser, and bolted the door from the inside, adding the safety chain. "Damn it," he muttered to himself. "Forgot ice." Wanting everything to be just right, Hack grabbed the ice bucket and observed Terri's negligee hanging just outside the bathroom door. He was aroused with feelings equaling those of teenage years and throbbed with sexual anticipation of something new and exciting as if it were an absolute first-time experience. Fumbling with the door locks, his thoughts continued. It would have been a lot easier for her if their initial night sleeping together hadn't been so spur of the moment. Such rationalization explained what he had sensed earlier in their embrace, as well as her prolonged visit to the bathroom. His pondering mind was relentless. Terri wasn't just another girl. What an understatement, he laughed to himself. She certainly had the right to her own ideas about sex. To her, there should be emotional need, and something beautiful with meaning, not just fun and pleasure. In a way, it was a little scary: involvement; marriage; being tied down again. He shuddered.

In his stupor, he somehow managed to locate the ice bin and finally became cognizant his shaking was as much from being cold as from fright. Cursing himself for his suspicious and serious mood, he filled the small bucket with as many cubes as possible. It had taken several minutes to locate the service area and he found himself hurrying, almost running, to get back. Entering the room, he expected to see Terri and had anticipated her lying on the bed in a seductive pose, clad in something provocative. She still hadn't emerged. However, the door was open and the negligee gone from its perch. "Where have you been?" she cheerfully called to him.

The sound of her voice immediately elevated his spirits. "Got some ice. I figured we could use a nightcap."

"Good. Is there anything to mix with?"

"Sorry. Didn't have change for the machine."

"Scotch or bourbon?" he asked.

"Scotch is fine. On the rocks."

Measuring the contents of her glass before the light, he decided to add a touch more. Terri walked from behind the corner and stood toweling her face. His disappointment was difficult to conceal. Even though she needed no frills or makeup to enhance her beauty, she was wearing a robe, tied around her waist, offering very little toward enhancing her attributes. He turned quickly away to pick up a cube inadvertently dropped on the floor. Welcoming the diversion, he resumed fixing his own drink.

Taking her glass from the table, she extended it in a toast as he turned to face her. Their glasses met. "To us and our trip," she smiled and stepped close, putting her arms around his neck. Her touch made him melt. His mind went blank except for desires beginning to swell like an inflating balloon. As their lips found each other's, there was the sensation he might explode. She pulled away, gently taking him by the hand, and moved to the bed. As they sat on the edge, he leaned back against the wall and watched her nervously finger the glass she held in both hands. Gazing into the liquid, it was as if she were staring into a crystal ball. He sat waiting in expectation of the revelation she would soon produce, observing her natural beauty. Her face, now void of any makeup, caused him to muse at the fact of not having earlier noticed an odor of cleansing cream replacing the beautiful aroma of cologne worn earlier. It certainly wasn't how he had pictured the moment.

"Hack, I . . . I don't know how to start," she began. "Earlier today, when you called and asked me about going, I was so excited and I never gave it a thought."

"What's wrong?" he pleaded as he raised to a sitting position.

Tears started to fill her eyes. "I've tried to tell you all evening. I wanted to warn you and couldn't find the words." She choked as the tears burst forth down her cheeks.

"Honey, honey, honey," he soothed, taking her into his arms. "Please. What is it?"

"I'm having my period. I just started this morning. It's very heavy," she cried.

"Is that all?" He laughed, pushing her to arms length and then pulling her back.

"Please, don't laugh. Don't make fun of me." More tears came and he struggled with words.

"Listen, sweetheart," he assured, "it's late, anyway. Besides that, we've got an entire week ahead of us. In fact, a whole lifetime."

"That doesn't matter." She sniffled as he kissed away her tears. "Our first time together, I had it all planned so perfectly. Now, this. It's been hard on you; me; the both of us. I want you so badly, but not like this. It's so important that it's perfect.

Please understand. Please?"

"Aw, baby, baby. It's all right. Please don't be sad. Don't cry."

Holding her even more tightly while caressing her back and hair, she felt his fingers generate vibrations of tenderness and understanding throughout her body. At the same time, he harshly accused himself for being so self-centered. Whether she was overreacting or not, her intentions were with great conviction. "Tell you what," he mused while bending over to pull a lace from his shoe. "Tie me up to that chair over there and you'll be safe."

A smile spread across her face as she laughed and the tension broke. "I might just do that." She winked.

* * *

Traveling via US 301 to 17A across most of South Carolina was wonderfully scenic. They stopped at a various spots catching their fancy and took pictures of each other. Originally, Hack had planned to continue on the alternate and skirt the heart of Savannah to miss downtown traffic. However, even considering the several self-imposed delays, they were making excellent time and therefore chose to confront the center city. The choice proved to be well made and provided a perfect sampling of the old town's charm. Eventually clearing the south-side suburbs, they returned to highway speed. Terri tilted her seat back to its farthest notch and curled into a semi-fetal position for a nap. As she slept, Hack's befuddled mind seemed to divide into sections, each having a tug of war with the other. Habitually, he shook his head as if it would shake everything straight. Since arising that morning, nothing had been mentioned about the previous evening. He glanced over at Terri and quickly turned again to the road. Damn it, he thought. Her beauty; her body; her charm -- it's like witchcraft. Every time he looked it was like being placed under a spell. He was beginning to despise his weakness.

Nearing Brunswick, Georgia, Hack decided to stop at the first chance of finding a decent eating place. It was almost three o'clock, and with nothing more than juice and coffee that morning, pangs of hunger were beginning to make his stomach growl. Spotting a diner on the opposite side of the highway, with a gas station nearby, he pulled across and into the parking spaces just off the roadway. Terri awoke and began straightening her makeup, using the mirror behind her visor. She scooted across the seat, kissed him on the cheek, then wiped the deposited lipstick from his face with her moistened fingertips. After helping her out of the car, he checked to make sure everything was locked tight and then headed into the restaurant. First things first, both searched for the rest rooms. Rendezvousing at the phone booth, Hack got there before Terri and found himself tempted to call Carin. It stirred him to consider the reasoning behind such an inclination. Did he miss her? Was he feeling guilty? Or, could it be because of the temporary physical alienation imposed by Terri? Had he developed a stronger tie and need for Carin than he could admit to himself? Or, was he being selfish in not being able to completely share or identify with Terri's moralistic and pure standards regarding their relationship? Whatever it was, he felt confused, and not at all pleased with the current events, or himself. "Hi," Terri said as she appeared from the powder room door, looking refreshed and bright. "Are you as hungry as I am?" She smiled and took him by the arm.

"Famished."

Finding a table near the long row of windows, they had barely completed their orders when a screech of brakes, followed by terrifying sounds of twisting and tearing metal, brought them to their feet. Stretching to see out of the window, they both gasped in horrified disbelief at the sight they beheld. A huge trailer truck attempting to avoid a stopping automobile, had caught its rear end, sending both vehicles careening into the parked cars in front. At first, they were too shocked to speak.

"Oh, my God," Terri almost whispered. "What are we going to do?"

Hack felt sick inside. He could only shrug his shoulders as they hurried out for a closer survey of the damage. Time seemed to stand still. His mind was functioning so fast it made all physical action appear to be in slow-motion. A crowd quickly gathered. Other car owners involved in the accident talked rapidly back and forth about their misfortune. Sirens screamed from everywhere. First, the police arrived, followed almost immediately by firemen. Then, not one, but three ambulances were on the scene.

They both stood hand in hand, staggered by the experience, and staring at the remains of the Caddy. Being the first parked car in the semi's path, it caught the full brunt of the impact broadside. Even though it was untouched, the force of the collision popped the windshield from its seal and it lay hanging on the passenger's side. State troopers responding to the accident were efficient and helpful. After taking care of preliminary paper work and setting tow vehicles about their chores, one of the officers assisted Hack with their baggage and transported them to a nearby motel where they registered. Before leaving, he provided names of a few local people who might be of assistance and other pertinent information relating mostly to the care of the vehicle.

When they were finally alone, Hack turned to Terri and managed a weak smile. "Sure looks like the cards are stacked against us."

"I don't know what to say or to do," she responded while almost falling into the chair. "Everything has been so unexpected and happened so fast."

Hack sat on the bed across from her bracing his elbows on his knees with his face buried in his hands. They remained silent for a long period of time. "We'll have to get back," he finally muttered with tremendous reluctance, rubbing his fingers hard against his forehead.

"I . . . I know," she stammered in return. "I guess I'll wait and call my brother when we get home."

"Yeah. Probably the best thing to do." He raised his head and stared at the phone. "Maybe. Let me see if I can get a local agent from the insurance company. He might have a few suggestions. Were there any insurance papers in the glove compartment?"

"I'm not sure," Terri answered as she leaned to retrieve a packet of documents removed from the car. Taking a long leather sleeve from a carry bag, she began to finger through its contents. "Here's something."

After searching through a local directory and trying several numbers, he eventually reached an agent.

During the conversation, he relayed information to Terri as she scribbled it down for future reference. The representative assured everything would be quickly processed and there was little need for further concern. It was also indicated, whether they desired to continue the trip or return to Washington, insurance would cover the cost of a rental car until the time their automobile was repaired and delivered to their satisfaction. Also, under any circumstances, they should retain receipts as there was absolute certainty of compensation for the inconvenience and interruption to their plans and unwarranted expenses.

Without consulting Terri, Hack immediately dialed the operator to get a number for the nearest airport. It was a tossup to either return to Savannah, or continue to Jacksonville. Solely based on being able to say they had made it to the sunshine state, the latter was a mutual choice. Not particularly in the mood to drive, and definitely opposed to coping with their abundance of luggage, the consideration of bus travel was unhesitatingly discounted. Jointly, they agreed they deserved the comfort of independent transportation and called a taxi company.

During the wait, Terri poured two tumblers of scotch and dashed them with water. Neither cared they were without ice. Lounging in the room, waiting for the cab, they indulged in trivial conversation, mostly about sports. Terri showed an unusual interest in golf, indicating she had taken a few lessons as a teenager. However, being female, tennis offered more immediate advantages and her peers strongly encouraged her in that direction.

Hack responded to a rap on the door. A broadly smiling cabby, tickled to death about the big fare he was soon to earn, in a heavy southern accent, announced his presence. He helped loading their belongings into the rear of his late 50's vintage station wagon painted bright yellow and they were on their way. It was dark by the time they left. Except for billboards and lighted structures, little could be seen of the surrounding landscape speeding past their view. Most of the trip, they both pretended to be asleep, but sprang to awareness when they reached the state line. After passing over the crest of a small bridge, they were confronted with a tropically decorated archway welcoming them to Florida. Following a stream of traffic beneath it, the entire area on the other side was flooded with lights enhancing endless numbers of palmetto bushes and tall palms.

An information center sat to the right of the highway packed with automobiles and tourists. Impact of the instant change of external environment left them astounded and with the sensation of entering another world.

"It's beautiful," Terri gasped, leaning forward in her seat. "Oh, I wish we could stay. There must be so much more to see."

Almost as quickly as they had entered the utopia, lights began disappearing from the highway and surroundings returned to silhouettes and blackened sky. Hack sat staring from his window concentrating on a glowing aurora of light on the distant horizon.

"That Jacksonville?" Hack asked the driver.

"Sho'nuff," he answered after spitting the juice from his tobacco chaw into a can that had been resting on the seat beside his hip. "T'won't be long for we be gettin' to that there airport."

Oncoming headlights exposed Hack's and Terri's smiles as they reached to take each others hand. "We could go on if you'd rather," he suggested in a low voice and sincere manner.

"I've honestly thought about it, and I really want to be with you." She squeezed his hand to emphasize the feeling of her emotion. "Is it wrong to want our first time together to be something beyond the ordinary and not overshadowed by all of the distractions we're facing?"

Backed into a corner, he again struggled between needs, wants, and reasonability. "No," he whispered. "It's not at all wrong. You're more than special to me." He moved closer and pulled her under his arm. She rested her head against his shoulder as he continued. "This won't be an end. It's a beginning. Maybe a little screwed up, but a beginning."

"I want so much for that to be true." She pressed her lips against his neck. "Kiss me." Lifting her chin gently, he lightly touched her lips with his. Completely void of passion, deep dwelling emotions were exchanged and shared in the tenderness of a brief moment. They held each other until arriving at the terminal.

Arrangements had been made for the evening's last flight bound for home. Flights into National weren't available and the alternative of landing at Friendship near Baltimore had to be accepted. The efficiency of their chauffeur placed them at the airport with adequate time to accomplish usual rituals of picking up tickets and checking luggage. On reaching the assigned gate, passengers for the flight were already boarding. Once on the plane, it was easier to relax and much of the deserted stranded feeling disappeared. Hack did his best to cheer Terri with bad jokes and a couple of quick drinks. The stewardess was very lenient and didn't restrict their needs.

Eventually falling asleep, due to exhaustion and the tranquilizing effects of the alcohol, neither stirred until the thud of landing gear being thrust into place harshly awakened them. It was a clear night and glittering lights of the nearing metropolis slowly began to overpower the twinkling stars supremacy of the sky. The plane banked in an exaggerated circle while the sensation of its descent became increasingly detectible. Soon the bite of rubber could be heard and felt as tires touched pavement. The roar of engines straining to reverse throttle caused the plane to shudder in rebuttal. At the end of the runway, without coming to a full halt, it spun on its nose wheel to the left and taxied toward the terminal to take its place among the other giants resting at various moorings.

Debarking and locating their luggage went unusually smooth due to the late hour. Terri's need for other transportation was the determining factor to rent a car rather than splurge on another taxi. Settling on an economy model, Hack arranged for a porter's assistance while Terri completed the necessary documents. Cramming the small Ford with all their belongings, they squeezed into the car and began the last leg of the trip home. Eventually arriving at Terri's apartment, at nearly one a.m., he pulled directly to the main entrance. After unloading, they transported every-thing into the lobby near the elevators before attempting to advance any of it upstairs. Hack dumped his things into the trunk of the Chevy. Terri had already accomplished moving the items to the fifth floor as he arrived via the stairway.

Hack manipulated the rest into her suite by himself and found a pot of water nearing the boiling point on the stove. A pair of cups sat on the counter containing instant coffee in one and a tea bag in the other. Adding cream and sugar, after the boiling liquid, he entered the living room, placed the drinks on the coffee table, and flopped on the couch. He was wasted.

Terri appeared from her bedroom door clad in the same robe

she previously wore. Moving to sit next to him, she appeared equally spent and tried desperately to be cheerful, but failed miserably. "It's all impossible," she began. "Unbelievable is a better choice of words. The deck's stacked I think you said." She sipped the coffee. "Do you realize . . . ?" She immediately answered her own question. "I know you do. Every time we make plans; no matter how hard we try, something goes wrong."

"It sure looks that way," he agreed.

"I'm so sorry, Hack, most of it seems to be my fault." She looked at him apologetically.

"Aw, baby. It's nobody's fault. Not yours or mine. It's just a run of rotten luck and bad timing." He stood and walked to the window, peered through the curtains, and returned again to sit beside her -- this time a bit closer. "Babe, it's really getting late. I better get going."

Terri appeared shocked at his suggestion. "Please. Please don't leave. Can't you stay this evening?"

"I could," he admitted while reaching to take both of her hands in his. "I don't think it's the best idea, considering everything, that is. We're both almost dead and have a lot on our minds. Better if we sleep it off alone, don't you think?" He really didn't mean a word of it. The thought of another night of abstinence lying next to her was too torturous to accept.

"I guess you're right," she sadly agreed.

They both rose simultaneously and walked holding hands to the front door. Taking his coat from the knob, she held it as he shoved his arms through the sleeves. As he turned, she moved into his grasp while slipping her arms around his chest inside the outer garment. Stepping away, she connected the zipper at the bottom and slipped it upward to his chin. Fastening the collar button, she kissed him lightly on the lips and whispered, "Call me tomorrow."

CHAPTER VI

Rain peppered persistently against the window, even as the sun peered from behind a cloud towering above the ten-story building across the avenue. Such occurrences were typical of the mid-Atlantic coastal region. The Washington area had some of the most unpredictable weather in the world. However, the winter having been exceptionably cold, Hack's southern trips did a great deal to diminish the snow season. Nevertheless, he was learning to abhor any weather condition limiting reasonable access to the outdoors. Spring was on its way, but with it came the proverbial, "April showers bringing May flowers." Fuck the flowers, Hack thought, sitting in a booth and staring through the blurred glass of the tavern window, turning his glass between his fingers -- his mind floating away on one of its frequent rampages.

After their ill-fated February trip, the ultimate decision to avoid Terri had seemed justified. However, as time passed, logic and reasoning loomed less important and he truly regretted his earlier reactions. He hadn't spoke to her since the following day after returning from Georgia, and then, mainly for the purpose of wanting to make sure her brother was squared away with the insurance problems. Their conversation having been limited to generalities, they were both guilty of misreading an unintentional but prevailing coolness. There were moments when he missed Terri a great deal. And, complicating matters to an even greater extent, Hack seemed unable to think of her without comparing circumstances to Sylvia -- both situations representing rejection in his life. He wondered how much of each relationship's failing was of his own fault. It was too easy placing blame completely on the women.

Then, there was good old reliable Carin; always present and

eternally understanding. Although, after the bullshit handed her regarding his reasons for the southern trip, he hadn't dared to take the chance to challenge her loyalties by returning too soon. He spent the remainder of the time he would have been away at Mitch's pad. Her consistent companionable attitude both blanketed his insecurities and raised his ire simultaneously. Feeling full of guilt, he cursed his conscience for accepting the truth in realizing advantages he had taken at her expense.

Hack motioned for another drink and returned to his thoughts. Never once had he ever doubted Carin's faithfulness. Maybe it was because he could account for practically all of her time. He knew all he had to do was say the word and she would marry him without a single hesitation.

As the waiter sat his order on the table, he gave Hack a conspicuous look and turned away. Without realizing his actions, he was actually laughing aloud. He was embarrassed, but continued to smile at the rotten luck shrouding his existence. At the least, the distraction was a saving influence bringing things back to the present, making him cognizant of staring out the window. The spring downfall had ceased and the skies were clearing as quickly as they had blackened. Umbrellas were being lowered and raincoats tucked over the arms of passing pedestrians. He did a double take at a familiar face of a woman standing at the curb attempting to hail a taxi. Without hesitating, he scurried from the booth and rushed out the door, informing the bartender he would be right back. As a cab pulled to the curb, in response to the lady's beckoning and she reached to open its rear door, he yelled emphatically, "Hey, Morty."

She spun around -- her expression expanding into a beaming smile. "Hack?"

"I'll be damned," he exclaimed, grabbing her hand.

"I'll be damned, too," the cab driver retorted, leaning across the seat and sticking his head out of the passenger window. "Ya want this cab or not, lady?"

"Up yours," Hack directed his vengeance against the transportation huckster while pulling Morty back from the curb. "Hope you weren't in a hurry."

"Well, I really . . . "

He interrupted her response. "You got time for a quickie . . .

150

drink that is?"

She giggled softly. "Sure."

Looking exceptionally relieved at Hack's return, the waiter appeared to be on the verge of laying claim to his attaché case and raincoat for ducking the tab. Hack ordered for Morty on their way past the bar.

"How the hell you been?" he cheerfully queried. "Tell me who you've been attacking?"

She laughed at his remark. "No one. Work, for the most part. I've been in D.C. several times since Richmond. You should have given me your number. I got lonesome on a few occasions."

"I'll bet," he teased. The waiter arrived with her drink. "How long will you be here?" he asked.

"Not long. In fact, I just got in about an hour ago. My next flight is scheduled for six-fifteen to New York. We'll layover there tonight and Lord knows where after that."

"Damn it," he groaned. "If it was tomorrow instead, I'd fly up with you. Screw the lousy luck."

Morty paused sipping her drink. Hack watched as she eyed the room as if in search of masculine challenge, wondering whether there might be more truth than fiction to her earlier claims at being a nymphomaniac.

"Tell you what," she offered. "Suppose I work out some way to catch a shift back here tomorrow. I might even get the weekend free."

"Damn, that would be great."

They talked long enough to finish their drinks, covered the check, and headed for the parking lot to get Hack's car. Dropping her at the main terminal, she blew him a kiss accompanied by a sexual indication with her tongue, and trotted toward the main entrance.

"Phew," he expressed shaking his head. Watching her disappear reminded him of their incredible weekend.

On the way back to his office, he knew he had to create a good excuse to keep him free from Carin for the next couple of days. Turning the corner, he saw her making an exit from the office's entrance and begin walking in the opposite direction.

"Hey, wait a minute," he called, jogging to catch her. "Where you headed?"

"A long trip to the mailbox on the corner. Wanna go?"

He did an about face. "See ya upstairs."

While Carin was gone, he took the opportunity to answer a few phone messages. Having taken care of most of the loose ends, he peeked into her office and was amazed she still hadn't returned. Usually more observant, it was of additional surprise he had missed noticing a fresh bouquet of flowers stuffed into what appeared to be an old mayonnaise jar sitting on her desk. Being nosey, he approached for a closer look and spotted a card tucked under the edge of her calendar pad. Hearing the downstairs' door open interrupted his chance to read the message, but it clearly ended "Love, Richard."

Scurrying back to his office, Hack felt bombarded by a conglomeration of conjured interpretations. Rushing through hurt and anger, his mind finally settled on fearing that he was probably on his way to losing her. Reverting to rationale, she had more than enough reason to get interested in someone else. After all, he had contributed little if anything of concrete value to their relationship.

"Can't you smile any more?" Carin remarked as she entered carrying a paper bag which she placed on the corner of his desk. "You look like you've lost your last friend."

"Yeah, maybe I have."

"What's wrong?" She reached into the sack and produced two large paper cups with a creamy substance oozing from beneath their lids. "Root beer floats," she explained. "Want one?"

He couldn't help himself. "You got a new boy friend?"

"Wha . . . . Oh, I get it. The flowers." She nodded her head in a positive manner. "No. As a matter of fact," she teased, "I've known the man who sent them for quite some time."

"You really like him."

"Yes I do. What's more, I love him."

Hack felt like he had been stabbed.

"They're from my brother, dumb-ass. He didn't forget my birthday."

"Aw, damn. Aw, shit." He was totally embarrassed. "Babe, I'm sorry. I . . . Hey! Your birthday's not 'til the weekend following this."

She was getting a charge from his uneasiness and laughed at the game she had played. "Men are all alike. You would have forgot my birthday altogether, and Rick thinks it's a week before." She faked a pout.

"Phew. You had me worried for a while. I should've known better."

"Known what better? That I wouldn't have a boy friend? Don't you think that's taking me a little for granted?"

"I didn't mean . . ."

She interrupted his response. "I know. Sorry. I got the rag on. You know how that is." Sucking on her straw, it made gurgling sounds as there was more air than liquid. "Seriously though, one of these days we've got to sit down and decide whether there's a light at the end of our tunnel or not."

Hack purposely ignored the remark and changed the subject. "About this weekend . . . "

Again, she didn't let him finish his sentence. "Glad you mentioned it. I hope you don't mind, but I've been spending so much time around here, a lot of things have piled up and I just have to get my act together. I really want to take tomorrow off to get a head start. A long weekend would give me a chance to get a lot done. You'll probably be golfing, anyway. The weather's supposed to be nice. You don't mind, do you?"

He felt like hugging and kissing her. "Naw. I hadn't planned anything. Guess you could use some free time." He tried not to sound too ecstatic. "In fact, there's a mess of things I should tackle myself, but keep the following weekend clear. We'll do something special for your birthday."

"That'll be nice. Why don't you help me to the car?"

Carin gathered a bundle of his clothes that needed laundering and a couple of shopping bags of items she bought earlier in the day. Strolling to the parking lot, she reiterated the list of chores on her agenda and, prior to driving away, she made a final suggestion. "If you want to have dinner at my place Sunday evening, I should be finished with everything by then."

"Sounds okay. I'll see you around eight unless I give you a call."

"Bye." She threw him a kiss.

Hack walked briskly back to the office whistling to beat hell.

He couldn't get over his sudden turn of luck. Part of his spiel wasn't exaggerated. There really were a dozen and one things to do. The rest of the afternoon and evening was spent working exceptionally hard, going on into the wee hours. Hitting the sack around two-thirty, he arose at seven, getting an early start for the day.

Morty had phoned after getting to New York confirming their date and planned to call when she got in town. Not having any idea when that might be, he anticipated her arrival in the late afternoon or early evening. Since breakfast was skipped, an early lunch was necessary. At noon, he ran out for a sandwich. On his return, a message was on the desk indicating Morty had called. Highly elated, he almost snatched at the phone and began spinning the dial.

"Washington National Airport."

"Would you page a Miss Friar, please? She's with Eastern."

Several moments passed.

"I'm sorry, sir. She doesn't answer the page. Would you care to call later?"

"Uh, okay. Thank you." "Son of a bitch." He banged the receiver down and rocked in its cradle as the intercom buzzed. "Yeah," he barked.

"Sorry, boss. The doll that called earlier is on the phone. Line-one."

"Great." He almost cheered his reaction. "By the way, I didn't mean to bite your head off."

"That's all right, it makes me feel like I'm home."

He pushed the button and changed lines. "Morty?"

"Who else," she responded in jest. "Just blew in and thought I'd give you a call and check your plans."

"I tried to reach you at the number you left, what happened?"

"I'm not sure. I must've been powdering my nose. Anyway, what's up?"

"Hell. I figured there wasn't much sense in you getting a room somewhere. You can stay here with me."

"Ooops. Small problem . . . about a hundred and twenty-five pounds worth, named, Pat. That's allowing two-and-a-half-pounds per tit."

Hack laughed. "She's welcome, too."

"Why not? The more the merrier," she giggled. "Think you can handle us both?"

He almost choked. "I don't . . . don't know. I'll probably die giving it a helluva try."

She ended the conversation trying to be sexy. "See ya real soon luv-ver."

The place was a mess. He was tickled pink they were managing their own transportation into town from the airport. With some extra effort, he could come pretty close to getting it cleaned before they arrived. Stopping long enough to phone Mitch, he changed his mind, terminating the call after the first ring. "Nuts," he said, talking to himself. "I better leave it up to Pat. She might prefer Gabe or already have plans."

* * *

A sudden burst of laughter and noise erupted on the stairway and echoed through the entire building. It was as if a herd of elephants were clamoring up the stairs and hall. He stood at the top watching the two girls in hysterics, laughing, struggling, bouncing their bags from step to step, as they tried to maintain their balance. Morty was the first up. She dropped her bag on his toe; threw one arm around his neck; shot her tongue in his ear; and, with her free hand, grabbed him by the crotch. "God you turn me on," she said in a husky voice adding much gusto.

Scrunching his knees together, he grunted. "You crazy sex fiend."

Hack's crew from the back appeared around the corner getting a kick out of his predicament. Pat didn't make it any less awkward by declaring, "Hurry up, I get dirty seconds."

Finally wriggling free, he tried to regain some semblance of composure as the guys were more than eager to help with the luggage. It was plain by the expressions on their faces, he'd hear about the episode for a long time to come. Morty and Pat settled down on the couch, kicking off their shoes, while Hack alibied his bug-eyed staff back to work. He decided it best to close the front hoping to afford at least minimal privacy. Pat had moved to his chair and was attempting an executive's pose by crossing her feet and propping them on the desk. It was obvious she didn't believe in wearing panties. "Something to drink?" Hack sheepishly asked.

Pat found one of the bubblegum cigars he was saving for the kids and imitated taking a big drag. "Natch."

"Me, too," chimed Morty.

"How about martinis? I've already got a batch made."

"Make 'em double."

They were quite a combination, and the afternoon full of laughs. Pat wasn't enthused about arranging a date, complaining of having a noon flight the following day and being dead on her feet. A good dinner and bed was all she needed. They both went shopping for about an hour at Morty's insistence, claiming there was nothing for her to wear. Before they returned, he took advantage of their absence and called Carin. She was quite concerned he would be okay alone, suggesting he was welcome to come by later. He squeezed out of a very touchy spot.

Around six, the girls were getting anxious to eat and started preparing for dinner. Neither one of them was much on modesty and freely disrobed without any concern. Morty's new outfit was astounding. There was less to it than there was more: a short mini; one piece, and, having holes and openings all over the place than there seemed to be material. She wore no bra, of course, just panty hose. Hack settled on a black blazer and grey slacks. Patty naturally wore items enhancing her biggest asset. The combination included a see-through blouse; dressy jumper-slacks; and, again, no bra.

Following a short jaunt over to Connecticut Avenue, reservations had been made at Paul Young's. The restaurant's street level entrance opened into a large lobby area emulating a grand hotel. Love seats and lounge chairs with end and coffee tables were selectively placed throughout the room. A pianist sat at a white baby grand, playing semi-classical selections. They were little more than a half-hour early, and after approaching the maitre d', agreed to have drinks in the lounge. Assisting in removing their outer garments at the coat room, Hack felt as though he were unveiling two pieces of sexy sculpture, considering all the eyes the girls were attracting. Celebrities couldn't have drawn more notoriety.

Eventually being notified their table was ready, the three descended the extra-wide staircase leading to the elegant dining room on the lower level. Again, all eyes focused on their entrance and the girls continued to capture the stares of customers and help alike throughout the entire meal. On the positive side, the service, dinner, and drinks, were outstanding. Negatively, the check looked like the national debt.

After walking Pat back to the office, Hack and Morty picked up his car. It had been decided earlier they would drop by the Sundowner's.

Mitch was tremendously surprised seeing her coming in the door. She rushed forward, jumping up in his arms, giving him a rather warm greeting. As she slid from his grasp, her feet settled to the floor and she turned to allow Hack to remove her wrap. Any of those not already distracted by Morty's grand entrance, immediately lent their full attention to her exotic appearance in the overexposing mini. Following Mitch, they wove through the tables toward the far side of the room. The hungry expressions of the males they passed boldly reflected secreted desires, surely undressing her in their minds. It was evident Morty was enjoying every minute of it. Mitch picked a spot next to the dance floor. He moved the chairs close together and they sat facing the stage.

Before returning to his post, Mitch strained to be heard above the music. "I'll see you in a few minutes."

Drinks were ordered and, while waiting for the waitress, they talked sparingly due to the blaring of the band that had started their first set as they arrived. Morty really didn't have to say much to express her feelings. Her hand was telling quite a story as she fingered the inside of his leg. He knew it was the beginning of a long and far from dull evening.

Appearing from nowhere, Mitch paid a second call to their table at about the same time the musical noisemakers were winding down. "When did you get in?"

"Around noon," she answered. "Swinging place you have here, but it would be better if someone would drown the band."

"Can't say I don't agree," he chuckled. "Those goofs you just saw are a group the owner shoved on us. If he'd keep his friggin' nose out of the manager's affairs, we wouldn't have these problems. Anyway, they were only a fill-in for an early set, as a trial. A pretty decent band will be finishing the rest of the night."

Feeling relieved, Hack interjected, "Man, that's great. I couldn't have taken much more."

Morty caught the double-meaning of his remark, also referring to the game she had been playing in his lap. She giggled overtly.

"Something I missed?" Mitch looked puzzled.

"Not at all," Morty squeaked. "It's something I've been missing."

Mitch shook his head as if to try and juggle his brain to accept her remark and finally gave up with a shrug of his shoulders. "Well, so much for that. By the way ol' buddy, are you going to be able to make the trip to Pennsylvania next weekend?"

"Yeah . . . No. Wow, it ain't next Sunday, is it? I thought it was the following week."

"Hummmmm." Mitch stopped and eased back into the chair he had started to leave. "You're right. It is at the end of the month. Sorry about that."

Hack breathed a little easier. All he had to do was screw up Carin's birthday and that would be it.

"Might not be able to go myself since that's the case," Mitch mumbled.

"Now, don't tell me you'd let some broad interfere with that dumb game of yours," Morty chided.

Mitch stood, slid the chair to the table, and reached to tap her nose lightly with his finger tip. "Don't be jealous, baby. I only like guys."

She mouthed something dirty Hack was unable to clearly decipher as he walked away. "Have you known each other very long?" Morty queried.

"Not really. Maybe a couple of years. Going on two, come to think of it. We met at the golf club."

"That figures. What in the hell do you see in that stupid game?"

"Don't knock it, 'til you've tried it."

She wrinkled her nose in distaste.

"I guess," he said, pausing to light a cigarette and then continuing, "golf's a complete departure from anything else I've ever done. You get be outdoors. There's clean air, exercise, . . . hell, it's a great way to ditch frustrations."

"You can accomplish that in an air-conditioned bedroom," she teased.

158

"Yeah, I know." He laughed.

Their waitress delivered another round as a much better band started the second set. Morty asked Hack to dance. The selection being played was one of Chubby Checker's hits and she was really enjoying bouncing to the upbeat rhythm. Getting her to take a breather was harder than having to make a fifty-foot putt. Except for the breaks between sets, they spent practically every selection trying to dodge the other couples packed on the floor. Morty wasn't the best fast dancer he had seen, but she knew how to cuddle on the slow ones. Before the evening was over, she easily accomplished stirring his blood. Between her teasing and the booze, by closing, he was feeling no real pain, only a pleasant ache between his legs. Morty suffered identical symptoms.

Mitch tried his best to talk them into joining him for breakfast. They refused with the excuse of being tired and having the long ride ahead. He was a bit disappointed, but Morty's way of saying goodbye did a lot to cheer him. They stopped in the restaurant long enough to get coffee to go, searched for the car in the lot, and drove for home.

Hack was faced with an impossible situation trying to keep her quiet as they giggled and stumbled through the door and up the stairs to his office. It was a miracle they didn't wake Pat or the old folks living in an apartment on the third level. Propping her against the wall and fumbling with his key in the outer office's door lock, it finally opened and he turned to help her. With legs spread apart, she had slid down the wall flat-assed on the floor. Pulling her heels together, he tried to drag her from the hallway.

"You damned fool," she giggled. "I'm only kidding."

"Shit," he grunted, dropping her feet to the floor with a thud.

She crawled past and literally climbed into Carin's chair, pushing away from the desk hollering, "Wheeeeee," as she spun on the seat.

"Shush. Damn it, be quiet. You're gonna wake Pat."

"Shhhhhhuuuusssshhhh," she mimicked.

"Listen. If you'll shut up for two seconds, I'll get the bed set up and you can expend some of that energy on me."

She clapped her hands across her mouth in a "speak-no-evil" pose while her eyes said "get-the-lead-out."

The cot wasn't the best of choices for two people, but beggars couldn't be choosers. Morty had a thing about leaving lights on. He talked her into the desk lamp as a compromise. Trying to lie beside each other on the cot was out of the question. Even getting onto it proved a problem. Hack laid down first and she carefully climbed on top. They were soon into heavy play, becoming uncontrollably captured in passions and totally oblivious to surroundings. Increasing physical response and almost violent movements began to conflict with the capabilities of the fragile bed.

"Ka-booooommmmmm."

The crash was thunderous. As the legs buckled, the cot had careened forward and into the side of a metal file cabinet. Morty groaned at first, then giggled hysterically. The double-doors flew open and there stood Pat in a nightshirt.

"Oh, hell. It's only you two. I thought it was a burglar or something," she moaned, stretching her arms high above her head. "Damn the lousy luck."

"Lord, why me?" Hack asked.

Managing to untangle themselves from the debris, they made their way to the open couch.

"Look's like she's going to play share'zies now," Pat joked. "Think we can all fit in one bed?"

"If you mean on top of each other, hell, yeah." Morty laughed. "He's got to get in the middle though."

Pat turned the lights off and was the last in bed. Morty was on one side and she on the other. Pat's abundant naked breasts sandwiched Hack's left arm as she cuddled against his side, indicating she had shed her nightie sometime after hitting the switch. Morty didn't delay in trying to get things rolling again.

As he lay enjoying their attentions, the thought occurred that his most recurring fantasy had always been sharing two women at the same time. He reasoned it had to be at the top of the list of erotic sex for practically every male. There wasn't much time for further rationalization as increasingly enhanced physical contact sent passions soaring.

Minutes passed as though they were hours. Enthusiasm and excitement abounding in the beginning, fizzled. Relief finally came with sleep as Pat continued unsuccessfully to arouse his lower body to attention.

Hack slept like a rock. Unfortunately, on awakening, he felt like he had lain on one, as well. His joints were stiff and the back pain complimented the surging ache in his head. Pat was tugging at his arm persistently. Still dazed by his recent unconscious state, all he could reason was she wanted some more.

"Damn it, Hack. Get up," she demanded. "Somebody's downstairs ringing the door bell. Damn it, come on."

Suddenly, he was aware of the constant buzzing. Morty sat up in bed as he rolled off the opposite side. Blood rushed from his brain. He reeled, groping for the corner of the desk to steady himself.

Pat grabbed his arm. "There you go, grandpa. Lean on me."

Morty started giggling at them as Hack strained in the effort of getting to the front window. Opening it barely enough to poke his head though, he almost knocked himself out, banging the back of his skull as he quickly withdrew.

"Mother of God. It's Carin," he almost shouted as the shock of the unfolding situation began to sober him fast.

"Holy shit. What am I going to do? I . . . "

"Who the hell's Carin?" Pat interrupted.

"Yeah," Morty chimed in, "tell us about Carin."

"It ain't funny," he blurted. "She's a, she's my . . . ." He paused very briefly. "Fuck it. Why lie? She's my secretary, and I mean a damn good one. She thinks I'm the greatest thing that walks. Almost. I can't fuck it up. Please?"

He knew there wasn't much time and was surprised the upper-floor residents hadn't already responded. He spun quickly and leaned out the window once more.

"Hey. Hey, up here."

Carin stepped back and peered upward toward the sound of his voice.

"It's about time. I thought you were dead or something."

He just stared at her.

"Well, are you going to let me in or not?" she asked, showing a growing frustration.

His mind was racing and he had to think fast. "You bring any coffee or tea with you? I ran out up here."

"No. But, I'll go to the corner and get some."

"Great. I need it. I'll be down and open up before you get back."

Being assured she was headed down the street, he turned suddenly to Morty and Pat. They were impishly enjoying his predicament.

"Oh, God. If you've got any compassion at all, you've gotta help me," he begged the girls. "I'll lose her, sure as shit. It could hurt the hell outta my business." He tried to emphasize work over personal involvement.

"Okay, okay." Morty tried to calm him. "Where are we supposed to go? Under the couch? In the attic?"

They started clowning again, making vulgar gestures and giggling.

He wanted to put them in the rear offices, but couldn't remember where Carin kept the key. "How about the walk-in closet?" Morty and Pat looked at each other and shrugged their shoulders simultaneously in an "oh, what-the-hell" manner. "But, damn it, please be quiet," Hack implored.

Like greased lightening, he sped around the room gathering foreign debris like a giant vacuum. The broken cot was the biggest problem. There was no way to fold it in its present condition. Cramming it into the bathroom was the only answer. Closing the couch, he then tugged on his pants, grabbed a pullover sweater, scanned the room quickly in a final check and purposely spread papers and job items over the area to appear he had been working all night. Having at least helped with their own paraphernalia, the girls had already retreated to their hideout. He warned them several times about their persistent moans and giggles. Satisfied he could do no more, he hurried down, unlatched the night lock and opened the door.

"Finally," Carin said as her face turned from a frown to a broad smile. He stood in a daze. "Well, can't I come in?"

"Ah, yeah, . . . sure," he stammered, reaching for her arm and kissing her cheek.

"That's a little better," she returned, closing the door with her foot and throwing her arms around his neck. Her embrace was long.

His mind marveled at the luck of having used the safety-latch when arriving last night, but didn't remember actually doing it.

Reasoning that the old folks from the top floor must have been disturbed and came down to check--thank the Lord for the racket they had made, he thought.

Going up the stairs, Carin explained she had forgot a needed package and decided to stop on her way to her mother's. Complimenting her for the way she looked, he falsely praised his good fortune in getting to unexpectedly see her. Once in her office, he went directly to the double doors and closed them tightly.

"What's up?" she asked.

"Uh, nothin'. The place is a mess. I worked late as hell and figured I'd catch some more shut-eye after you leave. You get the coffee?"

"Tea. Here you are." Carin shook his cup to stir it before removing the top. "I'm sorry. I shouldn't have woke you. Let me help you get it straight while I'm here. It's the least I can do." She moved toward the doors.

"No." He sounded more emphatic than intended. "I mean, that's okay. It's not as bad as I made out. Mostly my work. Organized mess, you might call it."

"Well, okay. If you say so." She began to appear a bit suspicious.

He spread the doors enough for her to have full view of the room. "See. Not so bad, is it?"

"Not really, I guess."

"Besides," he continued. "You've got a lot to do. Remember. That's the reason for the long weekend. Okay?"

"Yep," she smiled. "You must be tired. You don't look too good, you know. It must've been a rough night."

If you only knew, he thought before responding. "I'm still sleepy, but I'll be all right."

Reaching across her desk and grabbing the package she sought, Carin turned and started for the front door blowing him a kiss. "Damn," she said, stopping suddenly, "better go to the bathroom before I leave."

He could have almost vomited. All he could visualize was Morty and Pat nude, ready to pop out of their hiding place. Without realizing it, he was blocking Carin's way.

"You okay?" She was concerned.

"Uh, yeah. A little sick to the stomach. I'll . . . I'll be fine."

"No ifs, ands, or buts, you're getting back in bed."

Physically pushing him through the double doors, she took him by the arm and forced him onto the couch. Attempting to overrule objections against removing his clothes, he finally convinced her to leave them on. However, covers were tucked tightly under his chin.

She disappeared into the bathroom.

As the noise of the flushing commode could be heard, Morty's head protruded from the closet.

"Damn it. Hurry it up," she half-laughed in a loud whisper.

He waved frantically with his arms motioning her back inside while scrambling from the sofa in an effort to shut the door on her. No sooner had it closed and Carin reappeared.

"Did you say something, honey?" she asked.

"Uh, naw. Just mumbling to myself. I hit my knee gettin out of bed."

"Well, you shouldn't be up, anyway. If you need anything, I'll get it."

"I need some ala-seltzer." He groaned from despair rather than illness and crawled back in the sack while Carin dropped two tablets into a glass of water.

"What happened to the cot? It looks like a Mack truck ran over it."

He had forgot about putting it in the head.

"To be honest," he started, "I'm really not sure. Ted stayed downtown Thursday night and used it in the back, and it just gave way on him. I brought it up front so I wouldn't forget to take it to the dump."

"It's a miracle he wasn't killed. The way it looks, at least," she joked. "He must be gaining more weight than I realized. As skinny as he is, you'd think he could lay on stretched wet toilet paper without tearing it."

A chill ran up his spine in thinking he heard a giggle from the closet. Whether it was or not, Carin didn't seem to notice. Hack's wild coughing and choking spasm did much to distract her. Finally, after he had calmed, she put on her coat and moved toward the door.

"Give me a call later, after you get some rest. Bye-bye." She puckered her lips and wiggled her fingers in a waving motion.

He waited until hearing the downstairs front door close, sprang from the bed, hid behind a corner of the drape, and watched her enter the street below.

"Good Lord," he gasped in relief.

Continuing to stand at the window while watching her disappear in the distance, suddenly it occurred to him, in his preoccupation with Carin's departure, he had forgotten the girls. "Aw, shit," he muttered, hurrying to the door and yanking it open.

There they both stood clad in male attire. Morty was swimming in one of his business suits, including vest, while Pat came a bit nearer fitting into a blue blazer and slacks. Hack's astonished look preceded a nervous chortle. Panic-stricken seriousness quickly ebbed as the true ridiculousness of the preceding events surfaced. His laughter matured hysterically as he fell back on the couch.

"Damn, Pat. I don't think we look that bad," Morty commented indignantly.

Hack sat up trying to wipe a tear from his eye.

"Hell," Pat offered, "we figured if we got caught, maybe she might think we were just a couple of your golf buddies or something."

"Or something's the problem," he mumbled, still giggling.

They both looked at each other, shrugged their shoulders and in chorus said, "Aw, what the hell," then jumped headlong on top of him.

Under deep verbal protests, they managed removing his clothes. He was still weak from laughing and didn't possess the physical requirements needed to defend himself. They took turns trying to arouse him sexually, while the other was disrobing. Circumstances becoming impossible to withstand their efforts, he soon succumbed to the stimulation. The appeal of their bodies and the spirit of the 'ménage a trois' was tremendously magnified in the day-lit room.

As if a bell had sent a signal, they both leaped up simultaneously, leaving him alone to tumble from the euphoria.

"Jerk-off. We're going for breakfast."

* * *

After Pat left for the airport, Morty and Hack spent the

remainder of the day and Saturday night together without further complications. She caught her flight late Sunday afternoon and Hack kept his earlier dinner promise with Carin. He had been really tempted to cancel her invitation solely on the basis that she was sure to want sex. Considering the workout of the preceding two nights, he amazed himself in providing a reasonable performance.

It was the beginning of a good period between the two of them. They were together more than usual. Hack even arranged renting a cabin, spending four days over her birthday in the mountains.

Anticipated bad weather had postponed the Pennsylvania trip planned for the following weekend and the group mutually decided to wait until late May to reschedule. Early April was simply not the best time to venture any further north than they already were when it came to golf. It proved to be an unusually cool, windy, and rainy spring, hampering desires to spend any great deal of time at the club. Light mist could be tolerated. However, the downpours left courses in miserable playing conditions for days at a time. Hack was certainly not a fair weather golfer, but, even he had limits.

Virtually tied to his desk for the better part of two months, June was fast approaching, as was the change to warmer temperatures. Counterbalancing the promiscuous period previously experienced, his existence became virtually monogamous with Carin. In his preoccupation, he had thought of Terri on few occasions. Following the accident, their return home, and a few nimble attempts at getting together again, phone contact dwindled to no contact at all.

Hack leaned to reach the intercom and buzzed Carin's number.

"Hi."

"Didn't know if you were still there, or not. I couldn't hear you breathing."

She panted real hard. "I'm still here."

"Why don't you pant yourself through my door, if you've got a sec?"

"Be right there."

Carin cut the conversation short with her mother and strode

into his office. She took her usual seat on the corner of his executive desk, with pad in hand, expecting dictation.

"Put that away. No letters today."

"Good. I didn't feel like it, anyway. Wanna horse around?"

"I'd rather screw," he joked.

"You said the secret word." She jumped from her spot, pulled up her dress, and started to drop her panties before he called it to a halt.

"Cut that out." He laughed and shook his head. "Seriously. How would you like to do it in Miami and do it on the beach?"

"I'd probably stand a better chance on the 'Sands of Iwo Jima'," she quipped sarcastically. Pausing for a few seconds while observing the unemotional expression on his face, she became confused and then enlightened. "You're not joking, are you?"

"Nope. Wanna go to Florida?"

"Oh, my God, you're not joking. Tell me it's for real."

"For real," he assured.

Rushing around the desk, she plopped in his lap and began showering him with hugs and kisses. Carin's excitement caused her to ramble incessantly, leaving only brief opportunities for Hack to interject factual details regarding the proposed vacation. Her nervous energies eventually subsided to a point that reason ability and rationale were being slowly restored.

"I'll pick up the tickets tomorrow, we can leave the following day."

"I don't believe it," she squealed, leaping to her feet and turning to face him. "Can we really do it in the sand?"

* * *

Disembarking from the plane at Miami Airport was totally different than Hack's previous experience of entering Florida by automobile. Although exciting, except for the balmy weather, the initial aura of tropical beauty was confined to potted palmettos and plants throughout the terminal lobby. Paying a brief visit to the Hertz counter, papers were in order and quickly processed for a rental car. Gathering their luggage as part of the service, their temporary chauffeur drove them to a nearby pickup point and transferred the baggage to a jazzy 1965 white Ford convertible. It was an absolute necessity for Hack to be completely compatible with the Sunshine State. Carin gasped with enthusiasm and hurried to take her place on the companion seat.

"Like it," Hack taunted.

"Love it." Her smile accentuated her happiness.

Easily locating the expressway and using it to reach the proper exit to Miami Beach, they found themselves heading north on Collins Avenue toward their appointed motel. A large neon sign announcing the Pirate's Cove loomed ahead. Turning into the driveway, Hack pulled directly to the main entrance, parked, assisted Carin from the car, and proceeded inside to inquire about their reservations. Hack signed the register as 'Mr. and Mrs. Arnold.' Carin experienced a warm and wonderful feeling.

Finally finishing the unpacking, Hack sat on the edge of the bed gazing out their ocean-view window, watching the surf surge against the shore. Carin, having spent a brief interim in the bathroom, came to sit beside him.

"Let's go make love on the beach," she whispered in his ear.

"Are you crazy? It's still daylight," he laughed.

"I don't care. We can do it under a collapsed umbrella if you want."

CHAPTER VII

Miami Beach exuded all of the tropical splendor imagined and boasted through travel brochures. The seawater, although clearer and somewhat more colorful than that of northern shorelines, still held a major disappointment compared to what had been envisioned. They strolled along the beach, dodging erected barriers separating ownership of ocean frontage, feeling slightly dejected by the presence of commercialism and its affront to nature.

"It's beautiful, but not at all like I expected," Carin observed while stooping to retrieve a shell near her toes. "Oh, look," she beamed. "It's a shark's tooth."

Hack smiled, commenting about the size of her find, beginning to scrutinize the beach more carefully during their walk. After covering a reasonable distance, they came upon the patio of a restaurant overlooking the ocean and stopped for something cool. It was rare for him to ever imbibe any of the fancier mixed drinks, but a 'mai tai' for himself and a frozen daiquiri for Carin, fit the occasion. Snacking on an assortment of fruits and cheeses, they sat very close on one side of the umbrella-covered table.

"We should've done this last winter when it was so cold back home," Hack said, breaking the silence.

Carin smiled and returned gazing across the water at the horizon.

* * *

Hack lay in bed watching Carin stand in the middle of the open balcony doors spreading the drapes wide to afford full view of the rising sun. It had yet to clear the distant edge of the water barrier, but its preceding glow fused with the azure sky. The interior of their suite was still relatively dark, causing Carin to be silhouetted against the wall of soft light. The shapely and well-proportioned curves of her body were accentuated by the movement of her loose negligee flowing in the gentle breeze entering the room. Tempted to call her to his arms and quell the growing stimulation aroused by her image, he instead lay equally mesmerized by her, as she was by the unfolding seascape. Awareness was soon replaced by dreams.

"Come on sleepyhead." Carin hit him across the rump with a pillow. "It's almost ten o'clock."

Hack jumped with the impact to sit upright in bed, rubbing his eyes. Carin was fully clothed in a beach outfit.

"Where the hell you been?" he asked in a dumbfounded state.

"I went for a walk. It was beautiful." There was a special brilliance to her smile. "Got some juice and coffee." She busied herself doctoring the hot liquid and offered his cup.

"Damn, you look good," he garbled through sips of the brew.

She allowed him time to sit his drink on the night stand and reach for his cigarettes before she pounced on him. Literally leaping on the bed, the weight of her body forced him backward as she landed on top. Twisting and wrestling through all kinds of contortions, they laughed and played until the seriousness of passions replaced the frivolity.

Rolling quickly away, Carin avoided his lunge to grab her and managed to regain her feet on the floor at the end of the bed. "Take a shower, we've got a lot to see and do." She laughed at the pouting expression spreading across his face.

"Aw, come on," he pleaded, "I'm gonna have a hard-on all day."

"Good. It'll give me something to drag you around with."

"Bitch," he moaned, untangling himself from the maze of covers.

* * *

Typical of tourists, they spent the next few days visiting many of the popular attractions, including: jai alai, the dog track, John Deere's Villa Viscaya estate, and a boat tour of the inner waterway. Spending an evening at the Playboy Club having dinner, followed by a presentation of Minsky's Burlesque, was especially enjoyable. By their fourth day, they were exhausted and chose to lie basking on the beach and laze around the motel. Carin's rather fair complexion tanned slowly and was subject to burning easily. Hack stretched on a long towel, digging his toes into the sand and browsing through a tourist's attraction booklet provided by the local chamber of commerce.

"Let's go to Nassau," he said in a calm and deliberate manner.

"What?" Startled, Carin quickly turned her head in his direction.

"This ad. . . . There's an ad in here about a four-day cruise to the islands. It isn't very expensive." He offered her the publication. "See. Right here."

Carin raised to her elbows straining to focus her vision on a small box printed at the lower corner of the page. Initially, a surge of excitement swept through her as she read details pertaining to the promoted cruise. However, logic overcame enthusiasm as she returned the booklet to Hack. "The ship doesn't sail until Saturday. We'll have been gone a week by then. Don't you feel we should think about getting back?"

"Sound's like you want to get home." Hack appeared disappointed.

"God, no," she emphasized, "I could stay here forever. I was thinking of you and the business, more than me."

He leaned and kissed her forehead. "To hell with work, this is our vacation."

* * *

Excitement in finding things to enjoy, until the liner was scheduled to sail, became dulled by the anticipation of the cruise. It was considered the off-season in southern Florida and prices were extremely cheap on anything one would care to buy. Hack had been especially impressed with the low cost of dining, drinks and entertainment, comparing not only to his trips into "the Big Apple," but to those at home, as well. Taking some advantage of the situation, they visited a few of the larger shopping complexes in search of bargains. Hack's generosity abounded, lavishing Carin with numerous clothing selections: from swimming attire to summer clothes, galore; and, a sexy evening gown, specifically chosen for the boat.

Arriving at the dock early, they found boarding a very simple matter. Setting the mood for the venture, a Jamaican band played

Latin-American music as entertainment for the gathering passengers. Hack and Carin stood on the main deck watching the crew and longshoremen busy themselves with releasing the gigantic craft from its moorings. As part of the travel agent's pitch, they learned that the liner was relatively new and of Norwegian ownership. She had been christened the "Moonray."

Remaining at the rail, until the ship had cleared the inland bay and entered the vast Atlantic Ocean, Miami's coastline was breathtaking, even in the haze of the extremely warm day. Deciding to take a tour of the vessel, they walked holding hands from deck to deck continuing to be impressed in the craft's grandeur. There were two theaters, several shops, three nightclubs, two restaurants, a huge dining hall, and a lounge located above the uppermost deck fittingly named the "Crow's Nest." Hack constantly referred to a leaflet containing a map of the entire liner for directions to their next point of interest.

"We haven't even seen our room," Carin reminded him.

"Let's go." He smiled and tugged her arm.

Descending into what seemed to be the bowels of the ship, they located the number corresponding to their cabin key. Hack turned the lock and swept Carin from her feet into his arms to carry her over the threshold. She pushed against the door as he struggled to force them both through the narrow passageway. Simultaneously, they broke into laughter at seeing the closet designated as home for the next several days. Referring to it as being compact would have been too kind. There was just enough floor space for two people to barely manage manipulating. An adjoining compartment shielded by a folding door contained the toilet, basin and shower without a separation between any of the three. Lower and upper sleeping berths were positioned into one of the walls with cabinets and drawers, above, below, and between. Each and every inch of the room's available space was virtually designed for storage wherever possible. There was no way to sit up in bed and barely enough clearance for one to lie atop the other. They sat in the middle of the floor giggling hysterically.

* * *

Dinner was a true experience in itself. The drone of the ship's engines, seeming to be near or under the dining hall, vibrated the tables shaking the glassware in shivering tremors. They had been assigned the later dinner-shift at a sitting for eight. Among the other couples, was a pair of Canadians proving to be enjoyable company. Rounding out the group were very young newlyweds and a rather old and starchy husband and wife. Agreeing to meet later for drinks in one of the nightclubs with the northerners, Hack and Carin finished dinner and decided to attend a brief meeting provided by the ship's entertainment officer. There were any number of events planned. In fact, so many, it would have been impossible to cover them all.

Later, having fulfilled the obligation with their dinner mates, they ventured alone to the Crow's Nest lounge, hoping to find a less active environment.

Carin looked gorgeous in one of her new outfits. She attracted a lot of attention from the males, and especially from some of the crew. Hack always found it titillating to catch the reactions of men attempting to covertly ogle a beautiful female, especially if they were accompanied by another woman, and even more so, if the subject of attention happened to be with him. It was a tremendous boost to his ego.

In opposition to the previous club, the lounge was relatively sparse of customers and there was a wide selection of seats. Taking a table against the wall near the small dance floor, Hack recognized their waiter as being one of the members of the band playing on the dock. After serving drinks, he joined the other four who were getting ready to start another set of music. Gaining a rapport with the musicians added to the fun and enjoyment of the evening -- not ending until after three a.m.

Being a gentleman, and, a little more athletic than Carin, he had opted to use the upper berth. Hearing movement in the cabin, he raised quickly without thinking. His head thudded against the low overhead and he dropped back groaning and moaning with the added pain intensifying the previously existing throbbing in his temples.

"Are you okay?" Carin groggily asked, peeking her head around the corner of the bathroom door.

"Ahhhhh, I'm dead," he cried in agony.

"That's good."

Remembering the height between he and the floor only after

being halfway out of the bed, he lost all balance and tumbled to the rug. "Aw, shit." He groaned some more, rubbing his knee and the middle of his back.

"Do you have to be so noisy?" Carin's attempt at wit wasn't well taken.

"Up yours, . . . with my broken leg."

* * *

Reaching the main deck, they decided on fresh air rather than immediately attempting breakfast. Until they stood by the rail, it hadn't occurred to him the ship sat motionless in the water. Not having paid attention last evening, he now recalled having noticed the engines were silent when they had finally retired. Taking Carin by the hand, he pulled her through the lobby to the other side of the liner. On opening the door, they were embraced by the panorama of the island laying off the starboard side. Evidently, the craft had been lying at anchor, just off the coast, for the better part of the morning. Suddenly, the groan of the engines, followed by the violent thrashing of water, slowly sent the vessel in a forward motion.

"If we're gonna make breakfast we better hurry," Hack cautioned. "I really need some coffee."

Arriving too late for the full meal, a condiment table offered a selection of Danish and muffins. Undecided as to whether the waiter's motivation came from kindness or the simple desire to get rid of them, Hack accepted his offer of a small disposable tray arrayed with paper containers of coffee and a variety of sweets. They found a spot on the aft deck providing a vacant pool side table. Most of the passengers had already fled toward the bow and upper-decks to get the best view of entering port.

They had chosen to delay their own departure from the boat, hoping to avoid the onslaught of the anticipated crowd rushing ashore. The "Moonray" moored in a slip nearest the land. Two other vessels, one being even larger, lay at other points along the pier which jutted well into the bay toward a smaller island running parallel to the mainland. To the delight of the tourists, native lads perched themselves high on the ledges of nearby buildings and roofs, and some even on the masts of the other ships, diving distances of sixty or more feet into the crystal clear depths retrieving coins thrown by the passengers before they had

174

any chance to settle to the bottom. The clarity of the water compared closely to that of a swimming pool and was a beautiful azure in color. The diver's skills were uncanny and superlative entertainment.

Having made arrangements with the purser's office, a rental car awaited them near the dock. Entering a large center square immediately across from the pier's main entrance, they were confronted by numerous barterers peddling their wares. Weaving through the masses in the direction of the rental agency, they were stopped by a very young and tiny scrubby native girl attempting to sell them wild flowers. Hack was sure they had been pulled from someone's yard. Unable to resist her jabbering in horrible English, he stooped in front of her while rolling a ten-dollar bill into her hand and watched the child's eyes grow in excitement. She leaped forward throwing her arms around his neck and planted a big kiss on his cheek.

"You like my sister, too?" she asked quite clearly.

He laughed loudly, shaking his head in embarrassment and disbelief while regaining his feet. Carin joined his amused state as he related the little one's query. They watched her scurry between the legs of the crowd and disappear. Hack handed Carin the bouquet and she clutched them to her breast.

* * *

Driving on the wrong side of the road wasn't an easy adjustment to make. Fortunately, in town, all of the streets were one-way. They were so narrow in most cases, two cars would have been sorely tested to pass one another. However, the highways patterned across the majority of the territory were dual-lane, and he received any number of abusive insults regarding his driving mannerisms and tendency for the wrong side of the road.

They ventured to the opposite side of the island finding it virtually uninhabited. Except for the populated areas, the terrain provided trees and foliage more similar to the Carolina's than of the type expected in the tropics. It was disappointing. Covering most of the accessible areas in slightly over an hour, they returned to the urban district from another direction, entering through a very residential area. The homes were stucco and painted in a variety of pastel colors and shades. Huge degrees of moderate living and even poverty prevailed.

Hack jammed the brakes to the floor. In his preoccupation, he had not seen the horse bolt from an alley, directly across the path of his car. He barely missed hitting the animal and wildly cursed the pinto as it trotted away. Carin's amusement kindled his ire. Still mumbling about the episode and parking in a space reserved for the automobile, they decided to have lunch ashore before boarding ship for a nap.

Feeling rested, they had dinner in the dining hall with the others, except for the newlyweds who hadn't been seen since the previous evening. Following the meal, Hack invited the Canadian couple to accompany them to Paradise Island and the gambling casino. Having accepted the invitation, the four drove across a long bridge spanning the bay and connecting the land masses. They continued on a roadway paralleling the water, being stunned by the 'scape provided by the setting sun across the horizon. Arriving at the club, it sat at the base of a sprawling complex of apartments quite unlike anything seen on the mainland. Pulling directly to the main entrance and accepting valet parking, they entered a huge hall peppered with gaming devices. Having never been to Las Vegas or any other similar site, Hack and Carin stood gaping at the surroundings. Excusing themselves, their shipmates hurried in the direction of the roulette-wheel.

Hack and Carin were initially content in milling among the crowd for a while, watching the reactions of others. It was an education in itself. They observed a couple of jackpots scored on the slots, but for the most part, downtrodden and serious expressions prevailed.

"Wow," Hack exclaimed, "there's the blackjack games."

"You go play," she encouraged him. "I'll mosey over to the one-armed bandits and try my luck."

"Here, babe." He pushed several twenties in her hand before walking away enthralled by the prospect of winning big.

A line of bar-like tables ran in a staggered row for nearly half the length of the building. Each game was marked by a sign indicating the minimum bets accepted. Opting for the least risk, a two-dollar game, he sidled onto a vacant stool requesting fifty dollars worth of chips. Continuing to be observant, he noted that a "pit boss" sat in a position to supervise two tables at the same time.   From the seriousness of their faces and the cool mannerisms of the dealers, an aura of cold austerity hovered over the facade of eager gamblers.

"Place your bet, sir," the dealer repeated his demand.

"Oops, . . . sorry." Hack's attention was brought to the game.

Becoming engrossed in the play, Hack really wasn't aware of the passing time or Carin's extended absence.   The house provided any type of beverage free as part of the draw to get patrons to participate. Having faired reasonably well at being a two-dollar bettor, he decided to step up in stature and move to a ten-dollar table. Taking a brief break, he peered around the room and spotted Carin planted in front of a slot machine being encouraged by one of the officers from the liner. Failing to catch her attention, he returned to locate another spot. Eventually gaining a seat, he converted his winnings into ten-dollar chips and delved into the action.

Hack was a good card player and blackjack a popular choice for late-night games at the club. He knew better players would be at the higher-stake tables and felt qualified to participate. Sitting at the sixth position in the deals order, the seventh player dropped, and for a period of time he represented what is often referred to as the "anchorman" in the game. Having that honor, the rest of the players often counted on his good play and decisions to put the onus back on the dealer. His cohorts were pleased by his efforts until the seventh seat was again occupied. The addition of the new participant altered the flow of cards and luck, redirecting it in the favor of the house. The new number seven man was a lousy corner-stop and unlucky loser. It wasn't until Hack decided to quit that he realized the silver disks being lost by the newcomer, two or more at a time, were five hundred dollar chips.

Feeling satisfied at still being in the black, he went in search of Carin and found her at the bar embroiled in a conversation with the officer seen earlier in her company. Noticing his approach, she waved him to her and made the introduction to her friend.

"Eric, this is Hack, and Hack, this is Eric." She tilted her head each time in the corresponding direction. "Eric's the ship's male nurse. We were just discussing anatomy," she giggled, exposing her tipsy condition.

Eric blushed as Hack slightly reddened from other causes. "Pleased to meet you." Hack offered his hand in protested courtesy. Even though he realized Carin's attractiveness easily solicited the attentions of other males, and that he had no legitimate right to dominate or interfere, he felt threatened whenever she showed signs of interest in another man.

The officer acknowledged the greeting with an overly firm handshake. Becoming free of the Norwegian's grip, Hack immediately placed the scrunched hand behind his own back, plying all of the fingers to make sure he could still move them. Accepting Eric's offer of a drink, Hack's opinion of the handsome crewman began to mellow, becoming cognizant of the foreigner's customs and habits. Carin sat nodding as if to fall asleep any moment.

"She's not used to drinking very much?" Eric innocently asked.

"No, not really." Hack smiled. "I better get her back to the boat before I have to carry her."

"You have car?"

"Yeah. Thanks, anyway." He assumed being offered an alternative.

Carin gave little resistance and meekly rested against Hack's side as he ushered her from the casino. The valet quickly arrived with his automobile and Hack poured her into the front seat. Eric had tagged along in case any assistance was needed and persisted in getting a positive response to his invitation for them to join a crew party the last night of the voyage. Hack finally accepted.

* * *

Totally disenchanted with his early morning attempt at playing golf, Hack returned without bothering to test the second nine. The extended drought and extremely warm weather had burnt the course badly. Not having a complete watering system, fairways practically simulated giant sand traps stretching from near-like oases of tee to green. Adding to his dismay, lizards of all sizes and shapes scampered everywhere to be seen. Having earlier noted a native by the side of a road dangling a huge viper on the end of a bolo knife, there was no way he would have attempted going near any underbrush.

Carin was still asleep and he decided not to wake her. It wasn't quite eleven o'clock and having missed breakfast due to the early golf venture, he felt in need of food and didn't care to wait for the scheduled noon meal. Going ashore for sustenance, he spotted his little friend attempting to con another innocent passerby.

"Hey, sweetheart." He beckoned her to him.

Recognizing her benefactor, she rushed to Hack.

"You buy flower?"

"Maybe, but I need a hug first."

Beaming a beautiful smile, she grabbed him around the neck as he leaned forward. "You need my sister, now?" The earlier reaction of being funny was now replaced with the saddening conclusion, this was the child's way of life.

"You have mother and father?" Hack asked, slowly pronouncing each word with added distinction.

She looked puzzled. "My name Tina." She pointed to her chest.

"Where . . . sister?" Hack tried another tact.

"Sister there." Again she pointed, this time in the direction of the fountain.

Hack strained to see through the spewing beads of water and detected a scrawny child of no more than fourteen or fifteen years of age. Clad in an old cotton print dress, she intended to remain offstage until her presence was demanded. He felt sick to his stomach.

"Sister come?" He used a movement of his hand and arm to indicate his desire to Tina.

Tina looked in the direction of the other girl and waved with her hand. The sister walked around the fountain and they met her halfway.

"Hi," Hack said as a simple greeting.

"Hi, mistah. You want pussy and good tongue?"

He was amazed at the brashness of the youth. Although sure no one overheard the remark, he sensed embarrassment from having heard it himself. Hack held Tina by her hand and he motioned that they all sit on the fountain's edge.

"My name, Elisa. I speek good American. You see, I make good love, too."

"I'm sure you do," he smiled with his answer.

"Where is mother? . . . Father?"

"All gone. Brother," she started to continue and paused searching for words. "Brother, he work. He good diver."

Harsh reality exposed the truth of the situation — three children struggling to survive in a hellhole of a tourist's Eden.

"You hungry?" He mouthed as if he were chewing and rubbed his stomach.

Tina shook her head in a very pronounced positive manner.

Taking both of the girls by the hand, he led them to an outside café enhanced by a brightly colored awning that would shield them from the piercing rays of the sun. Still being early for lunch, by the standards of the locale, there was a choice of vacant tables. Hack opted on one near the rear to benefit in getting removed from the noise and bustle of the street. As they were seated, a waiter immediately responded, approaching them in a manner expressing objection to the girl's presence. He spoke to the children in their native tongue and they rose without argument to leave. Hack became vehement in his reaction realizing the situation. Urging the girls to remain at the table, he expressed in no uncertain terms his intention to see they were fed with all the proper courtesies afforded other customers. Fluently in command of the English language, the Bahamian completely understood Hack's determination and argued no further.

Selecting ala carte, Hack chose items from the American side of the menu no child could resist; hamburgers with all the trimmings; French fries; Coca-Cola, and, plenty of ketchup, mustard and pickles completed the list — a true juvenile fantasy.

Sating his own appetite through observing the eagerness of Tina and Elisa, he sat simply picking at his own plate enraptured by their pleasures. It was impossible not to think of his own children and make comparisons of lifestyles. These youths were no different in so many ways. Yet, in some of the most important phases, there existed a condemning nature of mankind to subject these fragile human beings to such desecration of mind, body, and existence.

Little if any verbal communication occurred during the meal. Other than an occasional comment of surprise registered between the two sisters, Hack's input was minimal. However, the enjoyment and fulfillment shared through the experiences of his companions epitomized any expectations he may have ever imagined.

The girls totally demolished the food from the table, including the majority of his own lunch. Hack was confronted with another challenging task. Now entering an area of extremely delicate concern, he dared to venture into the realm of ordering dessert for his companions. With great fortitude and expertise, not having the choice of hot fudge ice-cream cakes, he ordered banana splits. They went crazy when they were presented to them. The subdued atmosphere prevailing during the main course altered to excited jabbering between the little ladies. Their reaction was the greatest single thrill of his trip.

The waiter, having calmed compared to his initial reactions, reverted to acceptance of Hack's genuine efforts to make the children happy and contributed to the situation by adding chocolate bars under his napkin. His smiles and altered behavior more than indicated an appreciation of an alien understanding problems existing in his country.

Quite typical of youth, the girls started to become restless following their repast. Hack realized their need of returning to their own environment and made no effort to retain them any longer. As Elisa rose from her seat, he took her by the hand and pulled her to him. Without comment, she accepted the mass of paper he folded into her palm. Not being able to cope with curiosity, she stopped and inspected the gift--it was a hundred dollars.

Elisa spun on her heels and rushed into his arms. As tiny as she was, the strength of her embrace was sure to leave an indelible mark on his soul. Quickly, she withdrew and took a distant posture. However, the tears streaming down her cheeks related more truth and feeling than words could have ever expressed.

"Can I take picture?" Hack asked, choking back emotion.

Elisa snatched Tina by her hand, exacting her to a halt.

"Si. Come later to aqua. . . . Si?"

* * *

Opening the cabin door, Carin was in the shower and a rush of steam greeted his entrance.

181

"What the hell you doing, trying out for a lobster contest?"

"Don't talk so loud, you're hurting my headache. If you really want communication, come on in here and rub my neck."

"Are you kidding?" he joked. "If I tried to squeeze in there, too, one of us would probably wind up impaled on the doorknob."

"It's been so long since I've been impaled, I've forgot how it feels." She moaned.

"Turn the cold water on," Hack taunted as he scooted into the lower berth.

Carin emerged from the mist. She bent at the waist allowing her hair to dangle while pulling on it with a towel in long strokes. There was no attempt to hide her nudity. Hack lay in his berth unconsciously ogling her firmness and sensual manner of movements. Slowly, his body warmed with the growing surge of sexual arousal. Instead of immediately responding, he continued to watch, fantasizing contact and physical union. Carin stood with her arms above her head wrapping a towel around her gathered hair in turban style. Her profile exposed a trim figure of womanhood any man would cherish to share. Suddenly, his mind cleared with the impact of an innovative realization. In their intimacies, he easily became lost in their moments together. Lacking was any need to force attentions or concentrate on techniques and methods of making love. There existed a tender attraction that always drew them into deep emotional fulfillment.

As if Carin knew the revelations of his mind, she turned to face him, opening her arms in a welcoming gesture. He arose from the bed and stepped into the embrace. Silently and motionlessly, they stood molded into a single-being, savoring inner-tranquility emanating through their touch. He wanted desperately to sate the spiraling urges building in his body and cursed the chastisement of his clothes. Tilting her head slightly upward, Hack stared into eyes unable to conceal words otherwise feared to be spoken. Carin looked away, but her grasp intensified and he reacted in kind. Moments later, with mutual understanding, they eased from each other. Carin quietly busied herself with dressing for the day as Hack slipped from the cabin to wait on the main deck.

* * *

Stopping ashore for the meal that had continued to elude him,

Carin settled on coffee, supplemented by a glass of water and pair of aspirins. The afternoon had become extremely hot and the air still. Enjoying the comfort of an enclosed air-conditioned patio, subdued shafts of light softly filtered through an overhead trellis covered with tropical vines glistening reflections in Carin's hair. She was as tantalizing in her cotton spaghetti strapped sun dress as she had been without clothes. Struggling with lingering unfulfilled desires, Hack related his morning ventures, starting at the uneventful golf outing and ending with the episode involving the children. Carin listened intently as he gleamed with satisfaction and pleasure. From beneath a usually masculine and sometimes even crude exterior, his massive capacity of love and caring for others surfaced. At moments like this, when the angelic side of his sensitive nature emerged, withholding feelings and not expressing the depth of her love for him required a strenuous effort.

Hack had brought his camera. After leaving the restaurant, they went in search of the children at the water fountain. Waiting for more than a half-hour, their ship blew its final warning blast indicating its approaching departure. Tremendously disappointed, they returned to the pier. Frantic screeching coming from behind caused them to spin in their tracks. Tina and Elisa stood at the gate waving and calling loudly while being restricted from entering the area by a guard. Hack immediately rushed toward them as they broke free of their restraint and ran into his arms. Their faces bright and clean, they were dressed in new brilliantly colored patterned dresses, complimenting the vibrancy of their youthful vitality.

Carin watched with tearing eyes at the warming scene, realizing the importance of the care and love generated between them. Unfortunately, also present was a sadness and insecurity of it being only a fleeting moment before having to part and each return to their forced facets of life.

"We better go," Carin touched him softly on his shoulder as he still knelt with his arms around the girls waists.

"I know," he answered hesitantly.

Following a few quick snapshots and final hugs and kisses, he stood and removed two small packets containing condiments from the ship from his pocket giving one to each child. Taking

Carin by her hand, they turned and hurried for the boat. Being among the last to board, it was difficult to gain a position near a rail on the side docked next to land. However, venturing to the Crow's Nest lounge and taking a spot at one of the huge picture window's, they located the girls continuing to watch the departure. Carin placed her arms around Hack and they stood staring at the fading shoreline sharing deeply mixed emotions.

* * *

Where the night had gone was a mystery. Persistent pounding on their cabin door eventually evoked limited awareness and response from Hack. Moaning an answer of recognition to the stewards efforts of arousing them to prepare for disembarkment, he got up from the floor struggling to avoid stepping on Carin. An ache in his bladder was only superseded by the relentless throbbing in his temples. Attempts at standing were hampered by the rolling of the ship. Stumbling through the tiny lavatory door, he turned out of necessity to sit on the commode. Frantically, he tried to restrain his full descent on the stainless steel bowl. The seat hadn't been lowered and being unsuccessful in halting the downward motion of his body, his buttocks plunged between the icy-cold sidewalls. Wedged in such a manner there was nothing to grasp for leverage to escape the contraption, he passively called to Carin for assistance. First attempts failing, he became rather verbally loud in his efforts to revive her to consciousness.

Eventually responding to the commotion and noticing the unusual positioning of two legs stretching across the bathroom door's opening, she managed getting on her hands and knees, crawled to the bathroom, and peered through the doorway.

"Oh, my God," she moaned, "you've lost your hips."

"Damn it, Carin, shut-up and help me."

Bearing the pain, she broke into hysterics, writhing on the floor in agony.

"Aw, please Carin. Carin, damn it. Carin, help me."

* * *

Recuperating from their last evening aboard was one of the more difficult chores either of them had possibly ever faced in their lives. The crew's party lasted until nearly five a.m., ending only after killing the last available bottle of scotch. With less than an hour of sleep before being pounded awake, all senses of logic were dulled, leaving them as machines coping with the tasks at hand. For some strange reason, facing Customs seemed to be a formidable event even though they had little to declare. Other than the few trinkets bought for Sharon's brood, there were no other purchases remaining since the bottle of Canadian and Chivas Regal had already been spent.

Suffering in total distress, they constantly bumped each other in the confines of the cabin while salvaging belongings into suitcases and travel bags. As a saving factor, one of the crew, evidently aware of their plight, sent a steward to assist in packing. Totally appreciative of the helping hand, Hack graciously passed him a twenty-dollar bill, leaving him to handle the rest.

Taking the opportunity to finally go above deck for fresh air, the shock was too much, and the result, a beeline for the nearest rail to lose one's stomach. Hack stood by apathetically as Carin, looking extremely pale in complexion, contemplated the pros and cons of living or dying. As the liner entered Biscayne Bay, the water calmed as did the jostling of the ship, abating at least some of the distress. Braving the chance at coffee, they carried cups to a remote area and collapsed on deck chairs.

"Don't go to sleep," Hack demanded. "It's my turn."

"Bull-crappie," Carin blurted, expending last energies to lunge at him and tickle his ribs.

"Aw, damn," he exclaimed, dodging the spilling liquid from his cup. The deft and spirited reaction he displayed surprised even himself.

Settling down to bide the remaining time before docking, as leisurely as possible, they rested in the morning sun hoping its rays would absorb the poison from their systems. Their appointed steward appeared to keep them informed of landing details and request signatures on a final document for Customs. Indicating they would be paired with their luggage after landing, he took his leave while wishing them to return at an early date.

Until confronted with debarking, there was no concept of the masses of passengers present on the cruise. Waiting through the lines for inspection was not only boring, it was extremely taxing on bodies already dangerously close to crumbling. Custom's routine of fingering indiscriminately through certain choices and selections of baggage seemed fruitlessly ineffective. Hack reasoned search and seizure techniques viewed in movies as being dramatized figments of a screen writers glorified imagination.

"Do you have anything to declare?"

"Just these." Hack offered a small bag to the customs official.

He glanced at Hack in a typical agent's reaction to tourism while plunging his hands through items in their luggage without even looking. Shoving the baggage to the far end of the table, resembling a grocery store checkout counter, Carin assisted in helping close the grips and satchels. Fighting a great urge to comment about the ineffectualness of the system, Hack submitted to weariness and accepted a porter's assistance.

"I'll get a cab for you, sir."

"No, thanks. I've got my own car. Just take the luggage to the curb."

"Are you sure?" The youthful Floridian seemed strangely befuddled.

"Well, I think I'm sure. When I left here, my car was in the parking lot," Hack retorted, shaking his head, hoping he had at least a little bit of sound reasoning ability remaining.

Allowing the pier steward to cope with all the luggage, Hack retrieved the automobile, pulled it to the curb, and they filled the trunk. Taking refuge in the rear seat, Carin curled up and slept the distance to the Pirates Cove where they had made reservations prior to the cruise. Awakening only long enough to help Hack unload and dump everything into their room after he registered, they both crashed, one each per double bed.

"Holy shit." Hack grabbed his eyes. "I'm blind."

"It's just dark, lover," Carin quipped. "We slept all day."

"Damn, I don't feel like it. Are you sure?"

"Well, unless the sun took an extended vacation and those aren't stars . . . then, it's not night outside." She stood at the patio door spreading the drapes.

"Shut the curtains," he moaned. "The starlight's burning my eyes."

Pouncing on top of his body without warning, he gasped in pain. "I'm not long for this world. Give a guy a break."

"I'll give it a break." She grabbed for his crotch.

Seeming to know her intention in advance, he dodged the

effort and tumbled from the bed in the process.

"You hungry," he queried?

"What do you think I was after?"

"Knock it off." He smiled in reaction to her ambiguous question. "I mean food damn it. You know. Solid sustenance?"

"That's the most solid suste . . . "

Hack didn't dare let her finish the statement. "Get your ass up and ready. I want some food. Dessert, later."

* * *

Not feeling like driving, and also prompted by the advice of their Canadian friends met on the cruise regarding inconvenient parking, they called a cab for transportation to the Ship's Ahoy restaurant in North Hollywood. Halfway there, Hack realized he had forgot his traveler's checks. Out of absolute necessity, he instructed the cabbie to return to the motel. Double parking in the driveway, Carin remained in the taxi watching Hack hustle across the lot and to their room. Fumbling his key into the lock, he felt a hand at his back at the same time the door opened and a jolting sensation hit him in the chest.

* * *

It was good to sleep. Although, this time, dreams were fraught with screaming noises and frantically moving maidens dressed in white, dedicated to satisfying his needs.

Sometime in the past, there had been a similar fantasy. However, the lasses had then been more graceful and tantalizing. Now, the ecstasy was replaced by a crushing pressure experienced throughout his body and a spattering red substance obliterating his vision. The dream was gone, so too, was reality.

"Carin." He suddenly blurted her name in a loud frightened fashion.

"Oh, God, Hack. I'm here," he heard her encouraging assurance. "Please, God. Oh, please, Hack. Talk to me."

Nothing made much sense. He felt good and yet lousy at the same time. Everything seemed jumbled and unintelligible in attempts at comprehension. Opening his eyes, they focused on nothing at first. Slowly, Carin's face began to be recognizable among the mist of uncertainties.

"I hurt," Hack said, without realizing why.

"Baby," she wept with both relief and sympathy at his words.

"God, I love you. Don't you die, damn you."

He drifted into a never-never existence and popped back to awareness vaguely remembering some of the last words he had heard. "Die? . . . What do you mean? I'd rather play golf and . . ." His voice trailed into a whisper.

"Ooooh. . . ." Carin laughed in a frightened manner through her tears as she sat next to the bed, pressing her lips against his hand.

"Could I see you for a moment?"

Carin looked up to find a man standing at the foot of the bed. "Are you another policeman?" she asked disconcertingly.

"No," he smiled, "I'm Doctor Keane. May I speak with you?"

"God, yes." Carin's interest and reaction were immediate. She followed him through the door and into the hallway.

"Your husband's going to be fine," he assured. "The wound was very clean and nothing vital was damaged. He's a very lucky man. It could have been much worse."

"Are you sure, doctor? He looks so pale, and I'm so afraid."

"There, there," he soothed, placing his arm inside hers, leading her to a nearby couch. "You need to get some rest. He'll be here a few days until we're sure there's no infection. He'll be fine and ready to go by then." The doctor smiled as they took seats next to each other.

"It happened so fast. All I can remember is seeing him lying on the ground and his chest covered with blood." She grimaced and choked with tears recalling the incident.

"It's over now. Please believe me, he is doing fine."

Carin was definitely relieved and reassured, but the shock and terror lingered. Some time would pass before the horrible nightmare could be forgotten.

Doctor Keane stood and peered down at Carin. "You do need sleep. You've been up all night and it is morning outside, . . . if you haven't noticed." He smiled while leaning to pat her hand. "He'll be under sedation and asleep for most of the day. I'll make arrangements for you to use the nurse's quarters and be back to check on Mr. Arnold later this evening." He turned and walked to the floor station across the room.

Carin was escorted by a pleasant plump lady in white to a section of rooms on an upper floor. A hospital gown was provided and she was left in a small cubicle with just enough space for a bed and stand. There was no window and the room became pitch-black after switching off the lamp. She rolled to her side and was fast asleep.

Waking to the darkness and absolute silence was eerie. She lay on her back for several moments gathering thoughts and rationalization. A narrow sliver of shiny white affording little illumination seemed to be painted across a lower area of the black somewhere beyond the foot of the bed. Raising to a sitting position, she moved her legs over the edge and slid forward to touch her feet to the floor. Carefully proceeding toward the crack of light, she fumbled and eventually located the doorknob. Pulling the barrier widely open, the burst of immediate brightness was blinding. Turning quickly away, she faced the rooms interior and moved toward a hook on the wall holding her clothes. Finding her watch in the small handbag, it indicated the time to be nearly two-thirty in the afternoon. She had been asleep since eight.

After hurriedly dressing, she rushed from the room in search of Hack. Stopping to get directions at the nearest nurse's station, she proceeded to the third-floor and went directly to his room. There were two men dressed in suits talking to another clad in surgical garb in front of the door. They stopped her as she tried to pass.

"Are you the young lady who is with Mr. Arnold?"

"Yes. Who are you?"

"We're from the narcotics bureau. We'd like to ask you a few questions."

"Is he all right?" She directed her question to the doctor.

"Quite all right." He smiled in an assuring manner.

"I want to see him," she said indignantly, shoving her way past the officers.

They stepped aside.

Hack laid inertly on the bed, flat on his back. He seemed to have more color in his face and she leaned to kiss his forehead. His eyes opened, he smiled briefly and quickly returned to twilight sleep. She sat beside him for several moments before deciding she was as eager to talk to the authorities as they seemed anxious to question her.

"We can talk now," Carin said leaving Hack's room and closing the door behind her.

The doctor excused himself as Carin and the two business-suited men walked to an isolated far end of the hall.

"Are you aware of what happened?"

"Other than Hack being shot -- no." Her response was full of anger and bitterness.

The spokesman looked at his partner in a sheepish manner and continued. "Mr. Arnold walked into the middle of a drug related arrest. We're very sorry it happened and . . . "

"Sorry," she interrupted. "You're sorry. And, he's shot?" Tears stimulated by both ire and Hack's suffering welled in her eyes.

"Mrs. Arnold, I know that you've been through a terrible ordeal. But if you'd let me explain, I think you would better understand."

Carin calmed her temperament in realizing she did want to know the details.

"Our department has been working closely with customs relating to a rash of narcotics incidents. The Far East has been filtering drugs through Latin America using innocent tourists to smuggle drugs into the country on cruise ships. We've suspected a connection with the agency that made your trip arrangements for a good while. You and Mr. Arnold have been under surveillance since then and especially after passing through customs yesterday morning, not only by our agents, but the traffickers themselves. It wasn't difficult to learn you planned to return to the same motel following the cruise. Your Canadian friends were actually two of our agents. The drug dealers were informed by the travel people. That set the ball rolling and it was just a matter of time until you left your room long enough for them to retrieve the goods." He paused while taking a flattened pack of cigarettes from his shirt pocket. "Do you mind if I smoke?"

She nodded an approval.

"Unfortunately," he continued, "your unexpected return to the motel interrupted the arrest. One of our agents tried to grab your husband from behind to prevent him from opening the door . . . and . . . we were too late."

Carin began weaving slightly and the officer reached to steady her from possibly falling. He strongly suggested they go to the waiting area where she could be seated.

"Is that better?"

"Yes. Thank you." Carin smiled weakly as she leaned back against the couch's cushions.

The other officer arrived with a glass of water. She sipped it slowly.

"There were two men in the room when Mr. Arnold opened the door. One of them, obviously young and gutsy, fired several shots. The first hit your friend before we could get him inside the adjoining room. It was an awkward and a very unusual situation."

"But, why? How? I just don't understand." Carin was confused and even more bewildered.

"There's reason to believe the steward handling your things aboard ship placed several bags of cocaine in your luggage. It was confirmed during customs inspection and purposely allowed to pass. Our agents were immediately alerted." He lit another cigarette. "We knew there would be an attempted infiltration, but didn't have any idea as to who the carrier would be. We were covering all travelers having used the targeted service."

"You bastards." She nearly shouted in disgust. "You set us up."

"Not really. They were the ones setting you up. We had no control over who they might elect to use." He ignored her vehement reaction. "Of course, we could have halted the delivery during inspection, but that would have accomplished nothing. It was our intention to have you taken to your motel by an agent posing as a cab driver. He was to have told you of our plans and the arrangements made to keep you clear of the scene. As luck would have it, we overlooked the fact you had a rental car. There was no opportunity to approach you after leaving the dock. Even then, we felt there was never a chance for you to be endangered in the operation."

"You still had no right to do what you did."

"I'm sorry. I realize you became unwittingly involved in this matter, but our decisions were based on the best possible assessment of the situation. If the two of you hadn't returned when you did, the transaction would have taken place without incident and ultimately led to our locating their base operations . . . and you would have never even known about it."

"What would have happened if we had accidentally found the drugs in our belongings? We could have been killed," Carin countered.

"I don't think so." He smiled uneasily. "It was a simple matter for them to bug your room. They could do it from the outside. A simple gadget was placed at the base of your front window capable of transmitting all conversation inside your room. We were also able to do it from the room next door. Had they detected your finding the material, we were prepared to react in any necessary fashion. Under those circumstances, they would have probably tried to force an entry, but would have been stopped well before such a possibility. You must remember. We knew who they were, . . . and where they were."

"And, Hack winds up shot. That's a hell of a price to pay." Carin was determined no words nor explanation could ever justify the happening.

* * *

By early evening, Hack was beginning to ease from his overly sedated state and able to carry a reasonable conversation. Complaining little from the pain, it was a gallant attempt at trying to avoid placing additional concerns and worry on Carin. Until she related all of the facts, he had been totally unaware of what had actually occurred. The impact of the bullet and the shock that followed had sent him to sudden unconsciousness.

He listened to her explanation but was too tired to be overly inquisitive. Carin helped him sit-up in bed to eat his dinner. His right shoulder was heavily bandaged and his arm in a sling tied to his chest. She cut his food and he ate left-handed.

"What did the doctor say about the damage?" he asked between bites.

"Evidently, it was a pretty clean wound. From what I understand, the bullet . . . ," she grimaced at the word, "the bullet entered just below your shoulder joint and went all the way through. Other than a few bone chips, there wasn't anything vitally hit."

"That's good. Glad it wasn't my the other side. It might have affected my golf swing."

"Yeah, maybe so," Carin added, "but you'll probably rupture yourself if you try jerking-off left-handed."

They both laughed, helping to ease the tension.

* * *

Loaded with magazines, crossword books, candy, cards and a secreted bottle of Canadian, Hack spent the next day and night in the hospital. He was scheduled to be released the following morning. In the meanwhile, at his insistence, Carin rested in a new room provided them at the Fountaine Bleu -- courtesy of the federal government.

"Hi, babe." Carin poked her head through the door. "Look at what I've got." She carried two large bags.

"I don't know what it is, but it sure as hell smells good," he responded while moving to meet her.

"A little treat from the hotel . . . and our government friends," she joked. "I put it on their tab."

Removing the items exposed two huge stuffed lobsters, baked potatoes with scads of butter and sour-cream, clams casino as appetizer, an array of delicacies for dessert, and two bottles of rather expensive looking wine.

"What in the hell did all this cost? Not that I really care," he added.

Carin broadly grinned. "Two hundred and sixty-two bucks . . . with tip."

"Are you shittin' me?" He gasped.

"Nope. The wine was eighty bucks a bottle."

"Got those mothers by the short hair, huh?"

She responded with a wry smile. "Yep. Sure did."

Sitting on opposite sides of his bed table, they attacked the meal with great relish. Flowing through the courses at a steady pace, they fell short in leaving room for dessert, but did finish the first bottle of wine and opened the second. Carin busied herself in cleaning up the debris and bustled off to wash her hands.

"Could we come in? We're working on the case and need to ask you a few questions, if you're up to it." The man leading the other didn't wait for Hack to either agree or disagree, regarding their welcome. They entered the room and moved directly to him. Hack sat on the edge of the bed as the leader of the two offered his hand in a handshake and then withdrew it sheepishly, noticing the incapacitation of his arm. "We'd like to take just a few minutes of your time."

"Okay, what do you want to know?"

"On the ship, did you notice, or were you aware of, any persons handling your luggage other than the steward?"

"Nope. We hardly got any sleep at all the last night aboard. I gave one of the stewards a twenty to finish our packing that morning and handle the bags on our arrival at customs."

"Was there anything at all you might consider suspicious during the port call at Nassau?"

"Nope. Nothing."

"You didn't miss a piece of your luggage, . . . even briefly?"

"Nope. Not at all. We didn't spend much time in the cabin. What are you getting at?"

Carin entered the room and moved to the window, keeping clear of the meeting.

The agent followed her with his eyes. "Nothing important, we . . ."

Hack interrupted his response. "Nothing important? Hummm." He grunted and paused as he shifted his body position. "Tell me one thing. How in the hell did they get the stuff in our bags?"

"Evidently, at a time during the layover your golf valise was removed from the cabin. They rigged a false bottom inside it large enough to hide several pounds of pure heroin. Chances are the drugs weren't even put into the satchel until just before it left the boat for customs inspection. The odds of your ever detecting anything were virtually nil."

Hack shook his head in disbelief and caught the glare of anger emanating from Carin.

"Is there anything more we can do for you?" the second of the inquisitors asked.

"Yeah. You can get the fuck outta here."

Starting to mumble what seemed to be an apology, the agent decided it better to make his exit. The second followed his lead.

Just before they closed the door, Hack couldn't resist the opportunity for a last remark. "By the way, . . . dinner was great. Thanks."

Carin burst into laughter.

The agents looked at them like they were both nuts, gave each other a puzzled gaze, and disappeared down the hall.

CHAPTER VIII

Following the return from Miami, Hack had little choice other than heed the doctor's advice about avoiding active athletic endeavors. Even though the initial recuperative period was less than a full two months, each hour, day, and week, seemed like an eternity. Understandably, Carin was in her glory during his convalescence, having him confined to her presence. She was delighted in her role-playing as nurse and the fact they were together practically every moment of the day. With his dedicated attention to therapy, he responded in excellent fashion and found the early return to golf a convenient excuse for needed exercise. Work during the week was about back to normal. That meant about fifty-fifty course and office time.

The alarm rung at five-thirty. Hack reacted spontaneously, and with great vigor, considering the early morning hour. Rushing through a shower and shave, he then chose a pair of slacks and tried on several sport shirts before opting on a final selection. Mitch and a couple other players from the club were picking him up for their trip north. Nervously, he checked the clock any number of times and finally decided to have another cup of coffee during the wait.

Sipping the steaming brew, he tried remembering the last time he had drank tea instead of coffee. It seemed important, but didn't know why, and, on top of that, he really couldn't remember. However, his revelation was somewhat indicative of the overall radical change in his lifestyle since separation and divorce. Leaning back in the chair, his mind wandered through adventures of golf, trips and sexual encounters. It was staggering to realize the numbers of new experiences. Discontent with such a seriousness of mood, he altered his concentration, attempting to picture the layout of the course and how he might play it according to descriptions and boasts of several of his buddies. Originally, there were supposed to be five foursomes making the trip, but at the last count, it was down to three. He wondered if there would even be that many.

Picking up the phone, he dialed Mitch's number, waited for a dozen rings, then returned the receiver to its cradle. At least they're on the way, he thought as he carried the cup to the window. Staring at the street below, it seemed as if he had experienced the same feelings and identical moments, sometime before. It was unsettling. The last time he could recall spending any similar instance, there was snow on the ground, and . . . "That was the night I met Terry," he said aloud to himself. A strange chilling sensation surged through his body whenever he thought of her and the misfortunate lack of a relationship. His trance was so deep, he didn't even notice a car pull to the curb. Finally, the blare of the horn snapped him from his subliminal state. Al was driving his Lincoln and leaned through its window to see Hack motion he would be right down. Gathering his gear, he clambered down the steps and headed for the automobile. His clubs, shoes and golf valise were jammed into the already crammed trunk and they were soon on the road headed for Pennsylvania. Mitch rode up front as Al drove -- Mac and Hack sat in the rear.

"How long do ya think it'll take?" Mac broke the silence.

"Don't know," Hack answered shrugging his shoulders.

Mitch turned and peered over the seat. "A little over two hours. Depends on Sunday morning traffic. Shouldn't be too bad."

Al nodded his head in agreement and turned to quickly glance at Hack. "How's the shoulder coming?"

"Pretty good. I get a twinge every now and then."

"I got shot one time when I was a kid," Mac interjected.

"No shit," Hack responded.

"Yeah. A load a rock salt from a shotgun . . . dead in the ass." He laughed. "Got caught stealin' a watermelon from a farmer's field. Hurt like hell."

"By the way," Mitch said, changing the subject, "you took off for Florida so sudden after Morty was in town, I never did get to ask what happened after you left that night. If you don't remember, we were supposed to wheel the following day. How come you didn't make it?"

Hack chuckled. "Man, if you only knew."

"So tell me."

Hack began relating the entire events from beginning to end. Mitch called him a 'bastard' for not letting him know about Pat. Mac enjoyed the details so much he came close to getting his cookies. Al scared the hell out of everyone, twice, by not devoting enough attention to the road. Hack's story started the ball rolling and each of the others volunteered their own experiences and memorable tidbits. The conversation eventually spun around toward golf and they were soon planning wagers in anticipation of the rest of the guys meeting them at Penn National.

Time sped rapidly while they had been talking. Having just bypassed Hagerstown, calculations indicated they had traveled over halfway. Glancing at his watch, Hack realized there was little or nothing other than a golf date important enough to get him out so early. He gazed out of the window at the fleeting tree tops, after sliding down in the seat. Resting his head in the corner, he was soon cat napping. The swerve of the car making a sharp turn and coming to a halt jarred him awake. "I see the 'Mick' made it," he heard Mac comment. Raising up and taking a general survey, it was evident there would be at least two foursomes. Al continued into the parking area, found a spot, and they all piled out of the car. As stiff from the ride as Hack's group acted, it must have made them appear to be easy meat. Before they were able to extract their gear from the trunk, Mitch and Hack were being coaxed into wheeling. Mitch hadn't played for over a week and couldn't be swayed. After the attempt failed, all agreed to a series of independent four ball matches.

The course was said to be relatively long and an evident consideration for Mitch's hesitancy. Hack's game was more conducive to tighter and shorter courses. Furthermore, his injury had to be an added factor. Mick's foursome went off first.

Preliminary descriptions of the course proved to be true. It was long and also fairly new. Certain areas were still being landscaped and construction hadn't been totally completed on the watering system. Fairways were reasonably wide and the greens large and well trapped. By the third hole, Hack's muscles began to loosen and he started swinging more freely. Unfortunately, the rotten scores taken on the first two holes put him down on all of his one-on-one bets. Since there were individual and four balls with the other foursome, as well as among their own group, automatic presses were previously arranged on all two-down situations. After the seventh, Hack's legs began to feel the strain of covering the hilly layout. He cursed the decision to walk, rather than ride. Furthermore, carrying his bag over the left shoulder was awkward and bothersome.

Mitch birdied the eighth and Hack got the only par on nine -- both being a saving factor in most of their team wagers. The first group was waiting in the clubhouse after completing the front side. Everybody ordered sandwiches and collected or paid their bets. An open discussion began about what would get going on the second nine. "How about the 'Hacker' and me?" Mick offered.

Hack was sitting with his back to him. Not believing what he had just heard, he twisted slowly in his chair and gave him a curious glare. Mick was known to turn in some pretty good rounds, but both he and Hack could be rather erratic in their play. The point was proven by results of their first nine scores. Still dumbfounded and unable to muster a response, a sheet of paper rapidly circulated. An abundance of bets were recorded considering the small group. Mitch stared his disapproval at Hack while negatively shaking his head. Hack managed a meek shrug, slid his chair from the table, and retreated to the men's room.

Returning and viewing the list, it was easy to see why everybody was raring to go. All players had taken each other in the field. Having more guts than sense, Mick refused to put a limit on the amount that could be wagered. There were quite a few with twenty dollars across the board, and none less than ten. The groups changed positions on the tee with Mick moving to join Hack, Mitch and Al, while Mac dropped behind. Heading out of the door, a familiar voice yelled from the parking area. "Hey, Mick. Wait for us." Ape trotted toward them babbling his tale about car trouble, asking that he, and the other three with him, be included in the action. The two wheeler's chances, certainly not the best to start, suddenly took an even bigger downward turn. With the additions of the new arrivals, the total wagered was twelve hundred dollars. Hack had played for larger sums, but generally under better odds. Mick's personality exuded self-confidence, but he was usually considered as being fairly frugal with his money. God, Hack thought to himself, make him play good.

Sharing a cart together and riding down the first fairway, Hack began to feel a bit easier after Mick's explanation. "Listen," he began. "This back nine's not quite as long as the front and it's trickier than hell. There's only two of us out of the whole bunch that's played here before, Al and myself. Believe me, they've got their hands full and don't know it." Heeding Mick's advice carefully, whenever offered, Hack parred two holes in aiding the cause. They bogeyed number three, four and eight, birdied six, and finished two-over par. For what it was worth, Al and Mitch had an ample share of problems and needed help desperately from their partners. The anticipation of waiting for the following groups grew with each passing moment. Mick's self-assuredness bordered cockiness favoring their chances.

Mac's foursome lumbered into the clubhouse and gave their scores. Hack breathed a sigh of relief after a preliminary assessment indicated he and his partner were running well ahead. After everything was tallied, they split almost seven hundred dollars between them. Everyone was mumbling about how difficult and unfair the nine played. Hack bought a round of beer which hardly cheered them. Mitch continued flirting with the waitress and Mick eventually ordered and paid for a second round.

"Well, what the hell we gonna do?" Harry broke the brief silence. "I didn't drive all this fuckin' way just to sip suds."

"Yeah, we got time for another nine," Everett echoed encouragement, swallowing the last of his beer. "You going to do it again?"

"Don't know." Hack looked at Mick, searching for his reaction.

"Doubt if we can get that lucky twice in a row," he returned his opinion and smiled. "Hell, we're pretty well up. Let's give them a chance to get even or we'll never hear the end of it."

Mick had a superior short game. His biggest problem was a recurring hook. As well as he had been hitting the ball during earlier rounds, his tee shot deserted him. The more he tried to compensate, the worse it became. The both of them scrambled all over the course, miraculously managing to miss only one out of the first six holes. The eighth hole, they both double-bogeyed. On the ninth and final hole, Mick made par and the round was completed at three over par. After tallying the results, they lost a little more than half of what they had previously won, but were still ahead for the day.

It was late afternoon, but much too early to call it quits. Trips away from home to play golf were like marathons. It was rare to ever stop before dark. Everett and Mac decided to test their abilities against the field, and the group challenged for another complete eighteen. Hack was exhausted even before the last nine began and struggled on practically every shot. There was no real pain in his shoulder, only a growing weariness throughout his entire body from lack of stamina and physical weakness. The sun was disappearing behind a mountain as he entered the club and almost collapsed on a lounge sofa.

"Damn, I'm starving," Mick moaned. "Let's head to the inn and put on the feed bag."

"Uh, . . . well a, . . . I don't know," Al looked and sounded reluctant. "Wife wasn't feeling the best last night and I ought'a get back a'fore too late."

Other than being tired, everyone was in excellent spirits for the most part. Although, as usual, a couple of guys continued mumbling about an aspect of their game they must have left at home. Out of the twelve, Mick, Mitch, Ape and Hack were in no particular hurry. Al and Everett divided the remainder and struck out on the return trip. "What's up now?" Hack asked.

Approaching Mick from behind, Ape gouged him in both sides of his rib cage. "Hey, baby cakes. What about that swingin' place you been jawin' about?"

Mick jumped and rubbed his sides vigorously. "You big bastard. Damn it, that hurt. Don't know your own strength. Fuckin' Ape." Ol' Ape was hard to offend. His blush was his apology. "Damn," Mick continued. "Let's go. I gotta eat or I'm gonna be sick."

Ape hurriedly grabbed two more beers, offering one to Mick in a peace gesture. Mick hesitated, smiled, then affectionately poked the overgrown monster in his belly.

The inn, only a hop, skip, and a jump down the road, was quaint in decor, favoring Pennsylvania Dutch. It sat directly across the highway from yet another course. Having been greeted very cordially on entering the old historic structure, the hall and small lobby abounded with assorted pottery and handcrafted items. Except for a small counter occupying a corner, the room could have passed for a private home.

An older gent welcomed them, excused himself, and departed through a door behind the desk. He shortly reappeared from their rear. "This way gentlemen. Or, perhaps you would care to refresh yourselves before you dine." Mick nodded an approval.

Leading them down a hallway and into a large and very modernly equipped lavatory, the elderly gentleman made sure each was provided with fresh wash cloths and towels. "Hell, this is great," Mitch bubbled through the water he scooped to his face.

"Thought you'd like it." Mick was pleased. "Stay here whenever I get the chance. It's generally hard as hell to get a room for a weekend. Golfers gobble this place up."

After washing his face and hands, Hack ran cold water from the spigot, filling his mouth with the cold liquid. Finding it pleasantly sweet, like that of a mountain spring, he smiled at his own ignorance, remembering where they were. City water in such a remote area was a bit ridiculous. "All set?"

"Yeah," the rest of the group chimed.

Double doors led to the dining room. Many tables filled the area; some round; a few square. Handsomely carved wooden high-back chairs guarded elegant place settings. Except for two elderly couples, the other four or five groups present were all male. Out of habit, Mitch led the way, choosing a table offering a view of the highway. Taking a chair with his back to the window, Hack first stood and strained to see whatever possible of the course just beyond the road. "It's obvious you've played that spread." Hack pointed over his shoulder with his thumb, directing his question to Mick.

"Sure have. Quite a few times."

"What do they call it?"

"Caledonia."

"Well, I'll be damned. So, that's Caledonia." Hack turned to stare once more into the steadily increasing outside darkness. "Heard the guys talk a lot about it. What's it like, anyway?"

"Wicked little place." Mick smiled.

Mitch entered the conversation. "Nine holes, huh?"

"No, hell no. A full eighteen."

Ape gained interest. "You said little. You mean par three?"

"Naaah, I didn't mean small as little goes. It can be a rough son of a bitch." Mick shook his head in emphasis. "Distance ain't too long, but baby, I kid you not, there's holes like you've never seen before."

"Lotta doglegs, huh?" Ape asked.

"That's puttin' it mild. Hills and doglegs galore. It's built around the side and over the top of the whole mountain."

Strangely, until Mick mentioned it, Hack hadn't paid much attention to the gigantic mound hovering over the small clubhouse. Looking upward, the mass of earth's crest was silhouetted by a moonlit sky. Hack turned back to the table at the instant huge steins were being placed before each of them. After tasting the concoction, that definitely wasn't beer, the puzzled look on his face prompted Mick's explanation that it was a specialty of the house served complimentary on Sundays due to local blue laws.

"Damn," Hack moaned. "How the hell did we get served at the course? I had myself all primed for a few good, very chilled, extra dry, double, . . . martinis." He barely got the last word out, licking his lips as if to savor what he was being denied.

Mick laughed as he eagerly attacked the relish trays. "That was a private club. Only reason we got to play was because Pete's brother's the manager. If you need a transfusion that bad, I've got bottles in the trunk."

"Hey. Wonder how the stuff would taste spiked?" Ape joked.

Mitch motioned to the waitress. "I know you can't sell liquor today, but is there any reason we can't use our own?"

"Are you a guest of the inn, sir?"

It looked as though he considered lying, but replied, "No, mam." The sweet old lady looked so loveable, undermining the situation was impossible.

"Well, sir," she responded, "we have a policy of allowing only overnight guests to have their own bottle privileges."

"Why don't we order?" Hack suggested.

Mick didn't hesitate and blurted his choices faster than she could write. After completing her list, she smiled and moved gingerly away. Spending the interim waiting for the meal, subjects of conversation ran the gambit from one thing to another. The waitress eventually arrived pushing a serving cart loaded with food. "I spoke with my husband and, if you care to use the game lounge after the meal, you're welcome to have drinks there."

"Thank you." Mitch smiled with his answer. "I don't think we'll be able to be here that long, but it's very nice of you to offer."

The food was bountiful and delicious, being served family style. There was pickled carrots, German fried potatoes, fresh green beans, sautéed onions, and mounds of roast beef. Settling down to some serious eating, the more they ate, the more she brought. Finally having to force himself to stop when it began to feel like it was coming out of his ears, Hack took the napkin from his lap, wiped his mouth, and folded it neatly beside his plate.

"Damn," Mick mumbled, trying to suppress a belch. "You know, it's a quarter 'til eleven."

"We should stay over and play that course across the way tomorrow." Ape chuckled his suggestion.

"Baby cakes, I'm tempted." Mick responded. "What do the rest of you think?"

Looking at each other, the idea appealed to everyone.

After paying the check, Mick headed for a phone while the others registered at the desk. He decided to call his wife and alibi with car trouble. Mitch really didn't give a damn about his job and, as was becoming the habit, Hack generally dictated his own schedule. On the other hand, Ape had it made. Having retired on disability from the police department, he spent every day at the club. He was a huge man, but other than being slightly overweight--even for the tremendous bulk of his size--at least on the surface there was no evidence of physical insufficiency. He was divorced, living alone, no kids to worry about, and golfed whenever and wherever he pleased. At the tender age of forty-three, being able to have such luxurious freedom was envious, no matter what the problem might have been.

The inn, primarily being a weekend resort attraction, emptied enough of its occupants to provide accommodations for their stay. The little old man was very pleased with the addition of unexpected guests and went to extra extremes to assure their comfort.

Still on the phone, Mick was having great difficulty in convincing his wife of the delay. He dangled his car keys, motioning for Hack to take them. Hack approached in a swaying and effeminate manner. He took the keys, put his arm around Mick's shoulder, faked a kiss with puckered lips, and in as sexy a female voice as possible said, "Lordy, how you turn me on, honey."

Mick grasped the received to his chest. "You prick. You'll get me killed." Hack jumped back to dodge Mick's fake swing and retreated to the car. In the trunk, there were several various types of liquors. Selecting two bottles, one scotch and the other bourbon, he made sure the automobile was locked and returned to find the lobby empty. On a chance, he figured they would be in the game room and headed in the most likely direction. Nearing the end of the hall, he distinctly heard the sound of clacking billiard balls. The room afforded just enough space for two tables and a row of chairs along opposite walls. Ape sat on the edge of a table while Mitch and Mick took turns poking at the cue ball on the other.

Spotting a small stand covered with a tray of glasses, soda, ginger ale and a pitcher of ice, Hack placed the bottles among the other items. Ape joined in helping fix drinks. Everybody chug-a-lugged the first, and while getting refills, they elected teams and manufactured a pool wager. All of them being about equally proficient, the match was fair and alternated in wins and loses. However, the more they played, the more they drank, and vice versa. Ape was basically a beer man and not accustomed to hard alcohol as compared to the other three.

Eventually alternating partners, Ape and Hack were a team for the game that was just beginning. Every time Ape drew the stick back, he would miscue and giggle louder with each attempt.

Finally catching the cue square, he made two of their balls. Hack shrugged his shoulders and patiently waited for his turn. Ape had retreated to his perch on the edge of the other table. Before they knew it, he was passed out cold. Stopping long enough to hoist his legs with great effort, they drug his gigantic frame into a position so that his entire body rested lengthwise on the felt-covered slab. Failing to disrupt proceedings, the game continued until they were all highly inebriated. Occasionally, someone would test Ape without having success in arousing him.

Mick was aligning a shot while chalking the tip of his cue stick. He turned, looked at Ape pathetically, leaned across and twisted the square against the tip of his nose. "Damn glare was gettin' to me." He chuckled devilishly.

"Man, I'm tired. I'm gonna hit the sack," Hack declared and pointed at Ape. "What'd you want'a do with him?"

"Let him lay," Mick stated firmly. "Hell, we'd never get that lard ass upstairs without a truck crane."

Mitch retrieved the table's plastic cover and spread it entirely over Ape; head and all.

"Damn, brother, you can't do that. He might suffocate or somethin'," Hack warned.

"Yeah. Maybe you're right." They both grabbed a corner near his head, folded it back, and tucked it neatly under his chin. Mick caught the light switch as they left and staggered toward their rooms.

Once inside, Hack came close to jumping into bed without shedding his clothes. Barely enough reasoning remained to realize he had to wear the same things the following morning. Completely undressed, he eased between the cool sheets and floated into dreamland wondering which one it was in the next room he heard losing the contents of his stomach. Sleep came as a rush and overpowered his senses so totally, the pounding on the door seemed to be a million miles away. The persistent racket eventually prompted his response.

"Go'way."

"You planning on sleepin' all day?" Mitch's voice bordered between frustration and fun.

"Holy shit. I just got in bed. What time is it?"

"Late," he retorted. "Come on and get your ass up."

Hack's toes touched the floor as he edged slowly from the bed, making sure his legs would hold under the effort. He moved to the bathroom, twisted the faucets, and the shower sprang to life. The pounding beads of cold water worked very quickly to cleanse the fuzz from his brain. After toweling, dressing, and brushing his teeth with his index finger, he slowly and carefully proceeded to join the others. Mitch and Mick were already having coffee. "Where's the big guy?"

Both of the Irishmen started to respond simultaneously. Mitch gave way to Mick. "He's upstairs washin'. Must've slept on the table all night. He got me up this mornin singin' in the hallway."

As he spoke, Ape entered the dining room. "You bunch of bastards. You dirty bastards," he repeated. "Why the hell'd you leave me like that last night?"

"You gotta be kiddin'." Mitch laughed with his remark. "We couldn't have moved you with dynamite."

"Well, the least you could'a done was moved the fuckin' balls off the table. I slept on half of 'em, all night." He rubbed the small of his back.

"We're surprised you made it up at all," Hack joked.

"Oh, yeah." He began to blush. "Some poor ol' colored lady got scared shitless when she came in to clean up the mess this mornin'. She knocked over a pail and I must'a jumped up at the noise from under that damn cover. She hollered and took off like a bat outta hell." He plopped into a chair as they all chuckled at his misfortune.

"You big shit," Mick offered. "If you'd go on a diet, maybe we could carry you home next time. Besides, you've been gettin' kind'a heavy on the course, too."

"Fuck you."

Mick's remark about dieting didn't come close to phasing Ape as he ate enough for all of them. By nine-thirty, they were at the car getting their gear. Sometime during the night it had rained. The air contained a sweet odor of fresh and uncontaminated nature. Walking across the highway and the short distance to the clubhouse, they placed their golf bags in the rack and went inside to get green fees. The two small rooms of the shack were barren except for a counter and three tables with chairs. It was different from the majority of places they frequented. Most pro shops were abundantly arrayed with merchandise, and most public courses had halfway decent facilities. The nearest thing available representing a convenience were coke and candy machines on the porch. Hack imagined the course and its condition to be comparable to the rotting shed.

A roar of two gas carts being brought for their use diverted Hack's attention from the scorecard he had been reviewing. Electric carts were preferable and much quieter. However, combustion engines proved much more fitting in hilly surroundings. A four ball was agreed with Mitch and Hack as partners. The first tee was barren of grass and Hack smiled at himself, feeling gratified by his correct analysis in his earlier appraisal. "This is gonna be like a gravel pit," he mumbled beneath his breath.

Surprisingly, they all made good drives and had open shots to the green. The hole was three hundred and twenty yards by the card and doglegged rather severely to the right. Hack clearly noticed a sudden change as they neared the bend in the fairway. As he stood looking toward the first hole, the scene was breathtaking. A thirty-foot waterfall spewed from the side of the mountain, slightly behind and to the left of the green. A small trap filled with pure white sand that looked more like snow guarded the front. From tree line to tree line, there was plush and evenly mown grass. The rest of the course proved to be equally well tended. Except for the greens being a little too hard, it was fantastic. No two holes were the same -- each having its own individual character. It was suited perfectly for Hack's game and he was scoring exceptionally well.

There was no break between the nine holes. The first half of the eighteen were played going away, while the latter part wove its way back toward the shack, around and over the mountain. A light atmosphere prevailed filled with joking and laughter. There was little concern over the small amount wagered. They even gained an audience of kids for the few holes that bordered a narrow paved road servicing several rather plush homes set amid thick wooded lots.

On the fifteenth tee, Ape felt dizzy and plopped on a bench to steady himself. "You, okay?" Mitch asked.

"Yeah. Just short of breath."

"Take it easy. There's no hurry."

He sat for a few minutes and began cracking remarks, blaming the lack of sex as being the problem. Finishing the final four holes, his face was paled and lacking usual color. Any ideas regarding additional play weren't even mentioned. They all realized it best to get on the road for Ape's sake. On the return, he kept hitting the scotch during the long drive, hiding any indication as to how bad he actually felt. "You know what?" he began. "I ain't never enjoyed anything more than these past couple a days. Sure had a lot'a fun with you guys." The bottle top came off and he took another slug. "Never will forget when I got laid up and they pushed me into retirement. Didn't know what to do. That dumb broad I was married to, up and took off and never seen her since." He tipped the bottle again. "Got my divorce by mail. Then . . . then, I met you guys. Shit, my whole life's been the golf course ever since. Ain't got no other interests."

Ape was always the life of the party. Although a bit boisterous on occasion, practically everybody loved his pranks, dry humor, and ways of bringing out laughter. He was a fixture at the club. Unless he was on a golf outing elsewhere, not a single day passed without his presence. Hack watched nervously as Ape's difficulty to breathe was growing more apparent.

"Listen, baby cakes," Mick joked. "If anything ever happened to you, we'd bury your big ass under the first tee."

"No kiddin'." He grinned, taking the remark seriously.

"Hell, he'd feel more at home under a sand trap," Mitch corrected.

"You're full of shit." Ape started coughing as he tried to contain his laughter.

The clowning subsided and, soon, Ape slouched in the corner fast asleep. "He doesn't look very good," Mitch asserted. They all agreed.

"I was thinkin' about maybe gettin' by a doctor or somethin'." Mick versed his thoughts aloud.

"Damn good idea," Hack agreed.

Mutually deciding it best to stop by the hospital center, perspiration covered Apes forehead and they had trouble bringing him to consciousness. Mitch gained the assistance of a couple of interns who brought a stretcher and they wheeled Ape directly to the emergency room. Hack took Ape's wallet and retrieved a medical card for the purpose of obtaining his admittance. Following the necessary paperwork, they waited to talk to the doctor. He advised tests would be arranged, but early indications suggested a possible mild heart seizure. Ape was transferred to a critical-care section isolating him from visitors. Since there was nothing more they could do, Mick dropped Hack and Mitch at their places with the agreement they would meet later.

It was after seven by the time Hack finally got back. Climbing the stairs, it finally occurred to him, he had forgot to call anyone about being gone for the day. Before reaching the top, he could easily see the outer office door open, making it apparent Carin was either working or waiting for his return. Slipping quietly from his shoes, he peeked around the corner and tossed them ahead of his attempt to enter. Before he could take a step, one came sailing back through the door. Impishly, he picked it up and hobbled into his office. "I thought you weren't henpecked." Jerry roared with laughter. "You were my idol. Now, it's all destroyed."

"Up yours. What the hell you doing here, anyway?"

"A lack of compromise with the old lady. Carin left the door open for me. Just got here as a matter of fact."

"You finally did it." Hack shook his head. "It's hard to believe."

"Not much choice when you get caught fartin' around," he groaned.

"Are you shittin' me?"

"Nope," he affirmed. "Some dumb bitch got my phone number. I don't know how. Unlisted, you know." Jerry paused to swallow the last of his drink. "Anyway, she called and asked for me. When she found out I wasn't home, she bitched about getting stood up and banged the phone in Erica's ear."

Hack shuddered from the thought, almost personally feeling and sharing his dilemma. "Hummm, she booted you out?"

"You might put it that way."

"Well, you're welcome to stay here until you get things straight," Hack offered. "Got any other plans?"

"Hell, everything's happened so fast, I haven't had time to even think."

Hack moved to the bar. "What are you drinking?"

"Double bourbon. Straight," he emphasized.

"That's not going to solve anything. Just get you screwed up and feeling more sorry for yourself." Hack poured himself some Canadian and handed Jerry his glass. He plopped on the opposite end of the couch.

"Don't mean to bring more bad tidings," Jerry cautioned. "Carin was a bit disturbed at not knowing where you were."

"Screw her," Hack said, and then had second thoughts. "I don't really mean that."

"Guess it's none of my business, but you really ought to keep her a bit more up to date."

Hack started to respond.

"Now, wait a minute," Jerry interrupted and continued. "I don't mean because she's a woman . . . or . . . or anything to do with personal involvement. She is your secretary and you've seen fit to entrust her with an awful lot of responsibilities. You know damn well things happen. As on-the-ball as she may be, there's got to be a lot of things she just can't cope with when you're fuckin' around."

Hack nodded his head in half-hearted agreement.

"At least, if you had Tony here, it would have to help. Thought any more about it?"

"A little bit." Finishing the last swallow of his drink, Hack decided on another. Jerry handed his glass over to him for the same.

"Where you been, anyway?" Jerry asked, and moved to the couch to thoroughly enjoy Hack's story. It continued through a third drink, before heading across the street, and finished, as about the time they ordered dinner at Duke's. When they got back, Hack called Carin and there was no answer. He then dialed the hospital and had some problem in reaching the right doctor. Eventually, he was told Ape had definitely suffered a mild stroke, but was sleeping comfortably. No visitors for a few of days. The remainder of the evening, Hack listened to his brother's marital difficulties and finally dozed off with Jerry's interests diverted to television. Jerry made Hack get up long enough to open the couch and he barely remembered climbing back in the sack.

* * *

Carin woke them the next morning. Her initial irritation quickly subsided and altered to sincere concern after Hack explained circumstances involving Ape. By Thursday, Ape was out of intensive care. Later in the afternoon, Carin accompanied Hack to the hospital and was very cordial in helping to cheer the big man. Already in the best of spirits, there was little evidence he had suffered any malady. The doctor estimated his hospital stay to be at least another week, and he would have to avoid golf or strenuous activities for a few months. It was impossible to imagine Ape following either of the orders. They stayed for about an hour, leaving with the intention of returning to the office. On the spur of the moment, Hack headed the car toward the golf club. Carin was delighted when she realized where they were going.

As usual, familiar cars filled spaces near the front entrance. Their arrival, or more precisely, Carin's appearance, gained immediate attention. Wilt was the first on the scene. Hack made the introduction, then several more, and finally moved toward a vacant table near the windows overlooking the course. The pro joined them. "They out on the course?" Hack motioned with a nod toward the window with his query.

"About fourteen or fifteen of them," Wilt confirmed and immediately diverted his attention to Carin. "I hear you work for this duffer," he chided.

"That's right." She smiled at his remark. "When he's at work, which isn't very often, anymore."

Wilt chortled loudly. "Know what you mean."

"Okay, but don't complain ol' buddy, I help pay your salary." Hack winked. "By the way, you heard about Ape, I take it."

Wilt nodded affirmatively.

"We just came from the hospital," Carin filled in the void. "He looks great."

"Weird as hell how a big, strappin' guy like that comes down with heart problems."

"I know," she answered Wilt's comment. "It sure surprised me, too. I expected to see some shriveled up specimen. He'd put Hoss Cartwright to shame." Wilt giggled some more. Carin had

213

never been to a course and asked to move to the porch when it was mentioned the gang was coming into the last hole. Wilt kept her briefly occupied and informed while Hack ventured inside for beer. The pro was in his glory explaining events of the incoming play as she tried to return his interest on an equal basis. Mick and Mitch were in the lead group. Wilt confirmed they were wheeling, stimulating even more questions from Carin for him to answer. Hack left them sitting and went inside to watch them figure their results. Mitch wasn't in the best of moods. It was evident they probably hadn't faired too well. Muttering and mumbling to himself, he turned noticing Hack peering over his shoulder.

"You see that shit-ass putt I just missed. Hit the hole dead-center and it doesn't go. . . . Damn it. Son of a bitch."

"I hate to ask, but how'd you make out?"

"We won it all."

"You're shittin' me. Why in the hell are you so pissed off?"

"I needed it for an individual with Danny. Had him one down and blew it. I let him get off the hook." Beating Danny was more than a simple accomplishment and Hack truly understood Mitch's anguish. Seldom, if ever, did the man come out on the losing end. Danny possessed uncanny luck and ability to squeeze out of losing situations, time after time.

Mitch returned to his paperwork. Hack continued to idly watch, but his mind channeled to other things, highlighted by recalling a particular situation involving Danny. Sometime back, one of the young black workers at the club and Hack were wheeling. Danny arrived late and came running down the first fairway, wanting to get action so badly, he succumbed to their demands of one-up on all his bets. It was more of a disadvantage than it sounded, considering the wheel had already birdied the first hole. Danny played in the last group. Hack's partner Mel was tickled to death with their next few holes. After the fifth, they were three under par. Having missed number six, a birdie on seven, parring eight, and making another bird on nine, they finished four under. When Danny gave them his scores, they thought he was screwing with their minds. He birdied one, two and five, parred six where they missed, eagled seven, and closed them out on eight with a final bird. It explained his knocking a eighteen-inch putt fifteen foot past the hole on the ninth green. One of his trademarks was missing on purpose when he didn't have to hole-out.

Speak of the devil. "Hello, dere," Danny called loudly, bringing Hack back to the present, as he rushed toward him and boldly shook his hand. "Damn, it's good to see you. I heard you got shot and I was scared to death I'd lost one of my best turkeys." Mischief filled Danny's eyes as he winked and began to rub salt into Mitch's wounds. Suddenly, his attention was abruptly distracted by movement on the porch. "Hot damn," he said, practically drooling," who's that good-lookin' broad with Wilt?"

"My secretary."

There was a deafening silence among the entire group as they turned to stare in Hack's direction. Mitch spoke first. "Why, you stingy bastard. You've never said a word about havin' something like that around."

Before Hack could utter a response, Mitch and Danny dashed headlong for the porch and began beating Wilt's time. After visiting the men's room, Hack joined them and tolerated the lines and bullshit that was already knee-deep. Having allowed them to have their fun, moans and groans accompanied his declaration it was necessary for he and Carin to leave.

Carin had got a real thrill from all of the attention and, during the drive to the office, chattered on and on about how much she enjoyed the afternoon and his friends.

* * *

Attempts at limiting time at the club were becoming increasingly difficult. Hack found himself absolutely unable to resist the habitual infection affecting his existence. He rationalized subjecting Carin to his friends might offer grounds for her better understanding his need for them, and the associated environment of golf. However, the last couple of days hadn't reflected any change in her disposition relating to his absences.

Deciding there was no other choice, he desperately tried to recall Tony's home phone number. Fumbling through the stacks of unfiled papers without success, he resorted to flipping page after page of his desk calendar, terminating his search as the phone rang.

"Yeah."

"Baby cakes. Mick, here."

"What's up?"

"Got bad news. Ape kicked the bucket."

Hack groaned. "Aw, man. I don't believe it."

"Sorry to say it's true. I saw him yesterday and he took a quick turn for the worse last night. That was it."

"Holy shit. Poor guy. Poor bastard," Hack sympathized. "Supposed to have gone home today."

"That's right."

"Never know, do you?"

"Sure don't," he agreed. "Listen, I'd like to meet with you tomorrow afternoon, if you can. I already talked to Mitch."

"Well, yeah. Sure. What'd ya have in mind?"

"Figured we'd get together and work somethin' out for the funeral. There's nobody to take care of any details as far as we can determine."

Hack's first instinct was to deny the request. On second thought, he agreed. "Okay. Any special time?"

"Make it around two at my place."

Directions to Mick's home were provided in detail before closing the conversation. Hack pushed the button on the phone, sat holding the receiver in his hand, and tapped it against his forehead. The dial spun Mitch's number and on the first ring he answered. "Sittin' on the phone?" Hack joked.

"Not quite. I'm on the pot." He laughed. "Damn good thing this isn't one of those picture-type telephones. You'd see me at my worst."

Hack could hear him grunt. "To hell with a picture, I can almost smell the results."

"God forbid." He chuckled some more. "Naw, I drug the phone in here and was going to make a call. You rang."

"Yeah, just talked to Mick," Hack began. "Man. It floored me flat when he told me about Ape."

"You?" Mitch sounded equally exasperated. "Hell, me, too."

"Mick said you were going to meet him at his house tomorrow. He wants me to be at his place at two. You know any more than what he told me?"

"Did he mention the nurse?" Mitch asked.

"No, nothing at all. What nurse? Don't tell me Ape went while he was fuckin' his brains out?"

Mitch laughed. "Hell, no. Mick probably planned to fill you in later. I really don't know the whole story myself, but Ape must have had a premonition of what was comin'. He had his nurse scribble out what could probably be considered a last-minute will and testament, and things he wanted done."

"What things?" Hack interrupted.

"Not sure. She gave the list to Mick. I figured them to be typical of getting rid of his personal crap, or whatever."

"I forgot to ask earlier. Where's he at, now?"

"Still at the hospital. They're going to perform an autopsy sometime tomorrow morning. As much as there is of him, it'll probably last for a couple of days."

"Ol' Ape would've appreciated that remark." Hack chuckled while beginning to sincerely feel the loss of a friend. Mitch grunted again. "Sorry I interrupted your work," Hack forced the joke. "I can hear you're still hard at it. See ya tomorrow."

* * *

Wednesday afternoon, Hack's attentions were demanded by rather important office matters, making it impossible to meet with Mitch and Mick. Later in the evening, he talked with them and was provided with some of the details. Mick was handling all of the arrangements and scheduled the funeral for Friday morning. It appeared to be a rather quick burial, but hell, why affect weekend play. Gabe, Danny, Wilt, Mick, Mitch and Hack were to be pallbearers. The last-minute requests Ape had supplied to the nurse turned out to be only additions to already existing papers found in personal possessions at his apartment. A couple of other police force dropouts from the club pitched in, notified several of his old precinct pals, and made arrangements to fill certain provisions noted in the will.

Carin popped her head in the door. "Hey. You're going to be late. Better get the lead out and get ready."

"I am ready," Hack corrected.

"You're what?"

"I know. I feel odd as hell going like this, but it's one of Ape's ideas."

Her dumbfounded expression begged for an explanation.

217

"If you really knew the big man, you'd realize the reason for the outfit. First off, this was one of his last formal requests. Besides, other than a uniform, I doubt he ever dressed in a suit in his life. He'd turn over in his coffin if he thought this was made into a somber occasion. Ape couldn't stand to see anyone down-in-the-mouth. Hell, to him, everything was one big joke." Her expression never altered as she walked from the door shaking her head. It was clear she thought they were all insane, visually indicating her distaste as Hack walked past her desk and down the stairs.

Barely reaching the sidewalk, he confronted one of his better clients fast approaching. "Hello, Mr. Busher. How are you today?"

The customer's face contorted into a usual frown as his voice bordered on a growl. "Stomach's raisin' hell, again. I'm just on my way to see you."

"I'm awfully sorry I'm in such a hurry," Hack apologized, "but I've got to get to the funeral home. Could anyone else help you?"

"Guess they'll have to," he grumbled, as his eyes ogled him suspiciously.

Rather abruptly, Busher moved past and disappeared through Hack's office entrance. Suddenly, the truth of the matter struck Hack like a ton of bricks. There he stood ignoring a good client, dressed for no other purpose than golf, and evidently fabricating a lie about his true destination. There was no other conclusion to be drawn. "Maybe I should go back and explain," he expressed aloud, drawing the attention of nearby pedestrians. "Damn it," he muttered, suppressing further reaction to thought. He'll get over it. I wasn't lying. Why worry?

Continuing delays prevailed. Some idiot had parked illegally and blocked his car restricting any immediate possibility of escape. With the help of parking attendants, they managed to roll the obstructing auto clear. Taking advantage of every opportunity, and creating some for himself, he sped his way in hopes of making up for lost time. Finding a parking space near the funeral home was impossible. Four blocks away was the best available spot. Covering the distance fairly fast by running most of the way, he cleared the twelve steps leading up the front entrance three at a time, pushed the heavy door open, and struggled desperately to compose himself, gasping for breath. A directory hanging on the wall nearby listed Ape as being laid-out in the 'Rose Room.' "That's great," he mumbled, "the poor bastard thought only girls and qays liked flowers."

The building was an older structure reflecting many years of use. Typically high ceilings, bordered by hand-sculptured plaster moldings, undoubtedly once hooded a remarkable past. As hack started to move toward the stairway at the end of the long hall, the front door opened. "Hey, wait for me."

Recognizing Mick's voice, he spun around, a bit surprised. "Don't tell me you're late, too?"

Mick laughed. "Not really. I just fudged a bit on the time to you guys. Figured I'd play it safe and tell you make it a hour earlier than necessary.

"You asshole." It pissed Hack at first, but he quickly felt relief he wouldn't have to walk into the service after it had already began.

"Anyone else here?" Mick asked.

"How the hell should I know? I just walked in." Hack sounded exasperated.

"Walk hell," he chuckled. "I saw you tearin' ass up the street and takin' steps three at a time. I tried to holler at ya. You didn't even hear me." The dirty look Hack gave him made the smile on Mick's face only broaden as they walked to the rear of the hallway.

A small area set back from the wall housed an opening for an elevator, almost totally undetectable until one passed its location. The old lift looked as ancient as the building itself. An equally aged man sat perched on a stool, completely unaware of their approach. On noticing their presence, he tried desperately to conceal the racing form beneath his tail as he tried to raise and flopped once again on the seat.

"Gu . . . gu . . . good mornin'," he stammered. "Nice day for a funeral."

"Never thought of it that way." Mick snickered.

The outer doors slammed shut as the old gent struggled closing the iron latticed inner door. Cursing under his breath, he jerked several times on the lever before the gears engaged, jolting them into an upward movement.

"Third floor, please," Hack requested.

Whirring sounds, creaks and groans, echoed through the shaft as it strained to climb the distance to the top. Mick's face mirrored Hack's expression of disbelief and the wonder if they'd ever make it. The old guy seemed quite unconcerned by the events and never deviated from staring dead ahead through the entire trip.

"Holy shit, we could'a walked faster," Mick whispered as the contraption clambered to a halt and the doors finally slid open. They wasted little time clearing themselves and caught a glimpse of the old dude quickly returning his attentions to his paper.

"Hell. He looked like a corpse himself," Hack said, shaking his head.

"You ain't kiddin'," Mick agreed jokingly. "Probably lousy pay, but I'll bet ya' two to one he gets great burial benefits."

"Yeah, and all the formaldehyde he can drink, too."

A small sign pointed the way to the front where they found the room that held their big friend. They entered and stood before the bier.

"Don't look bad as a stiff, does he?" Mick offered.

"As far as being a stiff goes," Hack responded. "Hell, he looks about the same as he did that night on the pool table." No sooner had he finished his quip, he noticed the putter laying along side his body in the coffin. "Whose idea was that?"

"Mine," Mick answered. "Kind'a figured as old as the damn thing was, it deserved a decent burial, too." He turned and grabbed Hack by the arm. "Come on, let's go get a smoke."

On the second floor, they found a lounge and also the other four of the pallbearer's group. "What took y'all so long?" Gabe queried.

"Yeah," Mitch interjected. "We've been here almost an hour already."

"Sorry about that," Mick said as he reached for a cigarette from Hack's pack. "Knowin' you guys, I had to get you here ahead. Besides, I need to fill y'all in on some stuff before things get started." Hack flopped on the couch next to Danny. Mick stood in the center of the floor as he continued. "You all know by now that Ape wanted us to dress this way. He said he didn't want anything to be morbid at all to mar the event. Anyway, there's several other requests that he made. Between Mitch and myself, we've already covered a few of them."

"Like what?" Wilt asked.

"His old poker buddies for one," Mick answered. "I let them know and they were anxious to make a good showing." He paused to drag on the cigarette. "Catch this for size. Bet'cha didn't know ol' Ape was once in the police band."

"You're kiddin'." Danny choked on his heavy drag from the fat cigar clenched between his teeth.

"Like hell I am. Better than that, he played the flute."

Picturing his big ass tooting a delicate instrument was too much to grasp in reality. The entire sextet burst into laughter. Mick pulled a flask from his hip pocket and passed it around as he continued to fill the guys in on other procedures to follow throughout the ceremonies. His speech lasted much longer than his provided refreshment. Stretching the point, a few of the assigned tasks were logically reasonable. However, a few others bordered on an area of sacrilegiousness. In the middle of his speech, the funeral director interrupted Mick's oration. They briefly huddled together, whispering details remote to the ears of those in the room. Mick, in turn, related secrecies of the meeting, indicating that things were to be delayed. There would be almost another hour before services were rescheduled to begin. A motion was brought to the floor and unanimously passed to jaunt across the street for added fuel.

Hack never drank in the morning and only rarely in the afternoon. However, not wanting to be different, he joined the mood of the crowd. It was a crummy joint, but the booze tasted the same as anywhere else. Gabe was basically quite timid, and funerals, certainly not his forte. Having to attend, let alone participate in a wake, was very objectionable. Also, he really wasn't much of a drinker. The slug taken earlier from Mick's flask had caused his eyes to bulge indicating the overdose he gulped. After a couple of additional stiff ones at the tavern, increased giggling and an overall altering of his personality indicated his growing intoxication.

On their return to the mortuary a small but sympathetic group had gathered in the parlor where Ape reclined. Only a few females were present. They were evidently wives of Ape's police buddies or some of his old girlfriends they knew nothing about. In total, there were about thirty people in attendance. Mick led the way to a front row where they all discretely took seats, except for Gabe. He caught the edge of a folding chair and would have sprawled on the floor if Danny hadn't grabbed him by his belt.

"Oh, God," Mitch mumbled, as a sudden hush came over the room as the parson appeared.

The service started. After giving his religious opinions, the minister gave way to Lyle Lowater. It was difficult to restrain laughter at learning he had been chosen to provide the eulogy. He was probably Ape's closest drinking buddy, but had a horrible lisp and stuttering problem, especially exaggerated whenever nervous or excited. It took him twenty-five minutes to give what should have been a five-minute address. Gabe didn't budge an inch through the ordeal. He simply sat with a 'shit-eatin' grin the entire time.

Their group remained seated as other mourners filed past Ape and continued out the door. After the last had left, the home's manager and an assistant appeared. They immediately lowered and hooked the lid of the coffin. An eerie feeling passed through Hack as he watched Ape disappear. A third gentleman joined the other two and they wheeled the cart with Ape's casket down the hallway and onto the waiting elevator. "There's plenty of room for everyone." The man nearest welcomed them aboard.

"No thanks. We'd rather walk," Hack blurted, as he turned quickly for the stairs. "No offense intended to Ape, but he's got no worry if the damn thing drops to the bottom."

"You wouldn't catch me on that fuckin' rattletrap again for a million bucks," Mitch vowed.

"I see you rode up, too." Mick laughed.

They were downstairs and outside in a flash. Eventually, Ape came riding through the front door and instructions were given as to the proper method of carrying the coffin. Gabe was positioned in the middle on Hack's and Mitch's side. His condition wasn't any improved and he stumbled twice getting to the hearse. Hack was helpless to stop Gabe's incessant humming. The six of them were placed in what would normally be the family limousine and shortly the procession was on its way. Danny and Mick had bought half-pints during the earlier visit to the beer joint and broke them open. Gabe had his own and attempts to limit his intake weren't very successful.

The cemetery was located in the northern section of the city adjacent to one of the courses they occasionally played. The locale was quite fitting. Miraculously, they made it from the hearse to the grave site without losing Gabe. Standing as the last few words were spoken, Hack noticed only half of the people attending at the funeral home were present. One of the guys from Ape's old band stepped forward wielding a trumpet and commenced blowing taps. Before the last note faded, the bugler broke into a swing rendition of 'When the Saints Go Marching In.' Danny kicked Gabe in the ass with his knee when the latter started clapping hands and stomping his foot to the beat.

With the 'concert' over, and most of the onlookers beginning to drift away, Mick stepped forward and removed a layer of flowers covering Ape's old bag of golf clubs. He pulled out the driver and handed it to Danny. "Gabe was supposed to do the honor, but, under the circumstances, maybe you'd better do it," Hack heard Mick whisper to Danny.

"What the hell am I supposed to do?" he pleaded.

"Just tee up and hit one over in those heavy woods. You know, a last salute from his golf pals."

Reluctantly, Danny moved to a position near the bier, found a level spot, and teed the ball. He took a brief practice swing and then addressed the shot. Right at the top of his back swing, Gabe started puking. Between the unexpected distraction and his own consumption of spirits, he hit the ball square in the heel of the club. It was a low-liner, nailing a tombstone dead center about forty-feet away, ricocheting like a bullet straight back at them. It happened so fast, no one had time to duck. With the good Lord's blessing, the only casualty was a statue of cupid getting castrated in the process.

CHAPTER IX

Making room for his new business manager required only minor adjustments. There was plenty of space in the outer office even though Carin didn't particularly appreciate the invasion on her privacy. However, things being what they were, the two soon adjusted and a congenial atmosphere prevailed. Tony started work about a week after the funeral. It was hard to believe four months had passed and another winter rapidly neared. Hack missed Ape, as did all his friends. Stories regarding his burial, although dreadfully exaggerated, would be a topic of conversation at the club for many years to come.

Business had been relatively slow even though Tony seemed to be working extremely hard. His presence certainly helped in lieu of Hack's continuing and frequent absences. However, at the same time, it proved to be a hindrance for the boss, affecting his social behavior around the office. Tony's dedication to overtime at night and on weekends made it awkward to entertain during evenings or to sleep late in the morning.

Hack sat mesmerized in meditation, depressed at the fact cold weather would soon arrive.

"Got a minute?" Tony entered Hack's office carrying a handful of papers.

"What's up?"

"Nothing. And that's the problem," Tony quipped. "Everything is going down." He paused to offer the documents in evidence. "These records show a decline over the past quarter and I'm pretty concerned about it."

"Hell, don't be so upset," Hack smiled, trying to suppress a frown while accepting the papers. "After all, it wasn't our best season. Things always fall off during summer."

"I know," he corrected. "The fact is, my figures take that into consideration. If something doesn't happen for the better, you could be in real trouble."

His warning registered slowly as Hack scanned the journal sheets and tried to hide the uneasiness he was beginning to feel. The totals indicated made him curse himself for being so lax and not having checked the situation much earlier. "What do you suggest?" he finally asked, shoving the papers across the desk in Tony's direction.

"Simple. More sales."

"Okay, I'll buy that. But, how do we stimulate sales?"

"That's the problem," Tony answered pessimistically. "Look. May I be blunt and straight forward? Strictly business?"

"Damn, right," Hack assured.

"All right, but remember. Strictly business, and no offense intended."

"Okay, okay," he nodded. "Let's have it."

Tony took a deep breath and began to slowly pace the floor. "The way I see it, marketing capabilities can be simply broken into two major categories. One is new sales, but the most important, maintaining and nurturing already established business." Tony nervously walked to the double doors as if to make sure they were tightly closed. "The potential is great and among our clientele are a number of elite accounts. But, none of them are providing the quantity of projects they originally made available. Each and every customer on the books is doing much less than when they were initially gained." Hack nodded his head as if to indicate agreement or at least an understanding of the point made. "In the time I've been here," Tony continued, "the biggest problem that seems to exist is your lack of time spent in touch with clients. By cutting down on personal activities, you could sure as hell counteract a lot of the slack around here." Tony seemed relieved in having finally confronted Hack about his absenteeism and his tone became more positive. "Don't forget, you were once the cornerstone of production. You're no longer that even though you're still the backbone of this business. I fall in the same category. As business manager, my duties neither enhance production or sales. Counting Carin, you and I, we represent a third of the work force. I don't care how good the staff is, the work volume just isn't large enough to afford a highly paid crew and the proportionate percentage of nonproductive personnel as currently exists."

What Hack was hearing really didn't come as a total shock. It only brought into the open facts he already knew to be true, but inwardly tried to deny. He sat leaning over his desk with his face buried in his hands pondering Tony's words and weighing them against his own feelings. "Well, Tony, you see it's like this." Hack pushed away from the desk, rose from the seat, moved to the bar, and fixed two cups of coffee. "I know this business is far from being as successful as it could or should be." He handed Tony a cup. "By the way, I take no offense by your opinion. In fact, I have to agree with most of what you said and it's rather encouraging to find your deep interest in the situation. I agree, if things continue as they are, it will mean a disaster. That I certainly don't need or want." Tony nodded his head in agreement and waited for Hack to light his cigarette. "However," Hack continued, "that's why you're here. To keep things above water. Sure, I know I shouldn't fart around as much as I do, but understand this. I've worked many hard years, day and night, before I started easing up. Maybe it is too premature, but the way I look at it, why completely waste all of the good middle years without enjoying some of the fruits of labor? Why wait until you're too old and ready to kick the bucket?" He paused to sip from his cup. "I'm not about ready to give up. You ought'a realize that. As much as I may be away during the day, the hours I spend at nights working on the board add to a pretty good effort."

"No. I wasn't underestimating your efforts," Tony countered. "I meant they should be channeled in a more meaningful direction. Your value has superseded that of production. If you took an active role during the day in seeing old and new contacts, this business could blossom."

"Great, I want to bloom," Hack smiled in concurrence. "But, man. Believe me. Without the course as an outlet, I couldn't have handled all the heavy pressures and hours of work."

"We all need a shot in the arm occasionally," Tony agreed. "If golf is an aphrodisiac for you, then, fine. But in the long run, if you don't gain a control of the addiction it's become, there won't be the opportunity, albeit the money, to have the freedoms you're presently enjoying."

"Yeah. Maybe you're right." Hack didn't like to admit it. He proceeded to pour another cup. "So, what's the bottom line?"

"Workload. It has to be increased. It's either stimulate sales or decrease staff. The latter could only be considered a negative action and a step backwards. We've got good people here, but when you hired me, it only added to overhead instead of boosting production income. I know that bringing me aboard was based on the Hanford account. From what I can tell, their moving as slow as molasses in making a decision."

"They sure are," Hack confirmed. "I talked to Everett yesterday and he didn't have anything new to report. The final decision's hung up waiting for a meeting of the board."

"I thought the meeting was supposed to be last week."

"It was. Supposed to be, that is," Hack responded in a discouraged manner. "They postponed and haven't rescheduled a new date."

"Oh." Tony sounded equally disappointed.

"You don't think we should consider paring the staff?"

"Not really. At least not yet," Tony said shaking his head in disapproval. "Once they're gone, you'd have a hell of a time ever replacing them. I'd rather take the chance on getting more work. Which, brings it back to the point of marketing, and your involvement."

"Get out and do a little selling yourself."

"Who me?" Tony gulped as his eyes nearly popped from his head. "I've never . . . "

"Why not," Hack interrupted, pointing his finger at Tony in a challenging manner. "Tell you what. We'll both make an effort."

"Whoa, it's not all that simple." An uneasiness began to reappear in Tony's reactions. "You've always espoused that in this business, no matter how much talent is involved, it's more who you know, than what you know."

"True, but sometimes it's just a question of getting to know them. I've got quite a few prospects we could use for starters. I'll give you a brief sales education, 'Madison Avenue type,' and make a few calls with you. Then, you're on your own."

By the time the meeting ended, Tony had gained guarded

enthusiasm with the idea. They had sat for several hours discussing a plan of action. Carin entered as Tony was finally leaving. "Got some letters for you to sign." She smiled.

Hack motioned for her to lay them on the desk. "Want a drink?"

"Thought you'd never ask. Please." Carin moved to the couch, sat down, slipped from her shoes while leaning back, and wiggled her toes high in the air.

"Remind me to put a mirror opposite that couch," Hack joked, referring to the view afforded the wall in front of her.

"You know you don't have to use gimmicks on me," she blushed, reaching around to pinch him on the ass. He jumped, spilled some of the drink, then turned quickly to grasp her by the shoulders pinning them to the couch, and kissed her deeply. "Hummmmmm. I ought to pinch you more often," she cooed.

"You bet." He handed her a glass and moved to take a seat beside her.

Laying her arm across the back of the couch, her fingers played with the hair on his neck. "That was quite a meeting you had today with Tony. Got all the problems solved?"

Hack shrugged his shoulders in a 'don't know' manner.

"Are things really getting rough?" she asked.

"A little bit, but not impossible."

Carin sensed his need for contemplation. They sat quietly for a reasonably long period.

"You know what?" Hack broke the silence. "I'm going to buckle down for a while . . . line up new work . . . cut down on golf . . ."

"You're kidding?" She interrupted, blurting her response. "I didn't mean it to sound like it did."

"Forget it," he smiled. "Guess I have been going a bit overboard. Besides, the layoff might help my game."

"You are serious, aren't you?" Her eyes glared unbelievingly.

"One-hundred percent."

"God. I don't know what I'll do having you around for a change. You've been like a nomad since your recovery from the accident." She tried to sound facetious. "Maybe we'll even get an occasional chance to get together for lunch."

Hack took her by the hand. "Sorry, babe. Sometimes I can

get thrown pretty far off track. Maybe we can fit in a few dinners, too." Carin's eyes began to tear slightly as she sprang to her feet, pulling Hack along with her. Throwing her arms around his neck, she almost choked him in the embrace. "Let's make love," Hack whispered softly in her ear.

"Uhmmmmm." She hummed her positive reaction as she began to unbutton her blouse.

Moving through the double doors, Hack realized it best to check the rear offices and found the last of his staff preparing to leave. Evidently exhausted by the trauma of the meeting, Tony was long gone. When he returned, Carin lay on the couch, nude, extending her arms in an irresistible invitation.

* * *

Two months of dedicated work efforts passed as if they were eons. The first several days were a struggle, but by the end of the second week, it proved close to being unbearable. Withdrawal pains from cigarettes or even alcohol couldn't have been any worse. Instead of experiencing snakes and pink elephants, there were writhing golf club shafts and devouring sand traps in his dreams. Carin strained her patience and frequently coped with his bad and nervous moods.

Another year was nearing an end, unfortunately leaving several goals not attained. Still, Hack was able to accomplish a great deal. The Hanford board met and the decision had been made to place Hack's business on a year's contract. It was less than desired, but certainly better than nothing. On the plus side, among other things, the awarding of the contract placed his organization in a category above being simply a graphics studio to that of media-agency level. They would now be dealing in newspapers, television and radio as opposed to prior limitations involving only publications and institutional promotion. In addition to the Hanford success, Tony and Hack both landed a few other new accounts and there was little chance of an immediate crisis. Rather than layoffs, they pleasantly found the situation altered to an extent of needing to hire additional personnel.

Hack looked at his watch. It was slightly after one. Sitting behind the desk, he swiveled his chair to a position facing the window and stared at a small area of clear blue sky that could be detected above the buildings across the street. The warmth of the room camouflaged the bitter cold waiting outside. His mind wandered through times spent at the club. I wonder how many nuts are out on the course freezing to death, he pondered in thought?

The sound of sliding doors behind him interrupted his reverie. He spun quickly in the chair to see Carin standing just inside his office. "Sorry to disturb you." She winked. "You've got a visitor. Say's his name is Gabe."

"Hot damn," he said exuberantly and leaped to his feet. "Show him in."

Carin stepped aside as his unexpected guest ambled past her. "What say ol' buddy?" Gabe said, greeting Hack with a huge smile.

"You little, beautiful, SOB. Damn it's good to see you. What the hell brings you off the good side of the world?"

"Just in the area," he shrugged with his response. "Got a drink?"

"Hell, yeah. What'll you have?"

"Pussy on the rocks," he giggled and motioned with his thumb toward the direction Carin had retreated.

"Nothing doing. Anything else is yours."

"Sheeeet. Might've known. Bourbon and ginger."

It only took a second to make the drinks and they plunged into an appropriate subject. "Playing any lately?" Hack asked.

"A little bit," Gabe retorted. "Haven't seen you around though, what happened?"

"Work, brother. Work."

"Hell, that's no fun."

"You're tellin' me?" Hack laughed. "I almost went nuts gettin' my nose straight and back to the grindstone. Never thought I'd make it."

"Same thing happened to me. When I got drafted, I mean. Hell. I don't know which was hardest, given up golf for a while, or basic-trainin'."

They both shook their heads as if to rid them of the terrible experiences and simultaneously swallowed the last of their drinks as if to wash away the bad memories. Hack gathered the glasses and made seconds. "What's new?"

"Just got my final discharge papers last Friday," he beamed.

"Damn, that's great. Congratulations." He handed him his refill and touched glasses to salute his good fortune. "Hey, wait a minute," Hack said, breaking the mood. "I thought you got out a good while back. What's this discharge jazz?"

"Oh, hell. That was only from the regular army. I still had to do some of the 'weekend warrior' bit."

"Uh." Hack grunted in understanding his mistake. "So, anything planned?"

"Nothin firm," he replied. "Got a little dough saved, and believe it or not, I'm getting' tired livin' off my mother. Figured I'd spend a few more months playin' golf, and then, see if I can nail down an assistant's job round here, or somethin.'"

"What happened to the offer at your mother's club?"

"Still open I guess. But, I don't think I could handle bein' around my mother that much. Like I just told ya. I'm gettin' fed up with her runnin' my life. She's already screwed up a relationship with a girl I really wanted. I had enough of her interference. She thinks she can buy me, and everything else for that matter." His disposition was beginning to really sour.

"Hell, you shouldn't have much trouble finding some other pro job," Hack responded, trying to get his friend's attention away from his personal family involvements.

"Don't get me wrong," Gabe sensed Hack's intent. "I love my mother. It's just that she can't accept the fact that I'm not her suckin' baby, anymore. She really drives me nuts sometimes."

Hack realized the seriousness of Gabe's distraught confession. Even though his own parental problems were different, he could relate to other personal situations that seemed all too similar.

"Hey." He interrupted Hack's wandering thoughts. "What's chances of you gettin' some time off and maybe goin' south with me? Could get some damn good matches like we did before. Maybe pay expenses."

Hack's heart jumped and his body tingled with the suggestion. "Damn, you make me shiver. I don't think there's anything in the world I'd rather do more."

"Well, why not?" he coaxed. "Could sure have a great time. My family's got a cottage along the northern gulf coast. We

232

could use it as a home base. What'd'ya say?"

"Holy shit. I feel so damn fired up I might climax." Hack laughed. "Let me think for a minute."

Gabe's eyes followed him continually as he paced the floor.

Hack stopped suddenly, turned to the bar, and made a double drink before he spoke. "Can't pass it up," he muttered. "Hell, yes. I'll do it."

"Way to go." Gabe was ecstatic.

"Not so fast, now. Slow down a bit," Hack cautioned and waved his hands in a calming motion. "There's a couple of strings attached. A few matters I've got to take care of first."

"Like what?" He frowned his disapproval.

"Don't get shook. If there's a problem with waitin' a couple of weeks, . . ."

"Hell, is that all," he broke into Hack's rebuttal. "I didn't figure to go myself before at least the middle to the end of next month."

"I'll tell you what," Hack countered. "It's only a few weeks 'til Christmas. Why don't we leave between the holidays? That way, I won't cause any repercussions with friends and family," Hack offered.

"Done." Gabe beamed with anticipation.

The two acted like teens elated over their first piece of ass. During a few more drinks, they discussed plans in further detail. Hack made a decision to put up extra money since Gabe was covering their accommodations.

"How's that good-lookin' aunt of yours?"

Gabe seemed surprised. "Why? Your tongue still get hard thinkin' about her?" He laughed. "Ain't seen or talked to her since we were down there the last time."

"Aw, man. You got no compassion."

"I got compassion all right. Just don't try ballin' my mom or my sister." He laughed hysterically at his personal joke.

"Screw you, you sawed-off shrimp." Hack joined his laughter.

"It sounds like real fun in here." Carin opened the door and entered unannounced.

Her intrusion took Hack by surprise and he wasn't quite sure whether he approved or not. It was unlike her to interrupt him at any time, and especially in such a fashion. Obviously, curiosity fueled by diffidence was getting the best of her. "Why don't you join us?" he coolly suggested.

Carin ignored his antagonistic attitude and accepted. "I understand you're Hack's savior on the golf course. Are you really that good?"

Gabe made it apparent he wasn't sure how to respond. He looked at Hack, turned his head to observe Carin, and blushed.

Hack was shocked at Carin's uncharacteristic behavior, seething at her display of unwarranted irritation in front of his friend. "Yeah. He's that good," Hack said sarcastically. "Would you care to sit down, . . . or go home?"

"I am a bit tired from the day." Her voice trailed in submission, indicating she realized she had overstepped her bounds.

"Okay. I'll see you tomorrow." Hack was determined to show no quarter.

Smiling meekly, she bid Gabe a parting salutation.

Hack was in no frame of mind for further confrontation. However, as aggravated as he was with her, he inwardly knew she had been drawing all the correct conclusions.

* * *

Normally, time would have crawled waiting for the big day and his escape. However, between business matters and Holiday preparations, there was an abundance of diversions. Beyond her continuing suspicions, Carin was pleased with Hack's improving mood and took special pleasure in helping shop for his sister's children. In return, he promised to have a large tree at the office and share Christmas afternoon with her and the kids.

Initiating a master plan, he began to lay ground work very slowly regarding his intention to take another extended absence. To soften the blow, he arranged a whirlwind weekend trip to New York to see the opening of a Neil Simon play. The following Friday evening, he and Carin boarded an Eastern shuttle-flight leaving National en route to La Guardia Airport.

After being seated on the plane, Hack eased into various areas of conversation before eventually broaching his intended topic. "Babe, I, uh . . . you know, I've been hinting about wanting to get away for a while. I've almost made a decision to give it a try."

Carin looked up quickly, a bit surprised.

"There's some family. On my father's side," he paused, taking stock of himself. "Damn it." He shuddered from his guilt and reversed his tact. "I'm tired of alibis and lying," he corrected. "I'm goin' nuts inside. I've tried hard, given my guts, and made a lot of headway. And, I don't give a damn about it . . . any of it."

"I think you're going crazy." She shook her head. "I've seen your preoccupation with that silly game, but I'm just beginning to realize exactly how badly addicted you really are."

"I don't need lectures, I want understanding," he meekly stated.

"Understanding?" she echoed as a question. "I think all you're really looking for is my complicity in combating your guilt."

"But, . . ."

"Do you want my opinion, or not?" she interrupted, reaching for his pack of cigarettes he had laid on his convenience tray. "Sure," she continued, "sometimes I do get jealous of your other interests. I can't help it. I like to be with you. And, I love sharing and doing things together. I get high as a kite when you do something successful. You walk around like you're on cloud nine. You make me feel that way, too." She smiled as if visually recalling an isolated incident. Altering her expression to a frown, she added, "When I see you hopelessly wasting your time and talents, it hurts. I feel sorry for you." Smoking cigarettes had never been one of Carin's vices. It was apparent her momentary need was a result of nervousness, promoted by the awkwardness of the conversation and her attitudes pertaining to the subject. "How long will it be this time?" she asked with surety, sensing his decision regarding another trip to have already been made.

He reached to light her cigarette. "A couple of weeks."

"A couple of weeks?" She sounded as though she'd been stabbed.

The huge jet lurched from its terminal dock and swung in the direction of the runway.

"Sorry, babe. Didn't mean to put a damper on the evening or the spirit of the holidays.

Carin inhaled and choked on the smoke.

Hack took the cigarette from her and stubbed it in the ashtray.

"The no-smoking sign's on." He pointed to the front of the cabin.

They raised their trays to takeoff position and fastened seat belts. The airliner's engines screamed as the plane raced down the concrete slab until it began to steeply climb into the black sky. Following a sharp bank to the left, the craft leveled, and except for a droning hum, they might have been sitting in a living room.

"Getting shot affected me a lot more than I've let on. It's been on my mind quite a bit. I could've been killed." He paused and toyed with the creases of his slacks. "It's made me want to enjoy life even more than ever. You know. Here today, gone tomorrow."

"I understand better than you think I do." She covered his hand with hers. "Really. I'm sorry. It is some selfishness on my part. I just don't like being without you for that long, but I'm concerned for you, too, and what you've worked so hard for . . ."

"I know, Carin, but I'm not intentionally pushing you away or ignoring what you want in your life. Maybe, one of these days down the road, I'll get out of this frame of mind and come to my senses. But, right now, I can't promise you anything more than I have in the past. I'm really not sure what I want. Hypothetically speaking, there are times when constant companionship, and even the idea of remarriage, seems to be appealing. I do get lonely. Sometimes very lonely." He paused briefly to alter his tone and mood. "On the other side, I enjoy the freedom and flexibility that I've finally experienced for the first time in my life."

"Isn't the business important at all, anymore?"

"Damn right it is. I'm no fool." His anger surfaced. "I've busted my ass too friggin' hard to get where I am to lose it. I'm just tired. Damn tired. And I can't stay with my nose to the grindstone like in the past." The ire slowly subsided and he began to mellow. "You weren't around during the early periods. There's no way you could ever comprehend the effort that went into starting off on my own, and I'm not about to push myself back into another breakdown."

"Hack, I really don't know what to say. I'm always confused as to what our relationship is actually supposed to be. One minute there seems to be a future together. The next, nothing . . . nothing at all. We have more ups and downs than a horse on a carousel." Carin paused, lowering her head in thought. Finally returning to consciously confront the issue, she continued. "I love you, and I think you love me. That is, at least, in your own way. I've got no intention of walking away from you or leaving my job. I only wish I could better cope with watching you possibly destroy everything you've gained."

He smiled. "That won't happen. Not in a million years."

"At the rate you're going, you'll never last that long." She laughed.

Hack smiled. "You're probably right."

"There's no question about it? You're definitely going?" she asked.

"Almost sure," he corrected. "Unless something disastrous happens. Tony's doing great and the business is up. Between the two of you, I've got no worries."

"Would you care for a drink?" the stewardess asked, interrupting their train of concentration.

Hack shuddered in recognizing the sexy voice. Damn. It's got to be Morty, he cringed in thought before turning to confront her and his fears.

"Would you like the usual, or something special?" Morty winked as he met her devilish gaze. "It's a small world, isn't it?" She smiled.

"You've got that right." Hack struggled inwardly, but quickly covered the awkwardness of the situation by making simple introductions between the two girls while confirming a choice of beverages.

Morty continued down the aisle taking orders, frequently glancing in Hack's direction deviously aggravating his discomfort. Carin was both puzzled and curious, but said nothing to further incite the situation. As intense as their discussion had previously been, a sullen atmosphere prevailed dulling the importance of earlier concerns. Hack tried desperately to maintain composure in hopes of hiding the true extent of his distress. Dreading Morty's reappearance, he suspected only the worse. Being aware she was making her way up the aisle distributing drinks and snacks to the passengers, his mind rattled with details of possible anticipated responses to whatever she might decide to say.

"Have you seen Mitch, lately?" she asked as she placed the

drinks on their trays. "I really miss him. He never writes or keeps in touch." She pouted to emphasize the point.

"Oh," Carin said in a surprised, but welcomed manner. "You're a friend of Mitch's?"

"Friend? . . . Better than that. Extremely close friends," Morty expressed in a very untruthful, but convincing manner.

It was difficult for Hack to suppress his sigh of relief. Thankfully, it went unnoticed, and even more appreciated, was Morty's quick departure. Until they actually landed, Hack spent many anxious moments not knowing what might happen next. Fortunately, there was no other contact, and he and Carin disembarked without encumbrance or delay.

Since there was little baggage, other than the valises carried aboard, departure from the airport was expedient. Typically, it actually took longer to get into lower Manhattan and reach the Lexington Hotel, than time spent in the air from Washington National.

Arriving at the hotel, they deposited their sparse luggage in the room and immediately exited the premises in search of a decent restaurant. The streets were literally teeming with people. Taking a side street, Hack led them in the direction toward Times Square. As they neared the famous intersection, Carin's face and eyes gleamed in harmony with the lights of Broadway. She was astounded by the maze of theaters and gaudiness of neon. Selecting a fast-food steak joint, they first ate dinner and later opted on a movie. Finding the horror flick oppressing, they left in the middle of the film and walked next door to an amusement arcade. Being quite crowded with a majority of more undesirable types, they changed their minds about staying and caught a cab for the hotel.

Rising to the blare of traffic and wailing sirens the following morning, they showered and dressed with an eagerness to roam Manhattan. Plans for the off-Broadway theater weren't until the evening, leaving the entire day free for doing whatever they desired.

The morn's cold chill of impending winter proved invigorating. Strolling past an endless number of shops, each store seemed pent on outdoing the other in holiday season decor, and Christmas carols echoed through the city's corridors. Santa's bell rang on nearly every major corner as the towering buildings hid ominous clouds that soon began to shower large flakes of snow. As the storm intensified, looking upwards along the walls of granite, glass and concrete, the structures gradually faded and disappeared into the origin of the falling white. It was a breathtaking experience, greatly enhancing their enthusiasm for the time of the year.

Touring Rockefeller Center and NBC occupied most of the afternoon. They snacked lightly before the theater and honored their reservations at Sardi's following the show. Pleasantly tired from the day's crammed schedule and in anticipation of the next morning's return flight, they retired at a reasonable hour, falling asleep in each other's arms.

CHAPTER X

Christmas fell on Saturday. Under normal business practices, Hack wasn't obligated to give the staff anything more than either the choice of the preceding Friday or following Monday as a holiday. However, considering his good frame of mind and high spirits, he decided to close the offices for the entire week between the holidays, as well as Christmas Eve day. Having a very important business party to attend in the afternoon, Hack insisted Carin leave early on Thursday to finish some last minute shopping and he would meet her later. Since the return from New York, every evening had been spent together at her apartment. She left wishing him a good time during his afternoon rounds, but from prior year's experience, carefully warned against his drinking too much. According to plans, they were to have dinner early Christmas Eve so as not to hinder his schedule of managing family stops and seeing the children. Sharon had pleaded for him to play the customary role of Santa's assistant as in the past. There would be bicycles and other toys requiring his mechanical expertise, after the kids were asleep. Knowing in advance from experience the hour would be late before ever finishing, he would simply stay over and looked forward to being present when they woke in the morning and found the goodies.

Not particularly in a festive mood, Hack went through the motions of showering and dressing. Even though previous years of attendance proved the party to be a lot of fun, getting over-boozed just wasn't appealing and he almost dreaded going. He chose a three-piece dark-blue business suit, a pink button-down collared shirt, and a muted diagonally-striped tie. Standing in front of the mirror taking stock of his reflection, he winked at himself and smiled in egotistical admiration of the image.

Gathering packages containing gifts for several clients, Hack commenced his tour of nearby office buildings. By two-thirty, having completed the chore, he headed for the big bash. Things were in full swing when he arrived.

The big man of the corporation was a blustery individual and Hack's teeth gritted tightly in anticipation of his usual slap on the back greeting. It felt as if his shoulder blade had been shoved to his chest and would pierce his nipple.

Amidst the small group surrounding the boss, one of the secretaries began to rather boldly flirt with Hack and he quickly excused himself to avoid an awkward and possibly disastrous situation. The old-man had his private label on her and took great pleasure in knocking it off himself. Squeezing out of the sticky spot, Hack retreated to one of the liquor clad tables and poured his usual Canadian and water, then decided to mingle with a few friends from the editorial department, joining an ongoing conversation about the Redskin's lousy season.

Glancing across the large room, a lovely vision clinging to a young man's arm caught his attention. He almost dropped his drink. It was Terri. Void of control, he stood gazing in awe at her beauty, remembering her touch and the tenderness of their embraces. A twinge of jealousy surged through him as she seemed delighted by her escort's attentions.

Even though the youth looked familiar, until the couple was joined by the party's infamous back-slapper, he couldn't connect a name to her boy friend. Suddenly, it was obvious. "Holy shit," he mumbled under his breath, "that's the boss' son." The fear of what she might inadvertently say or do, should he approach them, gave him butterflies in the pit of his stomach. The kid was a real daddy's boy. Beating his time or complicating the scene was far from being a smart move. It was the type of incident that could swing the balance of a good account. Strongly considering sneaking out the door, he concluded their vantage point lent highly to the prospect of him being seen.

Several minutes elapsed as he continued to fake being interested in his immediate group's conversation. He noticed Terri and her friend headed in his direction, evidently on their way to the bar. "Hack. What a pleasant surprise." She abruptly stopped a few steps away, grabbing her escort by his arm. "Mark, you must meet a very good friend of mine that I haven't seen in ages. Mark, this is Hack Arnold."

"Hello, Mark. How've you been?" Hack acknowledged the introduction with a handshake. "We've met once, sometime ago in your dad's office." He directed the statement more to Terri than to the lad.

Mark smiled in agreement.

Following a brief exchange of several other polite remarks, Mark and Terri continued on to the refreshments. Although feeling reprieved, Hack fought desperately to ignore their presence and tried to avoid looking in her direction. Yet, his eyes were temptingly drawn to her like a magnet. Finding the situation increasingly difficult and awkward, he excused himself and made his way through the crowd wishing everyone holiday greetings. Having retrieved his coat, he thanked his host as a final gesture, and gave a last visual survey of the room. Terri had disappeared.

He was emotionally torn between being relieved and miserable. Entering the hallway, he turned the corner and pressed the down button. As the elevator opened, he stepped inside and turned to see Terri frantically impede the doors from closing.

"Oh, God. I thought I would miss catching you." She threw her arms around his neck and their lips met in a warm and long embrace. The elevator coming to its halt had no effect. As the doors opened, he pushed the button to the basement and they continued their descent. "It's so good to be in your arms," she whispered, pressing her body closer. "Why have we let it go this long?"

"I don't know, babe. I really don't know."

She pulled gently away and reached to hold his hands. "Where are you going, now?"

"Back to the office," he mumbled. "I couldn't stay up there any longer; . . . not without touching or even talking to you."

Terri smiled warmly.

"What's with you and Mark, anything serious?"

"Heavens no." She looked amazed. "I've been out with him a couple of times. Strictly social. We met at the club. He's a tennis-buff, too."

Hack leaned forward and kissed her on the nose. "You'd better get back. He's probably concerned by now."

"Please," she pleaded. "Wait for me while I get my coat and make an excuse. You won't mind, will you?"

"Lord no." He didn't hesitate, nor hide his enthusiasm. "I'm parked just down the street. I'll get the car and meet you out front."

They rode the elevator back up to the lobby floor where Hack made his exit after squeezing her hand.

"Give me ten minutes," she suggested with a wink as the doors took her from view.

Walking on air felt great. He flowed out of the revolving doors and ran to the corner. The threatening glare of a cop standing nearby gave him second thoughts about crossing against the light. He bounced on the balls of his feet, waiting his turn to proceed, finding it impossible to control his exuberance. After what seemed an eternity, the car engine roared into life and he wasted little time getting back. Terri was already waiting inside the lobby and she ran gracefully toward the car as he drove to the curb. Immediately sliding across the seat, she threw her arm around his shoulder, kissed him on the cheek, and said, "Home, James."

He turned his head and tenderly bit her on the ear.

"You've got just forty-five minutes to stop that." She tried to look mad.

"Make it a lifetime." He laughed.

The light turned green and Hack blended into the flow of traffic. Tiny flakes of snow began to flurry as a precursor of the predicted storm scheduled to hit the metropolitan area. "If there's nothing special you have to do at your place, why don't we go to mine," Terri suggested? "I've moved since we were last together."

"You've got the stage. Show me the way."

Traffic eased after leaving downtown congestion and their route was in the direction of an upper northwest suburban section abundant with expensive homes. Crossing the district line into Maryland, they proceeded along River Road until reaching a point where they veered to the right from the main highway. Several turns were negotiated and at the end of a narrow lane,

Terri pointed to the left.

Continuing up a long driveway, Hack became completely speechless, his eyes agape with amazement -- the structure before them shrouded in an aura of historical significance.

Terri took great delight at his expression and explained the circumstances of her mother's death. Her will divided the entire estate equally between the two siblings. Rather than sell the family property, for sentimental reasons primarily, Terri was awarded sole ownership of the house. In turn, her brother received other properties, plus controlling shares in the family business.

Standing in the huge foyer, it was almost as cold as the outside temperature. "Wow, it's freezing in here," Hack chattered as his breath frosted in the air.

"Sorry," Terri laughed. "It costs a small fortune to heat this entire place. I only use the downstairs most of the time. Usually, I try to keep the upper floors just warm enough to protect the plumbing and other things from damage."

Cold or not, Hack was unable to escape his astonished preoccupation with the immediate surroundings. His creative mind formed a mental image of the combined beauty and exquisite taste in furnishings and decor that surely had to exist throughout the dwelling. "Don't you feel a little lost? Here, alone, I mean?"

"Sometimes." She turned away in an emotional survey of the area. "I couldn't bring myself to let it go. There's so much of the family's past that clings to this place." She led the way into the living room toward a marble fireplace. A few moments later, the hearth, fueled by gas logs popped to life. Taking his hand, Terri moved to a nearby gorgeously carved cabinet. When opened, it exposed a small, but well equipped bar. She selected a bottle of brandy, looked for his approval, and poured generous amounts of the liquid into two crystal snifters. Before replacing the stopper, she spun quickly on her heels and threw her arms tightly around his neck.

"I've missed you so much." She emphasized her statement with an exaggerated squeeze.

His arms and body returned her embrace. "I know." Tilting her head slightly upwards, she invited his kiss. Hack felt such a fulfilling satisfaction in the caress, surfacing emotions brought a combination of ecstasy and confusion. He cuddled her head to his chest while his mind became more muddled and indecisive. Could he be in love? he wondered in thought. The concept was warming, but equally frightening.

"Don't leave me again; not like before," she pleaded.

"I won't. I promise."

Picking up their glasses, they returned to sit on the floor in front of the glowing embers. "Tell me. Please tell me everything that's happened."

"Nothing unusual, really." Hack sipped the warm biting liquid. "Mostly work, and golf."

"How about the love life?" Her face reflected sudden concern at what she had innocently asked.

"Been married to a golf ball."

She smiled and laughed softly.

"So, what have you been up to?" he asked, altering to the offensive.

"You won't believe it, but I've taken up golf." She stood and mocked a swing in rather excellent form. "I've been doing pretty well, too."

"I'll be damned. What prompted that?"

"The lack of good tennis partners mostly, I guess. There was a need to get involved after mother died. I really missed her at first. Not because we were so close, . . . it was more like losing my father for a second time . . . as if the last part of Daddy faded away."

"You were very close to him?" He found nothing better to say.

She walked slowly until stopping to stare out of a window. "I felt so lonely after he passed away. We did everything together. Mother had been ill for many years. I guess . . . I guess I substituted for her frequently. Dad and I loved the same things." She paused briefly in personal meditation. Turning suddenly, she threw her hands above her head. "Look at melancholy me. And, on the doorstep of Christmas." They both started to speak simultaneously. "You first." She managed a laugh. "What were you going to say?"

"Not much." He shook his head and handed her one of the

two cigarettes he had just lit. "I started to ask you, how come no Christmas tree?"

"It's funny. I never really gave it a thought." A glowing expression brightened her face. "Oh, Hack, I want one now. Let's put a tree up, . . . for the both of us."

Hack glanced at his watch. It was a few minutes past six. "Do you think we'll find one nearby?"

"How about the lawn?"

"Let's go." He jumped to his feet.

Ransacking the house, they had to settle on a keyhole saw. Like a couple of love-stricken fools, they entered the cold dark evening with reckless abandon. Terry picked a gorgeous spruce tree towering to a height of at least fifteen feet. She ignored any pleas Hack made to save it or find something closer to the house, vigorously insisting that no other would suffice.

Trying to achieve a position to cut out the top was as difficult as Hack had envisioned. The branches were like guarding arms doing their best to force him from the dastardly deed. Having had to remove both his suit coat and topcoat to manipulate the feat, needles bit into his flesh, and snow blanketing its boughs angrily clung to his hands until they began to burn.

Standing below his perch, Terri watched with enthusiasm and occasional supervision. Managing the last few strokes of the saw evoked her cheer. Shortly after the upper part began to topple, Hack followed suit. A limb caught him from behind and carried him head over heels to land at Terri's feet. Concern for his condition was brief considering the roar of laughter. After helping him struggle to an upright position and brush away the snow, they hurried with their chores, giggling and singing like children at play.

Hack gathered wood for the fire as she tugged at the trunk of the fallen tree, attempting to drag it across the lawn and through the kitchen door. Perspiration beaded on his forehead in defiance of the ensuing night's cold. He watched as Terri successfully accomplished the task of getting the tree inside and followed her with an armful of logs.

Terri briefly disappeared as he rid his burden in a nearby corner. She announced her return as she appeared in the doorway laden with a huge box. "Hey. Quick. Give me a hand."

Before Hack could reach her, the carton slipped and crashed to the floor. "Don't tell me," he gasped.

"You're right," she pouted with the response, shaking her head in a positive nod. "Decorations." Looking at each other rather stupidly, they broke into hysterical laughter and sat in the middle of the floor until they could control the insatiable giggling.

Terri was the first to speak. "Come on, 'Paul Bunyan.' We'll be more comfortable downstairs."

Hack rolled to his knees as a prelude to gaining an upright stance. He picked up the box and followed her to the lower level. The stairway opened into a contemporary-styled recreation room furnished as richly as the rest of the house. The carpet felt unusually plush and deep in pile. A polar bear rug majestically sprawled in front of a rustic fireplace that spanned an entire wall. Best of all, it was as warm as toast.

"This is beautiful, Terri."

"Thanks." She smiled in finding his approval important. "I redecorated it and spend most of my time here."

Hack nodded his approval. He stood holding the box, marveling at Terri's beauty being framed by the choice of her surroundings. The room, even though rather large, maintained a warm and cozy feeling aided by the low beamed ceiling. A small separate area, inset in a far corner, served as a bar and complete kitchen, if necessary.

"Going to hold that all night?"

Terri's voice startled him to awareness. "Sorry. I can't seem to get over the shock of this place."

Making additional trips to bring down logs and the tree, they eventually settled down to the game of decorating the Christmas spruce. "Pass me that pack of ornaments when you get the chance," Terri requested. Hack was settled in the middle of the floor untangling several strings of lights. He reached for the balls and tossed the box to her as she turned. "Oh, my God," she gasped, while making a shoestring catch. "You wonderful nut," she responded in a joking manner. She kicked her shoe loose in his direction and returned to adorning the tree.

"Terri."

"Huh?" She crooked her neck in an attempt to confront his

gaze.

"Got something I have to tell you."

"What is it?" She became immediately concerned at the tone of his voice and moved quickly to kneel in front of him.

Hack found it impossible to look into her penetrating eyes. "Sorry to spring it on you like this, but I should've brought it out earlier. I, uh . . . I know what I promised about not being apart, but I have to be away for a while." He cringed and continued to avoid her gaze. "I'll be gone for a few weeks. Maybe a month."

"Oh, thank God. You had me really worried for a second. I thought you meant longer than before." She leaned and kissed him on the nose and quickly bounced back to once again rest on her heels. "Business?" she asked passively.

"Uh, no. A pleasure trip. In fact, sort of a vacation I've been planning for sometime," he lied. "A buddy of mine and I are going to cover some of the courses through the south."

"Sounds like fun. Wish I could go," she added. "When are you leaving?"

"Christmas night, . . . or more probably, Sunday morning."

She moaned. "Oh, so soon."

"Afraid so."

"Well," she cooed, "we'll make the best of the time we have left. It will be wonderful spending Christmas together."

He held his hands in a stopping motion. "Another problem; I've made other plans that are going to be really rough to change. I'll have to see what I can do to work things out."

"Anything I can help with?" She was overly eager.

"Not really. Just invitations for dinner tonight and tomorrow evening, and the usual family stops."

"Oh, no," she contritely responded. "It's been very thoughtless of me. I didn't even consider your family, or their Christmas."

Raising to his feet, he attempted to pull Terri erect in the same motion. Unwittingly, his left leg was asleep and the blood rushed to his head making him reel. He caught himself on the edge of the couch, but caused her to tumble over his body. They burst into laughter and rolled back to the floor. "Old age," he alibied and continued to chuckle. They attempted the same maneuver the second time. "I knew I could do it," he joked. "Let me make a call and see if I can't break the dinner date this evening." Hack knew there was no other choice. If he didn't phone, Carin would be worried sick and manufacturing all sorts of terrible ideas about his being drunk. Moving to the phone at the bar, he picked up the receiver and dialed her number before suddenly realizing that being overheard talking to Carin wasn't very wise. Pressing his finger against the button to break the connection, he pretended the line was busy. "Tell you what," he suggested. "As luck would have it, my brother lives not very far from here. Just off Wisconsin Avenue, as a matter of fact. I've got presents for my nieces and nephew in the car. I'll run them over before the weather gets any worse and use the snow as an excuse to skip dinner."

"I don't want to be selfish. Won't they be disappointed?" Terri was sincerely concerned.

Walking around the couch, he placed his hands on each side of her face and tenderly kissed her forehead. "No, they won't be upset. And, yes, I want you to be selfish. I can't be without you tonight."

"Oh, Hack." She pressed her head against his shoulder and wrapped her arms around his chest. "That's wonderful. We'll have a beautiful evening together."

"Not if I don't get my tail moving," he said, patting her on the rump as a signal to let him go.

"Will you be gone long?"

"An hour or so at the most."

"You've got 'til nine." She winked and squeezed his hand. "That gives me the chance to get something together for dinner. We can finish the tree later. It'll be fun."

* * *

Roads getting to the highway had accumulated a great deal of snow, but were still passable. Yet, there were fears of possibly having problems on the return. Not being familiar with the immediate area near Terri's estate, he decided to head for a shopping area at Friendship Heights near the district line. As far as Carin was concerned, there was no chance of making it to her apartment. Not even considering harsh weather conditions, making a trip to her place and back before the deadline, was absolutely out of the question. Arriving at his destination, Hack found a newly built shopping mall replacing many of the older shops he remembered. Traffic was heavy, but would have probably been worse without the storm. Finding a space on the far side of the lot, he parked and trudged his way to a nearby drug store.

Carin's phone rang twice before it was answered. "Hello." A male's voice responded.

"That you Rick?" Hack queried.

"Yeah. Merry Christmas, Hack."

"Is Carin there?"

"Nope. She walked up to the store. She should be back shortly."

Hack breathed a sigh of relief. "Look, do me a favor. Tell her I've got car problems. It's a long story and I'll fill her in tomorrow. I'm waiting for my brother Jerry right now and I'll probably spend the night at his place."

"Aw, boy. She's gonna be pissed," Rick countered.

"That's the breaks. Just tell her I'm okay and not drunk, and that I'm sorry." Hack replaced the receiver and walked to the opposite end of the pharmacy and its mall entrance. The occasion demanded a gift for Terri. However, shopping for someone who has practically everything was no easy chore. After browsing through the concourse and coping with a great deal of indecision, he ultimately opted on a piece of jewelry as a proper choice. Disappointed with the array of items in the store's windows, he entered the shop and surveyed several of the display cases before being approached by a salesperson.

"May I help you," a middle-aged woman asked in a pleasant tone?

"Yeah, but I'm really not sure what to get. It has to be special."

Her smile broadened. "For a lady in your life?"

"Yes, mam," he confirmed. "A very wonderful lady." His face beamed with pride as his brain conjured a mental image of Terri's beauty.

Calling on her years of experience dealing in similar situations, she easily sensed the romantic aspects of his mood. "How serious is this relationship of yours? Possibly marriage?"

"Uh, no. At least not yet." He returned to gaze at several

diamond cocktail rings. "We're friends. Just real good friends."

"Oh. Just a moment." She reacted to an enlightening thought. "I may have the perfect item for her." Retreating to the rear of the store, she shortly returned carrying a small envelope. "Occasionally, we have goods that are never claimed." Hack accepted the packet, opened the flap, and emptied its contents into the palm of his hand. He was struck by the gleaming brilliance he held. "It would serve perfectly as a friendship ring," she suggested. "I'm amazed that the owner never chose to redeem it. I don't doubt that it could even be an heirloom, or certainly become one." The ring was a narrow coil of bright yellow-gold with a series of diamond chips set in the spaces between the coils. Hack was temporarily speechless and totally impressed at the selection. "It's apparent you like the ring," the lady observed.

"How much is it?" Hack was almost afraid to ask.

"Normally, as a new piece of jewelry, it would be priced in the thousand-plus range. However, falling into a resale category, and considering the circumstances," she smiled, "four hundred dollars should be a fair figure."

"I'll take it," he blurted with enthusiastic delight. "Thank you, it's more than I hoped for." He reached in his pocket and exposed a wad of bills. "Is there any tax on that?"

"We won't worry about it," she said, smiling and reaching for the four large denomination bills lying on the counter. Taking the jewelry, she placed it in a handsome ring case which was then fit into a small square box. Wrapping it in silver paper, a matching ribbon graced the gift as a final touch of elegance.

Hack was delighted with himself and the purchase. Repeatedly thanking her, he turned, stuffed a cigarette between his lips, and rushed from the store. He had barely left and realized his lighter was missing, he hurriedly retraced his route. Re-entering the shop, he noticed it lying on the counter. His unexpected return seemed to startle the saleslady as she was ringing a sale. Her face reddened as if from embarrassment and Hack offered a puzzled apology for apparently scaring her with his sudden intrusion.

Walking out of the shop, for the second time, Hack paused for a moment. A smile broadened across his face. The old biddy was on the take. There was no doubt in his mind that the amount showing on her cash register was the same total as it had been when he entered the store. It certainly didn't reflect his purchase. "Merry Christmas, you old bag," he said, chuckling to himself.

Consulting his watch indicated he had almost an hour before his promised return and calling the kids seemed to be in order. Billy answered the phone. After completing brief conversations with each of the children, he ended the call by assuring Sharon he wouldn't renege on his promises for Christmas Eve.

Listening to the second dime jingle in the box, he dialed Gabe. "Hello," he answered in a profoundly sleepy state.

"What's up?"

"I am now," he joked and yawned. "Naw, just takin' a nap."

"Too much to drink, huh?" Hack could readily empathize with his condition.

"Little bit. Stinkin' parties. All booze, no pussy."

Hack chuckled. "You've got pussy-itus."

"Don't laugh too hard, I've got a problem."

"Oh. What's wrong?"

"You know that jerk I mentioned who owes me fifteen-hundred?"

"Yeah."

"He's been puttin' me off and I'm gettin' really pissed. He's supposed to have it tomorrow and I wondered if you could meet him with me in case I gotta strong-arm him or somethin.'"

"No way. Are you kidding?" Hack questioned his sincerity. "I'm booked solid, up to my ass. And, besides, that kind of thing ain't my bag."

"Sheeeet, man. If I don't get the bread, I won't be able to go."

"Damn, damn, damn it." Hack's disappointment overpowered his better judgment. "Look. If there's no other way, I'll put the money up front." He paused, knowing the stupidity of his offer. "But, damn, do your best."

"Don't worry, I will." Gabe breathed in relief. "When do you want to get on the road?"

"Yesterday." Hack exaggerated his desire. "Only fooling," he quickly corrected. "I've got my hands full with family matters until later Christmas day. I think the best bet is to plan on leaving some time Sunday."

"All right by me," he agreed.

"Good deal. I'll pick you up as early as possible." Hack coughed, choking on the smoke filling the booth as he replaced the receiver.

Deciding flowers would definitely add to the occasion, he located the florist and purchased a dozen long-stemmed red roses and a gift card. Before leaving the mall, he added to his purchases, two bottles of Asti spumante. Finding himself now pressed with the deadline, he hastily rushed to the car and cleared it of snow. The roads had worsened, but remained passable.

Terri's greeting at the door quickly melted the chill in his bones. Adorned in a sheer and provocative negligee, she looked as if she had just stepped from a page of Harpers Bazaar.

"Miss me?" His nose was red from the cold.

"Not really," she teased. "You look like Rudolph."

Laughing together in an expression of their happiness, Hack turned from hanging his coat in the closet, swooped Terri from her feet into his arms, and carried her down the stairs to the rec-room. In his absence, she had certainly been busy. The tree was completely decorated and a low, Japanese-style table bordered by floor pillows sat in front of the glowing fireplace. Soft Christmas music blended in pure stereophonic balance. Oriental china concealed the contents that spewed forth a tantalizing aroma. Terri's feet lit lightly on the thick carpet as he gently released her to the floor. She continued to encircle her arms around his neck, pressing her firm breasts to his chest. Their lips met in a deep and tingling embrace.

With reluctance, she pulled away. "We'll never make dinner if that keeps up."

Her subtle invitation for Hack to join the feast was temporarily delayed as he remembered the wine and flowers left upstairs. With a simple excuse of being right back, he challenged the stairs, covering them two at a time, grabbed his packages and hastened to rejoin Terri.

She sat facing the flickering embers, apparently entranced by their dancing movement. He silently approached and knelt beside her, placing the roses in her lap.

She gasped. "Oh, Hack, they're beautiful." Her eyes watered and glistened, reflecting the flames leaping from the burning logs.

"You're so sweet and thoughtful." She pressed the flowers to her lips.

"I know it's not very romantic, but have you got a corkscrew?"

She laughed as she got up to fetch a vase for her roses. "Under the bar."

Terri initiated the meal by removing the lids and exposing an array of tempting foods. It mattered little as to what it was. However, the succulent taste furthered the pleasures they shared. The tree and fire twinkled and glistened the only available light.

Throughout the dinner, there was talk and laughter, with no recollection of any prior lapse in their relationship. Before realizing it, their first bottle was empty. Terri flinched as the cork exploded from the second and burst an ornamental ball hanging on the tree. She giggled, wanting him to try it again. Shaking his head negatively, Hack stood and retreated upstairs. Interrupting his intended objective long enough to visit the powder room, he then proceeded to the closet and his coat pocket for her gift. On returning, he found the table gone and only the wine bottle and glasses remaining.

Sprawling on the pillows, Terri soon took a place along side. A quick but tender kiss accompanied his placing the small package in her hand. Giving first attention to the card, she read its personal inscription. Finally opening the box, her delight was worth ten thousand. She sat dumbfounded with tears filling in her eyes. Not waiting for any other reaction, Hack took the ring from its case and slipped it on her finger. He whispered, "This has more meaning than just friendship."

"Oh, my God, I love you." Her exuberant lunge and embrace tumbled Hack to his back as she nearly lay atop his body. As their searching tongues caressed each other in full, front door chimes rudely interrupted the kiss and he tried unsuccessfully to coax Terri into ignoring the intruder. Her persistence to leave was disappointing, but forgiven. Considering the degree of stimulation experienced, Hack managed to regain a great deal of composure before her return.

Hearing mumbled conversation coming down the stairs, he stood in time to see Terri, now clad in a robe, followed by a rather tall attractive man near his own age, laden with a box of generous size. "Hack. This is my brother Jeff. And, Jeff, this is Hack."

Setting the carton on the floor, he extended his arm. "Hi. Nice meeting you."

Hack smiled while shaking his hand. "Merry Christmas."

"Want a drink?" Terri asked her brother.

"No, sweets," he refused. "I have to get back. I've got a lot to do. You know. Toys to put together and all that fun."

"Okay. If you say so," she smiled and kissed him on the cheek. "Thanks, Jeff. Love you . . . and tell all, Merry Christmas."

"You, too, doll," he returned. "It was a pleasure meeting you Hack." He started to turn and hesitated momentarily. "By the way, I hear you're a helluva golfer. We'll have to get together sometime."

"I've got a feelin' I've been overrated." Hack chuckled in return. "It would be great though. Whenever you say."

"Good. And, have an enjoyable trip, you lucky dog." He disappeared up the stairs.

Terri spent little time shedding her robe and rushed back into Hack's arms. "Now where were we at?" She smiled up at him and raised her hand to admire the ring on her finger. "It's so beautiful, and I feel so emotionally close to you."

Hack hugged her tighter.

Suddenly, she sprang away from his arms and grabbed him at the wrist. "Come. I need you to help me." She led him toward the package Jeff had delivered. "Sorry, I didn't have a card, or couldn't get it wrapped, but this is for you."

Until the moment, Hack hadn't paid much attention to the box and there were no detectable designs or labels to indicate its contents. In actuality, there were two cartons, one having been slipped over the top of the other. The awkwardness of its size and shape made it superfluous to move it any further. Lying lengthwise on the floor, he stood it on its end, and began to pull away the outer shell covering its upper half. He was shocked when the container disclosed a genuine leather pro-model golf bag, stuffed with a full set of Royal irons and woods, a rain suit, matching umbrella, and an abundant supply of balls. "My, God," was all he could manage.

"Pleased?"

"Good Lord, am I?" Regardless of what was said, his expression and excitement promoted all the thanks and appreciation necessary. Finally, his heart stopped palpitating and began to slow to a normal pace. He removed his gift completely from the bottom box and began to inspect each and every club and every pocket in the bag. Terri positioned herself on the pillows, elated by Hack's enthusiasm and childlike reactions to his present. "I can't wait to use them," he said with fervor. "How in the world did you know to get stiff shafts?"

"You forget, we're in the business." She laughed.

"Sorry. That's pretty dumb of me." He suddenly realized the only time available for her to have arranged the gift was during his trip to the shopping center. "Tell Jeff thanks. . . . That was really nice of him to come out on a night like this." He chuckled. "That explains how he knew about my trip."

"You're welcome." Jeff said, as his sudden unexpected reappearance startled both of them. He stood in the doorway with a fine dust of snow clinging to most of his lower body. "Oopps, sorry. I didn't mean to sneak in that way." He smiled broadly, disguising his true frustrations.

"What happened?" Terri managed asking, while attempting to conceal a giggle brought on by her brother's ruffled physical state.

"Nuts. I got my car stuck trying to turn around in the driveway. Stupid idiot. I should've left it down on the main road."

"Is there anything I could do to help?" Hack immediately offered.

"Can't think of anything. But, sincerely, thanks. It'll take a tow truck for sure. Wonder if I'll be able to get one tonight?"

"Not as late as it is," Terri affirmed.

Jeff moved to the bar continuing to speak over his shoulder. "Terri, I feel like hell putting a damper on your evening together, but I really don't have much choice."

"Don't be silly," Terri emphatically stated. "You're more than welcome to stay. You know that."

"Yeah, but it's not very . . ."

She interrupted again. "Shush. We don't want to hear

another word."

"Whoa. You don't know what I was going to say," he overruled, bending out of sight behind the counter. "It's cold as hell upstairs, and your converted apartment here just isn't made for more than two." Jeff located the bottle of Jack Daniel's he sought and his upper half reappeared. "Join me," he questioned, hoisting the fifth in the air?

Hack smiled, accepting the offer. "Why not."

Terri declined with a negative shake of her head while continuing her rebuttal of Jeff's concerns. "There's plenty of room. You can sack on the couch and we've got the floor."

Realizing the matter had been decided, Jeff ceased to argue and the three became involved in varied conversation sitting at the bar. A couple of hours and several drinks later, Terri's yawns were taken as a clue to consider calling it quits for the evening. Leaving the room only briefly, she returned with her arms full of blankets and bed pillows. On her appearance, Jeff excused himself and headed for the bathroom.

Hack, although thoroughly understanding circumstances, couldn't help but consciously feel fate was continuing to brutalize him and their relationship.

Terri laughed, dropping the items she carried on the floor and extended her arms to Hack in a beckoning manner. He lowered himself to his knees and crawled across the floor, burying his head into her abdomen. Pressing his lips against her stomach, she tenderly caressed his face and ran her fingers through his hair in long tender strokes. Hack drew her downward until Terri lay beside him on the pillows. He moved to rest his head on her shoulder and near her breast. She continued to caress his neck and back and they lay silently watching flames in the hearth coordinate their dance to soft strains of music floating through the room. Silence and total contentment ushered an unexpected rush of sleep overtaking their consciousness. The added drugging effect of the wine allowed an undisturbed interval until they were startled awake by a distant pounding and clanging of door chimes.

Looking at each other in a dazed state, Hack motioned for her to stay still and struggled to his feet. "Ohhhh . . . ooowww . . . uhnnnnn," he groaned, trying to straighten to an upright position.

"Are you all right? You sound awful," Terri showed concern.

"Yeah. It just helps to moan."

She laughed and rolled to her other side.

"Look's like Jeff's already up," Hack mumbled as he grabbed a cigarette, lit the unfiltered end, and proceeded up stairs as the pounding continued. Opening the door produced a sobering result. There was an elderly man sandwiched between two uniformed policemen. "Can I help you?" he asked, trying to comb his hair with his fingers.

"May we come in?"

"Uh, yeah, sure. I just woke up. I didn't mean to be rude."

"You'll forgive us," the officer sporting a pair of stripes began, "but this gentleman has complained that last evening he heard some small commotion on his property and found this morning one of his prize trees had been topped."

Hack inhaled the wrong way. It was difficult to determine whether he was coughing, choking or gagging to cover laughter.

"You see," the corporal continued, "Mr. Rubinstein claims he saw the lady of the house dragging something across the lawn and feels that someone here may be responsible for the vandalism."

Hack shouted at the top of his lungs. "Terri."

She appeared almost immediately as Hack stood amazed to note she was even vibrant in the morning.

The officer reiterated his tale as Hack subdued himself in the background and watched Terri turn on the charm. Lucifer himself would have been putty in her hands. Explaining she must have mistaken the property line, before long, Terri had the aged man agreeing to a paltry sum for his once priceless evergreen. She also denied Hack's offer of cash from his pocket, satisfying the obligation much more efficiently with a check noting a total immunity to further claims upon cashing. Since the matter resulted in such an amiable solution, the gendarmes retreated after exchanging holiday salutations.

They stood watching their departure and saw the old geezer, trying to take a shortcut across her lawn, fall flat on his ass down a snowy embankment. They slammed the door and slid to the floor in roaring laughter, noticing Jeff standing at the far end of the hall shaking his head in disbelief before he disappeared once again.

Hack twisted his position to pull her to him. The gaiety gradually subsided and they were soon resting quietly, slowly regaining a normal breathing rhythm. "It seems like I'm always apologizing for not making love," she said softly while toying with the buttons on his shirt. "It's just so strange. I've never in my life wanted anyone as I have you. It's unbelievable how much I need you at this very moment."

Hack silenced her by touching his finger lightly to her lips. "Last night wasn't your fault. It wasn't a fault at all. The evening couldn't have been more wonderful." Placing his opened hand against her cheek, he raised her face for their eyes to meet in full contact. "Honey, remember a good while ago when we first met. We agreed that the first time should be something special. That's the way it will be. Not with us having to part moments later."

* * *

As usual, Carin quickly got over her disappointment by directing a few verbal barbs at Hack. Having him in her presence was more important than carrying a grudge. To her delight, they visited the golf club in the afternoon on Christmas Eve day, did some last minute shopping, and prepared the early evening meal, together. After dinner, they agreed to each open a single present, keeping the balance under the tree to be shared with the children's Christmas the following afternoon. Carin swooned over the eighteen karat gold chain and immediately placed it around her neck as Hack raved about the unusualness of his new ceramic lighter painted with a scene from St. Andrew's Golf Club.

With a great deal to do, he kissed her at the apartment door and reaffirmed bringing the children on his return around noon the next day.

Visiting first at his mother's home, he pleased her by testing the homemade cherry tart and ritually accepting a generous take-home portion of her homemade fudge and divinity. Making the next to last stop at his brother's before completing the brief itinerary with the children, he unloaded presents for Jerry and his family. He and Erica had an unsteady truce, at least for the holidays. Taking only time for a single drink with his brother, Hack moaned excuses of what lie ahead in the way of toy construction and took his leave. He arrived at Sharon's shortly before ten o'clock and helped tuck the kids into bed. Waiting until it was obvious the children were asleep, Hack began working diligently on putting the toys together.

Involved in his mechanical skills until almost five in the morning before stretching out on the couch, the kids were up at seven. Struggling through the early hours half-dazed and allowing the children time to enjoy their gifts, around eleven he piled them in the car and headed for the apartment. All of them quickly adapted to Carin. In fact, as the day wore on, Josie wouldn't let her out of her sight. Hack snatched a brief opportunity to doze while she played games with them and occupied their time. Around seven, everybody bundled up for the cold, loaded presents in the car, and the kids took turns giving Carin a big hug and kiss. Hack returned by nine. The covers were down in anticipation of his need and he crashed on the bed without delay.

CHAPTER XI

"Why don't you get some shuteye?" Gabe suggested.

Still exhausted from the day before, Hack stopped staring at the passing scenery of North Carolina, mumbled an affirmative reply to Gabe, slid down in the seat, and propped his knees against the dash. His head bobbed from side to side, swaying with the movements of the car. Ages seemed to pass before dozing into an initially semiconscious state.

Although still being vaguely aware of sound and road noise, but unable to define a point between reality and dream, his mind floated in disarray and slowly focused on a burgeoning vision. A crowd of people stood cheering and shouting their approval as he strutted along a narrow path. His attire was that of a Russian cosmonaut. In the distance, loomed a towering missile-like object. Instantaneously, without rational sequence of events, a thunderous roar sent him screeching into the air. It seemed quite natural that the spaceship disappeared and his body continued to soar unaffected through the heavens. Numerous faces took form in the clouds. They all seemed to be feminine, but without identity. Their beaming smiles became giggles, gradually altering to total hysteria. The laughter grew to a thunderous pitch echoing over and over like a bullet ricocheting inside his head. Without warning, it ceased. The silence was equally deafening. They were gone. He was alone. Slowly, a ghostly image began to materialize as the stars moved dangerously closer together. He was sure that the emanation was an omen of things to come. Nearing the point of recognition, a distant voice destroyed the vision.

"Will ya' look at that?"

"Wha . . ." Hack sat up quickly, not knowing what to expect. He rapidly scanned the area and decided Gabe had to be referring to the late model car just ahead with its rear lid protruding in the air. "Ain't you ever seen the inside of a trunk?" He moaned, totally disgusted with being left dangling in limbo, never knowing the end of the dream.

"Not that. That." Gabe pointed through the windshield at a remarkable specimen of the female variety moving from in front of her automobile. He was already pulling onto the shoulder. Without hesitation, the second the car came to a halt, they each tried to beat the other out of the doors. It was a miracle the poor girl didn't think they had rape on their minds instead of helping fix the flat.

Purposely, Hack managed to be a split-second slower in reaching the lady. As a result, Gabe's quick action stuck him with doing the dirty work, while Hack kept the lonely Miss from being bored.

* * *

"Bastard."

Hack burst out laughing as the car swerved slightly in its lane. "Next time you'll know better."

Gabe glanced his way. "Kiss my ass."

"Now, you know you don't mean that," Hack goaded him. "Especially after I finagled a date with Barbie and a friend."

His eyes popped widely open. "You're shittin' me?"

"Nope. You're too big a turd for that," he cajoled. "All we have to do is head on down the coast before going to your mom's."

"To where?" He sounded skeptical.

"She's a senior at NC State and on the way to see her folks at their resort on Sea Island. Lots'a golf down there."

"Sum' bitch." Gabe stretched his southern dialect. "Hot damn, you're not such a prick, after all."

* * *

After spending the night at a small motel near Santee, South Carolina, they were back on the road Monday morning. The weather had gradually changed for the better since leaving Virginia. Nearing Savannah, clear skies aided in producing a balmy fifty-five degrees and their initial destination of Brunswick wasn't more than a couple of hours distant. Hack was delighted at the idea of spending some time there. Many of the coastal resort areas had often been topics in earlier conversations at the club -- both Jekyll and Sea Island offered scenic and championship courses.

Growing enthusiasm fertilized their discussion with ideas and plans, making the miles quickly pass. The new itinerary was to include getting accommodations at Jekyll, as suggested by their newly acquired roadside friend -- ten miles past the Sea Island turnoff, they reached their exit.

Driving along the final section of road leading to the island, it was bordered by an almost endless swamp. Picturing a resort area amid such desolation was difficult to imagine. A long low narrow bridge spanned a waterway separating the isle from the mainland. On the other side, the road split into a divided parkway lined with palms and tropical plants. Hack could visualize the absent flowers and beauty of wildlife that would return in early spring.

Shortly, the road ended at the ocean. Directional signs indicated they were to make a left. The route was adjacent to the seaside course and briefly brought them to their motel destination. All of the rooms were ocean fronted and the sea sparkled in the sun. Wasting little time checking in, they showered, dressed, and Hack made the call for their Sea Island rendezvous. Having better than two hours until meeting their dates, they took a quick tour searching for the other courses. Gabe seemed to possess an uncanny ability to smell out anything to do with golf. Not knowing differently, Gabe's direction was so intentional and unerring, Hack would have thought him a native of the area. In less than three minutes, they were parked in the country club lot and strolling toward the clubhouse.

Hack blew a low whistle as they surveyed the plush surroundings. Every inch of the landscape was immaculate and impeccable. From their vantage point, they could easily see the departure and arrival holes of both championship courses. Typical to the south, Bermuda grass fairways turned beige during winter. However, the color change made little difference concerning preferred lies. To enhance the greens during colder seasons, rye grass was substituted for the fall seeding and provided a year-round greening effect.

They quickly browsed through the pro shop, obtained cards for both eighteen's, and rushed back to the car for putters. Testing the practice surface was too great a temptation to resist.

Adding a bit of spice, they both agreed to play for a quarter a hole. At least in putting, their talents were fairly equal. An hour passed before it was realized. Gabe took advantage of Hack's trip to the men's room and got in a few last strokes. As Hack returned, he found Gabe chatting with a young guy while they both walked in the direction of the parking lot. Hack caught up as they parted toward their own cars. After tossing his putter in the back seat, Hack snatched the keys and jumped behind the wheel.

"Nice guy." Gabe motioned with his head toward the fifty-five Chevy pulling away.

"Oh. I thought you meant me." Hack gouged him in the ribs.

He laughed. "Sheeeet. That'll be the day."

"Wasn't he the one behind the counter inside?"

"Yep, assistant pro," Gabe confirmed.

"Jealous?" Hack detected envy in his voice.

"Might say that."

* * *

Hack was pissed. He had every reason to believe women were possessed with an inherent lack of ability to give good directions or to readily distinguish their left from their right. A simple misdirected turn sent them to the opposite end of the island. Needing gas anyway, they pulled into a station, filled the tank, and received proper directions.

The isle seemed to be basically split into two segments of social standing -- the middle-class, and the very rich. Nearing their destination, what they expected to be a smaller and less pretentious home, was virtually a resort in itself. Being awed was becoming quite commonplace for Hack and driving into the circular driveway in his rickety-old Chevy was embarrassing to say the least. Pulling to the pillared-porch, the two girls sprang from the front steps. Gabe quickly opened his door and eagerly accepted Barbie's introduction of her girlfriend.

"Come on in," she said in a slight southern accent while smiling and clasping Hack's hand in hers, "I want you to meet the elders." Barbie led the way as the rest of the entourage followed.

"Daddy," she called.

"In here, Peaches," a deep voice responded.

The four crossed the hall and entered a family room. "Someone I want you to meet. The two gallant knights who saved me from disaster on the open road."

"Hello," his voice roared as he grabbed their hands in turn, shaking them vigorously. "Pleased to meet'ch'all."

Before anything further could be said, Gabe's surprised stare at the figure sitting on the couch brought curious, but brief concern from her father.

"Well, I'll be . . ." Gabe caught himself in time, short of usual profanity. "Hack. This is the assistant pro. The fellow I met earlier at the Jekyll club. I'm Gabe; this is Hack," he said walking forward to meet the lad in the middle of the room.

"Barbie's not too swift sometimes," he smiled. "I'm Howard and this is my dad, Hy Jacobs."

The old man nodded and smiled his second welcome as Hack offered their names in return.

Barbie made a face at her brother and crossed the room to press a button next to the light switch. A butler soon appeared.

"Alfred, would you bring the liquor cart?" Barbie asked. "I'm sure our guests might enjoy a drink."

"Yes'um," the graying black answered and disappeared through the door he had previously entered.

"Down here on business," Hy asked from either politeness or possible interest.

"No, sir, we're touring the south to play golf," Hack answered.

"Oh, . . . on your way to Florida, huh?"

"Maybe," Gabe corrected. "We're really free-wheelin' it. Was originally on our way to Myrtle Beach and then to Aiken.

"Son of a gun. Aiken, you say. That's where I was born. You, too?"

"No, sir. I was born in Augusta, but my mother was, and is still there. We're on our way to her place, eventually."

Both Hy and his son became significantly involved in the ensuing conversation, touching on topics related to home, the south in general, and that of golf. The first drink led to two, and the second to a third. The girls were getting increasingly impatient. Barbie practically drug them away from the attentions of her father to make an escape. Accomplishing at least part of their purpose, Hy and his son agreed to a match at their private club the following afternoon.

Finally on their way, Barbie's remark took them by surprise. She said, "It's a damn good thing golf doesn't take care of your sex life; a girl wouldn't stand a chance." Although difficult to digest, truer words were never spoken.

Leaving the island and venturing to the mainland, they headed into Brunswick and the Holiday Inn. Dinner came first and dancing later. Primed for settling on a simple evening of entertainment with the girls, there was no expectation of any intimate physical contact. However, to their amazement, both ladies had already precluded events and made it perfectly clear they expected to spend the night. They had already gone to the extent of telling each of their respective parents they were each staying over at the others home. Hack hustled Gabe away to the head before leaving the nightclub and questioned him about the possibility of maybe blowing a good thing with Barbie's old man. As a mutual and ultimate decision, they considered it a risk worth taking.

Barbie insisted on separate rooms, and a condition easily arranged. Hack never was much of an exhibitionist and hadn't changed. If Barbie was as good in bed as she promoted herself to be, they were in for a long and prosperous night. The four registered at the desk and Gabe quickly disappeared with his date after declaring his assigned room. Hack and Barbie delayed going to theirs, first visiting the car to retrieve a bottle of scotch for a nightcap. Furnishings and decor were typical Holiday Inn. Two double beds, a couple of lounge chairs, plus adequate storage and bath facilities. Barbie zeroed in on the area normally set aside for hygiene, reading newspapers, and ridding one's self of personal waste, and eventually emerged wrapped in a towel. Specifically requesting all of the lights to be turned off, she crawled into bed and lay passively waiting for Hack's advances. The night continued as an endless cavern leading to nowhere. Hack had suffered disappointments many times in his life, but the current situation was ridiculous. Describing the unfortunate adventure as comparable to laying a dish rag would have been too kind. He wondered if his little buddy had better luck.

* * *

The entire next day Gabe rambled on about the date and his personal escapades in bed. From the appearance of his eyes, little of the night in the sack was spent on sleep, causing Hack further dismay regarding his rotten luck. Spending a couple of hours on the practice range lent much to clearing their brains and sharpening skills.

By midday, considering themselves in adequate shape, they ventured to meet their opponents for the scheduled afternoon match. Hy was in great spirits, exhibiting no evidence of suspecting any hanky-panky involving his daughter. Even though he and his son played a decent round, Gabe and Hack had covertly agreed between themselves to lose by a small margin to build the old-goat's ego and set them up for a later kill. They managed losing one-way on a twenty-dollar Nassau bet. Drinks and snacks after the round cost the winners a lot more than their winnings. Before leaving the club's lounge, Hy made them promise to have dinner at his home that evening.

Arriving back at the motel, they grabbed swimming trunks, deciding on a dip in the indoor pool. The water was cold, even though heated, but proved most refreshing. Splashing and clowning like a couple of kids and making fools of themselves, they finally tired and settled down on a pair of lounge chairs, basking under the warmth of sun lamps.

"Man, can't wait for tonight," Gabe said and swooned aloud.

"Screw you, you lucky bastard. How's about swapping?"

"No chance." He twisted on the chair to his side. "That's what you get for bein' in such a hurry to nail Barbie. The next time maybe you'll change the tire."

"Prick."

Gabe was tickled and giggled intermittently to himself until he fell asleep. Hack strongly considered letting him burn under the lamps, but decided it might affect his game. Instead, he went to the water cooler, filled an ice bucket, and took great pleasure in christening his entire body. The little man's choice of four-letter words made their presence at pool-side no longer welcome. On returning to the room, they showered, had a wet-towel battle, and dressed.

* * *

Dinner turned out to be a holiday party, including a patio cookout and numerous guests -- a small combo providing music. Barbie clung to Hack like glue. He had little chance to circulate among the many other available female possibilities. Around nine, a separation of the age groups occurred. Elders, representing the minority in presence, retreated to the upstairs den escaping the evenings increasing chill, while the more youthful commandeered the recreation room. With the absence of the older adults, festivities became a bit more lively. A few joints suddenly surfaced and Hack had a hard time convincing Barbie he didn't care to participate. His reluctance had little effect on stopping her.

Barbie's personality and behavior became totally opposite the previous evening's display of timidity and inhibitions. Between her intake of sloe gin, combined with grass, Hack had his hands full trying to keep her clothed. Considering it better to leave the crowd, he submitted to her coaxing and they returned to the patio. "Have you ever did it in the snow?" she asked in slurred speech and then giggled.

He laughed. "No, can't say that I have."

"Have you ever screwed in a pool?"

Second guessing Barbie's intention, he cautioned her. "I don't think that's such a good idea."

Ignoring his negative attitude, she drug a mat from a chaise lounge, tossed it into the deep end of the empty overgrown bath tub, and returned to take Hack by the hand. "Come on chicken-shit," she encouraged. For whatever reason, Hack decided not to resist. Except for limited light filtering from the house, it was quite dark. Following her down the steps of the shallow end and toward the awaiting cushion, she removed her slacks and panties and, with a giggle, threw them into the night. Without further delay, she pulled him to the mat, forcing his head between her spread legs. There was no awareness of the night air's chill -- their body temperatures soaring with the addition of passion abetting the alcohol already in their veins. His lips moved slowly up and across her abdomen to suckle her breasts through the blouse as he simultaneously removed his trousers and shorts.

Losing all earlier frigidity, Barbie reacted like a wild animal released from a cage. Her uncontrollable writhing made them twist and turn as she loudly moaned and groaned.

Without warning, flood lights encased in the pool's walls burst into life. Even though the sudden glare made it impossible to see, it was more than obvious they had a substantial audience, as cheers and applause echoed through the sunken abyss. Hack leaped to his feet, completely stunned, baring himself to the gathering crowd. Barbie had enough sense and composure to try and cover herself with the mat.

"What in the hell's goin' on?" Barbie's dad shouted, pushing his way through the gathering and arriving at the side of the pool. Hack's exposed condition and Barbie's half-covered body, combined with the onlookers shouting cheers, left little to the imagination. "I'll get you, you son of a bitch, he shouted, entering the shallow end.

"Holy shit," Hack hollered, grabbing for his pants and heading for the ladder in the deep end. Climbing up the steps, he barely got to the top when Barbie's dad snatched the dangling trousers from his grasp. Not giving it second thought, Hack streaked across the lawn heading for his car -- Gabe close behind. Reaching the vehicle at the same time, both jumped in, slammed the doors, and the good ol' Chevy roared into life.

"How in the hell did you get yourself in'ta that mess?" Gabe asked, shaking his head in disbelief, as the car sped down the road.

"I don't know." Hack laughed. "Put the damn . . . he . . . heater on, will ya?"

"You dumb bastard. Do you realize you left your pants, your wallet, and whatever else back there?"

"No, I did . . . didn't," Hack shivered. "I did . . . didn't have any back poc . . . pockets in my slacks. I only had about twe . . . twenty bucks on me. My wal . . . wallet's under your seat."

Gabe shook his head in disbelief. "Tell you what though. We better not press our luck. Let's clear out tonight."

"Fu . . . fuckin' good idea."

* * *

From Savannah they headed directly for Myrtle Beach along the east coast. Their getaway was without complications leaving little reason to push themselves as they did. However, with the adrenaline flowing at such an upbeat, they mutually agreed on not stopping along the way. It was well into early morning when they finally arrived and reached the family cottage. Even though rating among the nicer kept homes along the shore, it was certainly far less pretentious than their estate in Aiken.

Gabe was raised as a child in the beach house until his father became financially successful and bought the Aiken property -- the family moving inland for business convenience.

Although exhausted, they still struggled with the luggage, stacking it on the porch of a side entrance. In a startled reaction, Hack jumped backwards as the screen door cracked. Sylvia stood in the doorway. "Damn, you scared me. I thought you were a ghost."

"I may be, considering how long it's been since you've seen me," she joked.

"Son of a gun. What're you doin' here?" Gabe was equally befuddled.

"No one has used the house since last fall. I thought it would be a good idea to check on things and air it out before you arrived. It was my understanding you wouldn't get her until next week."

"Sudden change in plans." Gabe gave Hack a shit-ass grin.

Sylvia assisted in shifting their paraphernalia into the kitchen.

Denying her request to fix them something to eat, they trudged into separate bedrooms and collapsed on their beds. As tired as he was, Hack's mind was fired by the aspect of confronting the purpose of their trip. Lying on his back, he envisioned making enormous amounts of money, hustling innocent victims on the links.

Not far from the cottage was a course with a group of golfers well suited for their ploy. As a child, Gabe had been pushed into the sport by his father -- many of their early years spent at the nearby club where the same old pro remained. Even though 'wheeling' was foreign and only conducive to the DC area, as father and son, they had met all the competition and ultra-egos anyone could ever imagine. "Fuck," he mumbled aloud to himself in recalling the quick exit from New Brunswick. At that point, he could have kicked himself in the butt for blowing a great set-up. That crazy little bitch had sure screwed things up. Or, had he? Her old man had sure been ripe for picking, he thought, while wondering if they could be that lucky more than once.

* * *

Waking to the screeching of sea gulls, he threw his legs to the side and sat on the edge of the bed. The room seemed to be as bright and no different than when he had fallen asleep. He wasn't sure if he felt good, bad, or just tired. An aroma drifting through the door attracted his attention. His bladder felt as though it was going to burst and he left the room in search of relief. Finding the bathroom, and still too weary to stand, he dropped his slacks and shorts, and flopped on the commode. It was only after taking the seat he realized his shoes and socks were missing, vaguely remembering having them on when he succumbed to unconsciousness.

"Are you all right?" Sylvia's voice came from the other side of the door.

"I guess. I think I'm still breathing."

She laughed. "You'll find fresh towels on the foot of your bed. I just placed them there. If you need soap or shampoo, check the hall linen closet."

"Okay. Thanks." Hack slipped his slacks and shorts over his heels and risked darting across the hall to his bedroom. Snatching the towels, he wrapped one around his hips and stuck the other under his arm. He fumbled for his shaving kit and headed back to shower. The door was closed. "Shit," he said, "I thought I left it open."

"You did, you dumb dick." He heard Gabe's mumbled remark coming from inside.

"Who you callin' dumb?" Hack yanked the door open in fake anger. An utterly horrible stench burst through the opening like a blast furnace hitting him in the face. He reeled and staggered backwards, losing both towels in the process. He gasped, emoting in horror. "Gas warfare is against all morals of mankind. And, the Geneva Convention."

Disturbed by the unusual racket and reacting from natural curiosity, Sylvia rushed around the corner before Hack realized what was happening. "Ooopps, sorry," she said, spinning on her heels. "I didn't see a thing."

Hack grabbed for a towel, rushed into the bathroom as Gabe departed, slamming the door behind.

"You must have shocked the hell outta him," Gabe said to Sylvia's back. "There's not too much that would make him bear the torture of what's lingerin' in that room." He giggled in a fiendish manner.

"Gabriel." She shamed him with voice inflection and walked quickly to the kitchen.

* * *

Hack sang at the top of his lungs in the shower -- his spirits never higher. Pulling aside the curtain, he stepped from the tub and toweled dry. Deciding the room to be too steamed to cope with the mirror, he stuck his head out of the slightly open door and, finding the coast clear, started to make a naked beeline for his bedroom. Slamming on the brakes and stopping on a dime, he leaped back behind the jamb of the bathroom door and again stuck his head around the corner. "We've got to stop meeting like this," he said, peering at Sylvia.

"Forgive me." She blushed with her apology. "I'm not using my head very well this morning. I just wanted to make things comfortable and change the sheets for you. There wasn't much of a chance yesterday."

"Yesterday," Hack asked in a stupor. "You mean it's tomorrow?"

"You slept almost twenty-four hours."

"I thought it was still today. I mean . . ." The realization of his seriousness suddenly hit Sylvia and she burst into hysterical laughter. Hack utilized the opportunity and the distraction to hurriedly snatch the wet towel hanging over the shower curtain rod and hide his lower-half. He walked into his room as she sat on the edge of the bed holding her stomach, trying desperately to squelch the horrendous giggling.

"You look funny," her voice screeched, laughing herself to tears while pointing at his waist. The towels design was abstract in nature and a large ear of corn hung perfectly in relationship to his crotch. "Nibble, nibble, nibble," she weakly said, and roared even louder.

Hack lost all control due to the infectiousness of her reaction

274

and mood. He fell to his knees, too weak to stand under the pain of the prevailing craziness and hysterics. "Oh, oouu, I hurt." He cried a real tear, scooting across the rug on his hip. Reaching the bed, he pulled himself up to sit beside her. Placing his arm around her shoulder, she innocently laid her hand in his lap. Sylvia cried out, "Oh, my God, I'm touching your corn."

They both went berserk.

* * *

Gabe was already in the kitchen gorging himself with the breakfast Sylvia had prepared by the time Hack appeared fully dressed.

"You look different in clothes," Sylvia commented, unable to resist the opportunity to goad.

"He looks better, not different," Gabe corrected in a slurring, but joking manner.

Hack gave him the third-finger sign while she wasn't looking, and settled into a kitchen chair.

The food was absolutely delicious. Sylvia had outdone herself with nothing more than strict and simple 'good-old-home-style' cooking. Along with the gratifying meal came some tasty conversation. Gabe pumped his aunt for the local gossip and received details on the latest happenings. Her report wasn't completely encouraging. Gabe's one-time heartthrob had gotten married, his favorite cat got hit by a car, and as far as she knew, a lot of the old-time big gamblers weren't around Mrytle, anymore.

"Now, that you're both fed and satisfied, I've got to get back home," she said with the intention of putting an end to the gathering. "I hadn't planned on staying here tonight."

"Oh, Oooo, you're holdin' my corn. Do you really have to go?" Gabe made a grotesque grimace. "I was just savin' Hack the embarrassment of askin'."

Hack faked a swing at Gabe across the table.

Pretending anger, Sylvia chased her nephew out of the room waving a spatula, trying very hard to suppress a smile and a pressing urge to laugh. "Gabriel, shame on you." She scolded him in her pursuit. "Your mother taught you better manners."

As contrast to a usually prim and proper facade of surface personality, the other side of her character proved extremely delightful and pleasing to Hack, finding Sylvia to be a woman with many facets, living and enjoying each aspect of her life with honesty and sincerity. These were rare qualities seldom found in a single individual. Watching her busily rush through the ritual of rinsing dishes and clearing the kitchen counter, for the first time since last having been in her company, he felt very aware of how comfortable it was to be with her. Becoming cognizant of his stupor, he suddenly felt embarrassed at allowing her to clean the mess unassisted. He gathered the last of the items from the table, carrying them to the sink. "How's the golf game?" he asked.

"Not bad. How's yours?"

"Up and down," he smiled.

"That's the way it's supposed to be. Up in the air, and down in the hole. You must be playing pretty good," she teased.

As Hack reached around her, she turned and they were very close to each other. With no other part of their bodies in contact, their lips touched in a soft and mutually desirable embrace. As the kiss ended, Sylvia quickly turned her head away and resumed washing a pot. "That was very nice. I've thought a lot about you," she said, breaking the silence.

"Me, too," he feebly responded, trying to force a laugh to cover a sudden sense of awkwardness. "Sure missed dancing together."

"I know. That evening at the house was beautiful and something I'll always remember." She briefly glanced at him before continuing. "I started to call you a few times and even looked for an excuse to get to Washington."

"I wish you had," Hack assured. "I'm sorry. I really thought you wanted to avoid anything between us."

"I did," she interrupted. "That was before you left. And, there's no reason for you to feel guilty. I was the one to blame." She sighed and turned to face him. A growing smile replaced her previously solemn expression. "Want some more coffee?"

"Sure. That crazy nephew of yours takes more time to get ready than any woman I've ever known." Hack shook his head in mock disbelief while moving to sit at the table.

Sylvia poured two fresh mugs and joined him. "So, what have you been up to?"

"About a hundred and ninety pounds," he joked, provoking

both of them to laugh.

"You know that's not what I meant," she retorted, teasing him with a scolding glare.

Avoiding the mention of recent female encounters as much as possible, Hack began relating events, most of which centered on work and the lack of golf. Eventually touching on his misfortune in having been shot, Sylvia was horrified and exhibited much concern. Barely being able to respond to the first of her barrage of questions, Gabe burst into the room.

"I'm ready. Let's go."

* * *

Their plan was simple. It called for two days of becoming familiar with the course while getting introductions to other players through the pro. With any luck, a small match would blossom into a larger bet.

After arriving at the club, they learned the pro was on the course and decided to wait for him in the grill. Shortly after starting a friendly game of gin, the pro walked in the door. He stopped long enough to whisper to the waitress and then joined them with a cheerful greeting. "Gettin' much?"

"Action or pussy?" Gabe countered, with his usual devilish giggle.

"Take your pick," the pro retorted and laughed as he reached across the table to shake each of their hands in turn.

During the gesture, Gabe introduced Hack and the pro. "This is Crawford Thompson. Crawdad, for short."

Crawdad had gotten a little older and a bit grayer at the temples. He had been a fixture for many years at the club with no sign of any impending changes. First impressions indicated some of the reasons for Crawdad's success. Club professionals must always establish a priority of friendship and comradery with members. His personality, while being warm, exuded a witty charm, befitting the affectionate Cajun nickname he bore. Being a physically large man for his height, his hands were big with thick wrists and huge forearms -- an absolute benefit in playing golf. As he took a seat, the waitress placed three frosted mugs on the table.

"Thought you didn't drink during working hours," Gabe taunted.

"Don't. Just took the day off."

Hack drew a long sip of the icy cold brew and tipped the mug toward his benefactor. "Thanks," he said expressing his appreciation. "There anything around in the way of action?"

"Not like it used to be. Time was when they would be crawlin' out of the woodwork at the smell of new blood. Not like that, anymore."

"Yeah, that's what I figured," Gabe responded in a somewhat dejected manner. "So, what'd ya suggest?"

"I can get you a few matches, but don't expect any real sizable wagers. A twenty, . . . maybe a fifty-dollar Nassau is the best you'll manage."

"Well, we figured on starting slow, anyway. Neither one of us has been playin' a great deal, lately," Hack interjected. "Are you done for the day?"

Crawdad hesitated and then responded, "I usually hold it to eighteen, but what the hell. I haven't seen the little man in so long, I can't resist seein' how far he can hit it now."

The pro singled out a partner, making the group a foursome. Satisfied with a five-dollar Nassau, they piled their gear on a couple of golf cars and headed for the first tee. Except for a few interesting holes, the course was quite flat and fairly open. Not having to immediately face up-and-down and side-hill lies after such a lengthy absence of playing was a welcomed factor. Later in the afternoon, the sun appeared as the cloud bank began to diminish and roll away to the east. The temperature rose quickly. Sweaters and light jackets gave way to shirt sleeves in the upper-fifty degree balm. Rapidly beginning to improve his swing and sense the return of feel for the short game, Hack immensely enjoyed the round and looked even more forward to the back nine.

Nature was very kind, providing a continuing warming trend for the next several days.

By the middle of the following week, there was little if any action at all. As contrast to earlier conditions, a sincere respect for the little man's ability spread like a disease among their competition, making a reasonable bet no longer possible. After playing a late morning round on Thursday, they returned to the cottage earlier than usual. "Don't know about you, but I've had enough of this place," Gabe said, sounding down and discouraged. "We sure as hell ain't started the new year with much of a bang. Sheeeet."

"Yeah, we haven't won enough to even come close to covering expenses," Hack agreed while peering into the refrigerator. "Want a sandwich?"

"Naw. Hand me a beer while you're in there."

Hack tossed the can across the room. Selecting cheese and bologna, he moved to the counter and plopped it between two slices of bread. "What should we do?" he asked with his mouth full.

"I don't care. We could go back and down through Florida, but that's no guarantee we're gonna hit anything hot. On the other hand, we could run on over to Aiken."

"I like the second choice better."

"Thought you would. Got hot pants for my aunt, don't'cha?"

"Kiss my buttinski," Hack retorted as the phone rang.

Gabe jumped to snatch the receiver from the cradle. "Myrtle Beach Den of Iniquity and Socially Unacceptable Pleasures Department," he spouted into the mouthpiece.

There was a pause as he accepted the caller's response.

"Thought it was kind'a cute myself." He giggled with pride and shoved the phone toward Hack. "Speak of the devil, and she'll appear."

"Sylvia?" Hack questioned, expressing disbelief as he reached for the phone? "You got to be shittin'' me."

Gabe tried to wrestle it away to add a final comment. Unsuccessful at the attempt, he settled for shouting loud enough to be heard over Hack's objections. "He's usin' dirty language and watch out. He's in heat."

Hack aimed a kick at his rear end and missed. "Hi," he grunted, trying to catch his balance. "Happy belated New Year."

"Hi, and a Happy New Year to you, too." Sylvia laughed. "What in the world's going on over there? Gabe is sure wound tight. Has he been drinking?"

"Nope, being crazy as usual. They must've given him a section-eight from the army," he answered. "We just got back from the course and I guess he's getting rid of frustrations."

"Played bad, huh?"

279

"Not at all," he corrected. "We both played great. He's upset 'cause there's no competition or leftover rednecks willing to gamble their life savings."

"He's an image of his dad. Always trying to make things the easy way."

"His father was pretty successful though, wasn't he?" Hack appeared confused at what he considered negativity on her part.

"Jack was a good man and had his share of successes, but he was a gambler at heart and very lucky at it. Whatever he touched seemed to turn to a profit, one way or the other. Gabe will be very wealthy one of these days."

"Oh, lord. I'm gonna cry," Hack declared, attempting to alter the serious mood of the conversation. "I always considered him unfortunate and havin' nothin'. Nothing more than a wonderful and gorgeous aunt."

She laughed. "You may be right."

"So how's the weather your way?"

"It's been fairly warm, but a little cloudy, though."

"We might be headed your way before too long. When the phone rang, we were just comparing the benefits of Aiken versus hustlin' our way through Florida."

"That's one of the reasons I called. I decided to play this morning. Usually, I don't hang around long enough to get any of the gossip, but I overheard some of the men talking about the men's invitational tournament being held the last weekend of this month. I know if Gabe had known about it he would have probably wanted to compete. They have a Calcutta."

"Wait a minute," Hack said, holding the phone away from his head. Shouting over the blare of the television in the other room, Gabe appeared in the doorway. "Get on the extension for a minute."

In the ensuing three-way conversation, Sylvia reaffirmed her information regarding the scheduled two-man team event. Gabe's spirits immediately elevated and suggested she get off the phone so they could call the club. Sylvia yielded to the request, but insisted Hack call her as soon as they knew anything definite.

Following several attempts, Gabe finally reached the golf shop. Using his influence with the head pro, the best he could manage at the late date was to be considered as an alternate in the event of a team cancellation. They considered it better than nothing.

"So, what the hell, now?" Hack asked.

"The way I see it," Gabe offered, "there's no guarantee we'll get in the tournament, but I still feel there's a damn good chance. To tell you the truth, the more I think about it, I'd like to give Florida a try. We've got plenty of time to get back if we get a spot."

"You know what's funny," Hack countered. "I've tried two shots at Florida and still haven't made it to a golf course. It's something I've always wanted to do."

"I'll tell you somethin' funnier than that," Gabe chuckled with his remark. "I never played there, either."

"That's hard to believe."

"No bull. As close as we are from here, the opportunity just never came up."

"I gotta take a leak," Hack said, as he rose and headed out of the kitchen. "Make up your mind. I'll be right back."

Hack stood over the toilet and his mind rambled in turmoil. He smiled and shook his head in realizing he hadn't once thought of the office, Carin, or Terri, and cringed at the fact he hadn't contacted either since New Year's Eve.

"Shit, it's only Thursday," he commented, as he zipped his fly, moved in front of the basin and gazed into the mirror. Unconsciously, he spread toothpaste across his brush and found himself scrubbing his teeth. "Damn. They're gonna be pissed I haven't called," he said to his reflection through a mouth of foam. "I really shouldn't stay down here 'til the end of the month," he continued, altering his outlook. "Aw, fuck. I deserve the chance. It'll never be here, again." Hack spat into the sink and swilled several mouthfuls of cold water in a gargling fashion to rid the suds.

"What the hell you doin'?" Gabe stuck his head around the corner of the door.

"Cleansing my soul."

CHAPTER XII

Hack kept his promise to Sylvia, making her aware of their plans. Even though initially disappointed their arrival would be delayed because of the Florida excursion, she was elated they would see each other in a few weeks and boasted of having a scrumptious meal prepared on their arrival. Following her call, he touched base with Carin and Terri, suffering displeasure from both for being missed over the holiday and not having phoned more often.

They left the following morning, deciding to fly out of Charleston to Miami and stay at Doral. Gabe, using his mother's influence, had little trouble making the arrangements.

After a week of experiencing much success at nightlife, in contrast to failures of gaining golfing competition, they opted on renting a car and heading back to Myrtle, stopping along the way to test various courses and gambling opportunities. Instead of cashing a lot of tickets, the expenses constantly mounted. To make matters worse, reaching Gainesville, Gabe pulled a few more strings and arranged a match at the country club -- one that should never have happened. Fairing rather decently on the course, they had their pockets virtually picked by a couple of real pros, losing a considerable sum in an almost all-night gin game. With tails between their legs, they drove directly back to pick up Hack's car at the airport and begin the final leg of the trip over to Aiken.

* * *

After an excellent dinner, a few drinks, and attempting to teach Sylvia how to play gin, they all retired to a good night's sleep. Even though hitting the sack at a rather late hour, Hack and Gabe were up at the crack of dawn in anticipation of a change in luck and good things to come. Stan, the head pro from the club had called the house while they were still on the road, leaving a message with Sylvia indicating a team had canceled and their team entry was approved and accepted as an alternate. A practice round was scheduled for nine o'clock the following morning.

Almost out of cigarettes, Hack decided to drive down the highway to get a carton while Gabe was showering. The Chevy wouldn't start. Raising the hood and checking the battery cables, he gave a few good taps on the alternator, and tried the ignition for another unsuccessful attempt. Disgustedly, he slammed the hood and stalked into the house. "I'm ready to go if you are," Hack blurted, making his combined enthusiasm and anger quite apparent, "but we just lost our wheels. Damn stinking, no-good stinking car won't start."

"Sheeeet. We can walk up. No big deal."

"Yeah, I know. It's just that . . . aw, I don't know." Hack's volume wound down throughout the sentence. "Nuts, it ain't the car's fault. It's been good to me. I'm the one who hasn't been taking care of it."

"Cool your heels. It's only a few minutes after seven," Gabe assured. "The grill doesn't even open 'til eight. If you want coffee or toast, or somethin, we better get it here."

"Guess you're right," Hack muttered half-heartedly and flopped on a kitchen chair.

"I ain't your maid, asshole." Gabe said, pouring fresh grounds into the coffee-maker. "You want somethin, help yourself."

Hack grunted with the effort of trying to get out of his seat.

"Sit down," Gabe giggled with his demand. "Just jokin'. How about some English muffins?"

"Sounds fine. Sure you don't want some help?"

"Naw. Save it for the golf course."

Sylvia appeared in the doorway clad in a cumbersome beige robe. For a fleeting moment, she presented an image resembling the prim and rigid figure of propriety Hack recalled on their first meeting. "Good morning," she yawned, while covering her mouth, then quickly apologized.

"How come you're up so early? Want some java?" Gabe asked in the same breath, pouring a third cup without waiting for a response.

"I heard all of the cursing at the car and wanted to make sure you had a ride to the club. I'd let you use mine, but there's several things I have to do."

"You shouldn't have gotten up. We could've hiked up the hill," Hack commented.

"That's silly. There's no reason for you to have to struggle with all your gear." She discarded the objections while insisting burnt muffins weren't sufficient sustenance. Sylvia soon displayed an array of freshly cut fruits, rolls and jams on the table. Confronted by the appealing selection, Gabe's and Hack's focus was channeled to the intake of food. Sylvia disappeared to dress and met them at the car as they completed stowing bags and shoes in the trunk. After the short hop to the clubhouse, with almost an hour remaining until tee off, they each obtained a bucket of practice balls and headed for the driving range. Sylvia had time to kill and trailed along as an observer.

Gabe was generally constantly stable in his play. As normal with any truly good player, the short game, especially chipping and putting could occasionally prove a fickle nemesis. Consistency was also an important factor in Hack's ability. In his case, it happened to be the lack of it. The golf swing, when executed correctly, is a graceful and effortless stroke of artistic athletic ability. Each and every club selection should be swung without deviation to the swing pattern, whether it be the driver, or the wedge. No different than in any other sport, golf has its criteria establishing perfection. Among tour professionals, there are a number falling into such a category. However, there are several others extremely and often equally successful, that ignore accepted conventions. Doug Sanders, for one, with his abbreviated back swing proved an excellent example of independent style. Yet, his or anyone's ability to successfully implement such alien techniques, still requires strict adherence to standards of repetitious and harmonious execution.

Hack had always been plagued with being unable to groove himself. Without a semblance of automated mechanics, like all duffers, he was subject to many errant shots normally resulting in numerous over-par scores during any given round. In match play, he could be a formidable opponent and an excellent team mate.

In medal tournaments, double and triple-bogeys were insurmountable obstacles of his own creation. Even though experiencing prolonged spurts of quality play and low scores, they generally occurred during periods when he was able to devote a great deal of time to practice and on the course.

Since Hack's recovery from being wounded, his game had suffered considerably. Having probably returned too soon, compensating for the injury only magnified already existing discrepancies in his swing. As a result, whatever consistency he previously enjoyed, dissipated as his handicap soared. Coinciding with his comeback, the small public course back home had finally joined the USGA, benefiting its members by making them eligible for universally acceptable handicaps through the association. The old independent system listed him as a seven handicapper prior to being injured. However, only rounds played after the clubs qualification into the golf association counted. He was being entered into the current tournament as a legitimate thirteen.

Sylvia took serious interest in watching Hack's endeavors. Not being able to cope with his mental suffering any longer, she dared to make a few suggestions. Falling short of telling him to switch to volleyball, she provided compensatory tips to correct the more obvious and pronounced discrepancies. Before leaving the range, he saw some improvement. At least he had overcome the dreaded power-fade. Gabe warned of the fast approaching tee time. Relieving themselves of their bags to appointed caddies, Sylvia signaled a goodbye and threw a kiss in their direction.

"That's got to be for you, not for me." Gabe giggled as usual.

* * *

During the round, Hack was determined to work at Sylvia's suggestions. Gabe played his usual almost flawless round. The course was in fair shape, considering the season, and would offer a testy challenge for the tournament.

In essence, the Snowball Invitational was an open-event originally intended to provide a winter break for the members. The tournament, in its ninth year, had almost immediate success in becoming a big attraction, not only to members and local golfers, but to those throughout the state, as well. Members could select another member; they could invite a nonmember as a partner; or, two nonmembers could enter as a team. Whereas, the main focus was on gross score competition, net awards were to be presented on a somewhat lesser scale. As opposed to this particular tournament, Member-Guest's were usually the opposite. On learning of the situation, Gabe was elated, but probably wishing he had a much stronger scratch partner, while Hack was depressed, finding his wonderful handicap not as important.

Completing the practice eighteen shortly after midday, Gabe wasn't totally satisfied with his putting. Having no opportunity to play another round due to the capacity of waiting golfers and allotted tee times, he retreated to the practice green, leaving Hack to fend for himself.

The grill was unbelievably crowded with only a single table unoccupied. Arriving simultaneously with four others, he was hopelessly outnumbered, smiled submission, and backed away. Feeling a tug on his arm, he turned and faced an attractive middle-aged woman sitting alone. "This chair's not taken," she suggested, producing a broad smile while leaning to push it away from the table.

"That's very kind. Thanks," he acknowledged, accepting her offer. As he took his seat, he motioned for the waitress. "What would you like?" he asked his new found acquaintance.

"Another of the same, thank you." She handed her glass to the waitress.

"Canadian and water's fine," Hack smiled and winked.

"I'm Joy Larkin. Who might a gorgeous hunk of man like you be?"

Her forward and aggressive manner wasn't completely expected, but came as a refreshing stimulation and challenge. "Hack Arnold," he passively submitted.

"Well, Mr. Arnold, what brings you south, business or pleasure?"

"A little of both, but, how'd you know that I was from the north?"

"No tan, lover. No tan." Joy made her point. Their drinks arrived and she provided a toast. "Here's to whatever you're up to." Hack offered a cigarette and sat listening to Joy's prattle and incidental gossip, finding it totally foreign to viable comprehension or understanding. Without making her feel like she was talking to the wall, he timely offered denial and agreement coordinated with her expressions of speech and conversation. At the same instant, he found himself tempted and provoked into his usual male attitude of measuring her physical attributes and assets. A deep rich tan covering an evidently well kept body gave her a touch of youth belying actual years. Hack mentally contemplated her age at forty-two with tits that were probably a fourth of her weight. "They're real," he heard her say.

"Uh, I'm sorry. I didn't mean to stare."

"You can touch, but never stare." She laughed with the daring remark. "I always say, if you got it, flaunt it."

They laughed together, helping to hide Hack's evident embarrassment.

"Looks like I'm missing out on something good," a voice from nowhere commented. "Mind if I join you?" The feminine newcomer guilty of the interruption failed to wait for a confirmation and quickly occupied one of the two remaining vacant chairs.

"Should've known you'd show up and horn in." Joy continued laughing.

"Thanks a hell of a lot. I'm Peg." She grabbed Hack's hand firmly and didn't immediately release her grasp. "No matter what this old-biddy has said about me, it's only ninety-nine percent true. Has she propositioned you yet?"

"Geeze," he muttered, helplessly turning to Joy for assistance and found her taking pleasure in his apparent awkwardness.

Finally, Joy patted his other hand softly. "Hackie, baby. Reluctantly, I introduce you to my horny and unworthy, but longtime friend . . ."

"Listen to that crap. I already introduced myself," Peg interrupted and grimaced. "I want you to know," she directed the statement to Hack, "all my bad habits have been acquired from her."

Seldom, if ever, was Hack at a loss for comment or words. However, between the two of them, it was more than difficult to keep pace.

Peg reached for his drink, waved it under her nose smiling an approval, and chug-a-lugged the nearly full contents. "Damn, that hit the spot. Let's have another."

Hack ordered for the three of them and continued to be caught in the middle of their quips and parrying back and forth. The waitress returned to the table as Gabe and Stan approached.

"Damn, son. Are you in bad company," Stan shook his head and laughed.

"Well, I like that," Joy countered in mocked sensitivity to the remark and pinched him on the ass.

"Ouch, that hurt." He faked injury.

"Who's your cute friend?" Peg blatantly inquired, causing the little man to blush.

"My partner in crime," Hack chided. "Gabe, this is Peg and Joy."

"I know you. You're Sylvia's nephew," the latter acknowledged.

Gabe simply indicated a positive nod and excused himself to visit the men's room.

The following hour and a half proved to be one of the liveliest and nuttiest get-togethers they had ever experienced. During a brief interim, while the ladies powdered noses, Stan used the opportunity to provide a bit of background on the two. Like many clubs, some of his members gathered into cliques. Although basically harmless, one of the existing segments closely paralleled Peyton Place. Peg and Joy happened to be leading ladies among the troop and married to a pair of golfers Stan had previously indicated as high rollers. Seeing the ladies entering the far end of the room, Stan finalized his gossip by suggesting they not leave until their husbands completed play. As always, they were sure to join them in the grill.

Their luck was running almost too good to be true. Before finally excusing themselves, they not only got an introduction to the ladies' other halves, they also received an invitation to have dinner with them prior to the stag party and Calcutta later that evening. Agreeing on a time, followed by typical parting farewells, Gabe and Hack wove their way past the tables and exited through the nearest door. Having utilized available storage facilities and therefore not having to worry with their clubs for the next several days, they walked home agreeing to catch a few winks as a precaution against the expected long evening ahead.

* * *

Monday morning the house was like a mausoleum. Gabe's mother and sister, Bonnie, were still in Europe, and Sylvia had flown to Atlanta Sunday afternoon to handle a business emergency.

Starting Friday night off in a rather wild manner, the virtually sleepless weekend offered plenty of action, but little in favorable results. Having been guilty of alcohol inflated egos during the Calcutta, they were induced into bidding much too high for their own team in both gross and net categories. The field was comprised of many strong pairings with several at nearly scratch level, virtually ruling out any reasonable possibility of cashing a gross ticket. Faring slightly better in the net competition, they finished in a tie for fifth-place and split six hundred dollars. Considering the fact their auction expenses were near a thousand, it was a great disappointment and substantial loss.

Hack consulted his watch and found it to be ten-fifteen. He rolled to his back and closed his eyes, hoping to return to sleep. Instead of finding dreams, his brain ran rampant with details and concerns he had tried to ignore since leaving home. Mentally, he forced a visual reoccurrence of the past in his mind, searching for some clue that might shed light as to where he was going and what he really wanted in life. One thing was absolutely clear. Along the way, he had reached the proverbial fork in the road and made a decision to . . . "To what?" he said aloud and reverted to thought. That was the problem. Why couldn't he find the answer?

Over the last couple of years, problems hadn't been solved, they had simply changed. He had lost control of himself. Was the answer so easy? Could it be he had simply lost all interests other than inane self-gratification? Hack saw himself in his day dream. Strangely, he couldn't recall ever having the phenomena occur. He didn't like the experience, finding it presenting an image much different than he considered himself to be. There was selfishness, pride turning to egotism, and a prominent imbalance of moralistic values. His presence in the vision faded as the background became filled with distant stars. As they twinkled, they grew brighter and larger with each passing moment until meeting in a huge mass of brilliance. Slowly, the glare subsided into a haze which began to form shapes and indefinable faces. As always in the recurring dream, the women appeared, standing arm-in-arm. Again, their initially warm and loving expressions slowly evolved from smiles to giggling, and into hysterical laughter. It was maddening. He sensed that the sequence's following emanation could well hold the secret to his confusion and possibly a key to the future.

"Hey. Come on, let's go," Gabe hollered loudly from the end of his bed. "Get your ass up."

"Uhhh. What the . . ." Hack stammered, blinking his eyes in amazement at the surroundings.

"You've had enough beauty rest. Get a move on."

"You bastard. You no-good prick." Hack glared at him. "That's the second time you've done that to me."

"Done what?" Gabe looked at Hack as if considering him nuts.

"You've interrupted my dream twice. That's what you've done."

"Well, la di da. If you need a wet dream that bad, go back to sleep."

"Screw you." Hack grunted and half-laughed in frustration, flinging his pillow at Gabe as he quickly retreated through the door. "There's no fuckin justice," he mumbled to himself.

Taking his time getting ready, he spent quite awhile in the shower letting the beads of water beat incessantly against his head and body. It was as if he were trying to cleanse himself of guilt, moral corruption, and numerous emotional burdens. When his skin became pink from the combined pounding and heat of the spewing pellets, he twisted the faucets and stepped from the small cubicle. Toweling his hair while bending at the waist, he raised his head and met his mirrored image in an unwanted confrontation. Thoroughly disgusted, he quickly turned away and left the bathroom to dress.

"Morning," he half-heartedly said, entering the kitchen.

"Ahhh, we're speakin' now, are we?"

"Bite one. Got any coffee?" Hack walked across the room and flopped on a chair.

"Comin right up." Gabe filled a second mug and carried them both to the table. "You were really pissed this mornin, weren't ya'?"

"Uh. Yeah. I guess I was."

"Ain't never seen you so grouchy before."

Hack tried to joke. "Must be getting ready for a period, or something."

"Know what you mean," Gabe empathized, "I'm so friggin horny, your shavin' lotion's beginnin' to turn me on." He giggled.

"Yeah. Probably part of my problem. I mean, being horny, too."

Gabe paused to take a more serious gaze at Hack, observing he seemed to be in another world. "There's somethin more than that," he finally said in a challenging manner. "What's wrong?"

"I don't really know. That's the whole thing. I don't know."

"Probably just this weekend, I bet."

"That didn't help matters," Hack smiled and then became straight-faced. "When you woke me up this morning, I was having the same dream I keep having over and over. The damn stinking part about it is, . . . I think . . . I think it's trying to warn me of something."

"Wow, man, that's eeeerrriieee," he responded, stretching the word.

"I keep getting woke up before it ever gets to the end."

"Sheeeet. It's only a dream," Gabe chided while taking both cups for refills.

"Maybe, but it seems so damn real. Why doesn't it ever change? It's always about women and I can't tell who most of them are. They wind up laughing at me and before I can see what happens next, I wake up, one way or another."

"Geeezze," he whistled through his teeth, "sounds like you're scared shitless. It'd frighten the hell outta me."

"It's not that. I think it's something more." Hack hesitated and sipped from his cup. "You know, I was winging along pretty good until I got divorced and got so wrapped up playing golf. All the screwin around since then is really beginning to reflect on business, and my personal life."

"So, stop screwin off so much if'n it's botherin' you."

Instead of responding, Hack looked at him in an empty gaze. "I never cheated on my wife the whole time we were married," he finally blurted out unexpectedly.

"You what?" Gabe slapped the table with his open hand. "You're . . . No. You're not kiddin."

"That's right. I was over thirty before ever bein with a second woman."

"Damn," Gabe joked. "You've made my day. If makin the big three-zero turn means bein reborn like you made it, move over, I can't wait."

Hack chuckled. "Like everything else, you get bored with it sooner or later."

"Bullshit. Not me."

* * *

With the Club House officially closed on Mondays, they changed their minds about sneaking in a few holes of practice and spent the day lounging around the house until early evening. Gabe called for a cab around six to take them into town for dinner. No differently that the golf had been earlier in the day, Aiken was dead on a Monday night. Other than a few beer joints, most sources of entertainment were closed. Not particularly in the mood for a movie, they hailed a taxi and returned home. Sylvia was getting out of her car as they arrived.

"Hi." She greeted them with a wave.

"Welcome back," Hack said, sincerely elated with her being home. "Here. Let me help you." He carried her bag into the house as she followed him through the door. Gabe took the keys and moved her car to the garage. Sitting the valise at the foot of the stairs, Hack turned and found Sylvia immediately in front of him. She threw her arms around his chest, pleading that he hold her close. They stood for several moments in the silent embrace before she stepped away and took him by the hand.

"Come on," she smiled, "I really need a drink." Sylvia led him to the bar in the recreation room. Hack sensed a nervous energy exuded in her actions and allowed her to play bartender. They sat on stools and touched glasses before taking the first sip.

"You seem to be awfully tense. Is there anything I can do?" he asked.

"I'll be okay. I get this way every time I have to fly."

"Oh." Hack smiled. "No heights, huh?"

"Claustrophobia."

"Who's that, a new girl in town?" Gabe laughed as he popped around the corner of the stairway.

"He's got girl fever," Hack said, shaking his head. "No hope. Absolutely no hope." The conversation became a threesome until Gabe became bored with discussions about psychology and self-analysis. For a brief period, he piddled around the pool table before finally going upstairs to bed. "That's some nephew you have there," Hack commented as Gabe disappeared from view.

"You're really good friends." She smiled with the statement. Hack nodded in agreement. "I know he thinks the world of you," she assured and then laughed. "The only thing I've heard him complain about is your golf game."

"The little bastard." Hack joined her with a chuckle. "He's right though. There's a lot of room for improvement."

"Does your shoulder bother you when you turn?"

"Not really. Not anymore. But, off-the-record, I should have waited a bit longer before trying to start playing again. I think I pushed myself too quick and developed some bad habits. My swing used to be much better, or at least that's what I've been told."

"Make's sense," she said, pondering at the same time. "From what I can see, most of your problem is being too flat-footed and not having a high enough swing-plane," she paused to sip her drink. "If it doesn't affront your male ego, I'd be willing to work with you on the driving range."

"God. I'd love it." Hack responded before she barely completed her offer. "When can we start?"

"Tomorrow, if you'd like." His unrestrained enthusiasm pleased her.

"Tonight would be better." He rolled his eyes and paced back and forth across the floor in a Groucho Marx manner. She laughed and then began to giggle at his well-presented imitation. Continuing his act by pretending to flick ashes from the end of a make-believe cigar into her lap, he gazed into her eyes. "What's the secret word?"

"Sex. No, love. No, sex," she said teasingly.

"Taaa duhhhh," he sounded like a trumpet. "You've won the magic prize. A week's stay in lovely Port Noise, Tabasco. We'll fly you there on Crow Airways. Ah, ah," he emphasized, shaking his finger. "One way of course. You'll have to make arrangements to get back. And, you'll have accommodations in Hack Arnold's private penthouse . . ."

Laughing out of control, Sylvia slid from her stool and draped her arms over his shoulders. The unexpected weight caused Hack to stumble backwards, nearly tripping over a coffee table, as they fell on the couch. Rolling to the floor, they lay in each other's arms immersed in harmonious inanity and tears. "You're crazy. Totally cuckoo," Sylvia gasped, while trying to regain composure. They struggled to an upright sitting position and gazed into each others eyes. Giggling subsided to smiles, and smiles to serious contemplation. Simultaneously, they leaned forward to touch their lips in a brief embrace.

"Uh, come on." Hack leaped to his feet. "Time we went to bed."

Sylvia showed outward signs of disappointment, but failed to rebel against her better judgment. Holding hands as they turned off the lights and ascended the stairs, a magnetism continued to flow like alternating current between their bodies. Reaching the top floor and her bedroom door, they stopped and searched each other's eyes for something more than had already transpired.

Hack eluded her gaze and looked at the floor. "I'll see you in the morning. I'll be raring to go." Sylvia smiled and turned the knob to her door. "How about going dancing one night this weekend," he called over his shoulder?"

"I'd love to."

* * *

Gabe began to feel isolated as a result of Sylvia's attention and preoccupation of Hack's time. There was plenty of evidence to indicate her interests as being pertinent to something more important than his golf swing or game. For the next several days, Sylvia and Hack were constantly together. When not on the driving range, they were on the course. Confronted with little other choice, Gabe managed several matches with other partners and fared well considering his limited bankroll.

On Friday evening, Hack and Sylvia left the house early, having previously made reservations at a supper club in Aiken. The night evolved into a fantasy beyond possible imagination. They dined, danced and floated in a sea of tranquil harmony until the orchestra ceased to play. There would never be an end to the evening. At least in their minds, they would forever remember the beauty and peace between them. Driving home, Sylvia cuddled to his side and few words were spoken. Leaving the car in the driveway, they entered the house, silently climbed the stairs, and kissed while standing in front of her bedroom door. Hack turned and submissively began to walk away.

"Wait." Sylvia reached toward him, finding it impossible to part.

Hack spun quickly and grasped her hand. They entered her room, closing the door behind them.

* * *

It was very early Saturday morning. A large group of members were present at the club and Hack was surprised that Gabe seemed to be relatively familiar with many in the crowd. His reputation preceded him, and so too did that of their previous visit many months ago. Even though the locals well remembered the lesson served on several member friends, including Dave and Bill, a temptation to test their abilities lingered. Gabe had been using the week to promote the concept of wheeling. As popular as the concept was in the D.C. area, it was amazing the form of gambling was unheard of elsewhere.

Starting off slowly, Gabe began a list of the more curious and it slowly grew in length. Asking for handicaps for each of those listed, he created a classification for the individual on a letter scale from A to C.

At a point where there seemed to be an adequate number of players, Gabe confronted the group and explained the system. He and Hack would be the wheel, playing any combination of two other players with an allowance for match play handicap, based on the ratings of the players on the sheet. After thoroughly going into details and answering numerous questions, a fervor began to build among the crowd and even prompted several additional players to join.

Hack sat in the background daunted by Gabe's feat of magic. They would finally be going off the tee with a legitimate amount of money on the line. Understandably, the group remained somewhat skeptical, holding their wagers to the lower end of the allowable betting scale. A two-dollar minimum and ten dollar per partner maximum had been set. Even then, considering the number of players, there was a total of over eight hundred dollars riding on the line for each side. Unable to pause long enough in the middle of the round to figure results because of the heavy play, the wheel was based on the full eighteen holes, but each nine figured as a separate contest. It was similar to having a Nassau without having an overall wager on the total round.

Walking to the caddy shack, Hack and Gabe found their clubs already on a cart and ready to go. Riding to the tee, Hack said very little, allowing his buddy to bask in self-pride and savor his hustling triumph. From experience, both realized they didn't have a lock bet by any means, and their work still lay ahead.

Shooting even par, the front nine was questionable as to how they might have fared. Stopping briefly at the snack bar to get a coke, they were unexpectedly confronted by the old black attendant.

"Lawdy," he shook his head from side-to-side and smiled through jagged teeth. "In all my years, I ain't neb'er seen nuttin' like dis. You two gentleman's got dis course buzzin' like a giant flock'a killer bees."

Word traveled fast, and so did the opinion that odds were marginal on having either won or lost money. Going toward the tenth tee knowing the only guarantee against another losing day was to burn the back nine, Gabe faced the task with an unusual vengeance. More from aggressiveness than pressure, he placed himself in quite a few trouble situations, but except for three holes, was still able to at least scramble for par. However, when playing out of the rough and from behind trees, legitimate sub-par opportunities are rare. As if by script, Hack sprang to life, adding a first time ever three birdies in a row, on the fourteenth, fifteenth and sixteenth holes. A bogey on seventeen stirred the hopes of the field; the wheel finished the backside only one-under.

Perspiring from the warming day and the strenuous effort, Hack and Gabe entered the men's grill and quickly ordered a drink. The pro immediately joined them at their table.

"Son of a gun. Damn." Stan stumbled for words and loudly chortled. "Wow, I've never seen the club so alive. The two of you have made this place jump."

"That's what a little action and a fair bet can do," Gabe

countered as he unfolded the wheel sheet. "Got some paper?" he asked the pro. Stan immediately left the table and headed for his office.

"At it again, I see." Hearing the voice from behind, both turned to confront the source of the sour comment. Dave and Bill, two of their major adversaries on their earlier visit, sat at the next table like Cheshire cats. It was obvious that a tender wound had yet to heal.

"Hi. Good to see you." Hack and Gabe both stood and moved to the nearby table to shake hands.

"Come on and join us. No hard feelings," Bill said, reaching to pull an empty chair from the table.

"We'd really like to, but we've got a wheel to figure and it's gonna take a good while," Gabe apologized.

"Wheel? What's a wheel?" he asked in a blustery manner?

Hack noticed Gabe's growing irritation and motioned him away. Out of a feeling for forced courtesy, he remained at the table to explain what was happening. "Hummmm," Dave pondered audibly. "This wheelin'. How'd y'all do?"

"Don't know, yet. We won't be able to really tell 'til all the players get in and we get their scores," he answered, sensing a building frustration within himself. "You'll have to excuse me. I really have to help in figurin' the results."

"After you're finished, don't leave a'fore we get the chance to talk some more. Got a match y'all might be interested in."

Hack nodded an agreement to see them later and returned to his own table. "Holy shit," he mumbled under his breath to Gabe, "those assholes are really something else."

Finally computing the last of the combinations, they paid out two-hundred and fifty-six dollars while collecting three-hundred and fifteen. There were a few sad faces, but many more that were satisfied and enthused by the experience. Paying the tab for a round of drinks with their winnings did much to alter any thoughts of desertion by sore losers. They would be back again the following morning.

Earlier, while waiting for incoming scores, Hack had mentioned Dave's innuendo about another match. They were both of the mind to ignore his request, but decided him a fish too tempting for the hook to deny. By the time they were ready to leave, a pair of ladies had joined Dave's table. It was Joy and Peg.

"Hi. You two do get around," Hack joked, smiling at the women.

"I was wondering if you were going to ignore us." She reached to squeeze his hand.

"Won't bother to make any introductions since y'all seem to know each other," Dave grumbled, indicating a little bitterness at being denied satisfaction of playing his personal game of wits.

"Hack said you wanted to talk to us about a match." Gabe wasn't in a mood for horseplay.

Dave seemed to grasp his drift. "Yeah, I've got a friend of mine, a business acquaintance, comin in the first part of this next week." He paused to puff on his cigar and continued. "If y'all are in the mind for it, thought we could have a little game."

Hack had never seen Gabe in such an agitated state and remained silent as the controlled war continued to be waged. It reminded him of a movie scene between two southern plantation owners vying over who had the biggest cotton field. "What've you got in mind?" Gabe's voice became decidedly higher in pitch, building with his ire.

Hack decided it was time to quell the inflammatory situation that was rapidly being fueled. "If you've got a business card, I'll call you Monday at the office. We can make arrangements to play."

Dave accepted the interruption, taking a card from his wallet and handing it to Hack. "That'll be fine. I'll expect your call."

Taking Gabe by the elbow, Hack led him away from the table and to the bar. "Man, you've got a temper, you hot-headed little bastard," he laughed.

"Holy sheeeet."

"Now I'm the one who usually says that, but its 'shit,' not 'sheeeet.'" Hack poked him in the ribs.

"I know." He broke into a smile and then laughed. "We're goin get those bastards. I guarantee it." Hack patted him on the shoulder as if to agree.

It was too late for any more golf, and too early to go home. Ordering another drink at the bar, Joy and Peg stopped on their way out to apologize and contribute reinforcement regarding

Dave and Bill being out of place. They also changed their minds about leaving and accepted Hack's offer to join them. Gabe continued to mumble in an attempt to overcome his angered mood. Peg took it upon herself to attempt extinguishing his aggravations. "Let's go to dinner tonight." Peg grabbed him by the thigh near his groin.

"Okay," he gasped in delight without any hesitation. He turned to Hack and started to comment.

Joy beat him to the punch and literally commandeered the situation. "Oh, great. We'll all have dinner together. Why not my place?"

"Uhhhh. What the hell's going on?" Hack managed to ask. "I know you've both got husbands, and I don't think . . ." He was silenced before he could finish his objection.

"They're out of the country. They went to the islands on a convention," Joy moved her hand nearer Gabe's crotch.

"God," he exclaimed, blushing and writhing in his seat.

Hack knew he was in a world of trouble. Biding time, he finally found the opportunity to convince Gabe to meet him in the men's room. "What the hell you tryin to do?" Hack almost screamed at him.

"Get a piece of ass. It's been a long time."

"You idiot. If we screw around with those broads, word'll be all over this club before we even finish."

"Screw it. Who cares? I just want a piece of ass."

"Damn it, you little runt. If I don't go, you haven't got a chance."

"Oh, God, do it for me. Do it for me," he pleaded and went to his knees in fake appeal.

"You bastard, you're really gonna mess up my thing with Sylvia."

"Hooo, Hooo. You finally got in her pants, didn't 'ya."

"Kiss my ass, you friggin misfit," he laughed. "Come on, I'll never live it down unless you get laid."

Having agreed to meet them later at Joy's home, which also abutted the course on the fourth fairway, they parted and headed for the estate. "What the hell am I gonna tell Sylvia?" Hack asked, in search of Gabe's help.

"Tell her you're suppose'ta get fucked." He roared in

laughter and purposely fell to the ground to roll down the hill.

"Damn you, I'm serious." There was no doubting the emphatic importance of his mood. "If you make me screw things up with her, you can try and handle both of 'em by yourself."

Gabe quickly regained his footing and altered his attitude. "Wait a minute," he grabbed Hack's arm, pulling him to a halt and forcing him to sit on the ground. "Let's come up with a good story. I really don't want to mess things up between you and Sylvia, but give me a chance. You've had yours."

"Okay. okay," Hack succumbed to his pressure. "But, we've got to really convince her about being invited to a legitimate dinner by husbands and wives."

"Hell, she'll handle that. You forget she's a golfer. She's done a bit of hustling on the course in her own way."

"You better make it good," Hack warned.

Joy was her usual jovial self and Peg kept pace through the meal. After eating, they sat in crazy conversation, drank an overabundance of liquor from her bar, and danced until the midnight hour. Hoping the evening would soon expire, Hack was devastated with Joy's suggestion they go for a walk since it was an unusually balmy evening. Gabe was elated. The four of them headed across the patio, down a small incline above the fourth green, and onward toward the middle of the course. The two girls continually clowned until they were about to exit the woods and approach the fifteenth fairway. "I've got to take a piss," Joy declared without any hesitation or embarrassment.

"Me, too," Peg announced.

Retreating to a nearby rain shelter, the girl's giggling ruptured the silence of the brightly moonlit night. Gabe and Hack were dumbfounded by their sudden emergence. They were stark-naked, running hell-bent up the fairway in the direction of the lake. From Hack's vantage point, he lost sight of them for a brief moment, but telltale splashes and the scream of "Damn, that's cold," signaled their whereabouts.

Almost tumbling down the slight hill, Hack followed the little man who couldn't control his necessity to attack the creatures in the Black lagoon. "Damn it, Gabe," Hack sounded exasperated. "We're gonna break our damn necks in this dark if we're not

301

careful." Gabe paid no attention to his precautionary warning. Luckily, without mishap, they reached the shoreline. Hack finally realized Gabe had shed his clothes along the way. "Have you lost your friggin mind? Do you know what you're doing?" There was no response. He leaped into the dark water as Hack collapsed to the ground. There were no sounds affecting the still of the night other than the racket coming from the lake.

Suddenly, Peg emerged from the water in a burst of energy and called loudly over her shoulder. "If you want it, you've got to catch it." Gabe surfaced like the Loch Ness monster and chased his prey in hot pursuit.

"Holy shit," Hack muttered to himself, holding his head to subdue a growing ache.

"You all right?" Joy was suddenly standing over his prone position dripping water all over his slacks.

"Go way," he pleaded. "Come back some other year." She laughed and plopped on top of his body, unable to accept the seriousness of his denial. "I mean it. Get lost." His words and intent were unmistakably clear.

"Fuck you." Joy reacted with animosity as she rebounded to her feet. "You could kiss my ass, you bastard, but I wouldn't let you even do that." She rushed away into the night.

He hadn't wanted to hurt her feelings, nor really deny her of sex for that matter. Again, he found himself mentally troubled by trying to find respect within himself and a loyalty to things more important than instant pleasure. Having the urge to run through the night and seek Sylvia's arms in protection, he reluctantly stayed out of undying loyalty to his stalwart friend. Standing in the brush undetected, he became an unwelcome spectator to the events taking place. Gabe had evidently caught Peg after her challenge of escape, and she was on her hands and knees in the sand trap next to the fifteenth green. He knelt behind her buttocks, making repeated efforts at being successful in penetration. Wailing sirens and flashing lights were quickly approaching the scene.

"Aw, sheeeet," he heard Gabe yell.

Hack bellowed in hysterics as he watched the three of them scurrying to locate clothes in the dark. Suddenly, the realization became apparent it was a fruitless attempt. They all made a direct and totally nude escape in the direction of their homes. Reaching the back patio of the estate, Hack luckily found the doors unlocked and gently slid them open. Stepping inside, Sylvia was sitting on the recreation room couch watching the end of a late movie.

"You're out of breath," she noticed, getting up to greet him as he entered.

"Yeah," he panted, "your idiot nephew wanted to race from his friends house." Hack exaggerated his temporary distress.

"What happened to him?" she asked out of natural curiosity.

"I don't know. Must've fell in a gopher hole, or something."

They heard the upstairs door slam. "I'm home, you dirty bastard," Gabe called down the steps.

"Oooohh. He sounds upset," Sylvia observed. "What's his problem?"

"Rough night, I guess. Just can't stand losing."

* * *

Getting out of the shower, Hack was surprised to find Gabe standing in the bathroom doorway. Clad in a robe, he was grimacing in discomfort.

"What the hell's wrong with you?" Hack asked, beginning to towel dry.

Gabe turned his back to Hack and let the robe fall to the floor. His entire torso, including shoulders, arms and legs were spotted with scattered red bumps. Mosquito bites dotted his body, but the pesky insects had feasted on his bare little cheeks.

"You gotta help me. I itch like a sum' bitch." Hack started laughing, causing further irritation for his naked buddy. Finding calamine lotion and cotton balls in the medicine cabinet, Hack dabbed the thick liquid on every discernible lump. "I would say thanks, but I know you were gettin your kicks," Gabe giggled as he wrapped his garment around his waist.

"You asshole," Hack chuckled, "it serves you right."

* * *

When they arrived at the club, it was still misty outside and the air held a lingering chill. However, inclement weather did little to dampen the spirits of the growing crowd buzzing throughout the men's grill. Excitement intensified with their arrival, and the two of them sifted through the golfers in search of an open table. The pair of gents who had played in their foursome the previous day had already started a list that included handicaps next to each name. Opting to join them at the table, Gabe began assigning ratings as Hack ordered breakfast.

By the time they were ready to start the round, it was hazy, but beginning to dry. Other than occasional raindrops and a brief cloud burst while on the back nine, everybody managed to get in their eighteen before precipitation settled in for good. Results from the round were almost identical to those of the first wheel. Unlike Saturday however, the grill room cleared quickly of players as soon as bets were settled. An atmosphere of demure order slowly replaced the hustle-bustle activities of earlier morn. Hack and Gabe were invited into a game of partners gin, spending the rest of the afternoon playing cards.

Sylvia called to make sure they would be coming home and had dinner almost ready when they arrived. Desiring a bit of privacy, Hack closed the door and used the phone in the den. After unsuccessfully being able to contact Terri, he dialed Carin. "Hello." Her voice came sleepily over the crackling wire.

"Hi, babe. Did I wake you?"

"Oh, Hack, it's you. No. Yes. I'm sorry. I was just taking a nap." There was a brief pause. "I've missed you. I really thought you would phone. Why haven't you called before now?"

"Been busy. On the go and traveling around," he exaggerated, "but you're right. I should've called sooner."

"I need to talk to you about the office. A few things have happened you should know about."

"The building burned down?" He tried to joke.

"It's not funny." She showed irritation. "Tony's been getting pretty frustrated and feel's he's made some bad decisions."

"Has he?" Hack retorted.

"Yes, I think so, but it's not all his fault. He's comfortable in management and administrative authority, but you've placed him in a position of having to make production and technical judgments. He just doesn't have the experience or that ability."

A period of silence followed. Hack couldn't deny what she had said and sat for a few moments gathering thoughts. "So, what actually happened?" he finally asked.

"Well, starting at the top, there was a big mix-up on a job and

304

instead of letting the guys in the back work it out, he jumped into the middle of it and really got things screwed up. The situation got messier when he and Steve got into a pretty heated argument. Voila. You're minus an art director."

"Oh, my God," Hack gasped. "What the hell did he do that for?"

"Your guess is as good as mine. You want to hear the rest?"

"There's more?"

Carin chortled sarcastically. "We've lost the theater account, and if you want my opinion, there'll be a few more close behind."

"I don't believe it. I just don't believe it," he repeated.

"You better believe it, and get your butt back here."

"I've had trouble with the car. I know the alternator's bad, but there's some other kind of electrical problem the mechanic is having trouble finding. If the car isn't ready, I doubt if I can get a flight until sometime on Tuesday. I'll call you after I find out for sure and make arrangements."

She sounded relieved. "I'll meet you at the airport if you fly. And, listen. Try not to worry too much. I didn't want to upset you. I had no other choice."

"I know you didn't. I'll call you later."

CHAPTER XIII

Hack's sullen mood was evident during dinner, but Sylvia avoided any attempts to interfere. After the meal, Gabe made a call and borrowed her car claiming he wanted to go to a friend's house. Hack desperately needed to confide in someone and welcomed the opportunity to have Sylvia alone. They lounged on the rec room couch having coffee as he began to relate some of his immediate problems. Minutes turned to hours, and until well after midnight, Hack bared much of his past and emotions, using her more as a sounding board than advisor.

Both being conscious of the weariness they shared from the stress of the long evening, Sylvia took him by the hand and led him to her bedroom. Helping him undress as if he were still a child, she tucked him into bed, kissed his forehead, and turned off the lights. By the time she had slipped into a nightgown and crawled in beside him, he was fast asleep. They awoke in the morning still holding each other.

Gabe hadn't bothered coming home.

While Sylvia busied herself fixing brunch, Hack called the mechanic fixing his car. With no encouraging news, he contacted the airlines to arrange his return home. He was scheduled on a flight at nine-fifteen Tuesday evening. Before hanging up the phone, he dialed Terri at the shop and talked to Jeff in her absence, leaving a message he would call after getting back in town. Having forgotten about an earlier promise, he noticed Dave's business card while going through his wallet, deciding as a courtesy to call.

"Mr. Atkinson, please."

"His line's busy. Would you care to wait?"

"Yes, for a few minutes, thank you." Hack drummed his

finger's nervously on the desk.

"Mr. Atkinson's office. May I help you?"

"Could I speak with Dave, please?"

"May I ask who's calling?"

"Hack Arnold."

"Just a moment, Mr. Arnold." She put him on hold.

"Damn," he mumbled to himself, "I don't need this shit." The receiver suddenly clicked. Hack could tell by the echo effect he was talking into a speaker-phone.

"Hello there, Hack. How are you today?" Dave's voice was loud and irritating.

"I'm fine. I trust you're well."

"Never better, never better."

"You asked that I call. I don't mean to be rude, but I've got a very tight schedule this morning. Could we get down to business?" Hack was well experienced in dealings with characters of Dave's personality and realized the ensuing conversation would evolve into a battle of one-upmanship. He got in the first lick.

"Er-uuhhh, yes. That's a good idea." He cleared his throat. "As I mentioned last Saturday, I have a client friend of mine. In fact, he's here in the office with me at the moment. . . . Let me introduce you. His name is Gregory Brown." Hack acknowledged the introduction with a few polite remarks and waited for Dave to continue. "I don't want to deceive you at all. Greg's a pretty damn good golfer. We'd like to have a match with you and your partner on Wednesday if that's convenient."

"It's out of the question," Hack reluctantly responded, although dollar signs registered in his mind. "I have a flight tomorrow evening to return home."

"Oh. That's too bad." He sounded genuinely disappointed. "Just a minute, I'll be right with you."

Hack could hear whispered mumbling over the phone. Shortly, Dave resumed the conversation.

"I just discussed it with Greg. We can rearrange our schedule and play tomorrow morning, if you'd like."

"That sounds possible, but outta curiosity, how much are you planning to make the stakes?"

"The sky's the limit. . . . Let's say five a man?"

308

"That's hardly worth puttin on spikes."

"Okay," Dave corrected, "we'll make it ten thousand instead."

"Holy shit." Hack couldn't help his reaction and began coughing. "I'm sorry. I misunderstood. At first, I thought you meant five hundred a man," he lied.

"That's chicken feed son. Nothin but pure mash."

"I'll have to get back to you this afternoon. Gabe isn't here right now and I'll have to run him down."

"That'll be fine, but make it as early as you can. I don't want to alter my schedule unless I have to."

"You can count on us playing. It's just a question of agreeing on the stakes."

"That's great. I'll wait for your call." Sylvia knocked on the door as he ended the conversation, indicating food was on the table. Joining her in the kitchen, she was pleased with his uplifted spirits. About halfway through the meal, Gabe came through the back door and looked like he'd been up all night.

"Damn, I'm tired," he said, flopping into a chair. "I'll never do that again."

"Crap, not until the next time," Hack facetiously countered.

Gabe folded his arms on the table and rested his head as Sylvia brought a plate and a mug of steaming coffee.

"Move."

He didn't budge and she sat the items near his elbow.

"I called that guy Dave this morning. He want's a match with us."

"That's good," Gabe said without looking up or even stirring.

"They want it for ten thousand a man."

"What?" He shouted, rearing to attention.

Sylvia dropped a dish in the sink.

* * *

Conditions were established in the afternoon, only after a four-way phone conference. Finally agreeing to play a Nassau for a thousand per man. They planned to meet at the club and tee off at ten o'clock the following morning. As a further precaution, in not having any concept as to how good Dave's partner might be, there were to be no presses allowed and a half-adjustment after the first nine, if there was more than a one hole difference.

Later in the evening, after Gabe had a chance to get some

shuteye, Hack cornered him long enough to explain about the deteriorating circumstances back home and he really had to return as soon as possible. Gabe confirmed his willingness to drive Hack's car to D.C. at the end of the week. However, he also cautioned that Hack might consider staying at least an extra day in the event they might need a return engagement as insurance against a first day loss. Hack agreed and canceled his flight, rescheduling it for early Wednesday evening.

Preceding their departure for the course, Hack placed a call to the office hoping to get through before Carin usually arrived. Praising his luck, he left a message with one of the workers indicating his altered plan of departure and airport arrival. Having conquered guilt while regaining motivation, he was beaming with new found enthusiasm when he met his partner at the car.

No one could have asked for a better day. The sun was bright, the sky clear, and the temperature suitable for light sweaters. After the first several holes, Gabe and Hack both felt much more at ease. Greg was left-handed, but played an excellent game. On a scale, he would have been only slightly less proficient and shorter off the tee than the little man. Dave, although very unorthodox, did have a decided edge on Hack. Basically, he was much more consistent. Finishing the front nine dead even, they ignored the club house and went directly for the tenth tee.

The back nine became a seesaw battle until the sixteenth hole when Gabe and Hack went one-up and finished that way. They were flying high and a couple of thousand dollars to the good having won the last nine and the eighteen hole part of the bet. Neither one of them felt they had played to their potential as a team and they won, anyway. It was impossible to refuse a rematch for the following morning. Hack indicated his flight wasn't scheduled until later in the evening, allowing the opportunity to get in as many as thirty-six, if they desired.

Surprisingly, Dave and Greg didn't seem overly upset about the loss and accepted Hack's offer to treat them at the bar. Using an excuse of going to the head, he anxiously went for the phone and dialed Sylvia. She was ecstatic over the news and agreed on going out for dinner to celebrate. Tempted to call Carin and share his success, he decided it better to wait until the following evening. Instead, he contacted the operator and reached Terri's number.

"Hello."

"Long-distance calling," the operator cackled. "Mr. Arnold calling a Miss Lakewood collect from Aiken, South Carolina. Will you accept the charges?"

"Oh, God, yes. I'm Miss Lakewood." Excitement exuded in her voice. "Hack. Oh, honey, is it you?"

"For real," he beamed. "How you been, babe?"

"Miserable without you," she pouted.

"Yeah, I've sort'a been the same. I wasn't having too much luck until today. Gabe and I won a couple thousand."

"That's wonderful," she genuinely sounded pleased and then her tone altered to concern. "I thought you would be back before now."

"I had every intention to be. This opportunity cropped up and there just wasn't anyway to get out of it. I'll definitely be back tomorrow night. So, what have you been doing, besides missing me?"

"Trying to keep myself preoccupied mostly. I've got a big surprise for you, though."

"Great. What is it?"

"Oh, no. Hurry back home and I'll tell you all about it," she laughed, feeling pleased with herself.

"Damn, that's what I call all out bribery."

"Could be," she countered, "or you might call it love."

* * *

As for the weather, Wednesday was virtually a carbon copy of the previous day. That's about where any similarity ended. Gabe had a real off-day while Hack picked up the slack as best as he could. Having agreed to eliminate the Nassau and play a straight four-ball instead, it was also concurred that presses would be allowed. Finishing one down at the end of the first nine, Hack and Gabe lost half of what they had won on Tuesday. However, on the back nine, going into the last hole one-up, they agreed to Dave's request for a double-press and ultimately lost the eighteenth hole. The end result had them down for the two days by a total of one thousand apiece.

Dave's ego should have been soaring. Instead, he was extremely empathetic in expounding on Gabe's misfortunate and unusually bad round, stressing the extent of pure luck his team had experienced in accomplishing their win.

Both Gabe and Hack were at a disadvantage. Except for Stan's help, neither knew much about their opponents. Giving the benefit of the doubt, both began to consider Dave's earlier brash behavior as having probably been a temporary breech of usual southern hospitality. On the other hand, there was no doubting his wealth or questions about his ability to withstand any of the losses he had faced. As owner of a huge industrial conglomerate, and driving a late model Rolls-Royce, he should have been able to light his cigars with fifty-dollar bills.

Dave seemed to wait until Greg went to the men's room. "Well, you boys sure been showin us a thing or two," he said, shaking his head. "We're sure lucky to be where we are. No matter though, Greg has sure been enjoyin' it all." He paused to slip the wrapper from a cigar and bit off its end. "You know I'm footin' all the money on the bet? Couldn't let a client like him take a bath. Of course, since we won, I split it down the middle with him. It'll make a lot of good business in the future." Hack and Gabe smiled in understanding and let him continue. "Greg's a pretty good golfer, I tell you. He just didn't play up to standards these couple of rounds. Tell you the truth, cause I come to really like you boys, a'fore we played yesterday, I started to tell him to hold it back a little bit so we could get a bigger bet today. Didn't do it though, and sure as hell glad I didn't." He laughed and exposed a gigantic grin. "Wouldn't done as well as we did."

Both of them were impressed with his honesty and felt a little guilt at the same time. Being a moment for true confessions, Gabe admitted there had been times when he had used such a ploy. It didn't seem to shock Dave in the least and he laughed heartily at a story Gabe decided to relate. Greg returned at the end and Hack ordered another round of drinks with an array of snacks.

"What line of business are you in?" Hack asked Greg.

"Investments."

"Hummmmm," Hack responded, content in not pursuing the matter further. Greg had said very little at any time they were together. He appeared to be somewhat withdrawn or could have been a bit eccentric. Whatever it was, it could best be labeled as something strange. However, that was Dave's problem, and Hack could have cared less.

"You know. You fellows took me and some of my buddies for a pretty good piece of change the last time y'all was down here," Dave said. "Seem's that it'd be about six, maybe seven thousand dollars, all total. Not countin' what I lucked back today, of course." Dave relit his cigar. After several puffs, he took a healthy swig from his drink. "Think it would be right gracious of you lads if we could raise the ante for tomorrow's round."

"Tomorrow's round? What gave you the idea there would be a match tomorrow? I've got plane reservations for tonight."

"Ooops. Sorry about that. Jest thought you had more sportin' blood than to go out losin'."

"Whoa, I'm not a loser, dad. I'm still in your pocket." Hack's ire was quick to resurface.

"That you are, son. That you are."

"What do you have in mind?" Hack asked, not being able to immediately cool his blood or quench his curiosity.

"Like I said in the beginnin'. Let's make it for five. You want to go away winnin' big? Show your balls, boy. Show some balls."

Hack and Gabe looked at each other. Through an exchange of their gaze, they visually agreed the matter would have to be discussed. Excusing themselves for a moment, they walked outside to the terrace.

"Damn, I hate that bastard," Hack blurted his emotions.

"Join the club."

"You think we're getting suckered?" Hack searched Gabe's face for a sign of hesitancy.

"Figure we can rule Dave out right off the bat. That leaves the only one we really don't know too much about."

"I thought about it and I just don't see how. We've both seen some actors in our time, but he's no act."

"Yeah. It's easy to throw strokes in the short game, but that really hasn't been evident. There's no way he could alter his long-game swing and still keep it in play any better than he does."

"Would you agree he's been playing to his potential?" Hack asked.

"Sure as hell think so." Gabe tried to sound positive about his opinion.

"Well, there's another thing to consider. Dave's sure got a pretty big ego, and that's for sure. Could be he's just gone ga-ga over having the chance to get a hold of some real competition."

"That makes good sense," Gabe agreed. "Money to a guy like that ain't a shit-a-hill-a-beans."

"So what do you think?"

"Damn, I don't rightly know, Hack. I sure as hell would like to do it. I just ain't got the bread if we lose."

"How much can you scrape together?"

"Sheeeet. With what I come down here, . . . maybe a couple thousand. That's it."

"What about your mother, or maybe Sylvia?" Hack fished for solutions.

"Geeze. My mother wouldn't give me, or even lend me crap unless I do what the fuck she wants. As far as Sylvia goes, she sure as hell's got the money. Maybe I could hit her for a couple of thousand, but I really wouldn't want to."

"All right, . . . all right," Hack repeated and tried to ease the situation by waving his hands in calming motion. "Just tell me one thing. Do we have a good bet or not?"

"We've got a good bet. In fact, a damn good bet." He was emphatic. "You know I haven't been playin' to my best, and you haven't either. And, we're not that far down. We should'a been up five instead of losing a grand." Gabe walked to edge of the patio and spit into the middle of a large bush. Turning back to Hack, he continued. "If you can handle the money problems for now, I'm all for it. I'd say we should spend some time on the drivin' range this afternoon and early tomorrow mornin' and we'd really be set for those guys."

"That's music to my ears." Hack laughed his approval. "But, one thing. You carry twenty-five percent. I'll carry the rest. I really want to get into this guy's ass."

"Good deal." Gabe beamed a brilliant smile and they shook hands.

"Tell you what I'll do you little bastard," Hack said with a devilish smile. "If we win, for every birdie you make, I'll give you fifty bucks."

"Sum' bitch," was all he could say.

* * *

Staying on the practice range until almost dark -- Gabe having gotten Stan to work with him -- they finally called it a day and headed down the fairway for home. "Damn," Hack said. "We're gonna have to do something pretty soon about getting my car outta the shop."

"Don't worry about it," Gabe assured, "I'll take care of it first thing Friday mornin'."

"You all charged about tomorrow morning?" Hack asked.

"The way the pro got me hittin' it today, I'm as excited as a virgin 'bout to get laid." Gabe giggled at his own humor.

"Come on. I'll race you home." Hack got an unfair head start. Before they reached the hedge bordering the property, the little man whizzed past Hack like he was standing still and waited for him at the lower rear entrance. "Where the hell did you learn to run like that?" Hack rasped and panted with his query.

"Ran track in school." He was hardly out of breath and suggested, "Stop smokin', fool."

Sylvia wasn't home when they arrived and Hack missed sharing his story with her. Finding a note on the kitchen table, they raided the oven and refrigerator. While Gabe finished pulling Sylvia's meal together, Hack made a trip downstairs to retrieve a couple of bottles of liquor and made drinks. "Wish to hell you could stay down longer. Bet Sylvia would say the same thing," Gabe said, followed by his usual giggle.

"I do, too," Hack answered with certain remorse. "We started off slow, ol' buddy, but I think we're gonna finish up fast."

"You bet your ass," he smiled and chortled some more.

After the meal, Gabe started cleaning up the dishes without waiting for Hack to complete his chore of making phone calls. Saving the most difficult until last, he first tried Terri without success. Thinking about calling Jerry was nothing more than another subconscious delaying tactic. He also wasn't at home. Being a few minutes after seven, there was little doubt that Carin would be at her apartment. Having stalled as much as possible, he was forced with facing the inevitable and dialed her number.

The phone rang several times. "Hello." The salutation sounded stern and unusually cold.

"Hi, babe."

"Hack?"

"Yeah, doll. How's it going?"

"Damn you." Her voice was strained, clearly indicating she was on the verge of tears. "Why in the hell haven't you called back?"

Although expecting some flack, he really wasn't prepared for the reaction he was experiencing. Before he could respond, she continued.

"All hell's broken loose around here. Tony up and quit. You've finally lost the university. We're on the verge of losing the Hanford account. And, it's not going to surprise me if you lose the rest."

"Mother fu . . . ." He cut himself short. "What the hell's going on?"

"I just told you," she practically screamed her response. "If you'd been here, none of this would have happened."

"Baby, baby, calm down. We'll get things worked out when I get back."

"I really don't feel like talking to you."

Hack heard the receiver slam against the receptacle and the line go dead.

"Trouble on the home front?" Sylvia curiously asked as she entered the room?

"Something like that."

* * *

As high as he had been that morning, his current state of depression was lower than low. The combination of the day's events and Carin's report proved to be so emotionally and mentally deflating, his mind was oblivious to making love to Sylvia on his final night being with her. Lying in bed, his thoughts rambled over all of the unkind happenings in his life. For the first time, he was afraid to close his eyes. He didn't want to dream the dream. He was frightened to face the predestined outcome he knew was inevitable. Forcing his mind to dwell on the few better things that still existed, he visualized playing each hole of the morrow's round, and consistently came up winning everything.   Eventually, mental exhaustion sent him to unconsciousness.

* * *

Sensing he heard a cock crow, he reacted by sitting upright in bed. A faint light glimmered underneath the curtained wall and he instinctively moved across the room to open the drapes. There was no rooster, nor any farm. There was only a golf course.

"You up?" Gabe peeked his head into his room. Hack stood in front of the open patio doors, stark naked. "It's too early in the mornin' to get a sun tan," he quipped.

"Uh," Hack answered, turning to acknowledge the presence of his friend.

"You awake? Or, still asleep?"

Hack didn't respond and mechanically walked to the bed and climbed between the sheets.

"Damn," Gabe exclaimed and hurried to get Sylvia.

Shortly, she entered the room and went directly to sit on the edge of the bed, leaning over to caress Hack's forehead and kiss him on the cheek.

"That feels good," he moaned and turned to his back.

"Are you all right?" Sylvia asked, showing true concern.

"Sure. Just a little sleepy . . . and a little horny," he chuckled.

She pretended to smother him with a pillow, slowly succumbing to his resistance. He forced her across his body, pulling her to lay at his side, ending the faked struggle in a sustained kiss and embrace.

* * *

"You boys all set to go?" Dave asked in a jovial manner.

"Sure are," Hack responded.

"Well, let's get to it."

All the gear was in place and they ventured for the first tee. "We'll give you first honors," Gabe offered in true southern manners.

"That's all right son. It'll be a while a'fore you boys are around, again. The honors are all yours."

Certainly not superstitious, but at the same time not particularly wanting to tempt fate, Hack hit first as usual on his team. His drive sailed unerringly down the middle of the fairway. Gabe followed with a sensationally hit ball that landed slightly off the fairway and in the short rough. Silently gloating with great satisfaction, they moved from the tee to allow their opponents every possible courtesy.

Dave strutted from his cart wielding his driver, teed his ball appropriately behind the markers and proceeded to slice his shot into the trees on the right. Leaving the tee, Dave's cocky self-assuredness should have been an adequate warning that something was about to happen. Wrapped in their own egotistical sense of well-being, they continued to bask in expectation of making their big and final killing. Greg teed his ball a bit lower than usual. He stepped behind the ball to select the proper line and finally took his position to make the shot.

"The bastard's standin' on the wrong side," Gabe gasped in shock at seeing his opponent address the ball right-handed and sail it forty yards past his own lie. "We've been fuckin' had."

Dave continued to chuckle as he passed them on the way to his cart.

"You mother-fuckin', son of a bitch," Gabe shouted.

Greg was bigger than the both of them. He jumped into a position wielding his driver that was unmistakably intended to keep himself and Dave at a safe and adequate distance.

"Now boys. Just face reality," Dave said with a glowing smile. "You're both hustler's that's been out-hustled. You shit-assed pups. You think I was born yesterday? Grin and bear it." His smile became a stern and bitter grimace. "You had your turn. Now, it's mine."

"All right, you southern-fried asshole," Hack responded, beating Gabe to it. "But remember, this match hasn't been won yet. It's just beginning."

It was a gallant thought, but not a very realistic fantasy. They were closed out early on both nines. Good sports or not, they refused to play the last two holes since there was nothing at stake. Paying as much of their losses as possible in cash, Dave had at least the decency to accept the balance in the form of a check. Like whipped dogs, they walked down the fairway for the last time and headed for the house. The smartest thing they had done all day was not to have been dumb enough to press.

* * *

Philosophers are supposed to be considered prudentially

omniscient. However, odds are pretty good that Confucius, Plato, Aristotle, or any of their following contributors knew the first thing about golf. That would include the pervert responsible for cooking up the concept, "along with the bad can generally be found some good." Even Mother Nature had taken a turn at adding the shaft. The least she could have done was provide a hurricane, or anything in the category of a natural disaster for that matter, to avoid what happened to them that final day.

Again, the flight had to be canceled. Hack had very little money and was substantially overextended on his credit cards. With no idea as to what his reserves were at home, he just couldn't afford the luxury of returning by plane. Gabe's situation wasn't much better and he was in no position to idly lull around his mother's place for any further period of time.

Having withheld just enough cash to get his car out of the shop and cover expenses to get back, Gabe fumbled for change to pay their last toll fee just north of Richmond. Ever since leaving South Carolina, the weather had gradually gotten much colder. Thankfully, there was no sign of snow and the car had held up without further problems. Hack looked over at Gabe as he sat in a scrunched position, his head firmly wedged in the space between the seat and the door. It had been his turn to drive a couple of hours back, but for various reasons, Hack found sitting behind the wheel to be somewhat of a palliating therapy for his jangled nerves. A nagging ache formed in the pit of his stomach every time his mind inevitably drifted to their last day at the club.

As difficult as it was to admit and accept, the truth of the matter was simple. The hustlers 'had' gotten hustled. Greg wasn't Greg after all. He was Tom Seltzer, an Australian who had at one time been a sensation on the European tour and a phenomena in hitting the ball for distance. Having an excellent short game as well, his milieu was wide-open courses -- his downfall: too much alcohol and gambling, leading to a bad reputation, obscurity, and never being able to make the U.S. circuit. Following the initial impact, there had been no hard feelings. After all, there is an honor among thieves and the opportunity had existed they could have still won. Hack's thoughts began floating in the direction of home, equally split between Carin, Terri and the office. The two female rivals added pleasure to his daydreaming, while the office clouded his visions. To make matters worse, he had to worry about having enough to cover the check written to Dave. Gabe promised to repay the portion of his share as soon as possible. Being fairly aware of his financial picture, Hack knew it wouldn't be anytime in the near future.

A sign flashed past depicting the 'Springfield/Franconia' exit. Soon the lights and outskirts of Washington would be appearing. Hack preferred driving after dark, but welcomed the fact they would arrive home before midnight. To freshen up and get a good night's sleep before confronting Carin and the waiting hell was an absolute must. Lighting a cigarette, more for the purpose of warding off weariness than the desire for a smoke, he opened his vent window. A rush of cold air pouring into the car disturbed Gabe enough to make him groan. Hack chuckled to himself in sadistic pleasure cogitating how stiff his neck would be in the morning.

With near exhaustion dictating circumstances, and having no second thoughts, he pulled the car to the curb, parked, and cared less about the unavoidable ticket he would get in the early a.m. Coping with Gabe was enough of a remaining chore. Having him half-asleep was almost as bad as having him drunk. Finally managing to get upstairs and into the front office, Hack had further difficulty in keeping Gabe off of the couch long enough for him to open it into a bed. Ultimately turning off the lights, he groped through the dark until finding his side and literally collapsed on his back.

From that point, everything became a blank. There were no dreams nor tossing or turning. There was nothing but total oblivion. It seemed his eyes had just closed when he heard the distant and recurring ring of a phone. Taking an indiscernible length of time to clear his brain, it finally became obvious he was in his own bed and the double doors, open last night, were now closed. Gabe lay next to him, his head totally obliterated by covers. "Shit," he mumbled aloud to himself. "The little bastard probably smothered himself and took the easy way out."

Swinging his legs over the side of the bed, Hack noticed a blanket piled on his desk. Carin had undoubtedly been the considerate angel thinking to cover the phone and muffle its sound. He looked at his watch. It was ten forty-five. Standing erect, he stretched his arms toward the ceiling and then bent to touch his toes. Strongly considering visiting the potty first, he found it impossible to resist letting her know that he was alive. No sooner had his head appeared in the open crack between the doors, Carin flew around her desk and practically crushed him in her arms. As her grasp eased, the softness of her hands caressed his shoulders during the embrace, bringing with it the realization he was half-naked and clad only in boxer shorts. "God, it's good to hold you again," she groaned. Before Hack could speak, she covered his mouth with hers.

"Some guys have all the stinkin'' luck," Gabe moaned, coming to life and stretching his leg to goose Hack in the crack of his ass with his big toe prompting Hack to jump. The diversion provided an opportunity to drag Carin inside, eliminating exposure of his body to anyone entering from the hall. Carin moved to the desk, switched on the lamp, turned, and directed a befuddled glare at both of them.

Gabe sheepishly smiled, while Hack tried to avoid meeting her gaze squarely in the eye.

"How you been, babe?" Hack tried to break the icy chill hovering in the room.

"Busy as hell, . . . worrying about you."

"Aw, crap. You know I'm too damn rotten for anything to happen. Anyway, I carry a card with instructions to contact you and several others in case of an accident."

"Ten-to-one his golf pro heads the list," Gabe commented and giggled.

"That's a sucker bet," she responded sarcastically.

Hack laughed. "To hell with both of you."

Carin made coffee and the threesome sat around for quite some time in varying conversation. Hack and Gabe took turns relating their experiences, omitting sexual accomplishments of course, plus the actual severity of their losses during the trip. Even though she appeared to be enjoying the recount of their escapades, Hack noted a deeper inward sign of distress. Her eyes appeared tired and strained from pressure.

Gabe eventually left, after borrowing Hack's car. No sooner had he departed and Carin threw herself into Hack's arms, beginning to tremble, and suddenly sob. Sitting together, long after the tears had ceased, their only communication was through touch and Hack's tender caress of her face and hair.

"Any word from Sharon's kids while I was away?"

"They called a couple of times. Nothing important. Josie said you had called."

"I did," he confirmed. "I sent them some post cards, too."

"Tell me about Terri." Her words came very slowly in a low tone, showing a great reluctance.

Feeling as if he had been hit by a truck, his mind ran rampant with confusion and disbelief. He wondered if she could sense the esoteric tension and violent throes of guilt brought with the shock of her remark. "She's a friend," he mumbled hopelessly.

"A very good friend?"

Hack's mind continued to rush with jumbled and incoherent rationale, finding it impossible to imagine what might have happened to expose his hidden asset. One constantly recurring thought pounded in his head. He needed Carin desperately. Facing crises in both his personal and business lives, he couldn't dare afford to lose her at such a time. "You might say that," he finally answered. "What brings this all up?"

Carin had made no attempt to leave his arms. He couldn't decide if it was her desire to search for security in his grasp, or to avoid confronting him eye-to-eye. "Terri's very beautiful, young, and charming. I can see where she . . . ." Carin stopped abruptly in the middle of the sentence. "She came by the office Wednesday evening. It seems she had been told you'd be back and wanted to surprise you." Carin paused for a moment before continuing. "I happened to be here finishing up some work. We talked for a good while."

"About what?"

"We have something very much in common. . . . You."

In one way, Hack welcomed the ensuing silence. Yet, on a more important plane, it did nothing to help him interpret Carin's inner thoughts. Her voice had remained low and in a mellow monotone, leaving little to indicate the depth of her emotional feelings. Reluctantly he broke the stillness. "Listen, babe. I really don't know what to say. I don't want to lie to you. I . . ."

She suddenly bolted from his grasp, moving to the opposite

end of the couch to face him. "Hack. You're a bastard. That's right, a loveable bastard." Carin's voice still, remarkably, maintained its soft control. "I love you very much. Too, much." She ignored the pleading look in his eyes and continued. "What's worse is that she loves you, too," she said, slightly choking. "I don't give a damn about her, or her feelings. All I care about is my own and that maybe, just maybe," she repeated herself, as tears began to flow, again.

Hack moved toward her.

"Don't touch me." Her tone was loud and emphasized her anger. "God. Don't you touch me."

"Baby, . . ." He stopped his comment. There was nothing he could say. Shaking his head in disgust of himself, he rose, struggled into a pair of slacks and shirt, slung a wind-breaker over his shoulder, left the room and descended the stairs.

Oblivious to the bitter cold outside, or the stares of passing pedestrians as he sat in short shirt sleeves on the front stoop, he dragged hard on the cigarette, tasting the bite of burning filter. Flipping the butt to the gutter, he got up and headed toward the corner bar. Having immediately consumed his first drink, he ordered a second double. The dark dingy booth blended with his mood.

"Order me a scotch." Hack looked up as Carin slid into the opposite seat. "I'm not going to apologize," she started, "I can't. But, I regret that . . ."

He interrupted. "Stop. I don't wanna hear it. There's no reason for you to be sorry about anything." Hack paused as the waitress arrived bringing Carin's drink -- he ordered a third for himself. "Carin, I . . . I really feel awkward."

Hack hesitated, hoping she would say something to help, groping in his loss for words. Instead, she sat silently searching his face. It would have been easier if she showed bitterness, but her eyes mirrored his pain. "Please just listen," he finally continued. "This is really hard to express and I don't want you faulting my choice of words." Again he paused, leaning back and staring at the ceiling. "Finding a place to start is harder than hell. It should be pretty evident by my discomfort I'd rather face a firing squad."

The waitress arrived again, placed Hack's drink on the table, and walked away. Carin poured half the contents into her glass. Taking advantage of the lull, he clasped her hand in his, aspiring, but not sensing, any gesture of reassurance. "I care for you deeply, Carin. You've always been an angel. Never once have I had a need that you weren't by my side to help me. It's meant an awful lot. I can't imagine how things would have been without you." Carin sat motionless, her free hand tightly clutching her glass. "Right now you're hurt. God knows I hate to see you unhappy and I'd never do anything that would bring harm to you. It'll be difficult for you to understand, maybe, but, at least try to consider the possibility. Weigh your own circumstances. Just look inside yourself. See if you couldn't have either caused, or brought on some of the hurt." Her head came up quickly as her eyes glared in harsh reaction. "Come on, now. Let me finish before you shoot me down, although, I really shouldn't expect you to react much differently. In all honesty, I probably wouldn't want you to either. But, I did say it would be hard being objective. You have to remember one important fact. I haven't been dishonest with you, or anybody else, for that matter. A little secretive, maybe," he said, trying to joke. "I've just been me. And, damn it, I've tried to be clear about my feelings."

"Could I have another drink?" Her voice was as empty as her glass.

Hack nodded affirmatively, motioned for the waitress, and lit a cigarette. Moments passed, allowing time for his words to register. Only after the order was delivered did he attempt to continue his explanation. "Carin. I've never talked commitment, let alone marriage. Our relationship has been something great and wonderful, but to a large extent, it's also been incidental and associated with our circumstances. I've had no intention of bringing it to an end, although it's been apparent for quite some time you would have preferred more solid ground. In truth, I've had my moments as well." He paused for a drag of smoke, a sip of his drink, and to gather thoughts before proceeding. "Honey, there's a restless bug inside me I've been trying to get rid of. I've got one bad scene behind me and I don't want another. That doesn't mean I'd ever have the same problems as before. With you, there'd be no way. You've got the patience of a saint as compared to Alice. What I'm trying to get across, is that it would be me screwin' it up. You know I don't get any kicks out of always being alone. And, I know one of these days, . . . hell, maybe before you can even imagine, I might wind up settling down for good." Hack noticed a slight change in her expression denoting either relief or ridicule. "Maybe it's a rotten time to say this, but I'm not going to lie to you, no matter what. I'm still not ready to make up my mind about anything or anybody. I won't ask or expect anything more from you than you want to give. Honestly, I don't think I ever have. There's no denying that Terri exists, and for me to pretend that I haven't been strongly attracted to her, wouldn't only be stupid, it'd be an insult to your intelligence," he added, stopping again to sip from his glass. "There's one more thing. Terri and I've never been in . . . . We've never had sex, and that's a fact."

An astonished expression immediately appeared on Carin's face as if it were a response to having been slapped.

"It's up to you to believe it or not. There's nothing I can do about that."

"I don't know what to believe," she finally commented.

"Look," Hack continued. "I've known her for quite a while and, strangely enough, long periods have passed without seeing or even contacting each other. In a way, it might have been better if our relationship had been sexually consummated. At least then, maybe, she would have become just another good time. I guess, the way things have gone, it's only helped add to my confusion. Terri's no more moral than anyone else. It's just that crazy circumstances have never placed us at the right spot, at the right time. It's exciting to want something you haven't had. Maybe, that's the only feeling there is. Maybe, it's something more." Hack felt a tremendous relief at having released tensions and aired his guilt. Now there was only to wait for her reaction. Never before had he ever confronted Carin on such unequal terms, and trying to decipher her mood was impossible. It seemed like an eternity before she spoke.

"It's like I said earlier," she began. "You're a loveable, but dirty bastard." Her face twisted into a wry smile. "But, you're right. One-hundred percent right about one thing. You've never proposed, but I've sure as hell had hopes. I guess, if I'm really honest about it, you've made your desires to be unencumbered very clear. Sometimes, I lay alone at night wondering about many of the same things that seem to be bothering you. There's a big difference, though. I've never been married. I've never had children to love, even nieces and nephews. And, I'd like to experience those feelings and know what it's like. But, I have my fears, too. I don't consider myself a staunch feminist by any standards. Yet, I could never be satisfied with being shoved inside a kitchen, or behind an ironing board, for the rest of my life." Carin stalled by sipping from her drink. "You see, I do have two sides. One to love and be loved in a lasting relationship, and the other, to be productive and give something to this world instead of just taking from it." She leaned back and glared at Hack with a disconcerting smile. "It's a shame," she said, shaking her head in negative disapproval. "It doesn't matter which of the paths a woman chooses, she'll get screwed one way or the other." Carin grimaced at the earthy truth of her statement.

Hack felt like sliding beneath the table. Rarely had he experienced more guilt. "Wow. You believe in letting both barrels go."

"Why in the hell not?" She was extremely chagrined. "It's like you said. I made a lot of my own misery. Because I wanted you so much, I, and only I, am responsible for being such a fool."

"Damn it, Carin. How in the hell can you say that? We've had wonderful times together. And, what makes you think it's all over? I've hurt you, and you've hurt yourself, and for the most part, through figments of your imagination. Dear God, why can't you understand that we've built a lot together. This shouldn't necessarily mean an end."

"I know that. But, you're the one that doesn't understand. I love you and I've never wanted to share you. I don't know if I can settle for less." Carin motioned for the waitress, and another drink. "All you men are alike, you know. For the past several weeks, and especially after the other night, I've really felt used. I guess we women are guilty of placing too high a priority on our bodies. In giving ourselves to a man, we feel it should be for better reasons than entrapment or repayment; whichever fits the circumstances."

"God, I'm really sorry if you feel that way. The moments we've shared have sure as hell meant a lot more to me than what you're expressing."

"Don't be unfair," she harshly countered. "You've had your fun. Whether your escapades with Terri were chaste or not, you know damn well that you've expected an awful lot out of me recently. Give me at least the courtesy of blowing my stack and say the things that are pent up inside. And, to hell with it if half of what I might say isn't totally pertinent to us, . . . or doesn't mean anything at all. What I really have trouble understanding is why men feel they're the only gender socially accepted to be sexually promiscuous. If a woman does what a man might do, she's either labeled a slut or a prostitute. But, let me make one point very clear. A lot of faithful and trusting women feel they've bartered their bodies within a relationship a hell of a lot more times, and for a hell of a lot less, than most whores." Carin was on a roll, and her ire was steadily rising to a point above a level she probably intended. "Why? Why can't a woman sell her body or give it away, whichever direction she should opt? It's her prerogative. Man shouldn't be the judge. She should only have to answer to God and her own conscience. If she sells it, she knows what her return will be. If she gives it, it's either for kicks or for love. If it's for kicks, she can find her fun. If it's for love, she wants to fulfill her emotions. . . ." Carin began to choke from her own agony. Stalling purposely to regain composure, she used a napkin to dab at the corner of her eyes, quelling the sting of moistened mascara, and then continued in a more mellow tone. "If and when she finds someone capable of satisfying her physical, spiritual and emotional fulfillment, . . . she's found her world."

"The male's no different in that respect," he countered, "at least to the part about wanting and needing love."

"I know. I didn't mean that men are totally callous." She patted his hand. "It's not men I'm concerned about. Or, other women. It's us. What I need and want has to be two ways: felt by both, for both. Anything otherwise, it comes out hurt." Carin pulled a cigarette from the pack and Hack provided the light. Watching her take the first drag, he glared at her disapprovingly and took the cigarette to finish it himself. "If Terri hadn't popped up like she did, things would have undoubtedly gone on as they were. But, you know as well as I do, eventually, one thing or another would have brought us to a confrontation, sooner or later. God, Hack. Oh, Hack. I just don't know. Missing you the way I did, each day that passed longer than the one before. Tony walking out on top of all the other business problems. And, then, I get hit in the gut by her. It was a pretty heavy load."

Hack leaned across, cupped her face in his hands, and tenderly kissed her nose. His elbow tipped over a glass, spewing its contents over the table and into her lap. Son of a bitch. I can't win," he said, forcing a laugh.

"Well, if that's your way of cooling off my hot pants, you'll never win."

* * *

Accompanying the televisions test pattern, a high shrill pitch droning through the room was an unwelcome warning of the coming day. Glancing at the clock radio, it indicated he had awakened almost an hour prior to the time he normally arose. Deciding the sound emanating from the boob-tube too impossible to bear, Hack struggled to his feet, moved across the room, punched the off-button as he walked past, and stumbled into the bathroom. Plopping on the commode, he grunted from the effort, and sat nodding into twilight sleep. Snapping back to consciousness feeling himself urinate, it trickled down his leg. "Aw, geeze." He moaned. "It's gonna be another one of those days."

Standing in front of the mirror, he leaned forward bracing his hands and arms on the sink, not comprehending why he felt so exhausted. It was as if he hadn't slept at all. Running cold water from the tap and splashing his face, his mind struggled with reason. The last thing he remembered was watching Randolph Scott get into a fist fight with Robert Ryan. He wondered who won.

"No. . . . That wasn't all," he blurted into the mirror. Suddenly, like a rush, the sensation of having completely relived his life became almost a reality. "Was it a dream?" he questioned himself, shaking his head harshly from side-to-side, trying to rattle his brain clear. "I must be going crazy." He spoke again to his reflection.

Moments passed as confusion continued to reign. Abruptly realizing it was Sunday morning and there was no reason to be up so early, he trudged his way back to bed and crawled between the covers. Unwittingly, beginning to think again about being so tired, he concurrently sensed a lingering aura of the past clinging in the air, as if spirits were still present. Could it have been a dream, or was it actually experiencing all of his past moments overnight on some incorporeal plane? He tried even harder to find sleep as an escape. Finally suspended in a limbo-like state, somewhere between awareness and the unconscious, Hack's tranquility was rudely aborted when the clock-radio sprang into life, blasting gospel music that literally vibrated throughout the room. "Holy shit," he shouted, jumping in shock and lunging to slam his hand on top of the device. "Geeze. I forgot to reset the damn thing," he whined to himself and slowly leaned to lay his head softly on the bed. Attempting to ignore the racket that suddenly erupted from across the hall, Hack pulled a pillow tightly over his head and ears. Knowing all along he couldn't continue to avoid the chaos soon to encompass him, he opened one eye and peeked at the clock, dreading to note the time -- the clock read, six forty-five.

Swinging his feet to the floor, they instinctively found the waiting slippers. Flip-flopping across the room while tugging on his robe, he headed in the direction of the battle area. Sometimes wishing they were cages, standing in the middle of the 'arena,' were three cribs holding his little bundles of joy. His luck had continued to run true to form. Not only had their conception come before marriage -- who in the hell would have ever believed triplets? Gathering the sopping trio, Hack struggled through the ordeal of changing diapers. Opening the lid of the diaper pail did more than simply snap him to wide-awake alertness. He began gagging and heaved on top of the pile. Dabbing his forehead with the wet rag he had used on the babies' buttocks, his first thought was to stuff bottles deeply into their little mouths. Quickly succumbing to fact, he correctly determined such a move would only be a temporary truce to the 'war.'

Getting three eighteen-month-old kids down a flight of stairs, at the same time, was a knack finally mastered. Keeping them occupied was another matter. A girl and two boys were a rarity in multiple births, but anything could happen to him. Not without some static from their mother, 'daddy' found it clever and fitting to nickname them Tic, Tac and Toe.

Safely buckled into their highchairs, Hack pacified them temporarily with a chocolate chip cookie before hurrying to retrieve the Sunday morning paper. Cursing violently, discovering it hadn't arrived, he rushed back to the kitchen in time to find Tic, or was it Tac, about ready to test his ability to bounce when he hit the floor. Giving his ass a resounding whack, Hack shoved him back down, strongly considering the use of chains. In need of coffee to soothe his jangled nerves, the steaming hot liquid splattered from the pot, burning the hell out of his hand. He wondered where it would all end. Eventually, after adding sugar and cream, he sat watching the little monsters gobble their goodies as his thoughts ran back to years well into the past. Things could have been a lot worse, he forced himself to believe. The business was near collapse and he had almost pulled it through. Before getting remarried, having made Carin a full partner, the arranged merger with the Caldwell Agency in New York included her being appointed director of the Washington office, and a stockholder in the corporation. Carin's elevated stature and Hack's receipts from the sale, put them both in much better financial position than if they had tried to continue alone and without external involvement.

The agency, being primarily interested in the Hanford account and a few other media-potential clients, relinquished rights to several smaller personal institutional customers. Hack continued servicing the leftovers and was able to add a few more along the way while independently working out of a studio in their new home. Diligently concentrating on efforts to regain his own personal level of success, he wisely invested his comparably meager profit from the business sale into small investments and dedicated himself to goals even higher than those of earlier dreams. At the same time, convinced and content to share in equality of intent and purpose, he accepted the additional role of homemaker and housemother to the children in the necessary absence of his wife.

Why should he complain? Whether he owned it or not, here he was, living in a beautiful and sprawling home surrounded by several acres of property with its own private swimming pool. Already, he shared practically everything any man could want.

All he had to do was give up a stupid and silly game.

"Hot damn," he bellowed, glancing out of the window and seeing the paper boy peddle his way quickly down the drive. Hurrying to the front door, he retrieved the bundle and fingered his way through the bulky sheets searching for the sports section. A look of tremendous exaltation preceded his roaring cheer and leap into the air. Literally running back to the kitchen, not giving a damn that Tac, or was it Tic, had christened his sister with a bowl of Cheerios, he shouted, "Hey, gang. Guess what. Your old lady's coming home for a visit."

Sure enough, the storyline read: 'Leading money winner and spectacular sensation of the Ladies' Pro Golf Tour, Sylvia Arnold, steps in gopher hole and breaks ankle -- sidelined for rest of year.'

THE END

www.ingramcontent.com/pod-product-compliance
Lightning Source LLC
Chambersburg PA
CBHW032240010726
47494CB00002B/563